The Memoirs of Elikai:

The Children of the Solstice

D. Alexander

Book 1 in The Memoirs of Elikai Series

The Remastered Edition

Copyright ©2024 by Belltower Books
All rights reserved.

No part of this book may be reproduced in any form or by any electronic or mechanical means, including information storage and retrieval systems, without written permission from the author, except for the use of brief quotations in a book review.

ACKNOWLEDGMENTS

I want to say a special thank you to my fantastic editors, Joseph Daniel, Crab Editing, and Jenna Lynn. Without your help, dedication, and belief in me, this story would not have become what it is today.

Also, a special thank you to Craig DesJardins, who designed the cover. Please visit his website at:

https://cadesjardins2010.myportfolio.com/

Thank you all for helping to make my dream come alive.

Table of Contents

After the Final War
I: The Broken
II: The Promise
III: Remembrance
IV: Grenoff High
V: The Welcome
VI: The Hearts of Grenoff
VII: The Pure Heart
VIII: The First Day
IX: The Pianist
X: The White Funeral
XI: The Choice
XII: Michael Shepherd
XIII: The Warning
XIV: The Song
XV: The Soldier of Darkness
XVI: The King of Free Will
XVII: The Corridors of Creation
XVIII: The Children of the Solstice
XIX: The Final Child
XX: Alex's Secret
XXI: The First Crusader
XXII: The Two Philosophers
XXIII: The Third Funeral

Reader, please stop here.

Are you ready? Please ensure your heart is strong enough for this Dark Urban Fantasy series. This first book is told through the perspective of a fifteen-year-old boy who must pull himself out of endless torment and suffering to find the King of Free Will and bring him back.

This story will be disturbingly violent, with bleak outcomes that might break your heart, but if you can endure and find happiness in the moments of peace, then you will know, just as I did, that it is unequivocally worth it.

Please do not skip the prologue, as you will need to know how the Final War between Free Will & Destiny was won and what it cost us all.

Good luck, and know that I am always with you.

D. Alexander

After the Final War

~The Historian~

Her laughter warmed my doleful soul as she danced around the Meadow of Victory. I sat in the meadow, surrounded by breathtaking white lilies that represented peace, victory, and sacrifice. The honey-scented air made the flowers dance in the emerald grass.

I caressed the petals, and my finger touched the small sunbursts of red and yellow, with flecks of green and purple, that surrounded the sepal. This beautiful meadow had been created when the Final War ended and the Victor had at long last been crowned. The meadow was a remembrance of everything we had lost in the Final War.

The memory of standing next to the Victor burned in my mind. I watched as he sacrificed everything for his people. When the Children of Creation finally remembered the truth, their hearts ended the war. The crown had been claimed for all eternity, even though the throne currently remained vacant.

I wished that everyone had found peace, but due to the choices of the heart, it was not meant to be. I could still see their faces, the faces of those who fought against us, those who had believed in the misguided philosopher and his teachings, and even those who had turned away from his beliefs in the end. My eyes found the eternal white kingdom on the horizon, and I could feel those who had fought for the false ruler, those who, by the grace of the Victor, had been permitted a chance at redemption.

I gazed down at my flawless hands as the smell of blood and dirt flooded my senses. I relived my journey through the unhinged carnage that was the battlefield. I watched as broken families, lovers, and best friends opposed each other for the philosophy they would kill and die to ensure was the governing force of Creation for the rest of eternity. I moved unopposed, and any eye that fell upon me fell to their knees as they began to remember the truth, but their devastation did not matter. All that mattered was reaching my true love, who was at the heart of the last war Creation would ever endure.

Now, I am alone in the peaceful meadow of remembrance with the final undecided soul, and I still marvel at how the Victor sacrificed everything for the Children of Creation, even if I was the one who had to pay the price.

I glanced down at the simple, checkered flannel blanket, a blanket that had survived countless arguments, battles, loving embraces, and even the Final War itself. I turned to my daughter, the one I had promised to keep safe and to love forevermore. Her soft white dress had small golden flowers embroidered at the hem. Her golden hair was pulled into a small ponytail, and she looked as graceful as a fairy.

The tolling of the grand celestial bells of the Eternal Kingdom warned me that I did not have much time, and

I felt a tear stain my cheek. I knew that those who remained were ready for the final soul to decide. Their time was nearly over, and the Victor's unbelievable gift would finally pass into history, like everything else. My daughter was the last soul released after he was crowned. Every child born after his sacrifice had to choose their own fate, just like the countless souls before them.

"What's wrong, Papa?" I turned to her as my breath caught. She had those eyes, the same beautiful eyes of the one I loved, the one I had lost when the war ended. She had a goofy smile that spread across her face, and my heart yearned for my true love, the love that had slipped through my finger's countless times, no matter how hard I tried to hold on. My brother had seen to that with his curse that had been almost as eternal as myself, which is why things had to be this way.

I sat on the blanket, holding my arms close to my chest as the warmth of my love's embrace filled me, and the memories threatened to break my heart all over again. I looked into my daughter's eyes and found the steadiness, the calm that only those eyes could bring me.

"I have a story that I would like you to hear." I felt the remains of Creation fall silent to listen to a story it had already experienced countless times.

"The Final War?"

The atrocities were forming together as I reassembled the story, and as the Historian, I had been entrusted with every memory of this brutal war. It was not a blessing, but rather my punishment. My crimes, actions, and deeds, although noble and for the good of the people, had finally caught up to me. This was her punishment for me as well, but these were the chains I had to bear. I knew once my daughter had chosen—the last soul decided—I would finally be free.

I closed my eyes and tried to find the strength to relive it all one last time. After this, I would finally be able to let go of my lover, the Victor, and Creation. I would be allowed to fade into the past.

"I'm ready." Her soft hands touched mine, and it filled my heart with a feeling that had not been there since the day the Final War had ended.

"I know you are."

"But how will you do it, Papa, when I already know who won?" Her eyes were hopeful, and my heart ached at the knowledge that this might be the end of her existence. But I knew this was the way Creation and the Victor wanted it to be because this was how we won.

"I'm going to put all your memories of the Vi-victor and the Fi-final War behind a veil. That way, when the story ends, you will choose for yourself from what you have seen and felt and what your experiences have taught you to be-believe." The sorrow of reliving this story one final time made my voice crack.

"Veil?" Her graceful eyes brightened as if this would be something enjoyable like everything in her life had been until this point.

"It's a wall in your mind. You will not know the true outcome as you know it now. Not until you have experienced everything that had happened." I placed both of my hands on her temples. I shook away my fear and took a deep breath because I knew that this was the only way for peace to be everlasting.

My daughter closed her eyes and took a deep breath as I placed everything in her mind behind a shimmering wall.

Before I can tell you about the Final War, I must first tell you about a boy. My voice was only a small whisper in both of our hearts.

Why? The story was open in our minds, and I had to send her to the moment when everything started.

Because these are the Memoirs of how the Final War began.

Chapter I

The Broken

~Danny Elikai~

The pounding of my fists echoed through the darkness. My blood smeared on the invisible barrier that kept me from the Door of Light. I could not face this nightmare again. I screamed at the barrier as the door began to be consumed by the icy darkness. I felt the horrors that waited behind me, and I knelt before the light. I pleaded with it, I begged it, but it could not hear my pleas, or it chose to ignore them. It knew, as I did, that this was where I belonged, destined to an eternity of misery in the unimaginably icy remains of this fortress.

"Please, don't leave me here!" My breath made white puffs of warm air that sank to the cold stone ground of the small, claustrophobic room.

The Door of Light shuddered as the suffocating darkness consumed its light, and with a final wink, it abandoned me. The darkness crept all around me, curling around me like wisps of cold, black smoke. I huddled around myself to try and stay warm, wearing nothing but a pair of shorts.

I rubbed my palms together as the fire ignited in my hands to give a small flame, a pinpoint of warmth. I was trapped, alone in my nightmare. I let my fire warm me enough until I was able to turn around and face a small opening in the stone wall. I knew where this small room would lead me.

My bare feet dragged along the stone floor, the immense weight of dread slowing my movements in response to the nightmare below. I had to duck my head as I left the small room, my hair brushing against the ceiling. I moved a few yards into the next room, seeing nothing but pitch darkness around me and the small flame in my palm.

I approached the descending, grand, stone staircase; the smell of blood engulfing my senses as hushed whimpers from below broke the silence. They were the whispers of the damned, those who had been left in the frigid desolation to suffer. The fire was the only light in the darkness as it washed over me. I knew that even the fire in my veins would eventually burn out, so with a terrified breath, I continued to the edge.

I slowly descended the steps and felt the warmth of fresh blood under my bare feet. I could feel the cracks in the stone steps of this ancient grand staircase. My light wasn't bright enough to penetrate down the steps, the steps that I had walked down every night in this relentless nightmare. I carefully crept down to prevent slipping into the mangled bodies at the bottom.

I could feel my warden calling out to me in the darkness as he waited in his throne room.

Danny... I felt the whispering voices fall silent in response to his icy words. *Come to me...*

The cold stabbed at my exposed chest, and I continued to descend. The fire in my hand grew dimmer as if it were beginning to be suffocated by the sorrow, guilt, hatred, and misery that echoed in the darkness below. The smell of rotting meat assaulted my senses as I crept closer to the bottom.

When I reached the final step, an expansive hallway stretched before me with giant, spiraling pillars supporting the high stone ceiling. I raised my hands as the fire illuminated the darkness around me, and I saw them—the innumerable souls suffering and forgotten. They writhed on each other, their bodies mutilated and bloody as their agony echoed off the stone walls, and their purpose was clear. His words echoed in my mind, *They must suffer for you to continue...*

The horror and repulsion made me close my eyes, and I took a deep breath. The only way to continue was to burn them to ashes. I raised the ball of fire in front of me and commanded it to reduce their mutilated bodies to ash.

Their screams and torment weakened me as I fell back onto the stone steps behind me. The inferno engulfed the cavern of these tortured souls, but it provided no warmth to me. I felt the cold overcome me while my fire raged. I watched for hours as their bodies melted, disintegrating until nothing remained except for the rancid smell. The last scream continued to echo in my mind.

I could barely move; my fingers were stiff, and my body was violently shaking. I reached out to the tiny embers in the ashes, feeling the charred bones. I watched as the small fire removed itself from the ashes of the victims, and slowly returned to my palm. I held the small flame and breathed icy life back into it. The fire roared, consuming my hands and returning the heat to my soul.

I got to my shaking feet and proceeded through the ashes of the countless bodies I had just scorched. Their remains came up to my knees, and I felt bones crumble and snap under my feet as I made my way down the hallway. I wanted to vomit, scream, and run back up the stairs, but that would only make it worse.

I walked through an opening at the end of the hallway, and I stepped out of the ashes into a vast room with ceilings so high that the darkness kept them from prying eyes. I could feel more souls everywhere, the fire drawing them closer to me. The fire, the only light in the darkness, would call them, those lost in desolation.

A pair of large, beautifully carved stone doors loomed in front of me. I raised the ball of fire high into the air and focused the remaining strength I had into it. The fire breathed and flexed as it formed a small sun, giving light to the entire enclosure. I couldn't help myself as I turned around, taking in the scene around me.

Thousands of souls were curled up in the fetal position, whimpering the names of those who could not comfort them. They were all as pale as snow, their skin translucent, and I could see the blood on the stone floor where they writhed.

They were nothing more than forgotten souls of those who had come and gone. The screams brought me back to reality as they cringed away from the light and warmth. A few screamed and fled for their lives further into the darkness. Their eyes were hollow because they believed there was no hope for them. All they would have was an eternity of loneliness, sorrow, and regret, and I knew one day I would lie among them.

"Please," the desperate plead came from behind me. I spun toward the voice, and I wished I hadn't. A young man who had scars all over his body pulled himself across the floor toward my light, pleading with the sun to take him away from this place.

I walked toward the grand doors. I was not yet damned to the darkness as they were, reliving every mistake and atrocity they had committed in life, so I was nothing more than a ghost to them.

A small rusty blade was wedged in the seam of the grand looming doors. My energy was nearly depleted, and I struggled to pull it out, but the rusty blade eventually came out of its stone sheath. I placed a hand on the stone doors as the anguish thundered in my veins in response to what was waiting for me. The worst part of my nightmares was the masterpiece crafted by my warden.

Come to me, Danny... My warden was just beyond the doors, waiting with his final torture, the one that he knew would break me. This hell would end with me pleading for death, as it always did.

I stood in front of the doors, unable to move as I prayed, just like the souls around me. I prayed to whoever ruled the light to have mercy on me, to take me from this place. But, like always, I was left alone in the dark.

You deserve this. The truth burned in my heart as I slid the rusty dagger across my palm. The poison ripped through my body, robbing me of my abilities and my will to fight back. Blood pooled in my palm, and I smeared it on the doors. The small sun shuddered and quickly faded away.

I felt the world shake as the doors cracked open and slowly slid apart to reveal the most haunting light I had ever seen. I felt sobs against my leg and looked down at the young man who had crawled right next to me.

"I'm sorry," he said as he stared at the spot where the small sun had just flickered from existence. I wanted to comfort him, to hold him in my arms and let him know that he was not alone, but I could not give him false hope. He puffed white clouds as he whimpered on the floor, and I turned back to the slowly opening doors.

"Danny?" I turned away from the doors to stare into the depths of the darkness, where my eyes fell upon a startled woman. Her black hair almost touched the floor, her bright eyes were fierce, and she wore a plain white dress. Her features would have been beautiful, except for the frostbite that had eaten parts of her skin. We held eye contact, and I felt a single tear fall down my face. I could feel agony radiating from her.

"Tell him I'm so sorry. Tell him I love him and that I am proud of the man he is becoming. I know he doesn't miss me, but please, tell him how sorry I am," her voice rang clear and bright in the darkness.

"Who?" I stepped toward her.

Before she could answer, a burning whip appeared from behind her in the darkness and wrapped itself around her throat. The shock prevented me from doing anything as the whip quickly dragged her back into the darkness with a sharp snap. I remained frozen as another burning whip flew out of the darkness and lashed my face. The strike was so violent that it made me crumple to the floor.

The doors had opened far enough for me to slide through, so I forced myself to stand up and walk into the next level of his torment. His throne room was exactly as I remembered it. Nothing was out of the ordinary, and while it sent ripples of horror through me, I could not help but admire its majesty. It was a triangular room, and I entered at the middle of one of the sides. All along the black marble walls were large hearths that had crackling violet fires burning in them. Directly ahead of me, in the center of the room, was a glistening throne that had green and purple gems that glittered in the firelight. A cloaked figure sat gleefully on his self-proclaimed throne.

I reluctantly walked further into the room, and an uncomfortable wave of choking heat surrounded me. The shimmering violet flames felt unnatural, evil, and cast an ominous feeling over the throne room.

"Welcome, Danny," my warden called out to me in a deep voice that pierced my heart.

I felt the heavy stone doors close behind me, and the freezing air that had been creeping in dissipated. I didn't dare look back at the doors in fear of taking my eyes off the warden before me. He wore a shredded black cloak that had fragmented pieces suspended in the air. I had never seen his face, which was masked by the darkness of his hood. The only thing to be seen were his haunting violet eyes, the eyes of perdition.

"Hello," I forced the words through my gritted teeth.

"Come forward, my child." He raised his finger and crooked it toward himself. My legs moved, even though my heart screamed in wild protest. I struggled against him as his laughter filled my ears.

"Do not be afraid, Danny. This is your home, after all." He pulled me toward him, and there was nothing I could do to fight him. My legs finally stopped moving, and I stood only twenty feet away from him.

"Pl-please, don't do this." I didn't want to see this again, to experience it for the millionth time.

"Oh, Danny. Do not be so rude to your family. After all, they are just dying to see you." My insides tensed at his sadistic chuckle as he snapped his gloved fingers, and they appeared at his feet.

My parents and brother lined up in a row on the black marble floor. They were as lifeless as the day they were buried. My knees slammed to the floor, and I lost my breath, leaving a hollow ache inside me.

"Please, please don't do this." My pleas were ignored as he snapped his fingers again, and my dad's lifeless torso lifted to face me.

"This is your fault, Danny. We are dead because of you! We died because you were too weak! I wish I had taken you out before we lost our lives. We all died in agony, and it's all your fault!" His words reverberated in the vast throne room as if to make me hear the words a second time. I watched in horror as a hole opened in his chest and blood gushed out. All the warmth escaped from my veins as he bled profusely, and his body splashed lifelessly in a pool of his blood.

"I'm begging you."

He raised his hand again and snapped his fingers. My mom's corpse lifted her head just enough to look at me. Her hair had been completely burned away, and her skin had peeled back in places to reveal blackened bone. I could taste the bile rising in my throat as the smell of cooked flesh hit my nose. Her eyes had burned away, leaving mucous dripping from her sockets. Blood began to drip in various places as he forced her heart to beat again. She could not walk, so she dragged herself on the ground, leaving a growing trail of blood and flesh in her wake.

"I was once beautiful. Now, look at me! Look at what your actions have done! You were my greatest regret, my ultimate failure. You are an abomination, and you will burn this world to the ground!" She spat blood on me, and with a snap of his finger, she exploded into a pile of ash on the floor.

I could not plead with him to stop anymore; my voice was gone, and I just wanted to die. My throat was so tight that I could barely breathe. The tears were now pouring down my face. I couldn't even move my lips to apologize to my family for the agonizing pain that I had put them through.

I wanted this nightmare to end, and as if to honor my request to die, the warden snapped his fingers one final time, and Matthew got to his feet. His physique was not grotesque, and he looked as happy and vibrant as the last time I saw him alive. I remembered he was sitting next to me in the back seat as we approached Grenoff, and he was trying to make me smile by cramming popcorn in his mouth and talking like a chipmunk. Now he smiled at me, but I knew his punishment would be the worst.

"I know how much this hurts you. I know how much you want to end our suffering." Matthew looked at our father and the ashes of our mother.

"You can see what your actions have done to us. Danny, you know what will happen if you don't end it. Your existence is a disease upon Creation. Only you can bring us peace after all the pain you have caused." He knelt before me as our family's silver dagger appeared in his hands.

"It will be okay, I promise. End this before more people die, Danny. The darkness will not be a punishment but a blessing. You can finally be at peace and give us the peace we deserve." The cold hate in my brother's electric green eyes burned as he spoke the last words I needed to hear. The words that would pierce my heart like the silver dagger.

"I would still be alive if you had just killed yourself so long time ago." I took the dagger out of his hand, the guilt unbearable. I looked up to him, but I didn't see my brother—only the violet eyes burning through the darkness in the hood.

"Don't you understand yet?" The warden's vexation rang clear in his voice. "This is how it will all end, and I will rule Creation!"

The warden grabbed my hand with the dagger and pointed the tip of the blade toward me. I gasped for air, clutching the dagger as he thrust it into my chest. I stared into his eyes as my blood pooled around us. I felt his fury as he pulled the dagger out, and I fell into my blood, and everything went black.

****

My eyes opened, and I found myself curled up in a ball under the only apple tree in the graveyard. The sun was rising in the east, and I could hear the morning chimes of the bell tower. I began to sit up as my stiff body protested furiously, and I wiped away the dirt on my face. I had on nothing but the shorts I had worn in my nightmare, and I couldn't locate my shirt or shoes. I had black smudges on my legs and arms, along with dirt and dust that coated my body.

I pulled myself into a seated position to get a better look at their headstones. The nightmare was over for the night, but the true horror was waiting before me because three months ago, my family died in a terrible car accident, which I had survived.

I picked up the small silver locket from Matthew's headstone, and I could feel the pain and anguish they went through in my heart. I didn't have to imagine their mangled and burned bodies just below my feet. I never saw their bodies from that horrible night, and the ceremony that had been closed casket.

My aunt thought I had been through enough, but the warden made sure that I knew the horrors they suffered.

"I'm s-so sorry, Matthew." I touched my brother's headstone, my heart burning to be buried with them.

Matthew Philip Elikai
03.16.2000 – 06.08.2018
Beloved Brother, Nephew,
Believer in the Light.

Chapter II

The Promise

~Danny Elikai~

Their headstones were frozen in time, shaded by the beautiful apple tree on the hill, and my heart desired to be buried with them. I could see the beautiful script of their headstones, even from the edge of the graveyard where I stood. I closed my eyes and took a deep breath as I tightened my grip on the locket, trying not to let the guilt leave me breathless in the dirt.

Laughter echoed from the memory of my brother. It surged through my body. I felt its joy soothe my aching heart like it had when he was alive. I bit down hard on my lip, the metallic taste of blood washing over my tongue as I tried to avoid letting any hope back in. A single ray of hope would quickly fade and drag me deeper into the darkness.

I stood at the gate of the graveyard, lost in my thoughts. I gripped the iron gate as my knees faltered, and I felt the sharp pain as a jagged piece of metal sliced my palm. I watched as my blood slid down the rusted metal, and for a second, the emotional pain disappeared.

I glanced at my hand and watched the blood pooling in my palm. I felt empty as the blood hit the dirt by my feet. I looked back at my stinging hand, which had already started to heal itself. Small flames repaired the damage, stitching the wound more precisely than a surgeon could. Before I could wipe my bloody palm onto my dirty shorts, the wound had vanished completely without a scar.

I began to walk barefoot down the road that was lined on both sides with dense trees. The path wound its way back to the small town of Grenoff. This strange town was built at the epicenter of different breathtaking geographic phenomena, by which the town was encased on all sides. A massive lake was in the east, its crystal-clear waters shimmering brightly.

To the south, a magnificent mountain guarded the town against harsh winds and was capped with pearly white snow year-round. The graveyard sat at the base of a mountain. To the northeast was a vast cliff that overlooked Grenoff, but to the northwest, there was a deciduous forest with beautiful trails and glittering streams.

In the center of the town stood a jet-black marble bell tower that loomed over twenty stories in the air. The four-faced tower was my favorite part of Grenoff. At dusk, the clock faces turned four beautiful colors. The north was a warm red, the east, a bright yellow, the west, a dazzling emerald, and the south, a neon violet. It was the same neon violet color as the eyes of my warden.

I can still remember the first time I came to Grenoff when I was just seven years old. I remembered waking up when we cleared the dense wildness and came out into the open stretch that revealed the city. I saw the sun setting in the west as we descended from the north, the forest thinning as the bell tower chimed, and the northern clock glowed red. I felt like the bell tower was welcoming us home after an extended period away.

I was entranced as we pulled into this beautiful town. It was a hidden paradise in the middle of nowhere, a paradise that had been considered to be one of the most desired travel destinations by people from all around the world. Most people seemed to feel a pull toward this town as if it were calling out to people from every corner of Creation. The city of Grenoff had unique, incredible wonders about it that once made me feel safe, loved, and protected. But after everything that had happened, it was my endless nightmare.

My memories had carried me through the town to the place where I always ended up. I found myself sitting on a small bench, looking up at the northern clock of the bell tower. The jet-black tower was made from a rare ebony marble, and when the sunlight hit it at the right angle, the sides reflected tiny shimmering rainbows. The tower sat atop a small platform with a few steps, elevating it slightly above the courtyard. The bell tower itself had four arches, one underneath each clock face, allowing people to walk underneath it.

Surrounding these arches was beautiful, bright green, variegated ivy that, according to rumors from the locals, was planted by the man who built the bell tower. The tower itself was simple in appearance, but it stood as an edifice that had made Grenoff even more mysterious and breathtaking.

The best part of the bell tower was at the very top, just above the northern clock face. Even from where I sat, I could see the small three-pointed stone crown that rested above the clock's face. This was Matthew's favorite part of the town as well because he said that the crown belonged to the King of this city.

"A King?" I heard myself asking as the memory danced before my eyes. Matthew and I had sat on the same bench that I was sitting on. I could see him as if I were reliving the memory. He had been ten years old, and his strawberry blonde hair almost covered his green eyes. Our parents had left us on the bench while they went to purchase some ice cream from a traveling cart.

"Yes, a King!" His eyes were ablaze with passion. "A King to rule all of Creation!" he exclaimed, and I saw my parents look back at him with fear in their eyes. My brother leaned into me and said, "One day, the King will return, and I can't wait to meet him."

I stared at the crown as the memory faded. I could not help but wonder if Matthew had ever met the King. If anyone was worthy of meeting him, it was my brother.

"I'm sorry," I said to the crown, hoping my brother could hear me.

I gazed up at the cloudless blue sky and felt a tinge of pain, the pain of knowing that I would never see him again. I closed my eyes as I felt the light from the sun hit my face, and I knew that this was the closest I would ever get to the light.

A tear ran down my cheek as I pulled my knees to my chest, trying not to sob. *How do people survive this?*

How do I keep going when my life should have ended with my family in the car crash? When I have to face my loved ones every night and witness the pain they went through?

Another memory came back to me. I could still smell the hospital room where I woke up after the accident when I had turned to see my uncle sitting next to me. His luminous green eyes, the same electric green eyes that all Elikai men had—except for me—told me everything. I remembered resting on the uncomfortable hospital bed as the reality unfolded before me, and my warden's laughter echoed in triumph.

The funeral, a sea of white and yellow, was a night of endless tears. I didn't move or speak. I couldn't even cry because I was numb. It seemed that everyone in Grenoff had attended the celebration of their lives. My dad and uncle had grown up in Grenoff, so almost everyone knew them.

I received hugs, handshakes, sympathy, kind words, and best wishes from people I had never met, and it did not lighten the sorrow.

I was catatonic in my bed for weeks after the funeral, barely able to stay awake or fall asleep. I was trapped in my frozen hell, tortured endlessly by my warden. My depression escalated so dramatically that my aunt and uncle took me back to the hospital, where I spent another couple of weeks to make sure I wouldn't end my own life. The doctors concurred that I would heal in time and would start to feel again. The medication they gave me remained untouched under my bed.

Sitting on the bench, I could hear my warden's voice and my dead family's words echoing in my mind. I could feel his glee with my suffering, and once again, my mind was thrown into the darkness.

You made a promise. Matthew's words echoed like trumpets when I always thought about ending it. Even as I sat on the bench, feeling the sun's warmth on my skin, his icy words sent a shiver running rampant through my body. His words were slowly drowning out Matthew's.

Come to me, Danny... I was nothing more than the little red flag in an epic game of tug-of-war between my brother and my warden. I was being torn apart, little by little, with each passing day.

"Please." I opened my eyes toward the sunlight. "Please, let me die, just make it all end. Just make it all go away."

That was when I heard it. Its beauty was unparalleled by anything I had ever heard before. It was soft, like a child's lullaby, and it filled the surrounding air. I felt my guilt and depression melt away as the lullaby danced around me.

Danny. I felt the voice in my heart, mind, and soul. I sat there, astonished, as the warmth flooded through me, and the locket fell out of my pocket. I stared at it as the lullaby danced around it. I picked it up and gasped at the frigid cold that radiated from it. I could feel the lullaby was coming from the sealed locket. I stared at the seam, once again trying to make it open, but like the light, it ignored me.

"DANNY!" My uncle's voice made me jump.

His eyes found mine, and I could see the relief on his face from across the courtyard. The music disappeared as my uncle ran up to me and got to his knees before me, and I looked at him. He was classically handsome with a thick blonde beard, which highlighted those electric green eyes. His strawberry blonde hair wasn't combed to the side, and it was long enough that it almost touched his eyes. It reminded me so much of Matthew on the last day of his life.

My uncle looked distraught, with a drained look on his face, and wore a dirty T-shirt that was inside out. I could not mistake the worry that shined in his eyes, as well as the puffy redness that was framed by his black glasses. I looked into his green eyes, magnified by the lenses, and the guilt ignited inside of me like wildfire.

"I'm sorry."

"Danny." He placed his hand on my knee like he always did. "Did you sleepwalk to the graveyard again?"

"Yes." We both looked down at my exposed, dirt-covered chest. "I can't understand why I survived when they died." My grief strengthened its tight grip around my throat.

My uncle moved to sit next to me on the bench. He didn't say anything as he pulled me into a hug. As I hugged him back, I could feel tiny sobs coming from his broad chest. My uncle was one of those men who didn't showcase his emotions, but ever since he lost a large part of his family, I could see how it had devastated him.

"When I found out what happened, I wasn't sure how I was going to get through the rest of my life," he told me. "But when they told me that you were still alive, completely unharmed, I remembered that I had people I would continue to fight for. I am not ashamed to admit that I momentarily forgot about your aunt and my son. I know this pain eclipses everything, and it will for a long time." He pulled himself away slightly to look me in the eyes. "But I promise that we will get through this. I promise you that if you let us, we will protect you, and guide you through this. You are my family, Danny. I promise that everything will make sense one day. You just have to fight, and one day, you'll wake up happy, and your life will be beautiful." I could feel my grief and anxiety loosening their grip on me. My uncle's words were calming, and I was grateful to have him in my life.

"I hope so." I looked at his inside-out shirt and the stains from my tears and dirt. We must have embraced for a long time, but it felt like a single moment.

"Danny, you will see them again." His words were supposed to be comforting, but I knew in my heart that I was not going to end up in the light but lost, cold, and alone in the darkness. I would become one of the countless souls that haunted me in my dreams, clawing at the light and crying out for those that I longed for.

I turned back to my uncle and forced a smile. The last thing I wanted was to go back to the hospital because I was tired of everyone asking me what was wrong.

"Do you think they're in the Realm of Light?" I looked up toward the endless blue sky.

"I have no doubt, Danny, and I'm sure Matthew is watching out for you." My uncle smiled, but I could see the pain behind it. He got to his feet and looked at me. "I think it's time to go home and get you clothed again. Your aunt will be relieved to know that you are alright."

I nodded as I got to my feet, the day's horrors still before me.

We walked for several minutes in silence, lost in our thoughts of our family, as we approached the beautiful white Victorian-style house. It was two stories and had a white wraparound porch with large bay windows looking over a lush emerald, green lawn. This house had been in our family for several generations, and I can't remember a time when I didn't love coming here.

The Grenoff Sheriff's Jeep was parked in the driveway, and I had a feeling that my uncle was late for work.

"Danny? What's wrong?" he asked when he realized I had stopped following as I nodded toward the front door, which had just been ripped open.

"DANNY?!" My aunt seemed to fly out towards me, the relief washing over her face. She still had an oven mitt on her hand as she ran up to me and suffocated me in a bear hug. She was a beautiful woman with bright baby blue eyes and natural red hair that was pinned up in a tight bun. She had freckles on her nose—the reason my uncle had fallen in love with her the minute he saw her.

"Are you okay?" She scanned my face when she released me from the hug to see where I was hurt. "Where are your clothes?"

"I'm fine, I promise." I didn't need to lie, but it was easier to pretend at this point, not for me, but for them.

"Do I smell bacon?" My uncle diverted his attention toward the open door.

"Alex, save some for the rest of us!" She called over her shoulder as my uncle moved towards the kitchen. "Danny, honey, go on upstairs and get yourself cleaned up." She pointed to the dirt and ash all over my body.

I nodded as I made my way up the staircase to a large, tiled bathroom on the second floor, and I closed the door. I leaned my back against the door and breathed heavily, trying to pull myself together. I looked in the mirror and realized how haggard I looked.

My honey-brown hair was longer than usual, and I had dark purple bags under my sky-blue eyes that looked bruised against my ivory skin.

I hated my eyes because I was the only man in my family who didn't have the captivating green eyes of the other Elikai men. I moved closer to the mirror, and I saw the eyes of my mother, but around the iris were sunbursts of red and yellow, with flecks of green and purple. Everyone always said my eyes were breathtaking, but to me, they were a constant reminder that I was an outcast in my own family.

I scowled at my reflection. I balled my left hand into a fist, and I punched the mirror. The mirror cracked and created an intricate web of my sorrowful reflection. I watched as the blood from my fist trickled down my arm, tiny shards of mirror glistening in my knuckles. I felt the physical pain drown out the unbearable feeling in my heart.

I watched tears fall from my many faces before I raised my bloody hand over the broken glass and sighed deeply. I felt the warmth flow from my veins into my hand as the mirror slowly repaired itself. I watched as the fragments of the mirror were lifted from the black marble countertop and sealed themselves back into the frame. The cracked web began to disappear, and within a minute, the mirror returned to its pristine condition, except for smudges of blood and skin where I had punched it.

I looked down at my hand and saw that I was no longer bleeding. I knew that beneath the dried blood, there would not be any trace of a scar. I picked the glittery bits of mirror out of my knuckles and watched as my skin immediately repaired itself. The burning heat pulled back inside my veins.

"I hate you." I grabbed a towel and began to clean the blood off the restored mirror. I turned away from my reflection toward the shower, hoping the hot water would erase the exhaustion from my face.

Chapter III

Remembrance

~Danny Elikai~

The hallway was covered with the memories of my family, filled with the beautiful smiles of those I loved, who loved me and who were now gone. I looked at all their smiling faces, and I longed to be as happy as I pretended to be in the photographs. When I looked at the boy in the pictures, he seemed happy and was very well-loved. But what no one else saw was the darkness that continued to stalk him, whispering in his ear to kill himself before more of his loved ones died.

I held a picture of myself that was encased in a wooden frame. I was smiling while my brother was about to shove a marshmallow in my ear just before the picture was taken. The fire in my veins burned pleasantly at the memory. I remembered that day by the lake, the last day of our vacation before we headed back to Boston, where I would soon start my freshman year of high school.

This picture had been taken over a year ago and was one of my favorite memories. I remembered it so clearly because it was one of the few days when the darkness didn't touch me. I remembered waking up, the summer morning light filling my room through the open window.

I remembered taking a deep breath, waiting for the torment to start, but there was nothing but silence. I actually drifted back to sleep with a smile on my face. But in my sleepy haze, I clearly heard a soft, kind voice that said, *You are not alone, Danny.*

The words sent me into a cozy, dreamless sleep. I felt them around me, everyone I loved. I couldn't see them or hear them, but I knew they were with me. I knew they loved me and were always there for me. It was a beautiful, quiet moment we had all somehow shared before. The surrounding dark was warm and assuring as if I were asleep on a hammock in late summer. For once, I felt safe in the darkness, and I was not desperately searching for a way out.

I didn't want to be disturbed, but as if on cue, my brother gently pulled me out of the darkness and back into the light. I could smell a savory aroma, and Matthew was holding a plate that was piled high with bacon.

There was never a better way to start the day than with Aunt Shannon's bacon.

"Good morning, Danny!" He set the plate down next to me as he went to the chair next to the window, which was open, and a soft breeze gently twirled the curtains in a lazy dance. He stopped and looked at the open window and then back to me.

"Did you leave this open?" he asked as I shoved bacon in my mouth.

No, and I heard him chuckle. *What? The great thing about you being able to read my mind is that I don't have to stop eating to speak to you.*

"Well, how can speaking compete with bacon?" He gave that airy chuckle as he gently closed the window. He gave me a look, the same knowing look he always gave me when he knew more than I wanted him to. Even though I couldn't read his mind, I knew exactly what was upsetting him.

"Matthew, I promise you that I'm fine. Honestly, the warden is not in my head. I actually feel pretty good. I feel, I don't know, happy?" I felt it was important enough for me to stop eating for a moment to help make him believe me. His green eyes scanned me, and I knew he was looking through my mind with a curious, skeptical glare.

Okay, fine, don't believe me. I put my bacon back on my plate. In my head, I replayed how peaceful the darkness was and how I had felt that morning. I showed him the soothing voice that assured me I would not be alone. If I had blinked, I would have missed the look of surprise and the flash of anger that consumed his features for a fraction of a second. However confused that made me, I wanted him to know that, for the first time in a while, I was happy, and I wanted it to be a great day.

Happy? He turned to glare out of the window and seemed so distant and distracted, far from his usual focused and caring self.

"What's wrong?"

"Nothing." He ignored the heaviness in my tone as he turned to me. "We're going to the lake today, so you need to get dressed!" His emotions were completely hidden behind his big smile that always touched his electric green eyes.

"You're lucky I can't read your mind!" I threw a piece of bacon at him. I heard him chuckle again, and he whispered something as he walked out of the room, but I didn't hear what he said.

That was the day we went to Grenoff Lake. It was considered one of the most beautiful lakes in North America, due to its unique shape and beauty. The lake rested to the east of Grenoff. Every morning when the sun rose, its light reflected on the surface of the water and shimmered like the stars in the sky. In the fall, like that day, the trees on the far side of the lake changed to deep reds and yellows. The reflection of the swaying trees by the lake gave the illusion that the water was on fire.

I remember standing on the white sandy shore with a brand new red and white checkered blanket under my arm, staring at the blazing lake. My brother yelled at me, and I looked up to see him standing on the edge of a small rise that overlooked the lake about a few feet above me.

"Cannonball!" He jumped off and sank to the deeper part of the lake with a perfect splash. I rolled out the blanket as my parents sat down next to me. My mom handed me a soda as I sat down in the sand, making sure my toes were buried. I lost myself in the peaceful sounds of the water lapping at the shore. The calm I had felt earlier that morning seemed to return to me again, and I was perfectly at ease with myself.

It had been the perfect day, the final day before the darkness began what felt like its final assault. Since then, my days and nights were filled with endless suffering and darkness. I had horrible nightmares where everyone I had ever known died all around me. I felt helpless, paralyzed, and defeated.

It was only Matthew who understood because he could see what I was feeling every day. He could not feel its impact; the darkness would not touch him. Eventually, my parents became so worried that I was hospitalized for a week.

After intense psychological and physical testing, I had been sent home with an assortment of drugs that never seemed to work. It wasn't because of the darkness overwhelming the drugs, however. I could feel the fire in my own veins as it burned the chemicals out, never allowing them to work. It was as if my own body wanted me to suffer in the darkness.

I watched my reflection in the glass of the frame as the memory ended. I held the picture I had taken off the wall and wished I could relive that day over and over for the rest of my life. The memory felt like a long-lost friend, something familiar and beautiful but distant.

My trembling hands put the photograph back on the wall, and I turned back to head downstairs. I had barely moved before I froze in my tracks. I stared at the edge of the staircase across the landing, and I saw Matthew leaning against the wall. He looked at me with his arms crossed, and he looked exactly as he did on the day he died. He wore his ragged Yale sweater, but it was not stained with soot and blood like the one that was sitting in a sealed bag in my closet. My heart swelled with joy when I saw him standing in front of me, but I knew something was wrong. He stared up at me, his electric green eyes ablaze with urgency.

My mind went into gridlock as my heart plummeted to my toes, and I said in my mind, *Matthew?*

"Time is running out, Danny." His burning eyes betrayed the calmness in his tone. He didn't move or offer me anything but these simple words, "They are coming."

Wh-who?

"Find him."

"Find who?" I said this out loud because Matthew might not be able to hear my thoughts now that he was dead. I felt my body begin to twitch, so I stepped toward him as he began to disappear. "Find who?!" I heard footsteps coming through the hallway from under the stairs. Aunt Shannon stepped through the walkway and turned up to look at me standing near the landing. Her baby blue eyes were wide as she held up her wooden spoon like a sword. "Danny, who are you talking to?"

I looked back at the edge of the staircase where Matthew was standing, expecting him to be there still, but I stood alone.

"Oh," I shook my head. "I must have been thinking out loud." I tried to give her a reassuring smile, which she returned as if she had accepted my explanation.

"Oh, I do that all the time. I have your breakfast ready if you're hungry." She turned away and walked back toward the kitchen. I quickly moved to where Matthew had been standing and touched the part of the wall he had been leaning against. It felt slightly warm to the touch.

"Danny, it's going to get cold!" I shook my head in disbelief. Matthew had just been here; I could feel it. I could even smell the familiar scent of the laundry soap that our mom used on our clothes.

I knew that my doctor had told me that when someone loses a loved one, they could often convince themselves they had seen and spoken to those who were gone. I wasn't sure if that was what had happened because I had seen him, felt the warmth on the wall, and could smell that he had been there.

I shook my head in disbelief. This was just another trick; another elaborate ruse created by my warden to send me into another manic-depressive episode.

"I'll be there in a second, Aunt Shannon." I pulled my hand away from the wall. I turned around and moved back down the hallway to my room and threw open the closet door. I moved aside a few plastic crates filled with my various possessions to find a small wooden box. I opened the box and found Matthew's clothes exactly as I had remembered them: slightly burned and covered in dirt and soot but still intact. The Yale sweater was still sealed in a zipped bag, so I opened it and felt the fabric. I picked up the sweater and could smell smoke, sweat, and lilac laundry soap.

I felt the tears on my hand before I even realized that I was crying. I quickly wiped my tears away but felt an icy prickle move down my spine. I could feel the rage coming off him as if he were standing right behind me. His icy voice rang clear in my head.

Remember, it's your fault he's dead. The shiver ran down my spine, but it didn't send me into the suffocating darkness as it normally did. I got to my feet and brushed off my warden's attempt. I had seen Matthew, and it made me happy. I didn't care if it was a ploy from him, because it had failed.

"Not today, not now." I kept whispering to myself and felt him chuckle in the darkness. I put the sweater back in its proper place and walked out of my room without turning behind me. Even though I had avoided the pull of the darkness, I still felt the hollow feeling that usually filled my day. I let out a breath, knowing I had stood my ground and would not let him beat me. My warden felt like a million miles away, and I knew that Matthew was still protecting me. But I knew my small victory would end with another, more intense nightmare.

Chapter IV

Grenoff High

~Danny Elikai~

It was those twinkling navy-blue eyes of the boy who was sitting at the counter that pinned me to the entryway of the kitchen. We stared at each other for a long moment without saying a word.

"Oh, Danny, there's someone I want you to meet," my aunt said excitedly, and she led me to the table where the boy sat. "This is Jesse Daniels. He lives just down the road from here on the Daniels' farm, and I have been meaning to introduce you two for a while now."

Our gaze held as he gave me a wide grin. He was about my age, but his build was that of someone who worked outside. His cowboy hat rested next to his plate, and his hair was a warm chestnut brown with a classic military cut, buzzed sides, and a short top. He had a cluster of freckles on his short nose.

"Finally! I've been waitin' to meet you for quite a while." He had a thick Southern drawl, and I nervously glanced at Aunt Shannon, giving her a confused expression.

He smiled and chuckled shyly, saying, "Sorry, Shannon and Alex have told me all 'bout you, and I feel like I already know you as a close friend. My name's Jesse." He stood up and reached across the table to shake my hand. I grasped his large, calloused, pale hand in mine, and I was hypnotized by the way the muscles moved under his simple dark blue V-neck shirt that matched his eyes.

"Nice to meet you." I let go of Jesse's hand and quickly moved my gaze back to my aunt, looking for an explanation.

"Sorry, Danny, I forgot to tell you. Jesse is our babysitter for Alvaro." I looked at him, and the memory of his name came back. I remembered my mom telling me that my aunt and uncle had finally found a babysitter for my cousin. My eyes fell upon Alvaro, who was sitting behind the kitchen island, playing quietly with his blocks.

"Oh yeah, you are the one Alvaro is so fond of." I returned his smile. "I am glad that he is comfortable around someone outside of our family." He nodded, and we all turned to look at the small boy who was ignoring us. I moved to the table and sat down in front of my breakfast next to Jesse.

"That lil' man is certainly one of a kind."

The conversation brought back the sparse memories I had of Alvaro. About a year or two after my aunt and uncle were married, they tried to have children, but every time failed. Finally, after extensive visits to the doctor, they found out that my aunt could not bear children. Instead of being defeated, my aunt believed that it was the will of the light telling her to find a child in need of a loving home. Shortly after, they found

Alvaro. All they knew about him was that his unwed mother had died giving birth to him. He had been just a newborn baby when they had adopted him from an orphanage in upstate New York.

Alvaro was unlike any other child any of us had ever met, mostly because he refused to speak, and he had a stillness in his nature. He was not mute; he just had nothing he needed to say. Out of the seven years my aunt and uncle had taken care of him, he had spoken out loud only five times, briefly conversing with only the three people in the dining room, and my uncle. I believed the only person he had spoken twice to was my aunt, but one of those times had been an emergency.

Alvaro turned to look at us, and the young child stared directly at me with his bright hazel eyes. There were times when, if the light was just right, I could see flecks of yellow. He had straight black hair, and a soft bronze complexion to match. My aunt said he was going to be a heartbreaker when he grew up.

One thing I had always found to be curious about Alvaro was the fact that he didn't like to be touched. At first, he could only be handled by Uncle Alex, then Aunt Shannon. It was not for a very long time that they found anyone else that he was comfortable being touched by, and it turned out that person was Jesse.

I remembered the only time I heard Alvaro speak. He was sitting on the floor, and I had walked up to him, back when he was about four years old. He had looked up at me with a curious expression as if he could not decide if I were a friend or foe. He pointed at me and said, "Celestial." Then, he became confused and turned away, and that was the only word he had ever spoken to me.

The pat on my shoulder from Jesse brought me back from the past, and I noticed his smile was good-natured.

"Y'alright?" I shook off the past and moved to the plate of food that had been set out for me.

"Yeah, sorry, I was lost in my head." Alvaro was sitting completely still and staring at his blocks as if he were waiting for them to do something.

"So, I hear you're gonna be joinin' us at Grenoff High," Jesse's excitement made me look at my aunt again.

"I have been meaning to tell you that we are enrolling you at the local high school today, and we have a lot to do before Monday." She was not paying us attention as she looked down at the list in her hands. Since it was Saturday, I was surprised the school was even open.

"Has school even started?" I was unsure of how early the school year started in Grenoff. My summer had been a gloomy haze of darkness. I had completely forgotten about school and my approaching sophomore year.

"Nah, not 'till Monday. But everything you need to get will take a few hours," As Jesse spoke, I began to question why Jesse was here when I had seen him once over the several months I had lived with my aunt and uncle.

"Are you babysitting today?" I shoved the pancakes and bacon Aunt Shannon made for me into my mouth.

"Well," my aunt started, "I felt bad. Since everything we have dealt with over these last few months, we haven't really needed Jesse, and I thought today would be a good excuse to have him babysit." She absently mindedly waved her hand in our direction, making Jesse chuckle. "Plus, Alvaro kept standing by the door as if he were expecting him to walk through it."

"Don't worry 'bout it. I was startin' to wonder if the little guy had forgotten who I was." He turned to me with his eyes downcast, and I could see the nervous tension in his shoulders. "I'm so sorry to hear about your brother. I met him several times, and he was a good guy."

His soft words were genuine, but they felt as empty as they always did every time someone tried to console me. I knew everyone meant well, but for some reason, words did not help. They certainly didn't bring my family back, and it didn't fill the chasm they left in my heart.

"Thanks." I finished the rest of the meal in silence as Alvaro tugged away Jesse to help him stare at his blocks, and my aunt went upstairs to finish getting ready.

"Ready?" My aunt entered the kitchen as I was washing off my plate to place it in the dishwasher.

"Yeah, let's go."

"Jesse, if you'd like, you're more than welcome to meet us at Bear's Piano Diner at seven. We'd love to treat you to dinner."

"I was actually planning on meetin' Izabelle tonight," he waved over his shoulder as Alvaro placed a block in his hand.

"Oh, well, she is more than welcome to join us."

"You'll have to ask her; she's the boss." He turned around to smile at us as I put on my shoes. "Ya'll should see her at the school today."

"That sounds fantastic! I can't wait for Danny to meet her." Aunt Shannon twisted the doorknob to the garage door and left it open for me. I began to leave, but I stopped myself and went back to the kitchen.

"It was nice meeting you."

"Oh, don't you worry 'bout it. We'll be seein' a lot more of each other, Danny." He stood up and shook my hand again with a firm, warm grip.

This time, the minute our hands connected, I felt a deep and distant sorrow that echoed through his body. I looked into Jesse's deep eyes, but the feeling didn't match the gleefulness. Confused, I turned and left through the garage.

"How are you feeling?" My aunt turned to me once we were inside her sedan.

"I'm fine." I lied with a smile, "I just miss them."

She grabbed my hand and squeezed it, saying, "Me too, honey."

After a few minutes of driving, we walked around the parking lot of the high school. The grounds of the school were covered in trees, with a few benches along some walking trails. The campus itself was composed of three buildings that were four stories tall. They were arranged in a triangle and overlooked the massive lake. The walls of the buildings were built from traditional red brick with ivy climbing up the sides, giving them an established appearance. The building that was closest to the parking lot was surrounded by a brick path that was inscribed with the name of every graduate from the school. I looked around, and I couldn't help but admire its incredible beauty.

"Danny!" I could hear the excitement in her voice. She stood a couple of yards away from me, closer to the main building. She waved me over, pointing at the brick pathway, and I saw what she wanted me to see.

Alexander R. Elikai
1998

I stared at his name, and I couldn't help but wonder.

"Do you know where my dad's name is?" It took us less than a minute to find his name. It was more comforting than I ever could have imagined.

Joshua P. Elikai
1991

"Soon, Danny, your name will be engraved into this path. It will serve as a reminder to future generations that you can do anything you set your mind to." She smiled and placed a comforting hand on my shoulder. I felt the joy swell inside my body, and I looked toward the school. "Are you ready?"

The wooden doors were old and elegant with old-fashioned bronze knockers. They were heavy, but they swung open easily with a groan. The foyer inside was cozy and had the feeling of an upscale mansion. The walls were adorned with paintings, the couches lining the walls were plush and comfortable, and the fireplaces were made of black marble. A couple of students were walking around talking, while some were reading by the fireplaces, and others were setting up a banner, which appeared to be welcoming the new school year.

The walls were a dark gray, which allowed the bright colors of the couches and armchairs to stand out. I could see the levels above me, and they all had different color schemes, similar to that of the bell tower. The bottom floor had an assortment of bright green couches and chairs that complemented the dark walls. The second floor had vibrant yellow furnishings, while the third was a violet scheme, and the top floor had maroon decor.

The furnishings of Grenoff High were very peculiar, like something out of a dream, but it all matched tastefully. The colors of the walls were coordinated with each other, and the building seemed to have a calming effect. I felt at home, which may have explained why so many students were hanging around on a Saturday morning before school even started.

"Aunt Shannon, I don't think I'll be accepted here. My grades weren't spectacular, and I don't want you to pay a ton of money for my tuition," I said, taking in the majesty of this school.

"Danny, this is a public school." She practically forced me along to the offices. "This school only looks this way because it's purely academic, so all of the funding goes to the school. The people who attend this school come from all corners of the globe and generally donate for years after they graduate. They believe, like many of us do, that education should be the prime focus in a youth's academic career. I have no doubt that you will be incredibly successful here."

When we entered the admissions office, I found myself in a very modern room, standing by a sleek desk. Glass bay windows overlooked the beautiful lake, and a large computer monitor was sitting on the counter before me.

"Hello, Shannon!" Another Southern drawl sounded from behind us. When we turned around, a short, plump woman with curly blonde hair and bright green glasses greeted us with a warm smile. I had a feeling she was Jesse's mother.

"Hello, Blaire." My aunt put on a very forced smile that I knew all too well.

"Well, howdy," she patted me on the shoulder. "You must be Danny." I nodded as she moved past us to sit behind the desk.

"This is good timing. I just pulled your file." She was holding up a manila folder. My school records must have been in there, but I noticed the folder was extremely thin.

"I can't believe my whole academic career fits on two sheets of paper." If I were to die, that was the only record of my existence.

"There weren't any problems obtaining his records from Blackwell High?" My aunt ignored my comment as we sat down in one of the conformable chairs.

"No, problem at all. They were very understanding, and they sent them quickly," she said, smiling the whole time before turning back to me. "Danny, I am genuinely sorry to hear about your family. It was such a tragedy. Your family was very well-loved and admired, and they will be missed. However, I'm sure you will be very happy here." Her words were supposed to be comforting, but they only sent a surge of emptiness through me.

"Thank you." My words were not at all sincere, and they came out hollow.

"Danny, head upstairs to Room 217 and get fitted for your school uniform. We have the measurements, but we need to make the final adjustments. Your aunt and I will finalize your school schedule." She waved me out of the office, and I gladly left. I walked past the green couches and started to head up the glass staircase. I walked around the school and slowly took in all of the immaculate architecture. I wanted to experience the beauty of this school before I started classes.

I reached the second floor and made my way down the hallway. I saw a sign that indicated Room 217 was down in the south wing of the building, but I looked down at the eastern wing and stopped in my tracks. Down the eastern hall was a pair of giant wooden doors, which seemed out of place compared to the smaller yellow doors on both sides of the hallway.

I looked around and saw no one, so I walked down the hallway and stood in front of the ornate doors. I pushed one of them open slowly, which groaned as it moved, and I peeked in the room. Inside was one of the most beautiful libraries I had ever seen. It didn't look like a high school library, but rather a library at an Ivy League university. Plush leather chairs surrounded black marble fireplaces, and the bookshelves and desks were made of polished mahogany. Tall glass windows reached the high ceilings and let in the morning light to illuminate the rows of books. The polished hardwood floors creaked with every step, but it only added to the rich atmosphere of the breathtaking room. I walked toward the windows, and I saw that they overlooked the lake. It was a library that made me want to dive into its collection and be lost in its pages. I could have spent the rest of my life in this library.

"Is there something I can help you find?" I turned around to see an older woman wearing rimmed glasses on the end of her crooked nose. She had a warm smile, and she wore a simple two-piece wool suit.

"Oh, I'm sorry, I got distracted. I love libraries and books."

"Don't trouble yourself, dear. Are you new to Grenoff High?"

"Yes, I will be starting Monday."

"Well, welcome! Is there anything, in particular, you were looking for?"

"Sorry, yes. I'm supposed to be looking for Room 217."

"Oh, please, follow me." She led me out of my new favorite library and pointed to the southern hallway. "You will be looking for the last door on the left."

"Thank you."

I walked down the hallway toward Room 217. I kept thinking about the library, and I had a feeling that Matthew had spent a lot of time studying at those mahogany desks. Matthew's warning was deep within my mind. *They are coming,* but I had no idea who Matthew was referring to, and it left a pit in my stomach.

I walked past several doors until I finally saw a placard that read *Room 217*. When I opened the bright yellow door, light flooded into the hallway. I stepped into the room, and I felt like I had entered a fashion designer's workshop. A girl about my age was fussing with a dark gray blazer with a yellow badge pressed on the right breast. Even from the doorway, I could tell it was the school's coat of arms. She turned around and smiled warmly at me.

I felt butterflies explode in my stomach. I stared into her hazel eyes, which were filled with kindness and beauty.

She had long, straight black hair complemented by her bronze skin and highlighted her gentle features. Her beautiful smile touched her eyes and revealed a set of pearly white teeth. I could not take my eyes off her.

She looked at me and said, "You must be Danny. I'm Izabelle!"

Chapter V

The Welcome

~Danny Elikai~

"Hey, Izabelle." Her smile was infectious, and I smiled back at her because it felt like being around an old friend. I held out my hand, but without hesitation, she flung herself into my arms and hugged me tightly. I could smell her perfume, which made me think of summer with hints of lavender.

"I am so sorry about your family. Your brother and I were good friends." Her touch surged through me, and I could feel her sorrow and compassion. They were not empty words, and for the first time, they made me feel warm. I inhaled her intoxicating scent as tears began to fill my eyes.

"Thank you, Izabelle," I whispered. When she let go of me, she wiped away a tear of her own. She looked up and down at me and smiled again.

"Matthew wasn't kidding."

"What do you mean?" My curiosity flared inside me. She had moved back to the mannequin with the uniform and from across the room, and I could see there was something new in her eyes. It was a look that I could not quite place, but one that I had seen before. It was the same expression Matthew would give me when he knew more than he was saying.

"Your brother was right about you, that's all," she said again with another beautiful smile.

"How did you know him?" The words escaped my mouth before I could stop them.

"I met him last summer. I had just moved into town. I was in the main courtyard looking up at the bell tower…"

Her words faded away, and before I realized it, the walls of Room 217 disappeared. Sunlight blinded me, and I could smell the sweet scent of honey around me. I found myself standing in the center of the Grenoff courtyard, looking at the bell tower.

"Uh, what?" I looked around, trying to figure out what was happening.

"Izabelle?" I walked up next to her, but she didn't respond as she stared at the ivy-covered bell tower. She wore a simple blue sundress with small white flowers that seemed to dance around the hem as she moved. Her hair was down, tied with a matching blue ribbon that was moving gently in the soft breeze.

We stood silently as her sorrow and frustration washed over me. She absentmindedly ran the fabric of the dress through her hand. A warming sensation rippled through me, and her heart opened to me. I knew that her dress had been the last gift her mother had given her before she died. Grief radiated off her as she swore under her breath. At the time, she hated the dress, and had even told her mom to take it back, and...

"No!" I stared at my shaking hands as her entire life began to play out before me. "What's happening?" But my words fell on deaf ears.

"I hate you." She brought me back to the bizarre situation, and the secrets of her heart opened to me again before I could stop them.

I watched as her widowed father brought her to Grenoff for a fresh start. They had left everyone they had ever known and loved behind in Fayetteville, North Carolina.

"Stop!" I clenched my hands over my head, and the sensation dissipated. I felt sick because I had just intruded into her past, her emotions, and her life without her consent. I also wanted to comfort her, but my feet were rooted to the spot where I was standing. I reached out to her, but my fingers were just inches away from her shoulder. I wasn't even sure that I was there with her, but my heart told me not to fight it.

"Are you okay?" His words sent a wave of sorrow through my body. I turned around and saw Matthew sitting on the same bench as when he told me about the King. My brother wore simple blue jeans and his black Yale sweater, which he wore everywhere. I noticed that he hadn't shaved in a few days, and his blonde beard was beginning to show. He held a sandwich in his hands, and his vibrant green eyes were trained on Izabelle. I stared at Matthew, and I realized that I was witnessing the moment she had met my brother.

Matthew's power were creeping toward Izabelle. I knew that he wanted to read her mind, just as he had read mine many times before. I jumped in front of her, but neither of them gave me any indication that they knew I was there. I stood between them, guarding her against Matthew's probing mind. Seeing how vulnerable she was, I knew her emotions were not for my brother or me to know.

"No, Matthew." And to my amazement, his eyes snapped to where I stood as if he could see me. He glared at me knowingly, but just like Izabelle, I knew he could not see me. He must have felt me there with them.

Leave Izabelle alone. I don't know how Matthew had heard me, but his powers pulled back into his mind.

Thank you. I stepped back to watch as the past played out before me. I didn't understand why I was witnessing this moment, or how Matthew knew I was here while Izabelle did not, but my gut told me to let it happen.

"Yes, I'm fine," Izabelle answered Matthew, wiping away her tears.

"Would you like half of my sandwich?" My brother reached out half of his peanut butter and jelly on whole wheat. I could feel the swelling emotions and the confusion forming in her heart. I reached out again and was surprised that I could touch her.

He can help you, and that beautiful smile lit up her face. I was unsure if she could hear my thoughts, or even feel my touch, but I knew Matthew could help her through her regret.

"Thank you." She walked over to him, took half the sandwich, and sat beside him on the bench.

"My name is Matthew. Matthew Elikai," my brother said to her with a warm smile, which she easily returned.

"I'm Izabelle Pescador. It's very nice to meet you, Matthew." They stared at each other and giggled. It was nearly impossible to tell that Izabelle had been upset just a moment ago. My brother's presence had calmed her and had given her a quiet peace.

The sunny courtyard faded, and I found myself back in the present with a blink. Izabelle was standing in the same spot before I had disappeared, almost as if nothing had happened.

"Your brother was always kind to me." I looked at her, trying to figure out how I had experienced her memories. I blinked at her as she continued her story without a pause. "He was the first friend I made in Grenoff after I moved here last summer. We even used to send letters to each other over the past year while your family was back in Boston. He introduced me to a couple people here, and I have been better off because of it. He was a great friend."

"Yeah, he was a great brother as well." I really hoped my confusion didn't show on my face. I had just seen a memory or rather had been in the past to witness the moment when they met. I stood there, racking my brain for an explanation, but none came.

"I was so happy when he was accepted to Yale." She took a piece of fabric off the counter and wiped away the tears.

"I remember he wore that sweater for a month as a good luck charm before he even applied." My words trembled as I tried to keep the conversation going while thinking about her memories. This wasn't the first time something like this had happened. I had been completely confused when I discovered I had the ability to create and manipulate fire. My life was a series of confusing events, so why should this be any different?

I turned my attention back to Izabelle, and my words came out stable and confident. "He loved wearing that raggedy old sweater."

"Yeah, he was wearing it when I met him, even though it was hot that day." Izabelle layered different pieces of fabric on top of one another. It took every fiber of my being not to say, "I know."

We stood in Room 217 in hushed silence as we remembered my brother. She was busy with her work, and she seemed to be making decent progress on my uniform. After a lot of consideration, I decided that I could not tell her that he had never mentioned her to me, even though he had told her about me. She pulled the uniform off the mannequin.

"Here, try this on," she said, handing me the blazer.

"Do we all have to wear uniforms?"

"Yes." She gave me a small wink. "Everyone wears pretty much the same black slacks or skirts with a white button-up shirt and black loafers. However, the crests on the breast and the ties are based on your academic level." She pointed to the yellow crest on my blazer.

"Sophomores are yellow?" I wondered if that was a stupid question. I buttoned the blazer and moved my arms around to see how it fit.

"Yes. Freshmen are green, juniors are violet, and seniors are red," she answered kindly. She started to tug slightly in different areas of the blazer. She grabbed a measuring tape and began to take notes.

"The same four colors of the bell tower?"

"The whole school is built around those colors." She continued working on me and the blazer, pinching the fabric here and there, trying to fit the blazer to my athletic frame. I was taller than most of the young men my age, just barely over six feet. For the next twenty minutes, Izabelle took measurements and fiddled with my uniform as silence eclipsed the room.

"Are you alright?" She seemed to snap out of whatever thought had been eating away at her.

"You should join me for lunch on Monday!" Her face lit up with excitement, but I knew that this wasn't the thought that had been bothering her for the last twenty minutes. I decided not to probe, and I went along with it.

"Sure! I would definitely like to have a familiar face with me on my first day of school." I was relieved that I wouldn't have to transition into this school completely alone.

"Oh, hey!" The memory came flooding back to me. "Do you know a guy named Jesse?"

"Yes, I know him. He's my boyfriend. He texted me to let me know you were coming." She smiled, but I felt disappointed. A cold shiver crept down my spine as I felt the icy laughter of my warden. His amusement was unmistakable, and I felt a little unnerved by it.

"Oh, of course!" I exclaimed, trying not to sound too disheartened. I remembered Jesse mentioning her name earlier. "I met him this morning, and he seemed like a nice guy."

"Yeah, he's pretty great." Her eyes were filled with that dreamy daze. "He wanted me to keep an eye out for you! I was glad to hear you were starting on Monday." I didn't know what to say, so I just smiled.

"Danny, are you ready?" My aunt stepped into the room and smiled at Izabelle.

"Hello, Izzy."

"Hey, Shannon! How are you?" Izabelle greeted her with loving excitement. A warming sensation rippled through me again, and for the third time, I began to see inside her life, and how much love she had in her heart. I pulled myself away from her heart and concentrated on myself. I didn't want to probe any further into her life.

"No," I whispered under my breath as they carried on their conversation.

"I'm good, thank you. How are you?"

"I am just wonderful. I'm very excited to have Danny join us on Monday!" Izabelle said.

"I finished getting Danny's classes situated, and he's ready to go." Izabelle turned back to me and pointed to the blazer, which had been once again pinned to the mannequin.

"I'm almost finished. I just need to make a few adjustments. Is it alright if I drop this off later tonight on my way home?" She asked.

"Why don't you just bring them to dinner? We hoped you and Jesse would join us tonight, right, Danny?" My aunt shot me a look.

"Yes, we'd love to have you, Izabelle." I was failing to pull myself from her past, secrets, and emotions. I needed to get out of here before I knew everything about this girl.

"I'd love to!" Her bubbly personality was pulling me closer to her heart, and it was becoming difficult to pull myself away from her past.

"Wonderful. We were planning on meeting at Bear's Piano Diner at seven. Is that going to be enough time?" My aunt asked.

"Yeah, I'll have this finished before then. The measurements you sent me were almost spot on, but it seems that he has lost a bit of weight and grown taller since you last measured him." My aunt shot me a concerned look but didn't comment on those weeks when I couldn't eat.

"Danny, here is your class schedule. I registered you for classes and added two that I thought you would be interested in." She handed me a folded piece of paper, trying to pass over that awkward moment.

I began to read what my next few months would hold. Before I had a chance to analyze my schedule, I felt Izabelle move from the mannequin to stand over my shoulder.

"Oh my gosh, Danny! It looks like you have World History with me! And P.E., too!" Izabelle exclaimed as she scanned over my schedule. "Oh, you have Biology and Math with Jesse! Also, I think my friend Claire has the same Home Ec. Class as you!"

"Well, it looks like my first day is going to be more inclusive than I first thought." I wanted nothing more than a distraction from the crippling depression and the darkness stalking me. I wanted to dive into schoolwork, and hopefully, get to know Jesse and Izabelle better.

I noticed my aunt was watching me with a pleasant surprise in her eyes. She could see I wasn't pretending, and that made her smile. I felt myself smiling at the idea of potentially being happy. I felt rage explode in the distant darkness, and I knew my warden would try to break me, but for the second time today, I ignored him.

"I think Michael has English and Creative Writing at the same time as well!" Izabelle exclaimed. She was more excited about that fact than I was.

"Michael?" I subtly became aware of the look my aunt gave Izabelle, and for whatever reason, it made me uncomfortable.

"He's just a family friend around your age," my aunt said with a smile, waving her hand like it was no big deal.

"He's a really great guy." Izabelle turned away.

"Come on, Danny, we have a million other things to do before we can head home." Aunt Shannon waved Izabelle goodbye, and she left the room.

"See you tonight, Izabelle!" I smiled at her, and I followed my aunt.

****

The doorbell rang, and I looked up from the book my aunt bought me while we were running errands. We had a bustling afternoon that involved school supply shopping, clothes, and a desperately needed haircut. I had not had a haircut since the beginning of the summer, and my aunt insisted that I looked presentable for my first day.

The minute we got back to the house, I showered off the loose hair, grabbed a soda from the fridge, and spent the next several hours reading in the window seat in the sitting room. The book was one of my new favorites, and I was only twenty pages from finishing it. Books had always been an escape for me, and they captivated me enough to ignore the darkness for a little while. My aunt had left to take care of a couple of things at work, and Alvaro had been taken to the park by Jesse.

I heard a knock at the door. I got to my feet and shuffled to answer it, never taking my eyes off the pages. I reached the door and looked through the peephole, but there was no one standing on the front porch. I began to open the door, but it slammed into me with such an immense force that I was thrown against the stairs behind me. My body broke the stairs as a sharp pain ripped across my arm. I gently touched it and felt the sickly warmth of blood.

"Danny!" The darkness began to consume the house, and I looked up at the doorway. Matthew had fear in his electric green eyes as the darkness began to consume everything.

"Danny, he's here!" Matthew ran to me and grabbed my shoulders. "You need to run!"

I ignored the immense pain as the fire inside me repaired my broken bones. I ran up the stairs, looking behind me as the growing darkness began to consume him. While looking into his terror-stricken eyes, my feet collided with something solid at the top of the stairs. I tumbled onto the wooden landing. The metallic smell of blood hit my senses as I felt the body underneath me. I felt a chilling horror creep down my spine as I stared at her. My aunt was sprawled at the edge of the top stair, blood still trickling from the fresh slit on her throat that pooled on the landing. I looked at myself and saw I was covered in her blood, as a scream caught in my throat.

I crawled away from my dead aunt toward my bedroom, the swirling darkness overtaking her body. My heart ached for her, and I knew I had to escape this horror. Alvaro stood at the end of the hallway, and a sense of panic washed over me as I jumped to my feet and ran to grab him. He held out his arms to be picked up, but when I reached him, he became nothing more than smoke in my arms.

I turned to see a shadowy figure standing at the top of the staircase as the inky darkness swirled toward me. I ran into the master bedroom, slamming the door shut, but a feeling in my gut told me it wouldn't do any good.

I heard a small whimper come from behind me. I slowly turned around, afraid of what I would find. I didn't see the familiar master bedroom that I was expecting. Instead, there was an expansive, ancient, dying forest around me.

"Run…" The trembling words of my uncle escaped his bloodstained lips. My uncle was pinned to a large tree by six arrows.

I stepped toward him and felt a harsh crunch under my foot. I looked down to see a fractured human skull and countless other human bones interweaving the roots of the overgrown tree.

"They're coming for you. Run!" He whimpered as a seventh arrow flew from the darkness and pierced his heart.

I began to run into the woods, briefly looking back to see that the darkness had consumed my uncle. I ran until the light of the forest had faded, and I stood alone in the blackness of night.

How many must die before you realize that you are wrong? My warden's whisper echoed in my mind while I stood in the forest, blind. He did not have anger in his voice but rather a desperate, gentle pleading that made my skin crawl.

"Stop!" I fell to my knees, my hands covering my ears. "Just leave me alone!"

They will all die because of you! The warden proclaimed, and the guilt burned hot in my body. My heart was pounding, and I wanted nothing more than to escape. I slammed my fists on the soft ground, and fire exploded around me. My fire's self-determination stunned me as I watched the fire crawl up the trees of the dark forest. The flames climbed higher and higher until the inferno towered over me. The bright fire burned as it danced, spelling out a message for me in the darkness.

Welcome to Grenoff, Danny.
I've been waiting for you.

Fear rooted me to where I knelt as the fire disappeared. The darkness circled me and began to consume me. I watched as it conquered me, swirling around my feet and up my legs. The heat that usually burned inside me faded, and I felt nothing but the chilled hands of darkness. The darkness crawled up my neck and around my face, choking me as it entered my gaping mouth.

The sunlight made me open my eyes, and I woke up in a cold sweat. I was breathing rapidly, fear keeping me paralyzed on the window seat. The book I had been reading was still on my chest, and I looked around the room. Nothing seemed out of place in the sitting room I was in. Except, of course, Matthew was sitting next to me as if he was made of sunlight. I bolted upright and stared at him.

"Wh-what was that?" The fear was clear in my voice as confusion, anger, and denial ran rampant in my mind. The fire in my veins demanded answers, but Matthew's soft expression contradicted everything. He looked at me with sheer joy, as if seeing me were beyond his wildest dreams.

"I never thought..." he began, tears filling his eyes. I noticed he looked different than normal; his skin looked airbrushed, and I could have sworn he looked older.

"Matthew?" I reached out to touch him, but the fire inside me screamed against it. I was about to touch his cheek when I pulled my hand back.

"I'm sorry." He wiped away the tears on the back of his hand.

Matthew, are you really here?

"We don't have much time, Danny." He ignored my question. "He is coming, and they are going to rise." I could see the worry and the fear in his green eyes, but it was nothing compared to the peace that burned through him. I could feel his heart, quiet and unburdened.

I don't understand.

"I know you don't. That's our fault, and that's why I'm here. We should have told you before we came to Grenoff this summer."

"Told me what?" I noticed he was fading again, and I could see through his fingertips.

"We were going to tell you on that trip. We thought it was time, but we were too late. However, I have been given a second chance to help you."

Help me how?

"He is coming, and they will soon rise," he said again, becoming so transparent that he was barely here.

"Who?!" I felt the frustration building in my chest.

"The dream you just had, the burning message. That was his welcome to you. He has found you, and soon they will all come."

"WHO?!" I pounded my fists on the window seat.

"The Crusaders... his Crusaders..." he whispered.

The jingle of keys unlocking the front door echoed in the intensely quiet atmosphere, and I reluctantly turned in time to watch my uncle walk through the door. He looked at me and waved, carrying the mail in his teeth. I returned to where Matthew had just sat on the window seat. I was left with a million questions but only sunlight to answer them.

Chapter VI

The Hearts of Grenoff

~Danny Elikai~

Confusion burned through me as I stared at the place my brother had just been. His words rang clearly through my mind as a sickening feeling rippled through me. *The Crusaders? His Crusaders? Who and what were the Crusaders?*

"Danny, are you okay?" My uncle stood in the entryway to the sitting room. His Sheriff's uniform was in his hand, and the white T-shirt he was wearing was drenched in sweat and mud. His face and blonde beard were discolored with dirt, and he looked exhausted. He looked at me with curiosity in his luminous green eyes.

"Yeah, I'm alright. I just dozed off for a second," I lied as I turned away from him, trying to be casual. He walked into the living room and stared at me, crossing his arms.

"Danny, you've always been really bad at hiding your emotions. You know you can always talk to me about anything, right?" By the look on his face, I could tell he wanted the whole truth. His years of detective work, with countless interviews and interrogations, had given him the ability to tell when someone was lying to him. He would get the truth out of me, one way or another.

I looked at him, and I felt uneasy. I didn't necessarily want to relive everything I had just experienced, and I didn't want to bring up my confusion and frustration. While my family knew about my abilities, and my father had trained me to control them and only to use them for self-defense, I had rarely discussed them outside of those training sessions. It was not because they were afraid of me or because it was taboo, but because I never wanted to discuss it.

Since Matthew could read minds, I didn't feel the need to lay out all of my private thoughts for everyone to analyze. Matthew and I never even talked about my warden or the darkness surrounding me because it made everything worse, and Matthew understood that. I looked into my uncle's eyes and explained.

"I just had a nightmare where I was left all alone, and everyone I loved was gone." The image of my uncle pinned to the tree as the seventh arrow pierced his heart dance in my mind. The look on my face must have convinced him I was telling the truth, and he knew not to probe any further. He sat down next to me and gave me a hopeful expression.

"One day, you'll understand that you will never be alone." He smiled. "You will be surrounded by your loved ones and all of the people whose lives you have touched. You will look back on your life, and the darkness will be forgotten." My uncle wrapped both of his arms around me.

"I can't wait for that day." Even if it was never going to happen, it was nice to hope. He got up, but I knew that dream would never come to fruition. I was destined to be alone in the darkness, cold and afraid.

"Give me half an hour, and we'll head out and meet up with everyone, okay?" I nodded, and he moved upstairs. I picked up the book that rested beside me, marked the page I was on, and closed it. I didn't even realize that I was walking until I reached the top stair of the staircase, where Aunt Shannon's corpse had been in my dream, and a crippling weight pressed on me.

Matthew's warning blared in my mind as fear rooted my feet to the stairs. My breath left my lungs at the realization that everyone I've ever known would soon be in danger. I lowered myself to sit on the step as I tried to quiet my racing thoughts and my worrisome heart. The rage built inside me, and nothing made sense as I clenched the book harder in my hands, and I closed my eyes.

I don't understand, I repeated in my mind, each time my voice growing louder as the frustration, anger, and confusion burned through me.

The sharp sting of smoke entered my nose, and my eyes flew open. I looked at my hands in shock since I had not realized the book I was holding had caught on fire. I had burned away the outer edges of the book where I was grasping it. I watched as a clump of ash hit the oak floor beneath my feet.

I set the burning book on the pile of ash and closed my eyes again. I breathed deeply and tried to calm my shaking hands. I placed my hand on top of the cover and breathed in again, slowly exhaling. I felt the heat escape my hand, but I knew these flames were not meant to destroy. This fire was to heal, restore, and recreate.

When the fire returned to my veins, I opened my eyes. The book on the ground before me had returned to its unburned state, but it seemed different. When I picked it up and looked it over, the book appeared to be in better condition than when my aunt bought it just a few hours ago.

I looked down at my palm and released the fire as it consumed my hand, and the warmth filled me. I had never seen my fire as evil or destructive but rather as beautiful. To me, fire was life; fire was creation when wielded properly.

I stared at the flames in my hand in wonder, and I could feel the untapped power inside of me. I pulled the flames back inside my veins, got to my feet, and picked up my book. I walked the small length of the hallway to my room, locking the door behind me. I looked at the bookshelf in my room; the one Uncle Alex built for me many years ago. He knew I loved books, and he wanted me to have my own space when I came to visit over the summers. I placed the new book on the shelf, and I sat down on my bed. I placed my face in my hands, still warm from the fire.

"I don't understand what's happening." I looked around my room, trying to think through everything that had happened to me since the accident: the relentless nightmares of my family, seeing Matthew and hearing his voice as if he were still with me, Jesse and Izabelle, Grenoff, the high school, and now this warning—this vision of death. I ran my hands through my hair as my brain tried to understand the events of the past few weeks.

My ears twitched as I heard a gentle and barely audible lullaby playing around the room, and I felt peace flow through me. I felt my body respond to the soft, calming music as it did early this morning next to the bell tower.

I felt an icy weight in my left hand, and I saw the small locket. I didn't even remember grabbing it from the nightstand. Even though it was sealed shut, I knew the music was coming from it. It felt as if it were breathing in my hand, and I looked at it closer. Its surface was scratched and worn because it had been passed down through generations of Elikai men.

I had never been able to open the silver locket, but I had seen it open in the hands of my brother and my parents. I remembered asking them many times how they had opened it, but they never gave me a proper explanation. All they ever told me was, "In time, it will open for you." I sighed and placed it back on the nightstand, stood up, and turned toward the door.

"Danny." A wave of shock went through my whole body, as the voice spoke directly behind me, but there had not been anyone else in the room. It sounded fuzzy, like a voice over the phone or from a speaker. There wasn't something exactly right about it.

I couldn't move, my body seemed to be paralyzed, and I struggled to breathe. I had made sure the window was locked, but I heard it creak open slowly, and I felt my heart jump into my throat. I could feel the warmth coming from behind me, and a sweet, calming aroma surrounded me. I knew someone was in the room with me. I was not sure why, but my body grew peaceful. My pulse slowed down because I felt that I had known this person since the beginning of Creation when we were nothing more than stardust.

The knock at my bedroom door rang loudly in the silent room, making me jump violently, and the moment was broken.

"Danny, are you ready to head out? We don't want to be late for dinner." My uncle's voice was cheerful through the door. The lullaby and the person had vanished abruptly. I turned around and scanned the room, but the only different thing was the open window.

"Yeah, I'll be out in a minute." I shook my head and dismissed what just happened because it was most likely another trick played by my warden. It wouldn't have been the first time he did something like this, trying to make me feel safe just to have a horrific episode waiting around the corner. I brushed it off and left the room.

****

Bear's Piano Diner was a small restaurant on the northwestern edge of Grenoff next to the wilderness. It could seat about fifty people and had glass ceilings to let natural light illuminate the restaurant. The interior had a cabin feel to it, with a large fireplace that was encased within the log walls. A black grand piano was featured in the middle of the restaurant, and a small, stuffed black bear sat on top of the piano's closed lid. Along one of the walls were autographed pictures of celebrities who had visited the restaurant over the years. Another wall was lined with large glass windows that overlooked the northern forest, with a small patio that allowed for outdoor dining in the summer months.

Uncle Alex and I walked into the restaurant, and I saw our group before they saw us. Izabelle and Jesse were sitting next to each other in the largest booth in the restaurant; his arm draped around her. My aunt sat to Izabelle's left, and Alvaro sat next to her, leaving the seats on the right side of Jesse open.

"Hey, guys!" Jesse had a bright smile.

"Hey, Danny! How are you?" Izabelle pulled me into a hug.

"I'm fine. I'm just a little tired, is all. What about yourselves?"

"We were wonderin' if you wanted to go with us to the bonfire tonight?" Jesse's eyes were vast and twinkled like the stars. "It's a tradition!"

"Yeah, that actually sounds great!"

"I'm glad," Izabelle let go and it felt nice that they wanted me to come.

"Hello, Claire!" My aunt said as my eyes fell upon a girl approaching the table. She had waist-length black hair, a heart-shaped face, with soft dark eyes that matched her rich midnight skin. She wore tight blue jeans and a black button-up shirt with a small red apron tied around her waist. She had a cute bear name tag pinned to her low-cut shirt.

"This is Danny Elikai. He has Home Ec. with you!" Izabelle jumped to introductions before Claire even said anything.

"Hey, Danny!" She extended her hand, and I smiled sheepishly. "I'm glad I will have someone to sit next to on Tuesday!" She didn't let go of my hand. "I am so sorry about your family. Your brother and I were very good friends."

I shook my head and smiled. *Of course, she knew Matthew.* Everyone knew him. During our summer breaks, Matthew had been busy volunteering on community projects and working at internships around Grenoff. While he was padding his Yale application, I was trying to stop the depression from drowning me.

"Thank you. Matthew was a great guy," I nodded. She had a beautiful aura around her, but when I looked into her eyes, I knew she had experienced immense sorrow, yet she didn't let it change her. The longer I looked at her, the more I knew her. I could see that she missed her father…

I looked away quickly, pretending to look at the menu. *It had happened again.* I can look at someone and know their deepest secrets. I snuck a look at Izabelle, and that warming sensation rippled through my body as I dove into her heart and her secrets. I looked back at the menu, disgusted with myself because I hated violating people's privacy. I remembered how much I didn't like it when Matthew read my thoughts at first.

"How's your mother, Claire?" My aunt's words brought me out of my thoughts and back to the diner.

"She is as well as can be expected. My aunt and my cousin Amari have been an immense blessing these last few months." I watched as the sadness crept into her eyes, and again I felt her anguish over her father.

"If you need anything, will you please call us?" My aunt touched her arm comfortingly.

"Actually, I was hoping that you could take over the Back-to-School Bake Sale next weekend? I'm afraid my mom is not quite up to it at the moment," she asked quietly.

"Of course, dear, I completely understand. Just have her call me with the details, okay?"

"Thank you, Shannon. I really appreciate it." She then wrote down our drink orders and disappeared.

"That poor girl," my uncle said, and everyone else nodded in agreement. I didn't ask because I didn't want to know what had happened to her unless Claire told me herself. All I knew was it had to do with her father, judging by what I had seen and felt when I looked into her heart.

"Are you excited about starting school on Monday, Danny?" Izabelle pulled me out of my thoughts. I could feel her eagerness.

"I really am excited. The school looks beautiful, and my classes seem interesting. And I'm really excited to spend time in that library!" It was easy to match her enthusiasm. "But I'm glad that I met you guys, so I'll have someone to talk to on Monday."

"Good." Izabelle took my hand again and looked into my eyes. "I just wanted you to know that we are here for you," she added, smiling brightly. "That's what friends are for!"

"She's right, y'know." Jesse smiled at me. "We take care of each other here."

When I glanced around the table, I felt the peace within all of them, and I felt it calming me. I could feel the warden's fury, but it felt like it was miles away at the end of a long, narrow tunnel.

Claire reappeared with the drinks. She quickly placed them in front of us and turned to leave but stopped abruptly. She turned back to Izabelle and whispered,

"Izabelle, Michael asked me to tell you that he won't be able to make it back for the beginning of classes. His mom passing is taking more time than he originally thought, and he's still taking care of the arrangements."

This time it was like being hit by lightning as his name sent an odd tingle through my body, and I felt that weird sensation of familiarity again. I felt like I knew him, but I couldn't recall from where. It was like trying to remember the lyrics to a song I had heard only once, many years ago. I shook my head in frustration.

"Oh! That's so sad, but it won't be a problem at all. I'll make sure the professors know on Monday," Izabelle whispered back. "Do you know how he has been this past summer? I haven't really heard from him." I noticed her eyes flickered toward me for a split second.

"It's been rough for him. I only hear from him once a week, but communication is not his strong point, so that isn't anything new. I miss him, though." She quickly straightened up and asked, "Are you ready to order, or would you like any recommendations?" It was clear that she wanted to change the subject.

When she took our orders, she spun on her heels and walked away. The moment Claire was out of earshot, I leaned over and spoke to my aunt.

"Is that the same Michael from earlier?" She nodded, and the atmosphere around the table changed as Izabelle, my aunt, and uncle all gave each other glances. It was hard to miss, but Jesse didn't seem to notice.

"Michael is Claire's boyfriend," he said casually. "He's the golden boy 'round here. Everyone loves him."

"Have I met him?"

"Trust me, Danny, if you met Michael, you would never forget him," Aunt Shannon responded.

"Why?"

"Well," Izabelle began awkwardly, "he's one of the most beautiful men to walk the face of the earth. You'll understand when you meet him." In my astonishment, I noticed that even Uncle Alex and Jesse nodded in agreement.

"What makes Michael so incredible is that he's not arrogant or conceited about anything. Just from my experiences with him, he seems to hardly pay any attention at all to his looks. Michael's true beauty comes from his quiet, gentle nature." My uncle took a sip from his drink as everyone else again nodded, and I became somewhat anxious about meeting him.

"You'll see Michael every Sunday at the local soup kitchen and volunteering every chance he gets. He's very kind," my aunt confirmed as she helped Alvaro with his juice.

"I'm surprised you've never heard of Michael before," my uncle said. "I mean, Michael and Matthew were really good friends. They used to send letters back and forth to each other all the time."

I turned to look at my uncle, and something horrible formed in my gut. Matthew had known all of these amazing people, but he never once told me anything about them.

"You know Matthew kept his friends a secret, Alex," Aunt Shannon gave me a strange look. My aunt was right, of course, but Matthew rarely had been secretive with me. He always felt that since he could read my mind, his secrets would be open to me as well. But now, I was beginning to know that my brother had kept a lot of things from me.

"It's alright, honey." She had that knowing smile on her face that all mothers have, and like Matthew, she knew what I was thinking. I smiled back, trying to reassure her, but I couldn't ignore the feeling in my gut.

"Don't overthink it. Your brother had his reasons, just trust him." I nodded at my uncle as the conversation turned from Michael, and I did my best to weigh in every once in a while. The arrival of the food brought me back from my confusion and a bit of anger. I had taken Claire's recommendation and ordered the baked Mac and Cheese, and it smelled incredible. The atmosphere around the table changed as the food was passed around.

The meal was filled with laughter, questions about my previous school in Boston, and details on how a politician's daughter was kidnapped from Rosario, Argentina. Apparently, her entire family had been brutally murdered. The story was even more gruesome since the kidnapper had drawn a symbol on the wall of the house with the blood of her family.

"That's disgusting," Jesse griped, but his words seemed hollow as if he didn't quite believe his own words.

"What time does the bonfire start?" my aunt asked, taking our attention away from the gruesome story.

"Actually, we should start headin' out." Jesse checked the watch on his wrist.

"Thank you for dinner!" Izabelle said warmly to my aunt as my uncle pulled out his wallet.

"Of course, honey. We'll see you two at the bake sale next Saturday, right?"

"Yes, of course! I'm the president of the sophomore class, so I'll be there!" Izabelle exclaimed cheerfully.

"Danny, have fun tonight, okay?" my uncle said as he stood up to let me out. "The bonfire is a time-honored tradition."

"I will, Uncle Alex." I nodded and turned to my new friends as they waited for me.

"I love your aunt and uncle." Izabelle wrapped her arm around mine. An explosion of butterflies erupted in my stomach when she touched me, and she reached out to hold Jesse's hand.

"They're amazing people." We had left the dinner and began walking toward the beach. The chilly evening air reminded us that summer was coming to an end as we walked past several groups of people, all smiling and waving at us. The walk was beautiful, and we were a couple of blocks away when Izabelle stopped in front of a small rundown yellow house.

"Henry." A guy about our age was sitting on the porch steps with his hands over his ears. He was humming to himself as the shouts from inside the house reached us.

"His parents must be fighting again," Jesse said and walked down the little stone path to sit next to his friend.

Henry looked up when he felt Jesse's approach, but his eyes made my blood run cold. There wasn't anything peculiar about them since they were just a normal dark brown that matched his hair. What I saw was the burning rage in them that I could feel from several yards away. I could see the darkness surrounding him, and I felt uneasy about Henry. The darkness didn't seem to haunt him, as it had with me, but it seemed as if it were a part of him.

Jesse looked at Izabelle, who nodded and gently pulled me away. We continued walking toward the beach.

"Is everything okay?" I asked a block or two after we left Jesse with Henry on the porch.

"Henry has a bad home life, and Jesse is the only person he'll talk to. Don't worry; he'll catch up with us later." I didn't press as we walked down the path toward the shore, we kicked off our shoes. The white sand was soft as we moved toward the roaring fire that accented the brilliant sunset in the west. Night was rapidly falling upon us, but the fire kept the chill away as Izabelle pulled herself closer to me. People were sitting on logs and chairs around the bonfire, talking and drinking from plastic cups.

The bonfire was warm, and I could feel the roar of the fire radiating inside me. I felt the urge to engulf my hand in it, to absorb it, but I knew that would freak out my classmates and raise way too many questions that I did not want to answer.

Izabelle and I sat down on a log, and she introduced me to a couple of people in our grade. Izabelle told me about a girl with black hair named Alyssa who had the same History class that we did. We sat on the log and talked for about an hour before Jesse joined us.

"Hello." He was cheery as he put a plastic cup into my hand and handed another to Izabelle.

"Thank you." I took the cup, and as he moved, my eyes fell on Henry, who stood a few feet away, staring at me.

"Henry, get yer butt over here!" Jesse waved over his shoulder. He reluctantly approached us and sat down.

"Bottoms up!" Henry ignored his command as he continued to glare, his fury unmistakable. I knew it was directed at me, but he said nothing. After a moment or two, he got up and walked away. I watched him leave, and Jesse said, "Don't take it personally, Danny. He looks at everyone that way."

I nodded and took a long gulp from the cup. The taste made me gag, and I felt the fire in my veins roar in disgust.

"What's in this?" I retched as I stared at the fizzy amber liquid.

"That, my friend, is an IPA," proclaimed Jesse. "Go 'head and take another sip, you'll get used to the flavor."

"I'm alright, thank you, though." I set the cup in the sand.

"I should go check on Henry," Jesse got to his feet and walked away. I looked at the cup in the sand, and I could taste the vomit in the back of my throat. Izabelle sat closer to me, sipping her beer as she stared into the fire. She looked at me, and when she noticed that I didn't have my cup, she quickly sat hers down next to mine.

"Not a drinker?" I looked at her and gave a half smile. The firelight danced in her eyes, and those butterflies erupted in my stomach again.

"Honestly, I've never had a drink before," I admitted, "and I don't think I will again." The fire in my veins purred in agreement. She nodded, grabbed both cups, and threw them away in a trashcan just a few feet away.

"Well then, I won't drink either," she laughed. "I never really liked the stuff anyway, but Jesse loves his IPAs." I couldn't help but enjoy the way she smiled, how it lit up her face and made her eyes even more beautiful.

Jesse came back, holding another cup in his hand, and Henry was nowhere to be found. Izabelle looked up at him with captivated look, and guilt rippled in me. They were in love, and I needed to respect that.

Jesse laughed as he took another swig from his cup and put his arm around Izabelle. She rested her head on his shoulder and looked up at him. I could see the love, the beauty that surrounded Izabelle, but Jesse was not as easy to read. He had a wall that kept me from seeing anything but the light swirling around his heart. I couldn't help but watch them, and I was comforted that they had found each other. I looked down at my hands, folding them together in my lap as the bonfire crackled next to me.

"Danny." Izabelle pulled me away from my thoughts. "I can't wait for you to meet Michael. I believe you and he will be best friends." I looked at her, and I noticed Jesse rolled his eyes and scoffed.

"Izabelle, you can't just assume people will become friends. For all you know, Danny and Michael could hate each other." He spoke without taking his eyes off the blazing fire.

She placed her hand on his face. "I just have a feeling that they will be amazing friends."

"I'm sure we'll get along just fine," I lied, knowing myself and knowing I was not the best at making friends. Most people seemed to pass through me without noticing, and I was sure Michael would do the same. I had been mostly ignored at my previous high school in Boston. If it hadn't been for Matthew and his friends, I probably would have sat by myself daily at lunch. I looked back at Jesse and Izabelle.

Danny... That still, small voice came from the depths of my mind, and I felt a pull behind me. I looked toward the sky above the bell tower.

"I'll be right back," I said to Izabelle and Jesse, standing up and turning away from the bonfire. I walked down the beach toward the courtyard. I passed people who waved at me, so I smiled and nodded in response.

While I passed them, I looked upon the hearts of Grenoff, and I saw beauty in them. The night sky was filled with stars, and I walked down the beach with my shoes in my hand. I had always loved the feeling of sand between my toes. I reached the paved path that ascended uphill toward the center of town.

The voices and other noises of the party disappeared the minute I entered the trees. The city park felt eerie as I walked along the grass in silence. I moved toward the bell tower that loomed in front of me, and that still, small voice called out to me in the growing darkness. I felt my pulse spike as I moved toward the bell tower. The yellow clock illuminated the night sky as I moved closer. I felt the pull, the anticipation growing as I moved toward the spot where my brother had first told me about the King.

I approached the tower as my eyes fell upon the bench, and I stopped in my tracks. A young woman sat with her back to me. The only thing I could see was her vibrantly red, silk dress.

"Hello?" She looked up at me with deep brown eyes as I approached.

"Hello." She looked bewildered as her mouth hung open. Her jet-black hair had been pinned up. Even in the dim lighting, I could see she was beautiful and familiar.

"May I sit with you?" I indicated to the bench, and she nodded politely.

I sat on the bench, and the scene around me began to change. I found myself sitting on a plush chair inside of a beautiful gazebo. I looked around and saw a perfectly manicured garden with an assortment of exotic and colorful flowers. I saw a small pond with large koi fish lazily swimming around in circles. There were several trees around us, many that were a gorgeous shade of red, very similar to the woman's dress.

"Where are we?" I turned and looked at her. I noticed she had a black feather quill pen in one hand and a book in the other. There was a white feather quill that was tucked away behind her ear, almost as if it were woven into her hair.

"We are in my family's garden." She answered my question calmly, but she seemed somewhat distracted as she looked at me with amazement.

"South Korea?" I guessed, looking at the architecture of the gazebo and the scenery around us.

"No, Danny. We are in Xi'an, China." She was more composed now. "What brings you here?"

"You know who I am?"

"Yes, of course I do. Do you know who I am?" I could feel the hope beginning to consume her as tears began to fill her eyes.

"I'm sorry, but no." I felt ashamed that I didn't know her name, but the fire inside me stirred in protest.

"Then you do not know the truth yet," she sighed and closed her eyes. She put the black feather quill inside her book, set it on the little table in front of her, and the scene around us changed. Once again, we sat on the bench in Grenoff, looking up at the bell tower.

"Grenoff." She jumped to her feet, looking around in wonder. I noticed she wore expensive-looking black heels with bright red soles.

"What truth do I not know about?"

Her eyes were filled with wonder and awe, but she ignored my question. She spun around as if trying to memorize everything she saw. She stopped and turned back to look me in the eyes.

"The truth about who you are," she said.

"What do you mean?" I could hear the anger in my voice. I was tired of not knowing what was going on and what was happening to me. *How could I be in Grenoff and Xi'an at the same time?*

"I can't tell you if you do not know." She sat back down next to me. I could see in her eyes that she didn't feel worthy of telling me the answers that wanted to explode from her lips.

"What's your name?"

"My name is Sun Ying, and I am a General of Light."

"What does that mean?"

"It means I am a General to the King of Free Will, the King of Light, and the rightful ruler of Creation who is about to be at war." That was when I noticed the power inside her. I could see the magic glowing like pink light in her body. When I looked into her eyes, she smiled as a tear slid down her face.

"I, uh, I am sorry, but what are you talking about? Who is the King, and who will he be at war with?" A pit was beginning to open in my stomach.

Before she could answer, a beautiful yellow butterfly that looked as if it was made from lightning began to flutter around us. We both spun on the bench as we felt him approach. He wore an elegant white robe that highlighted his tall, muscular body. His hood covered his face, but Sun jumped in attention to him. She clearly knew the man and wrapped her arms around him. She stood more than a foot shorter than him.

I could hear their hushed conversation but couldn't make out the words as a deep tremble ran through me as

I stared at his immense arms. The man pulled her out of the hug, holding onto her arms. They stared at each other for a few seconds before she nodded. She pulled the white quill from behind her ear and turned toward me.

"I will see you again one day, Danny Elikai." The quill began to glow pink, as she gently caressed the feather over my face.

I felt myself falling backward, and I blacked out.

Chapter VII

The Pure Heart

~The First Crusader, 1958~

The night sky was filled with beautiful glowing stars as the bell tower read five minutes until midnight. The four faces of the tower clocks glowed their normal bright white lights, and from the cliff, I could see everything in Grenoff. The bell tower was level with me, and if I were closer, I could have touched the small stone crown.

I watched time pass on the northern clock face as my stomach filled with butterflies. I had waited for this moment for such a long time, and I could not believe it was finally happening. I knew she would be here any minute. I gently touched the small object in my wool coat pocket for the millionth time, and it felt unbearably heavy.

The town of Grenoff was silent, and I knew how much trouble we would be in if we were caught by the Sheriff. Although we were both eighteen years old, we could still get in trouble for being out past curfew. But midnight was her favorite time of the night. It was the exact time when we first met.

The memory played before my eyes. I had come here, to the edge of Star Cliff, every night for a week, trying to prepare myself mentally for high school. That was when I first saw her. She stood at the edge of the cliff, the wind gently blowing her dress and her hair, looking like an angel. I stood there for a long time, watching her. She finally turned around and saw me. She smiled at me, and I felt like I had known her my whole life. Now, I stood at the edge of the cliff, waiting for her for what seemed to be forever.

"I got your note." Her soft words were filled with such love and warmth that it made my heart race. I turned around to see her standing behind me, looking as beautiful as ever. She wore a simple white sundress with yellow lilies stitched around the hem. I knew it was a Lily original, created by her exactly for this moment. She loved making her own clothes, and I knew her passion in life was to create her own clothing line. She was my beautiful girl, my light, my guidance, and the reason I got out of bed every morning. Her long brown hair curled around her soft face, and her blue eyes looked nervous. A small feeling of unease ripped through my body, and a small voice in my head echoed,

This is not my life.

"Are you okay?" My usually deep voice sounded a little off. She shook her head, but then she smiled.

"I am now that I'm with you." She flung herself into my arms. I could smell the scent of lavender from her hair. It was the most intoxicating aroma I had ever smelled and was one of the reasons I had fallen in love with her.

"I am glad you came, Lily," I whispered into her ear, and I felt my heart begin to race.

"Me too." Something inside of me felt wrong. I kept hearing the same voice in the back of my mind, echoing, *This isn't me! This isn't my life!*

She pulled away and looked up at me, giving me her lovely smile that I found to be absolutely captivating.

"Why did you want to meet here tonight, Austin?" She placed a soft kiss on my lips.

I am not Austin!

That voice screamed in my head, and I felt something hot burn within me. I shook my head because it was nothing more than nerves.

"I have something to ask you." I knew my nerves were engulfed in flames. I felt uneasy, and I staggered a little as I put some distance between us to do it properly.

I had dreamed of this moment for the last year and a half, and I would not wimp out again. I steeled my nerves and ignored the panicked voice in my head that didn't know what was going on. The voice felt strange and unreal, and it didn't help my confusion either. I stared into her beautiful eyes and felt myself stabilize.

"Lily, I have loved you from the minute we met. I remember seeing you the night before we started high school, and I knew I would spend the rest of my life with you." My vision blurred as that voice pounded in my head. I could feel his presence but did not understand who he was or what he wanted.

You aren't the only one who doesn't understand, his voice whispered in the depths of my mind, allowing me to take control again. She took a step back, and I mirrored her movement.

"I knew you were the one for me from that moment, and when you finally kissed me, I knew you believed that I was the one for you. Now, four years later, I still look at you, and I know. I asked you here tonight to make forever a reality." I took out the black velvet box from my inner coat pocket and knelt on one knee. "Lily Amelia Jones, will you do me the honor of becoming my wife?" I revealed the beautiful engagement ring.

The tears in her eyes were not filled with joy but regret and sorrow. She panicked and backed up slowly as she put her hands behind her body, fear masking her features.

"I'm sorry, Austin, but I can't marry you."

Her words burned white hot across my heart as tears threatened to break my composure. She swung her arms forward, revealing that she held a silver dagger in her hand.

That's my family's dagger!

"Lily? Lily! What are you doing?" The words tumbled out of my mouth as the voice in my head grew in strength and began to fight inside me for control. I found myself giving in because of my heartache and sorrow. I did not want to face this; I could not believe this was happening.

"I can't marry you, Austin!" Darkness slowly formed around her as silent tears fell. It grew until it resembled a human figure, and it placed a ghostly black hand on her shoulder. The darkness around her laughed wickedly in triumph as a pair of violet eyes flared to life in the face of the shadowy abyss. The voice in my head roared in protest, and I felt its fear and confusion. I stood there, my legs shaking and my heartbroken, and I surrendered total control to the screaming voice.

****

~Danny Elikai~

"I'm so sorry, Austin." My words finally escaped Austin's lips. I forced his eyes onto my warden. "What's happening?" I demanded, and I felt my fire burn through both Austin and me.

"Hello, Danny." The icy voice called out from the dark figure, and everything inside of me flared in its need to protect Austin. I wanted to make sure he stayed safe, but my power was burning him up from the inside. He was not capable of containing my raging fire. I knew that I needed to leave his body to protect him.

With a blink, I felt the separation. I wasn't sure how it happened, but I was pulled outside of Austin's body. I knelt next to him, whose navy-blue eyes were almost lifeless as if all the fight had left him. He was still on his knees, hands trembling as he clutched the small black box. There was something familiar about him, with his short brown hair and strong, calloused hands. I could see a tear running down his face as the love of his life stood in front of him with my family's silver dagger still in her hand and my warden's hand still on her shoulder.

I looked around, trying to figure out where we were, as the bell tower chimed. I realized that we were on Star Cliff, which overlooked Grenoff, but the town looked older and less developed. I stared at Austin, and I noticed his vintage clothing, like something at a drive-in theater in the fifties. My mind seemed to gridlock itself as the realization hit me: I was in the past again. I was witnessing another event, just like I had with Izabelle.

Furious, I glared back at my warden. His shadowy hand tightly gripped Lily as he whispered into her ear.

"You have to kill him. It's the only way to stop the nightmare from coming." His words were soft, kind, and filled with compassion. It reminded me of a parent consoling their child.

"I don't un-understand, Lily! What's go-going on?" I allowed myself to look through his eyes. I saw that he could no longer see me or the warden, only Lily, but he knew someone else was here.

I pulled myself out of his head after an invisible force dragged me out of reach from Austin. Gravity increased its pressure, pinning me to the grass. I grunted in protest, but I couldn't move.

"I love you, but I cannot let him escape." Her fear rang clear in her voice. I stared into those familiar violet eyes, and they turned to look at me with pure glee.

"What are you talking about?!"

"Last night, a beautiful spirit of Light visited me in my sleep, and he warned me about a war that is coming. A war that will destroy all of Creation. He gave me a warning about an ancient evil that was about to be released, and he told me I had to stop it from happening." She raised the dagger and stepped toward Austin. His face reflected my stunned disbelief as his eyes narrowed on the dagger's tip.

"What does this have anything to do with me? Lily, please stop! I love you!" His pleas made Lily cry even more, but she held the dagger with steady hands.

"And I love you. But, Austin, you are the key to opening his cage. You will release Emperor Phantonix, and he will lay waste to Creation. That is why I must do this to stop that from happening."

Everything in my body cringed as his name echoed through the night and within my mind. I felt the force around me shudder at the name, and I stared at him. His eyes were stalking my features, and while I could not see it, I knew he was smiling.

"You are Phantonix." I finally knew his name, which made me want to puke through my gritted teeth as the truth finally sunk in.

"Yes, Danny, I am Phantonix," he said gleefully. "Now, watch as I destroy a pure heart." His laughter echoed throughout the night, but I knew we were the only ones who could hear it.

"I do-don't understand!" The silver dagger was trembling in Lily's hand, and I wanted to take it from her.

"Austin, your heart is pure. He needs to sacrifice a pure heart. Then, he will be able to shatter his cage and destroy the world before the King of Light returns. The King of Light's angel warned me, then gave me this dagger." She looked at the silver blade, and I looked at my warden.

"She saw you, didn't she!" His soul-crushing chuckle confirmed it. My anger burned hot in my chest. I felt the fire wanted to roar out of my hands, but I couldn't do anything.

"Lily, stop!" I knew she could hear me because her eyes flickered to where I was pinned to the ground, but I couldn't tell if she could see me. "Don't listen to him! He's using you for his own gain! He is not a spirit of Light!"

"No! I know what I must do!" she yelled as Phantonix growled at me, and without any warning, she lunged at Austin's heart.

"No!" I watched in horror as the blade dove toward Austin, who dropped the small black box and rolled back out of the way, barely dodging the blade as he landed upright on his feet.

"Lily, please stop!" Austin jumped on her and tried to wrestle the dagger away. I could see he wasn't using his full strength. He still wanted to protect her, to make her see reason as she tried to cut him to pieces.

Phantonix slowly gilded toward me, as his shredded cloak danced in the night air. The immense gravity kept me flat on my stomach. He touched my cheek as an icy pain rippled through me, and I screamed.

"You can do nothing but watch as my plan unfolds!" Phantonix hissed sweetly in my ear.

The struggle seemed to go on for an eternity until Lily finally slashed Austin. The silver blade made contact with his chest, and he staggered as he fell onto his back. She lunged, the blade aimed at his heart, her eyes burning with determination. Austin jumped to his feet and wrapped Lily from behind, trying to stop her. The blade cut his hand in her thrashing movements.

In a moment of self-defense, Austin grabbed her wrist that was holding the blade, and amid her wild bucking movements, the blade plunged into her chest. Time seemed to freeze until the blood began to pour out of her wound, staining her white dress.

The horror on Austin's face was heart-wrenching. He let go of the blade as his hands trembled. Lily looked down at the dagger sticking out from her heart and looked into Austin's watering eyes. I could feel the pain between them as she crumbled forward into his arms. I watched as he lowered her to the ground, sobbing as he pulled the bloody blade from her chest.

"No! No, no, no!" he cried as he tried to stop the blood spurts with his hands, but the white dress was almost entirely crimson. Lily coughed, spattering blood on Austin's face.

"Yes!" Phantonix hissed in my ear. He moved toward Austin and Lily. I could see the light invading Lily's body as another light caught my attention. Austin's heart lit up like a lighthouse. It was a pure white light, and it was beautiful to behold. However, when he looked upon Lily's dying body and the blood on his hands, the darkness ate into it. He was desperately trying to stop the flow of blood with his stained hands, but it was too late.

"Witness the rise!" Phantonix proclaimed to the night, to the stars, and to us. He stopped before Austin, whose sobs echoed through the darkness as Lily looked up into his reddened eyes.

"I am sorry," she said through shallow breaths, "I couldn't save you." She coughed blood again, touched his face, and closed her eyes.

"Lily! No!" Austin drew in her as her hand hit the ground, and she went still. He pulled her closer as he began to rock her in disbelief. I could feel his agony, his defeat, and his sorrow. The darkness in his heart had grown quickly.

"Enough, Austin," Phantonix whispered. He froze when he found the violet eyes of Phantonix. Panic drained his face to a pasty pale. "Lily is dead, and you killed her."

The heartbreaking wail echoed through the night as Phantonix placed a hand on Austin's shoulder, waiting for him to calm down.

"Who are you?" he asked as I frantically tried to move closer to him to stop whatever was coming.

"My name is Phantonix." Austin went cold. "And I am not here to hurt you, Austin."

"Don't listen to him, Austin!" Phantonix raised a hand to me, and I felt my body go stiff again. I couldn't move, and worse, I couldn't speak.

"What do you want?" His anger was letting the darkness eat away more of his pure heart.

"I want to help you, Austin. This tragedy should have never happened." I felt the blind fury towards the warden.

"You just want to use my pure heart, like she said," Austin said through gritted teeth.

"No, Austin. The King of Light lied to Lily. Only breaking the Seven Seals can truly release me from my cage. They tricked her into killing you because they are afraid of you." His tone was soothing and gentle in a creepy way.

Rage boiled inside of me, and I wanted to scream that Phantonix was the one lying, not the King of Light, but I couldn't even open my mouth. I watched helplessly as Phantonix broke him even more.

"Why are they afraid of me?" Tears were still streaming down his blood-spattered face.

"Because of who you truly are."

"Who...who am I?"

"You are my Crusader," Phantonix said. "My soldier, my warrior, my first General of Destiny." I felt my blood run cold. This was the Crusader. I was witnessing the rise of the first Crusader, who Matthew warned me about.

"But I'm not evil!" Austin screamed. "I don't want to serve the darkness!"

"Evil is a word they use to describe me, Austin. They use it as a way to discredit me, to discredit my beliefs, and they label my philosophy as immoral. But they are wrong. I am not evil, and neither are you. I simply believe in Destiny, just like you, Austin. I want order, structure, and a world without pain. If Destiny were the governing force of Creation, you would have married this girl, and you would have had the family you always fantasized about. You would have been happy because that was your destined path. But, because of the choices offered by Free Will, you have to suffer. The King of Free Will, of Light has allowed you to suffer unnecessarily." Phantonix touched Austin's chest, where the darkness was conquering the light.

"Why does the King hate me?"

"He does not hate you, Austin, but he is afraid of what you can do," Phantonix said. "He believes that people should have the right to choose their own paths. He showed Lily a false image of what is to come and gave her a choice. He wants Free Will to reign so badly he drove a wedge between you and the love of your life and convinced her to try to kill you. Look at what happens when Free Will is allowed to run rampant—true love dies. But, when Destiny reigns, betrayal and murder will become myths of old." I could feel Austin hanging onto his every word. His red eyes were focused on Lily's body.

I felt something gently touch my back. Lily knelt beside me, her hand on my shoulder. She looked whole and undamaged but also several years older.

"I'm sorry, Danny." Her regret was fierce as she looked at the shadowy figure and the young man she loved, the man she had so desperately tried to save.

"Don't be, Lily." My words met no resistance. "You weren't the first person to be fooled by him."

She nodded but continued to stare at the man she loved, holding her lifeless body.

"I'm so sorry, Austin," she choked, and without any explanation, she faded into the night.

"Join me, Austin, and there will be no more pain. When I win this war, I will bring back the woman you love. I will hold the King accountable and make him pay for his crimes. Help me win, and there will be no more suffering." Austin's sobs echoed through the quiet night, and I saw his heart was consumed in darkness.

"Just kill me!" He shrieked at Phantonix. My warden raised his shadowed hand, and the silver dagger lifted into the air in front of Austin, dripping in Lily's blood.

"I cannot, Austin. Unfortunately, it must be your choice, your sacrifice. Take this dagger and swear your loyalty to me. Swear never to let Free Will destroy the lives of anyone else."

"No…" The feeling finally returned to my body, but my words were nothing but a whisper in the surrounding despair.

The need to protect Austin raged through me. I slowly got to my feet as Phantonix roared in anger. I ignored him as I slowly made my way toward Austin.

"He's wrong, Austin. Please, don't listen to him. He did all of this!" His puffy eyes finally found me.

"I don't understand."

"I don't know either, Austin, but Phantonix planned all of this. Please, you cannot believe him!" I knelt in front of him, taking his hands in my own, and let the tears fall down my face. "He's lying! He's using you for his own benefit. Don't let the light in your heart go out! You have to fight him!" I pleaded, but Phantonix merely chuckled.

"Ignore him, Austin. The King allowed Lily to have the choice to try to kill you. It is because of the freedom of choice that the woman you love is now dead." I felt Austin's rage turn toward me. "He believes in the philosophy of Free Will, and you see what the freedom of choice can lead to. Those who follow this philosophy will always blame everything on me. But in reality, it was because of choice, because of Free Will, that Lily acted this way. If this disease continues, more people will continue to lose the ones they love. If Destiny had been the governing force, she would have never had the choice to kill you, and she would still be alive." Phantonix hissed the last words while pointing at me. "Help me defeat those like him."

Austin looked at me, and I saw his decision in his heart. He grabbed the handle of the floating dagger and stared me in the eyes as he said, "Her blood is on your hands, and I will make anyone who believes in Free Will suffer. All hail Emperor Phantonix!" He turned the dagger toward his chest and plunged it into his heart.

"No." The word quietly escaped my lips as the tears streamed down my face. Phantonix's laughter eclipsed us as the darkness in Austin's heart exploded out and consumed him. Phantonix turned to the bell tower that was now chiming uncontrollably.

"Do it!" Phantonix fury was out of control, and the midnight chiming of the bell tower stopped. Everything became silent as the darkness tore Austin apart. Phantonix stared at the bell tower.

"Do it!" Phantonix screamed again, and the change of the bell tower happened slowly. The warm red light of the northern face and the yellow of the eastern face began to consume the white light. I didn't need to see the other two faces to know the other colors were appearing too. Within minutes, the four lights engulfed the night sky, and I felt a change in the air. The four colors marked the beginning of something horrible.

"It has begun, Danny." He turned to face me, and I trembled as I locked onto that violet gaze. "Do you not yet understand? I will win this war." He looked to the darkness that had swallowed Austin. "I will win because the hearts of Creation are weak, selfish, greedy, and self-righteous. They cannot be allowed to govern themselves. Destiny, forced agency, is the only true plan for their happiness."

"No! I don't believe that! People are good and kind and loving! We may falter, and we may stumble, but we know when to help others, when to fight, and when to protect those around us. We should have a right to choose how we want to live and to love. Free Will is the only plan that allows that! I will do whatever it takes to stop you!" I would not allow him to tarnish the hearts of those I had loved. I would not let Phantonix beat me ever again.

"Free will and the King will fall at my hand, and Destiny will rule Creation! You cannot stop me, Danny Elikai. The Eternal Throne will be mine!" I looked at the darkness where Austin had been, and it began to form the outline of a new body.

"Tonight, is the night of the rise of the first Crusader of Destiny! Rise, Ieiunium!" I looked at what was once Austin, and I knew that the boy with the pure heart was gone forever.

Chapter VIII

The First Day

~Danny Elikai~

In a blink, I found myself alone in my room. The afternoon sunlight shined through my open window, the curtains dancing gently in the breeze, filling my room with a sweet scent. I stayed under the covers, afraid to move as my heart thundered against my chest. My vision blurred as Austin's wails echoed in my ears. My body felt heavy, unable to move as the past repeated itself in my mind. I watched time and time again as Austin became a Crusader, a General of Destiny for Phantonix.

I felt the rage burn through me like an open flame. Phantonix had manipulated that young girl to try to kill the young man she loved because she thought he would be used for evil. As it turned out, Phantonix had been right. He twisted Austin's mind to sway him to give in to the darkness, to exact his revenge, and to calm his fury. I remembered looking into his eyes as Lily's death convinced him to join Destiny.

Free will and the King will fall at my hand, and Destiny will rule Creation! Phantonix's words echoed in my body.

I touched my chest as the idea of the King burned in my heart. I believed in him, and I barely knew anything about him. I believed in him because it felt as natural as breathing. I thought of everything that had happened, and I understood. I could feel the truth blazing in my heart.

The words of Sun's echoed in my mind, *I am a General to the King of Free Will, the King of Light.*

"Is it possible that I can choose to be in the light? That I am not destined to an eternity of misery in the darkness?" My words sent waves of emotion through my body. "That's why the King of Light didn't interfere."

He did interfere, Danny, the still small voice said in my heart. *Austin chose to believe in the anger and pain of his tragedy, and from that, he chose Destiny. He will not be the only one who will choose Destiny.*

"The King could have fought harder for Austin!"

It wouldn't have mattered, Danny. Austin would choose Destiny because it's easier to blame others than oneself. He truly believed Destiny was best for Creation, even before the death of Lily, the still small voice said, more patient than ever.

"I don't believe that. I believe he could have saved Austin if he had been there."

The King was there. He was with Austin until the end.

"I didn't see him! I was the only one there with Austin."

Trust me, Danny, even if you couldn't see him, he never left his side.

"Who is the King of Light?" My words echoed in the empty room. I felt something heavy appear in my hand, and its warmth spread through me. I raised my hand to my face and saw the locket.

"You belong to the King, don't you?" I asked it, and it pulsed in response. "Will you open?" The minute I said the words, I knew it wouldn't open just yet.

Only when the King is ready to return, the voice said again. I tried to focus on it to recognize who that voice belonged to, but the more I tried, the harder it was to focus.

"Who are you?"

I am your friend, Danny.

"Do you know the King of Free Will?"

Yes, Danny. I have known him since the beginning, and I miss him deeply. I could feel the raw emotion pulsing from inside the locket that felt like a crack in the earth.

"Where did he go?"

The King is on Earth.

"Where?!"

That is something I cannot answer.

"Will I ever meet him?" I had focused so hard on the locket that the soft knock on the door startled me.

"Danny?" My aunt spoke through the door.

"Come in." The door burst open, letting all four of them come crashing through. Izabelle lunged at me and wrapped herself around me, her hair covering my face. Her tears rolled down my neck, and her apologies were coming in rapid-fire Spanish. My uncle sat down to my left, my aunt to my right, and Jesse sat at the foot of my bed.

"Are you okay?" My uncle asked.

"Well, I can't breathe," I choked through Izabelle's hair, and she jerked away as if she had been hit by lightning.

"I am so sorry!" she said as she sat next to me.

"What happened?"

They all started talking quickly, and soon I heard the full account. They had found me unconscious next to a park bench in the town courtyard, and they called my uncle. They had tried to wake me up, but I wasn't responding. They had argued about taking me to the hospital, but they decided against it. I had woken up long enough to tell them that I was okay. They had brought me home and left me to sleep off whatever had happened. I decided not to tell them about Sun, the pink feather, the dream, or Phantonix. Not until I knew more about what was happening.

"What time is it?"

"It's 2:45 P.M., Danny," Jesse said, looking at me with a curious expression. I looked into his eyes, and I felt a weird sensation crawl through my body as if two people were looking at me. He smiled, and the feeling went away as quickly as it came. "I'm glad yer feelin' better. Y'all gave us quite the scare." He sat next to me. "Thought we lost you."

"I'm okay. Actually, this is the best I've ever felt."

"Then tell me, what was it like? Did it hurt?" He leaned in as if he planned to whisper in my ear.

"What?" I tried to look at my loved ones, but his twinkling blue eyes captivated me.

"When you failed to save me." I jerked back and found myself alone with Austin. His eyes held such pain, animosity, and fury as blood oozed out from the wound in his chest. We were kneeling in front of each other on the beautiful grass of Star Cliff, the place where he had given himself to Phantonix.

"What?!" The fear was drumming in my veins.

"You failed!" He pulled the silver dagger out from his chest, and blood gushed from his body all over me. Without any warning, he stabbed me in the heart.

"I will win Creation." Phantonix's words whispered in my ear, and when I looked up, I saw his violet eyes.

"No!" In another blink, I found myself back in my bed, looking into Jesse's shocked, scared face.

"Danny?" He grabbed my hand. "What's wrong?" I looked at Jesse, and panic tightened my throat.

"Austin?" I stared into his eyes. He looked at me with a shocked, bewildered expression.

"No, I'm Jesse." His thick Southern accent did little to calm my nerves as the fire roared in my veins in defiance. I stared at him as bile rose in my throat.

Are you the Crusader? My eyes were drawn to the white light dancing in Jesse's heart. Not even a smudge of darkness diluted that beautiful light. I relaxed as the room began to spin.

"Danny, y'alright?" The fear pranced in his eyes.

"Sorry, I don't know what came over me," The edges of my vision began to darken. "I think I should lie back down."

It was just a trick, another message from Phantonix, I told myself as sleep overtook me again.

****

My alarm was blaring, and as I woke up, I tumbled out of bed and smacked my head hard on the floor.

"Ow!" I rubbed my head, rolling onto my back on the cold wooden floor.

"Danny, are you okay?" The sleepy voice of my uncle called from the armchair by the window.

"Jesse!" I jumped to my feet and looked around my quiet, still bedroom, and I noticed the sunlight had just touched the horizon.

"What happened?!" My uncle looked up at me, and I felt the worry radiating from him.

"You passed out again." He got to his feet. I could see he still wore the same clothes he was wearing when I woke up yesterday.

"Was Jesse here?"

"Yeah." He yawned deeply. "He and Izabelle were here for the rest of the day, but Jesse had to get going. Izabelle ended up staying the night." He smiled and looked over at me.

"Danny, are you okay? You really scared us for a minute there. First, we find you passed out on the ground, and then you passed out again in your bed."

"I'm so sorry, Uncle Alex. I didn't mean to scare you. I do not know what happened. I must have not been sleeping well, lately." I had to shake off another one of Phantonix's mind games. I was not going to let him distress me anymore. I would not allow him to break me, and I would not believe his lies ever again.

"It's alright, Danny. Are you sure you're okay?" I could not mistake the fear in his green eyes. I walked up to him and sat on the window seat.

"I feel good, Uncle, and I am going to lean into that." The thought of the King made me smile. "Trust me," I said as I touched his hand.

He gave me a curious look and then nodded. "Okay." He looked at his watch and said, "You'd better hurry and get ready so you aren't late for your first day of school." He wore a warm smile, hugged me, and left the room. I stood there, looking around the room, and laughed.

"I am not going into the darkness without a fight. I choose the light," I said to myself again, and I knew I would be saying it a lot more over the next couple of days.

I went to the bathroom, ignoring the sarcastic laugh that echoed from Phantonix. I showered, washing away the sweat I had been soaking in from the day before, and changed into my new school uniform. I made sure I had everything packed before I headed downstairs.

"Izabelle!" I walked down the stairs and watched her emerge from the guest bedroom. She wore an outfit similar to mine, but with a skirt instead of slacks.

"Morning, Danny! How are you feeling today?"

"I'm doing better."

"If you need anything at all today, you let me know, alright?"

"I will thank you." She turned in time to not see the blush come across my face.

We walked into the kitchen, and she sat down while I pulled out eggs to make breakfast.

Danny!" My aunt exclaimed as she came into the kitchen, placing in an earring. "I wanted to make you two breakfast this morning." She removed the eggs from my hand. She quickly turned on the stove and poured us all a glass of orange juice.

"Are you excited about your first day at Grenoff High?" Izabelle asked me.

"I'm excited to get started." I wasn't talking about the coursework. I had a feeling that the answer to my questions about the King of Free Will had something to do with Grenoff, and I hoped the school library would hold some answers.

"Well, you're certainly going to learn a lot," she said with excitement as the doorbell rang.

"I really hope so." I loosened my tie as my uncle opened the door.

"Hey, Danny." I looked up and saw Claire walking into the kitchen with a smile on her face, and Jesse walked in behind her. They were both wearing their school uniforms and sat down next to us at the table.

"Hey! Look who's alive!" Jesse held out his hand towards me. I looked into his eyes warily, but I didn't see two people staring back at me like I had the day before. I sighed in relief because it had just been another mind game from Phantonix.

"Yes, I'm alive. Good morning, Claire."

"Hey, Danny. I thought I would walk with you guys to school today." She returned my smile and turned to greet Izabelle.

"I went ahead and told Michael's teachers that he wouldn't be back in time for classes. They're going to upload his homework to him," Izabelle said to Claire with enthusiasm. The odd feeling surged through my body again as she said his name.

"Oh, thank you, Izabelle."

"There's been another kidnapping," Jesse said in a hushed whisper as he watched the news program my uncle had left on in the next room.

We all got to our feet and went to the flat screen. A young newscaster stood outside of a small yellow house that had a broken tricycle in the front yard. Izabelle turned up the volume, and the story began.

"Thank you, Tom. I'm standing outside of the house of the latest gruesome kidnapping. The newest victim comes from the small town of Yellow Springs, Ohio. Authorities have identified young Benjamin Kahrs as the child who has been abducted." A picture of a young child named Benjamin picture flashed before us. He had ashy blonde hair and blue eyes. I stared into his eyes, and I could not help but see Matthew in his face, and my heart ached for the missing child and his family. "Authorities are baffled by the latest crime scene, and have concluded this to be the same kidnapper who has already taken two children: one from Argentina, and one from Ireland. This symbol has been left by the killer, drawn in the blood of the Kahrs family." When they showed the symbol that was drawn in blood, my skin crawled.

A single word burned through my mind: *Crusaders.* The fire in my veins roared hotly. My legs went shaky, and I had to sit down on the sectional couch to stop myself from falling over.

"Authorities are asking anyone to come forward if they know anything about this symbol. An international hotline has been set up for these kidnappings. If you can provide any information that is connected to these cases, please call the number below." The television was clicked off, and I looked up to see my aunt holding the remote.

"Well, that's enough of that. Breakfast is ready!" She almost pulled off the brave face, but I could see the fear in her eyes and the slight green tint in her cheeks.

"That's just awful," Claire said, her hands covering her mouth. Izabelle embraced her, and they held each other as the wave of mixed emotions passed.

"Come on," I said, and we all sat down at the dinner table, even though none of us were hungry after that horrific scene we witnessed. We all remained silent until we arrived at the school an hour later.

I stood outside the doors, looking up at the beautiful school. I could not stop thinking about how things were so different from just a year ago. My family had been alive, and I had nothing but darkness haunting me. Now, I was standing outside of a beautiful school with people I actually liked, and who liked me back. My parents and brother were gone, but I was filled with a purpose, and that was finding the truth about the King.

"Danny?" Jesse held the door open for me. "Y'alright?"

"Yeah, just thinking about my family," I said with a sheepish smile.

"I miss Matthew, too, man."

"I'm ready." I moved a couple of steps before my eyes fell upon a name engraved into the stone path.

Lily A. Jones
1954

My heart fell to the ground as I stared at her name. I looked around the steps, but his name was nowhere to be found. I stared at the brick walkway of all the graduates and reached down to touch her name. It was all true, and here before me was the evidence.

"I'm sorry." I followed Jesse into the school.

The amount of school spirit at Grenoff High was incredible. Banners that matched the four colors of the bell tower welcomed us. The office staff offered free coffee, hot chocolate, and a variety of healthy snacks. Students were visiting in the hallways, excitedly reliving their summer vacations and showing off their new bags and accessories.

Izabelle wrapped her arm around me, and we headed upstairs with hot chocolate in both of our free hands.

Our first class was World History, with Professor Herzog. When we entered the classroom, I discovered there were no desks, but couches, recliners, floor mats, and plush love seats.

"What is this?"

"I know, it took me some getting used to as well," Izabelle said as she pulled me along. Izabelle and I sat on a small couch near the windows and pulled out the tablets that were required for the classrooms. Grenoff believed technology was a vital part of education and could help save the environment. There was a note on the board in the front of the classroom for login and instructions to set up our class profiles.

The teacher was a woman in her early fifties with long, silvery hair. She wore rings on every finger and had a classic hippie vibe, even though her dress was very professional. When she welcomed the class and introduced her course, she spoke with passion about history and why it was important to study it. The next hour and a half was a clear indication that this class and this school were unlike anything else I had ever experienced. The expectations were higher, and the curriculum was harder than at my last school. But I found myself eager to learn because she made the content relevant and interesting. When the bell finally rang, she looked at us and smiled.

"I expect those personal essays due first thing Wednesday morning before class, outlining what you hope to learn this semester, your favorite part of history, and how you think it will impact the future. I hope you have a wonderful first day back." She smiled and waved us out. Izabelle stopped me out in the hallway and smiled.

"I will see you at lunch, okay?"

"Yeah, I'll see you then," I replied.

When I entered my English classroom, I found it had the same layout as my history class, with no desks, only couches, and recliners. The classroom was just as open and bright as the last one. The teacher, Professor Hoff, was another woman who had a rigorous attitude. Even though there were no desks, she had an assigned seating chart. I found my seat on the couch, and when I sat down, I looked at the board again. When I read my name, I found my couch partner, and it read:

MICHAEL SHEPHERD

I felt my hands go clammy and I had to force myself to shallow. The couch would sit both of us comfortably, but I wasn't sure why I felt uneasy about sitting next to Michael, considering I had never even met him.

I sat down and followed the instructions for logging in to the classroom material. The bell rang, and Professor Hoff started class. Just as Izabelle and Claire had discussed in the kitchen, Michael did not show up.

****

"The funeral was yesterday. He should be back before Monday," Claire said later that week when I brought up Michael's absence. Claire and I had grown closer over the last two classes, especially Home Ec., which was turning out to be one of my harder classes.

I had been to all my classes, and I knew I would hate Math and Biology, but luckily, I had tutors for both of them. Izabelle loved Math and wanted to make it a career. Jesse was incredible when it came to the human body and seemed to know how everything worked and fit together.

While Home Ec. was not a hard subject, the demand for the class was overwhelming. In class on Tuesday, we received a list of the different dishes we would be making that day, and we had to complete two dishes before the hour was up. Fortunately, Claire and I were partnered up, and because she grew up at Bear's Piano Diner, she had the upper hand. She told me she wanted to be a chef and own her own restaurant in Paris.

"I will introduce you to him when he gets back." She smiled at me, and I nodded.

The more everyone mentioned him, the more I wanted to meet Michael. I had heard the other students talking about him in the hallway, or in P.E., where Izabelle liked to tell me all about him. Everyone lit up when they talked about him, all except Jesse, who was very quiet when the subject turned to Michael. He just gave basic information about him, although I didn't pry too much.

I walked home alone after school, planning to meet with Claire, Izabelle, and Jesse after dinner to start on our homework. For the past several days, all I could think about was Michael Shepherd and the King. *Why did they impact me so much? Why did my mind continuously go to them? Was it possible that Michael was the King of Free Will?*

I had spent every free moment I could in the library looking at various books, but so far, nothing had told me what I wanted. While I was not even through a fraction of the vast collection in the library, I was beginning to lose faith that the information I was searching for was among those books.

"Hey!" my uncle called as I walked up the steps to the front door. He was walking out with a mug of coffee in his hand, wearing his Sheriff's uniform. My uncle had been working the night shift for the past couple of days.

"Hey."

"How was school?"

"It was great! Claire and I threw flour at each other while the professor wasn't looking," I said with a smile. "I'm going to meet everyone tonight to start on Biology homework."

"That sounds like fun! Do you want a ride home tonight?"

"I don't think we will be out that late, but I'll keep you posted." I turned to head inside.

"Please do!" He waved over his shoulder as he walked to the Jeep.

The house was warm and filled with the scent of honey-glazed chicken and garlic potatoes. Alvaro was in the living room playing with his blocks. I walked into the kitchen, tossing my backpack on the counter, to talk to my aunt.

"You're going to the library after dinner to study, right?" She asked without looking up at me.

"How did you know?"

"Izabelle called to confirm the time."

"Oh, great! Yes, it has a lot more room to spread out and work." She put a plate of food down in front of me.

"Sounds wonderful! I'm glad you're making friends and seem to be enjoying yourself here." I nodded before she left to take Alvaro upstairs for his nightly bath.

I sat alone as I shoved the delicious food in my mouth. I wanted to be able to start on my Math homework before I had to head over to the library.

"Danny." Matthew's voice echoed in the silence. I turned around and saw my brother standing in the hallway. "Hello." His smile lit up those green eyes in wonder.

"You are really here, aren't you?" I got to my feet, and he nodded at me. "Why didn't you tell me?"

"About what?"

"The King of Free Will, the Crusader, and Phantonix. I know you knew," I said, and the truth became clear in his eyes as rage lined my words.

"I did, yes. However, you had to find out on your own. You had to choose, Danny, but I knew you would figure it out when you were ready." He walked up to me and placed a hand on my shoulder. His touch was warm, as if he was still here.

"I don't understand what I am supposed to do." I watched as the sadness eclipsed his face, and he seemed to slump.

"We should have told you sooner."

"It's okay, Matthew, I understand." His eyes held such regret and sorrow.

"No. No, you do not understand."

"Understand what, Matthew?"

He looked at me, and I saw the conflict in his green eyes. I watched him arguing with himself, and I saw him decide.

"The Crusader." The look in his eyes told me that this wasn't what he wanted to tell me.

"I saw the vision of Austin!" My voice growing high pitched in confusion and annoyance.

"No, Danny," he shook his head, and I could see the frustration in his eyes, "there is still so much you do not yet know."

"Then tell me!" He stared at me with sympathy.

"I can't, Danny. You have to find out when you are ready."

"Ready for what?!"

"Danny…" His luminous eyes widened in fear.

"What?"

"Danny, the Crusader is here…"

"Where?!" The fear rose in my throat.

"…behind you."

Chapter IX

The Pianist

~Danny Elikai~

My body reacted quickly. I spun around and saw the jet-black blade descending upon me. I brought my hands up in a defensive stance, and fire ripped out of my left hand, colliding with the black blade with a loud crack. I saw the fire had formed a flaming sword of its own.

I looked at the Crusader and saw that he wore a fitted black cloak that defined his strong body. The fabric itself looked as if it were breathing. I could not see the Crusader's face, because he wore a fitted hood, and the darkness concealed everything but his haunting pale eyes. I stared into them, and they reminded me of bones breaking and decaying into dust. I felt a scream growing in the back of my throat.

The Crusader began to laugh and stepped back, moving out of his stance. The black sword seemed to wink and turned to nothing but smoke that coiled itself around him like a constricting snake.

I did not move out of my defensive stance as my body screamed with adrenaline. The sword made from fire was clutched tightly in my hands, ready for his next attack, but it did not come. We stared at each other for a long time.

"That's it?" I finally asked the Crusader. "Why are you here?"

He didn't respond but raised a black-gloved finger to where I assumed his rotting lips should have been, and he hissed as if he were silencing me. Then, he pointed it up. I knew that directly above us was the master bathroom, and that was where my aunt was right now with Alvaro. I didn't take my eyes off my enemy.

"You leave them alone!" I demanded as the fire grew hotter.

The Crusader began writing with his finger, and the black smoke began to form words that floated in the air.

*Death soon befalls
someone close to you*

"That is not going to happen." The fire cracked in agreement. But before I could do anything, the Crusader moved with impossible speed. He jumped and spun in the air, and the black smoke whipped around him, reforming the black blade as he descended upon me. I turned my fiery blade sideways in front of me to block his strike, and the impact nearly threw me off my feet. I held my burning blade in front of me, straining from his immense strength. The dark blade tried to cut through my fiery sword, and I had to use both hands to keep steady. Both the fire and smoke blades were beginning to crack, and I felt my strength waning.

In an act of desperation, I broke the connection by throwing his blade to the left as I spun right. I quickly slashed his left side, and the dark robe caught fire. A tortured scream echoed through the house as he staggered away, and I began to follow.

Before I could even move, he raised his left hand as darkness formed around it. I felt the blast coming before it shot toward me like a missile. My strength gone, I raised the burning blade sideways to deflect the inky blast. The force made me slide back onto the wooden floor, but I did not lose my balance. I stood there as the blast of darkness relentlessly pushed against me, trying to break through my defenses.

The Crusader moved quickly as he prepared to attack me from the side, but I would not allow him. I followed him with my eyes as he approached me, and before his blade touched me, I hurled the inky blast back at him.

The darkness collided with him, knocking him back into the wall of the kitchen. The collision was intense; it tore a gaping hole in the side of the house. The Crusader disappeared into the backyard, and I jumped after him without thinking.

I turned to find the Crusader standing calmly on the opposite side of the pool. He had his hands on his hips, and I could feel a superior attitude coming from him. His cloak was dusty, but otherwise, he appeared undamaged, as if this were nothing more than a game.

"Enough, Austin!" My father's training came back to me. I knew that I could not make the first move. For the first time, I was glad my father had put Matthew and me through all that endless, exhausting training.

"Wonderful! You're beginning to learn the truth. I wonder if you know the truth about yourself yet?" His voice sounded like it had been dead for a while and was worsening with decay. I could feel the strength, the raw power in those words, and I knew this fight would be nearly impossible.

"What truth?!" I could not take my eyes off his haunting pale gaze. I forced another burning blade in my right hand. I stood at the edge of the pool with two burning swords, waiting for him to make the next move. However, he did not do anything but stand in silence, ignoring my question, as if he were waiting for something.

"Danny!" My stomach dropped, and I took my eyes off the Crusader towards my aunt, who stood in the gaping hole, horror clear in her eyes.

The Crusader moved, and I watched him with my peripheral vision. He raised his hand at her as another explosion of darkness sailed toward my aunt. I moved to get in front of the blast, but I was too slow, and it was on course to hit her square in the chest.

I watched as she dove sideways and rolled out of the house, the blast making the hole even larger. She rolled into a crouching position and hurled a knife straight at the Crusader. Before he could defend himself, the knife plunged into his right shoulder with flawless precision.

I quickly brought the two flaming blades together and forced them into a small ball that was suspended on the tip of my middle and index fingers. I took aim with my left hand; the same way children do when pretending to play with guns. With my thumb serving as my guide, I released the inferno. The Crusader turned just in time to see a single beam of fire sailing toward him. Even though the thin beam of fire looked feeble, I knew that it could reduce a full-grown tree to ash upon impact.

The Crusader tried to defend himself again, but he only had time to try to lessen the impact. As he raised his right arm, the knife cut deeper. I heard his agony as the small beam of fire tore through the left side of his chest, and his body began to disintegrate.

My aunt and I looked at each other, and she smiled at me as if to tell me she was not harmed. We turned back to watch the Crusader, who was now burning. He stumbled around before his shrill, dying laughter filled our ears, and he jumped into the pool, extinguishing the flames upon contact. The darkness spread out like ink in the water, touching every corner of the pool.

A wisp of black smoke rose from the middle of the pool and danced around me before fading away into the shadows. The water returned to its natural, clear state; the Crusader had vanished back into the darkness.

I stared at the water, my body pulsing with adrenaline. I felt the rage burning inside me as I focused all my anger and animosity toward him.

"Are you okay?" Aunt Shannon asked me. Her touch brought me back to my senses. I turned to look at my aunt, who had a big smile on her face.

"Do you think he's dead?" My voice quivered, and my hands shook with fury.

"I doubt any Crusader will go down that easily, even with that powerful of a blast," she said warmly. I snapped up to look at her.

"You kn-know about the Cru-crusaders." My fury dissipated with the realization.

"Yes, and I am so happy you know now, as well. I believe it is about to start."

"How?!" The tears began to sting my eyes. "How did you know?"

"I know because I am a believer," she said.

"A believer?"

"A believer in Free Will, Danny." She touched my face gently.

"Why didn't you tell me?"

"I couldn't. None of us could. You had to find out on your own and, more importantly, when you were ready."

"Ready for what?"

"Enough." His words echoed in the space around us. We both turned to see Matthew staring at us.

"Matthew!" Her face lit up with pure joy. "I've missed you!"

Matthew stood in the gaping hole in the side of the house with a warm smile on his face. I watched as the tears flowed from my aunt's eyes.

"I missed you, too, Aunt Shannon." He moved toward us. "You cannot say anything more, it is not time yet," he said sternly, and she nodded. My brother turned to look at me. "You need to go to your friends. You need to protect them."

"But I still don't understand!"

"Yes, you do, Danny. You know about Phantonix, his Crusaders, and the King of Light. That is all you need to know for the moment. I promise you will know everything soon enough, but for now, you have to go protect them." I felt the finality in his words, and I nodded. I trusted my brother, and I trusted that I would soon know the whole truth.

"I will protect them," I promised Matthew just before he disappeared in the blink of an eye. I felt the stillness surround us, and we stood in the backyard for a few moments without moving.

"Before you go, can you fix the side of the house?" My aunt asked without even looking at me. I looked at the gaping hole, and I nodded.

I moved toward the house and held out both hands. I had never repaired anything this large, but my fire had never failed me before. I felt the fire reach my fingertips as the magic in my blood touched the house's broken, beaten pieces. My aunt stood behind me as the fragments of the house rose in the air, and neatly assembled themselves back into the hole. Within seconds, the house looked exactly like it had before the fight.

I felt exhaustion taking over my body. I hadn't used that much of my power in a long time, but it felt good.

"We have to get moving." She ran to the back door, opened it, and dashed inside. I stared at the wall, and I felt Sun's words in my bones.

I am a General of Light. I found comfort in these words, but I did not believe I was worthy enough to be a General of Light, even if I could wield fire. I believed in the light and choice, but to hope for more was dangerous.

I sighed and followed Aunt Shannon back into the house. I knew what I had to do. I grabbed my bag off the kitchen counter and repaired my uniform to ensure it was in pristine condition. With a little bit of my fire, they were as flawless as the day Izabelle gave them to me.

I walked down the hallway from the kitchen and met my aunt in the foyer. She had the silver dagger tucked into her jeans, and Alvaro stood beside her, holding her hand. His hazel eyes were staring at me, but before I could say anything, a loud knock echoed through the house, and we both turned to the front door. I moved to check the peephole and smiled. I opened the door, and Izabelle's warm smile greeted me.

"Hello, Danny!"

"Izabelle, you're early." She entered the house and looked at both Shannon and me.

"I thought we could get started on the assignments," she responded cheerfully.

"Sounds great." I turned to my aunt. "I'm going to walk with Izabelle to the library. Are you okay?" She smiled at me and winked.

"I'm going to head over to see Alex at the station and update him." She walked past us and went out of the house. Within seconds, I heard her car start.

"Everything alright?" Izabelle asked as she watched my aunt drive away.

"Yes, we're all good. We just had a little family talk before you showed up, nothing too stimulating. We should probably head to the library anyway."

We left the house and began walking down the street before she spoke again.

"Jesse and Claire will be waiting for us there," she said, and I nodded as my body was on alert.

We walked along the path toward the school. Nothing seemed out of place, but the Crusader's warning made me feel like everything was an illusion. I couldn't shake the feeling that blood would be spilled tonight.

"I have always loved this time of day," Izabelle said as she looked up to the sky. The sun had just descended as the bell tower chimed, and the four faces of the clocks lit up. The southern clock face burned violet, and I felt the fire burn hot in my veins.

"I have always been more of a dawn type of guy. The sun rises, and I'm hopeful of what possibilities a new day can bring." I kept the fire at my fingertips in case I needed to protect Izabelle.

We made it to the school easily enough, and my aunt texted me, saying she was safe with my uncle as we walked through the doors. We had just started to walk up the stairs to the second floor when Henry appeared at the top step.

"Hello, Henry," but he didn't say anything to her as his cold eyes held my gaze.

"Hello," I said to him as my fire roared in distaste. It wanted to be set free, but I held it back just barely under my skin.

"Why are you here?"

"We're going to study in the library with Jesse and Claire. Would you like to join us?" Izabelle interjected cheerfully. He didn't take his eyes off me, and they burned with hatred.

"Is something wrong?"

"No. Nothing's wrong." I do not know how, but he was lying, and I felt his animosity toward me. He moved past me, bumping into my shoulder, and within seconds he disappeared out the front doors.

"He clearly doesn't like me."

"He looks at everyone like that," Izabelle sighed. "Don't take it personally."

We continued walking up to the library, and it felt like home as we entered. I found Claire sitting alone at a table for four people. She had a pen behind her ear, and she was focused on a small book in front of her. Jesse was nowhere to be seen as we approached the table.

"Hello!" Izabelle pulled out a chair next to Claire. I took the chair on the opposite side of her, and I saw she had a joyful grin.

"Michael just told me he'll be coming back soon!" I felt my stomach fill with those electric butterflies I had seen when I met Sun. "It feels like I haven't seen him in so long. I can't wait to see him!"

That odd sensation rippled through me again just by hearing his name. I noticed Izabelle glanced at me with a curious expression on her face, but the moment our eyes met, she looked away.

"I'm glad he is coming back! I miss that boy." Izabelle gave Claire a side hug.

"Well, I can't wait to meet him," and my fire purred in agreement.

"I have a feeling you two will be great friends," Claire said.

We studied for about half an hour before Jesse finally joined us. He looked worn, exhausted, and even a little annoyed.

"Sorry," he whispered as he took the seat next to me and smiled at me. "My mother wouldn't stop fussing about me. I barely escaped." This sent a round of laughter from our table that received a stern look from our classmates around us.

I tried to keep everyone at the library as long as possible, but everyone started to yawn constantly. I was desperate to keep everyone together, and I asked if they wanted to spend the night at my house. To my dismay, everyone refused for various reasons, and they all left. I watched the three of them walk in different directions as I stood outside of the school and waited for my aunt and uncle. I was alone under a streetlamp, but I felt the darkness starting to enclose me. I couldn't stop worrying about them and the emperor.

"Phantonix?" I asked the surrounding darkness, but no one responded. *If the King is both Free Will and Light, does that make Phantonix the Emperor of Darkness, since that is where his throne is?*

I stood in the darkness, and I knew I was right. I could also feel the light burning within me. I looked at my hands, and I sensed the fire that burned in my veins. I wasn't scared of the darkness anymore, and I wondered if *I could actually be a General of Light.*

I dismissed the idea. There was no possibility that I could be a General. I believed in Phantonix and the King, and I knew I was somehow a part of it. I watched the fire burn around my hand, and while everything in my life seemed insane, I knew deep down that it was the truth.

I was lost in my thoughts again as the headlights in the distance gave me a start. I watched as the Sheriff's Jeep came to an abrupt stop in front of me. My uncle smiled as I got in the backseat with Alvaro.

"You both okay?" I asked my aunt and uncle as we pulled away from the school.

"We're fine, Danny. Nothing happened to us. What about you?" My uncle's voice was layered with concern.

"Nothing happened at all."

"Danny, this is a good thing."

"It means that the Crusader won't attack, and we called his bluff." My aunt finished for him.

"Danny, when did you find out?" My uncle looked at me in the rearview mirror with his green eyes.

"About the Crusaders?" He nodded. "It's been a few days. I had a dream, or I was in the past, I'm not sure, and I saw the first Crusader. I watched him as he was created, I guess, is the way to put it."

My uncle slammed on the brakes.

"What?!" He sounded angry as he turned around to face me. His anger caught me off guard as I stared into his eyes.

"Yeah, he was a Grenoff High School graduate named Austin back in the 1950s." I told them the whole story while we were stopped in the middle of the street.

"We need to head back to the station. That is one of our only cold cases." We had almost arrived at the house, but he turned the Jeep down a different street. The atmosphere of the Jeep was tense as he gunned it.

We drove away, well over the speed limit. We were passing Bear's Piano Diner, and when I looked out the window, I saw something that made my blood run cold.

"S-Stop the c-car!" Fear tore through me like acid as a root of panic burrowed into my stomach. I was not sure why the scene had caused me alarm, as there was nothing sinister about what I had seen.

Claire was standing by the piano, holding a stuffed black bear. She was talking with someone who was playing the piano, even though the restaurant should have closed over an hour ago. Maybe it was that I could not see the pianist or the unease of the Crusader's threat, but the fire inside me panicked.

I threw myself out of the car before it had even come to a screeching halt, and I screamed her name. Claire looked up at me through the window with a smile. As I ran toward the diner, I saw the swirling darkness begin to consume the man sitting at the piano.

Chapter X

The White Funeral

~Danny Elikai~

I let the fire rip out of my hands as I charged toward the restaurant. I watched as the realization lit Claire's eyes with fear, and she slowly turned back to the pianist. She jumped back in alarm as her eyes fell upon a dark shadow where the man had sat only moments ago. The monster was formless, massive, and looked like swirling ink, similar to the darkness the Crusader exploded into when he entered the pool.

I watched as the darkness made an enclosed fist and slammed it into the piano, shattering it into a million fragments. We heard a burst of high-pitched, ice-cold laughter as the creature turned toward me, his haunting pale eyes staring at me. I stumbled to the ground, and fear rooted me to the pavement. I watched in gut-wrenching horror as the black monster formed a bloodthirsty smile. I looked at Claire, and I noticed she didn't scream as she turned to face me through the glass door.

"Help me," she mouthed as a tear fell down her face. I ran toward her, fear and anger hammering in my veins. I ran as fast as I was able, and I saw her at the door, trying to shake it open.

I moved faster toward the front door—a door that was sealed shut by magic. I could see a symbol burning in shimmering violet light, and I knew she couldn't escape. I slammed into the door, but it didn't shatter upon impact. I slammed my burning fist against the seal, but it didn't break. I put my flaming hands to the glass, and Claire put her hand on the other side. I stood just three inches away from my friend, who was trapped with the Crusader of Destiny. I looked into her eyes as the purple ink glowed, and the darkness began to eclipse the diner. The swirling black smoke grew until it covered everything, including Claire's wide brown eyes.

Her scream tore through the night. I stood outside, and fear broke out of me in a continuous blast of fire. I aimed the flames at the seal, trying to break through to save her. The seal still glowed a victorious bright violet in the suffocating darkness, so I forced the fire to be hotter than I had ever tried before. I could feel the intense flames as they began to warp the asphalt beneath my feet.

I need to break through; I need to break through; I need to save her, I kept repeating to myself in my head.

Though I was immune to the powerful heat, I could feel my skin ripping under the intense force I was exerting. My skin began to heal itself as my energy slowly drained away, but I would not stop. I would save her, and I would protect her, just like I promised Matthew. I screamed into the void.

Danny... I felt a desperate plea in my heart.

I felt part of myself leave my body, just like when I was pulled from Austin's mind the night, he became the

Crusader. I found myself next to Claire in the darkness as she frantically banged her bloody fist against the unbreakable glass. I could see her, but I could also see myself outside as I forced my fire to try to shatter the seal on the door. I watched as my flesh ripped under the immense force of the blast as if to solidify my failing attempt.

"I'm here." I moved closer to her in the darkness. I tried to reach out and comfort her, but my hand passed right through her. I stared at my transparent hand, and I understood. My physical body was outside, trying to save her, while my soul stood with her in the darkness so she wouldn't be alone.

I slowly looked all around and saw the inky darkness from the Crusader had consumed the entire restaurant. I could not see anything except for Claire, and I could barely breathe as the darkness suffocated me. I turned to Claire as she held her throat in her hand, desperately trying to catch her breath. I touched my own throat and had a similar choking feeling. A startling realization crossed my mind, and I knew I would experience everything she felt.

The darkness of the Crusader surrounded us as an immense force bore down on Claire's leg, shattering it. Pain shot through my leg, and our screams held the same high-pitched agony as we both crumbled to the floor. I looked back outside at my physical self, but I saw that my leg was completely undamaged, despite the pain I felt. The fire still roared from my draining body.

"Danny…" Claire's whimpering cry called out to me, and I refused to leave her alone in the darkness. I would experience everything she felt, regardless of if she knew I was with her or not. I could not leave her alone to suffer. I was with her as she attempted to drag herself away from the Crusader, and the pain overcame both of our senses. I got to my belly to be with her, and I looked into her beautiful crying eyes.

I am here, Claire. My voice had not echoed in the darkness but was in our hearts, and she smiled through the pain.

The Crusader pulled her up by her hair, and my scalp burned too. I felt her legs kicking wildly in the darkness, trying to find something solid to stand on. After a moment, a long, sharp blade stabbed through her stomach. We both screamed in pain as her blood poured all over the floor, and she vomited from the pain. I felt my physical body crumble on to the asphalt as my aunt's scream filled my ears. But none of that mattered because I was only concerned with Claire.

"No!" I screamed, both into the night and in the darkness. I refused to fail; I refused to let her die like this.

I blinked and found myself in my physical body kneeling outside the restaurant. My fire sputtered and disappeared, and I could taste bile in my throat. I looked at the glowing seal and felt my heart jump in surprise when I saw it had cracked. The fire sparked back to life as her scream gave me my second wind, and it exploded out of me. I put everything—my pain, her pain, and our suffering—into shattering the darkness. The Crusader's force was slowly, playfully tearing her apart, and I wanted to vomit, to blackout and escape his nightmare, but I would not leave her.

"Danny!" I heard the scared cry of my aunt behind me. I turned my gaze over my shoulder to see my aunt and uncle standing by the road. My fire was burning so hot that they were drenched in sweat. I dropped both of my hands, and the immense fire surrounding me disappeared. I felt the cold night air swirl comfortingly around my aching body.

The darkness danced around the building, and I stared at it with wet eyes, completely out of breath. My friend was dying, and my power was not strong enough to break through. I could not protect her or even save her.

I screamed in defiance as I stood up on my sore legs. I used Claire's screams, pleas, and whimpers to continue to fight. Fear ran rampant inside me, but I refused to let him win, to let her die.

I moved closer to the front door as the fire again exploded out of me. I forced the heat and the uncontrollable fire into a small beam at my fingertips. Tears stung my eyes, and I forced my fire to penetrate the darkness.

"Claire," I whispered as my fire shot at the symbol. I closed my eyes and forced myself back into the darkness to be with her. Her eyes found me as I tried again to touch her face, but my hand passed through her.

"I am here." She nodded, her eyes beginning to lose the life in them. She was dying, and I could not even comfort her the way she deserved. Her face was twisted with devastating anguish that I experienced with her. I lowered myself to the ground as the sharp blade stabbed her repeatedly. Blood was everywhere, and I could feel the cuts all over my body.

"I am so sorry."

It's okay, Danny. She touched my face, and I knew she was beginning to give up.

"Please, help me!" I pleaded in the black void and the cold night air outside as the tears stung my eyes.

"Danny." I was dragged unwillingly back into my physical body as a robust and immovable presence stood behind me. I could not miss the unmatched strength and compassion radiating from the person who was holding me. I had that feeling again, that feeling that I had known this person since before we were stardust.

"You can do this, Danny. You can save her." It was that filtered, distant voice. The presence was directly behind me, comforting me, and the warmth coming off him was reviving.

He reached from behind me to put his white-gloved hands on mine, and I knew, even through the fabric they were strong and rough. Together, I knew that we could break through this barrier. I focused everything into our combined strength as my fire turned white. I felt the immense power in the white flames, and I let the fire take over my senses.

"Danny…" Her words sent a shiver down my spine, and I found myself back in the darkness. I wanted more than anything to hold her in my arms, to shelter her from the darkness, as I knelt outside trying to break in. I was experiencing her death by the passing seconds.

"I won't leave you," I whispered in her ear as I felt her soft skin. In astonishment that I could touch her, I quickly wrapped her in my arms and held on through the pain. She could feel me there, and together we would face this. Nothing was holding us apart now, and I could be with her at this crucial moment.

"Thank you." Her fear slowly drained, and I barely felt any pain in her body as acceptance began to form in her heart. She was safe with me. My hand itched, and we looked down as a small white fire had consumed my left hand. It gave a small light in the darkness, and we could see the formless Crusader looming over us. I stared into its haunting pale eyes as it smiled. I pulled Claire closer as her life was slowly slipping from her body. A hand formed in the inky blackness and shot forward, piercing her chest.

Goodbye, Danny. She closed her eyes, I found myself kneeling outside of the restaurant.

"Claire!" The white inferno overtook the dark barrier and burned it away. I fell back into the man behind me as the sorrow and exhaustion flooded through me. The violet seal on the door had burned away in white golden flames, the front door completely disintegrated, and ash drifted lazily into the cold breeze. The white golden flames conquered the inky darkness, leaving nothing but the restaurant in flames.

I felt the man behind me pull me up to my feet, and as he held me up, I knew it was too late. I had been with her when the Crusader had devoured her heart.

In its celebration, its absolute glee, the dark shadow had torn her apart and began to devour and mutilate her body. I was thankful we didn't have to experience that horrific pain.

"Well done, Danny," the man behind me said in his strange, beautiful voice. I didn't care about who he was at that moment. All I could do was stare at the burning building, which held the dismembered corpse of my friend.

I felt a gentle brush of air moving around me, and I knew the man had vanished. I barely moved my head to see that in the distance, my uncle was calling in his deputies. He shot me a look before he ran into the building, which was slowly being consumed by the golden fire. I laid down on the warped asphalt, letting the numbness, exhaustion, and phantom pain become the only things on my mind.

I found myself staring at my uncle, who had fallen to his knees in front of Claire's body. The Crusader had ripped her apart, and what remained of her was splattered all over various overturned and broken tables.

I looked down and saw an odd design in the warped asphalt. I touched the design, sending panic and fear through my broken body, and I knew the Crusader was coming for me next.

"Danny, honey," my aunt whispered gently into my ear, "you need to pull the fire back in." I sat up in alarm and watched as the burning red flames attempted to destroy our surroundings. The heat from my inferno had caused almost everything around us to catch on fire.

I nodded to my aunt as I shakily got to my feet and took control of the wildfire. I wanted it to repair the damage it had caused and to heal and create instead of destroying. The destruction caused by the fire was intense, and my body violently shook as I pulled it back. The fire slowly crawled across the asphalt, repairing the damage and returning it too normal.

I fell to the ground in defeat. I knew that I could sleep forever and that reliving the nightmare that had haunted me since my family's funeral would be a vacation compared to this night.

"That was incredible, sweetie," she said, wiping sweat off my forehead with a handkerchief. My uncle stepped out of the restaurant, and his horror-struck face told me everything I already knew.

"Danny," he said, getting to his knees and kneeling over me, "I am so sorry." He wrapped me up in a hug. As he held me, I felt my exhaustion take over as I faded into sweet oblivion.

****

Everything stood still over the next few days as the news broke out that Claire had been brutally murdered. No one knew that I had done everything I could to save her and failed. As a result, my body was broken and defeated in my vain attempt. No one knew that I had been with her when she had died, that I had held her in my arms and experienced everything with her. The official story was that I saw something strange in the diner, and when my uncle went to investigate, he found Claire's mutilated body. The police ruled the death to be caused by a bear, but we kept the truth to ourselves.

I could still relive her death with absolute feeling and recollection. The memories were just as intense and horrifying as when I experienced them. Every time I closed my eyes, I went through it again, and it was worse than the first time when I lived it.

I had stayed awake in bed, watching the falling sun, and now it seemed I was out of time. I had dreaded this moment for the last few days.

Tonight would be the celebration of life, and tomorrow morning was the funeral. School had been scheduled to start back up on Monday. I hadn't been able to get out of bed since that night, and if it weren't for the funeral, I would not be leaving it.

In my attempts to save her, I had drained not only my strength but also my power. My fire and magic had finally returned to me this morning, and for the last several hours, I had been playing with it to distract my mind from the nightmare. My phone kept going off, but I ignored it. The doorbell rang, and I heard whispered conversations that I knew were about me. My aunt and uncle were telling people, mostly Izabelle, that I was in shock and not ready to be with people, which was kind of true.

My phone buzzed loudly on the nightstand. I turned to look at it, but my eyes fell on the silver locket instead. The locket hadn't left my side, and the lullaby still played quietly, even though it was sealed shut. Since that night, I had not heard from Matthew, the still small voice, or the mysterious man who helped me destroy the seal of darkness. I wanted it to stay that way. I had failed to save my new friend from the Crusader, and the guilt threatened to eat me alive, just like the Crusader had done to Claire.

I remember when I finally woke up and saw my uncle sitting on my bed. He was looking at me with sympathy and regret. He held a photo in his hand, and I felt dread flaring in my chest.

"What is that?" I barely managed to croak, and my uncle sighed. He got to his feet and handed me the picture. I stared at the proclamation written in her blood and guts. The message was for me and no one else.

Phantonix will rule Creation forever!

I felt dizzy and sick every time I pictured it in my mind. A soft knocking sound came from my door, and my eyes focused on the lock, making sure it was secure. I didn't want to see anyone. I didn't want to go through another funeral. It would be another sea of endless tears, and I would have to face the white casket that they had picked out for Claire. I figured it was my aunt that was knocking, and she was going to try to get me into my white suit. It was the same white suit that I wore to my family's funeral.

Grenoff had a different tradition when it came to saying goodbye to people you loved. Instead of black veils and endless casseroles, we dressed in white and yellow, honored their life, and celebrated their passing into the Realm of Light. Right now, the city of Grenoff was preparing for a party that would be dedicated to the short life of Claire Childs.

"Danny," my uncle's voice whispered through the door. "Please, Danny. Open the door." He sounded broken and defeated as he called through the door, and I slowly got out of bed, my body straining in protest as I got to my feet.

I opened the door and looked into my uncle's tired eyes. He wore a suit that was similar to mine, except he wore a yellow shirt with a yellow pocket square. In his hands, he held my suit in a zipped black bag. His blonde beard and hair were trimmed, and he gave me a weak smile.

"I thought we would do something different with your suit." He handed it to me, and I turned away tiredly without saying anything.

I walked into the bathroom and looked at my haggard face. There were deep purple marks under my sky-blue eyes, my skin looked pale and ghostly, and patches of a beard lined my face. I looked into my eyes and saw the failure bright and alive in them.

I showered, shaved, brushed my teeth, and styled my hair to be combed to one side. I looked at the blonde streaks above my ears, which looked out of place. I grabbed my suit and unzipped the bag, and I noticed a stark difference from when I wore this same garment about four months ago. While it was still the same white suit, the dress shirt was a warm red, and there was a purple pocket square. The same violet as Phantonix's eyes, the same violet as the bell tower, the same violet as the seal on the door that kept Claire from living. Rage burned inside of me as I put on the suit, leaving the violet pocket square crumpled in my fist. I walked downstairs into the kitchen, where my uncle was standing.

"What is this?" I demanded of my uncle when I saw him, a cup of steaming hot coffee in his hand. His eyes locked onto the violet fabric and gave me a weak sigh.

"You need to wear it, Danny," he returned his gaze to his coffee.

"This color represents Phantonix, and Phantonix's Crusader murdered Claire!" The venom was clear in my voice, but my uncle nodded and walked up to me.

"I know you don't understand this just yet, but this color represents something more important." He took the silk pocket square out of my hand and began to fold it. "This color represents a different philosophy, another choice, another way to govern Creation. There will be countless people who will turn to this belief, and whether we agree or not, we must respect their choice. That is what separates us from them, Danny. You need to understand that and respect it." He put the folded fabric in the front pocket of my jacket. "The King of Free Will gave us the freedom to decide, and I will respect his gift, and I hope you do as well. Unless you believe in Phantonix's ideology of Destiny?" When my uncle asked this question, his fierce green eyes held mine.

"No. I believe in Free Will." The relief was clear on his face.

"Then we must respect Phantonix's ideology, even if we disagree with it, and his methods. We are the light, the compassion, and the understanding. We must demonstrate that in everything we do, alright?" I nodded and he hugged me.

"Are we ready?" We both looked at my aunt. Her hair was pulled back into a stylish bun with a yellow lily woven into it. Her white dress hugged her fit frame, and she wore classic white heels with a yellow rose on the toes.

The doorbell rang, and I volunteered to answer it. I looked through the peephole and saw a tired, but familiar, handsome face.

"Danny," Jesse said, as his eyes twinkled at me, and I felt my knees shake. He wore a simple shirt and jeans, and he took a long look at my attire. "That's an interesting suit. A blend of the two different philosophies." He sounded defeated.

"Free Will and Destiny." The annoyance clear in my voice, but all he did was nod.

"Crazy town." He stepped over the threshold.

"You don't believe?" He looked at me and shook his head.

"I believe in what I can see, touch, feel, and experience. I don't believe in anything else. If there is a great governing force, then one day, I'll see it." We hugged, and I felt him wince.

"Are you okay?" I asked as I pulled out of the hug. He sheepishly smiled at me, rubbing his shoulder, and nodded.

"I hurt my shoulder in wrestling practice," he waved it away as he walked into the living room.

"Thank you so much for babysitting tonight, Jesse," my aunt said as she gently hugged him.

"It's no problem at all, ma'am. I'm just not in the mood for a party tonight." He gave me a soft smile.

"We should be back after the funeral." She was referring to tradition in Grenoff when the celebration of life kicked off at midnight, just after the bell tower turned white. The party ended as the morning light touched the coffin that would descend into the ground.

"Try to have a good time tonight," Jesse said to us all before we walked out of the door. Izabelle was standing outside on the porch, about to knock.

"Danny!" Izabelle threw herself into my arms. I hugged her tightly and swung her in the air.

"How are you holding up?" she whispered into my ear. "I heard you were one of the first to find her."

"I'm just trying to get ready to say goodbye." I placed her back on the ground.

"I'm trying to keep a smile on my face because that is what Claire would have wanted," she said, smiling. She then turned to my aunt and uncle. "Michael's here." I caught the glance she gave me, and I felt that strangely annoying heat radiate through me once again at the sound of his name.

"Well, it's about time!" My aunt said with a smile. "We have certainly missed him. I hope he is getting through everything, considering the two funerals he's had to attend."

We all walked to the bell tower, where a grand stage had been quickly built, and Claire's smiling face beamed down at us. I felt guilt building in me, and the shame I felt ran cold through my body for not being able to save her. Izabelle and my aunt grabbed my hands, and my uncle wrapped an arm around his wife. My heartbeat faster when Izabelle's soft hand wrapped around mine, and I felt my breath catch in my throat. We all stood there, holding on to one another.

The celebration was beautiful, just as beautiful as the one for my family. The mayor, my aunt, Izabelle, and many other Grenoff citizens gave wonderful, inspired speeches dedicated to Claire. Finally, her mother slowly walked onto the stage, eyes red from crying. She thanked everyone for the love and support everyone had given her over the last sixteen years of Claire's life, and how well she had been treated through the death of her husband, and now daughter.

She felt her time in Grenoff had ended, and she said, "There is too much sorrow and grief in this wonderful town. I am leaving after the funeral to stay with my sister in Washington. Thank you all for everything."

She then walked off the stage, and the band took her place. My heart went out to her, and I could feel her sorrow as I stared at her heart. The longer I stared at her, the longer I saw fragments of Claire's childhood. I was watching a young Claire in a pink shirt with overalls learning to ride a bicycle when I heard him call out to me.

Danny. Matthew's words echoed in my mind.
Yes?
Come to the place where the Crusader was born. My eyes darted to the northern cliff above town. In the distance, I saw Matthew standing at the edge of the cliff. I looked at my uncle, and his eyes were locked on the same spot. He glanced at me and nodded tersely.

"I'll be right back," I let go of Izabelle's soft hand.

I began to walk toward the cliff on the other side of town, but it took me a while to shuffle through the crowd. The band began to play, and when I looked up, I saw it was one of my favorite bands, and I couldn't help but smile. My smile didn't last too long, however. I blended in with the crowd easily enough, but I couldn't help but feel as if I were being watched.

I finally reached the start of the trail that led to the top of the cliff, and I began to climb. The noise from the concert was mixed with the endless sounds of sorrow. I walked up the dirt trail, but I knew I was not alone.

I looked to my left and saw three figures covered in white robes, similar in design to the Crusader. They were walking next to me, just within arm's reach. On my right were another three cloaked figures, walking up the path with me. I was not afraid of them, and I felt their calming presence. They were not solid, but spirit-like, and I could see through them.

There was a voice in the air, the same voice as the man who helped me break through the barrier. I heard him whisper in my mind, *These are the Generals of Light, of Free Will.*

"We walk this path with you because we believe in Free Will," a soft, beautiful voice said. I felt a warm feeling flooding through me as her voice filled the night air. Her name was at the tip of my tongue, but I could not recall it.

"We are with you, Danny Elikai," another voice said. This voice was also familiar and thick, with a Russian accent that I remembered hearing before. I looked at the person on my far left. I stopped and moved to face the six cloaked figures. While I could not see their faces, they had always been with me, and I knew they always would be.

"In the name of the King of Free Will!" The deep, masculine voice that spoke had a thick Scottish accent. The voice came from the hooded figure that stood second from the left. I fell back into step with the Generals of Light, of Free Will, and we continued to walk up the slope. I could feel their power, their undying faith in the King, and their belief in his philosophy. I knew they all had deep experiences with the King; I could feel it. I didn't have to question whether or not I was a General of Light. Walking up with them, feeling their hearts, I knew this was where I belonged.

I turned to my right and glanced at the cloaked figure who was staring at me. I couldn't see his face, but I had that same warm feeling wash through me.

I stopped again, and I noticed that the person closest to me on the right was not translucent. While all of the other Generals were slightly transparent, this one seemed actually to be here.

Danny, Matthew whispered in my heart. I looked up, and I knew I was almost there, almost to the truth. I started walking again because I knew I would meet these Generals again one day.

I reached the top of the cliff, and Matthew stood at the edge with his hands behind his back, looking down at the concert. He was also wearing a white suit, but his was far more elegant than mine. His fabric was threaded with actual gold instead of just yellow thread, and when he turned to face me, the Generals of Light walked up and stood next to him.

"It is time you learned the truth," Matthew waved his hand, and the familiar scene around me disappeared as my breath caught. I was no longer standing on Star Cliff, but on a different cliff that was covered in emerald grass, which was surrounded by beautiful white flowers. The soft breeze was filled with the scent of honey, and I looked upon the most beautiful sunrise I had ever seen in my life. I walked out to the edge of the cliff and looked down into the crystal-clear sea, bordered with soft white sand. I felt at peace in this beautiful realm.

Chapter XI

The Choice

~Danny Elikai~

Where am I? I turned back to him, but he stood alone. His emerald eyes were filled with a peace and kindness that I had never seen before.

"You are in the Realm of Light." He smiled and pointed to his left. In the distance loomed a breathtaking white golden kingdom with soaring towers that shined like a diamond in the otherworldly sunrise. I fell to my knees as I took in my glorious surroundings.

Matthew, I looked into my brother's eyes, *are you the King?* He got to his knees and pulled me into a hug.

"No, Danny. I am not the King of Free Will. The King and the Realm of Light have given me the power to interact with Creation to help guide you here." He spoke into my ear as we hugged each other. The sorrow, the guilt, and the time apart seemed to melt away as we hugged. I was not sure how long we held onto each other, but neither of us wanted to let go as we sobbed into each other's arms.

"It's time you learned the truth." He finally pulled away and looked into my eyes.

"Everything?"

"Everything you need to know," he began. "Danny, I should have told you this a long time ago, but for many reasons, I kept it a secret. I wanted to protect you, but that time has now passed, and you need to be ready. As you already know, the warden that has haunted you for several years is the embodiment of absolute Destiny. Phantonix is an ancient entity that has been sealed away before the first life touched this world. He is the Emperor of Destiny and Darkness who is attempting to overthrow Free Will, the governing force of Creation." I felt everything around me go silent as the truth was playing out before me.

"Who sealed him away?"

"The King. He imprisoned him and his Crusaders inside the Realm of Darkness. You bore witness to the rise of the first Crusader, which broke the first seal on Phantonix's cage. That is why you and the Generals are on Earth. When Phantonix is set free, he will begin the Final War and lay waste to Creation as we know it." I felt my blood go cold as Matthew explained everything. "That is why I am here now." I noticed Matthews's eyes no longer held fear but instead hope and excitement.

"Danny, you are here to bring the King back."

His words hit me like a freight train, but I didn't even have time to process anything before Matthew continued his story. "That is why Phantonix is so hellbent on destroying you. He wants you to fail, and that is why he ordered his first Crusader to kill us." Matthew spoke solemnly.

"What?!"

"Danny, our parents and I didn't die in a car crash. We died because of the Crusader." I had forgotten he was slightly taller than me, as I looked up at him.

"What?!" He held out his hand and I knew he wanted me to experience his death. My heart was beating to the drums of fear as I took his hand.

****

~Matthew Elikai~

"Matthew!" The agonizing scream brought me back from the depths of oblivion as a searing pain left me paralyzed on the highway. I saw my life flash before my eyes for the second time today.

I couldn't help but think of how I ended up here, graduating with honors from my high school, my acceptance letter to Yale, and our summer vacation to Grenoff, Wisconsin. It all seemed pointless now due to the black-cloaked figure that had been standing in the middle of the road. I turned my head, agony escaping my lips, to see that the bell tower loomed over the forest of deciduous trees just a few miles away.

It was a beacon to the believers, unfailing like the sun. The northern clock face glowed a bright red in the distance. It blazed in the magnificent night sky, where the stars danced above me as they witnessed our destruction. I didn't have to see the other clock faces to know they were lit. It filled me with a certain peace as death's shadow crept around me, waiting.

I still remember seeing that phenomenal bell tower when we drove from Boston for my uncle's wedding. I couldn't have been more than ten years old, and I woke up in the car on this very highway. The sun had just disappeared, and the northern clock burned as if it had stolen its light. It was at that moment that I knew I had found paradise; I had found the Eternal Kingdom.

My fingers moved to the impaled glass fragment protruding out of my side, and I couldn't believe this was where I was going to die, just a few miles away.

"Matthew!" The voice pleaded again with such intensity I could feel the sorrow in my gut. I forced myself to turn my head away from the hope and peace of the red clock.

I realized it was not my mother's voice that was screaming and that I had not heard my mother's mind since I saw the cloaked figure in the road. I reached out with my mind to hear my mother's thoughts, but all I could hear was a clashing echo. I turned toward the immense heat that lit up the road, and my eyes fell upon my mother, who was still strapped in a car that was not only demolished but ablaze. The enraged fire was billowing black smoke into the night sky, starting to blot out the stars above.

"Mom." The tears fell as I watched her body burn in the fire. Her caramel brown hair had become nothing more than ash in the wind, while her charred skin peeled back to reveal white bone beneath the blackened tissue. The smell of her burning flesh almost made me black out from revulsion.

"Please, son, get up!" My father's voice tore my blurred eyes away from my mother. I glanced at my father and noticed he was standing in the middle of the road. His strawberry blonde hair was covered in ash, his white shirt was stained with blood from multiple slashes across his chest, and he looked exhausted. The crystal broadsword in his hand was gleaming in the firelight as he circled toward me, forcing the dark-cloaked figure away.

The figure stood in the flickering light, but his entire body was encased by a black cloak that fitted his body like a suit of armor, making his features indiscernible. The fabric danced as if it were made from the finest silk, and it moved effortlessly. The blackness of the robe looked unreal, almost as if darkness itself had formed his cloak. The cloaked figure held a black sword that seemed to absorb all light around it, even the flickering light from the flames of the burning car.

My father glanced at me for just a moment, but I could see those dazzling green eyes, the same eyes I had, were alight with fear.

"Find Danny!" His terror echoed in the devastation.

I can't move, Dad. I can't even wiggle my toes, as I began to slip into the loving arms of death. The clashing sounds of the swordfight seemed to be coming from miles away.

Will you give up? The still, small voice echoed in my mind. The voice had always appeared when I held the silver locket, which had somehow found itself inside my enclosed fist. I remembered packing it in my suitcase, which was now a pile of ash in the back of my dad's car. It was warm to the touch, although not from the roaring fire that had engulfed the car and was beginning to spread to the nearby trees lining the road.

Never. I fought to get to my feet, but the searing pain left me breathless on the road in a pool of my blood as I gripped the locket. Its silver, rounded body, shaped like a pocket watch, pulsed in my hand.

Will you do whatever it takes to save him? That still, small voice asked again.

"Even after my dying breath...please..."

A warm light appeared through my fingers, and as I opened my palm, the virtuous white light from the locket enlightened everything around me. Its warmth flowed through me, healing me, the glass fragment disappeared, and I felt it lift me and set me on my feet. Then, as quickly as it had appeared, the light vanished.

"Find him!" My father's eyes locked onto mine, and in that moment of distraction, the cloaked figure knocked the crystal blade out of his hands. The gleaming sword clanged to the ground as it shrunk to form a small silver dagger.

"Killing us won't change anything, and you know it!" My father's words did not tremble as the triangular tip of the black blade touched his throat.

"The blood of your family will change everything." That voice sent a shiver down my spine because I recognized it. I studied the darkness shrouding his face for a clue, for any indication that could help me remember the face.

Who are you? I heard my father think, and I realized that was the first time I had ever been able to read his mind. I had tried for many years, but his mind was the only one that had never opened to me. Whenever I reached out to hear him, all I ever heard was silence. His mind had its secrets and kept all manners of information from me, and I loved it.

I remembered the first time I found out I could hear and see into people's minds. It was when we arrived at Grenoff for my uncle's wedding, just after I had seen the bell tower for the first time.

"No!" The image of the hooded figure burned in my mind. I remembered who he was, and I felt a sting of betrayal because he had been my friend. He was the first person I told that I could read minds because his mind was the first I heard.

However, the traitor ignored me, forcing my father to his knees and putting a gloved finger to his forehead. The symbol burned hot across his mind, and I felt my heart drop to my stomach because we both knew what it meant.

"You're a Crusader." I felt the shock and wonder course through his mind as a black city with violet lights played across his memories. Before I could dive deeper into his thoughts to find out what was important about the city, he grabbed the hilt of the silver dagger. It shimmered to reform the crystal sword, and with an immense swing of the blade, he sliced the chest of the Crusader.

Find him! My father's words screamed in my head. He moved toward the Crusader, who had staggered back from the blow. He clutched his bleeding chest with one hand and wielded the black sword in the other. His blood hit the asphalt as the bell tower chimed in the distance.

"Danny!" I frantically spun in circles to find him. My eyes fell a few feet away from the road, and I noticed a large willow tree that gently swayed in the breeze. I didn't see anything, so I looked toward the swirling inferno, and I noticed how quickly the wildfire was expanding. The clash of swords behind me thundered in my ears with every blow.

I scanned back over my surroundings, and I found him propped up against the trunk of the willow tree as if he were merely napping. I stood there confused, unable to believe that I had not seen him there before.

As I ran toward Danny, I took in his appearance. His honey-brown hair was matted, and blood and dirt had stained the blonde streaks just above his ears. We had always joked that he looked like a raccoon when those blonde streaks grew in when he was younger.

"Don't lose this." I placed the locket in his open hand as he rested against the tree, unconscious. I stared at him, trying to look into his mind to see how badly he was hurt, but like my mother, his mind held nothing. The thunder of the battle behind me and my father's curses at the Crusader made my heart start to pound. I knew I was running out of time, and as if to emphasize that thought, I slipped in the pool of his blood that surrounded us. I stood back up to touch his right hip, and I felt that a tree branch had impaled him.

"No." My terrified word came out hoarse and was ringing with fear. He was going to die, and I could not heal him.

I grasped his cold hand, and the realization knocked me to my knees. His hands were never cold because of the fire that roared in his veins, the fire that should be healing him but wasn't. I felt tears slide down my face as the truth hit me. My brother, our hope, was going to die at the hands of Destiny.

We'd failed before we had even started.

An agonizing scream made me turn away from my dying brother. The scene before me was terrifying. The inferno from the car and trees was now illuminating the entire road with a flickering light. I turned to see the black silhouette of my father as the Crusader's black blade pushed deeper into his chest, the blade protruding out of his back. It was hard to miss the blood that was streaming from the tip of the sword as my father fell to his knees. The crystal blade fell out of his hands and hit the asphalt. It shimmered back to the small silver dagger, splashing in a pool of my father's blood.

"The reign of Phantonix begins," the Crusader whispered in my father's ear. He flicked his wrist, the black blade disappeared from my father's chest and faded into the shadows cast by the inferno.

I watched as my father turned to stare at me with fading green eyes. When his eyes found mine, I felt peace radiate through him as a faint, bloody smile froze on his defeated face.

"I trusted you!" I screamed at the cloaked figure I had once considered to be one of my best friends. He stepped over my father's body. With a sweeping motion of his hand, the darkness reformed the sword, and he pointed it at Danny. The black blade didn't reflect the light from the sky, the bell tower, or even the inferno that had spread around us.

"He's going to die, and there is nothing you can do to stop it," the Crusader's tone was more playful than I remembered.

"You can't kill him! Phantonix won't allow it!" I stared at the man in the black cloak, feeling the raw power of Destiny and destruction before me. However, fear didn't course through me. It was not bravery or courage that made me stand between my brother and the darkness, but the simple fact that I could not allow him to kill Danny. I stood my ground in a feeble attempt to stop him from destroying our only hope.

"No, I cannot kill him. But that doesn't mean I cannot stop you from saving him." The Crusader moved toward me in long steps, and I could feel the glee pulsing through him as he prepared to end my life.

"Goodbye, Soldier of Light." The black sword was aimed at my heart as he lunged for me. I watched as my death sailed before me. I could not take my eyes off him, and I would not give the traitor the satisfaction of making me feel fear or hopelessness. I watched as the black blade entered my chest, and I waited for the pain to overwhelm my senses, but I didn't feel anything. The black blade penetrating my chest felt as if it were nothing more than a soft kiss. Adrenaline surged through my body, giving stability to my shaking limbs.

I looked into the swirling darkness around his face and moved quickly while the traitor stood there stunned. I grabbed his hand and twisted it behind his back, all while hitting pressure points under his arm to disarm him. I felt his arm go limp as he loosened his grip on his sword; the blade faded from my chest and back into the shadows. Before he could react, I jumped and kicked him square in the jaw. He twisted around and fell to his knees by the willow tree while clutching his jaw with one hand.

I followed him, to take advantage of his shock and pain, and moved closer to the tree. Faster than I expected, he overcame his momentary weakness, and I watched as he stumbled with surprising speed to grab a low-hanging tree branch. He swung from the branch and landed both feet into my stomach, projecting me into the trunk of the willow tree. I felt the air leave my lungs as I slid down and came to rest next to Danny.

He loomed over us, and I felt his piercing eyes, his vengeful hate and animosity boring into me. The black sword reappeared in his hands, and I did not need to read his mind to know what horrifying demise he had planned for me. I didn't care what he did to me, as long as Danny survived. He stalked slowly, savoring the final moments of the end of the light, the end of Free Will.

I turned to look at my bloodstained brother as a jet of lightning shot through the air and burrowed through the Crusader's right shoulder. The agonizing scream tore through the smoky night air, and he sprinted back to the road.

"I am so glad you are here." I turned toward the General, who wore a shimmering white robe similar to the one the Crusader was wearing. I could not see his face, but I didn't need to. I knew who he was, and I knew he would come. I also knew he would do whatever it took to save Danny.

"The Crusaders have risen." All he did was nod and point to Danny.

"Save him." His voice was more beautiful than the wind in the trees or the air in my lungs. Even the most beautiful melody sounded like a dirge compared to his voice. I looked up at him as he lowered his hood, and I saw his familiar face. The beautiful green forest around us grew dimmer, despite the roaring fire, and became ugly in comparison to his angelic face.

The General moved back toward the Crusader, ready to fight. I turned away as the General of Light clashed with the Crusader, filling the night with the gut-wrenching sound of thunder and darkness. I moved behind Danny, holding him in my arms while my back rested against the tree.

He's going to die, Matthew. Please save him. I could hear that still, small voice from the locket, even though I was not touching it. I felt the voice in my heart, in my mind, and I knew I was safe.

"How do I save him?"

What does your heart tell you? My heart grew heavy because I knew what I had to do.

There was a light coming from Danny's lap. When I glanced down, I saw that the locket was encased in a ball of fire, suspended in Danny's open palm. The fire was not meant for destruction but for protection. Relief rushed through me like an open floodgate. There was still light in my brother's veins that pulsed faintly with his slowing heartbeat. He was still alive, and I could still save him.

I realized how quiet the night was, despite the roar of the fire. The flames had spread around to several trees, nearly encircling us, but it never seemed to move any closer than the farthest branch of our willow tree.

"You said you would do whatever it took to save him." His beautiful voice called out from the darkness and the flames. I turned my head to watch as he folded his muscular arms across his broad chest. I looked around, but I didn't see the Crusader. He had either fled or was a smoldering pile of ash on the road.

"Did you kill him?" Again, all he did was shake his head. The traitor must have fled, but he would return later, and my brother would again be in danger. I looked at one of the most devoted Generals, the one who had saved me one last time.

"Time is up, Matthew." There were notes of fear ringing in his voice, and I knew I could not put it off any longer.

"You'll keep your promise?" I pleaded with the General of Free Will. Even though I knew his answer, I just needed to hear it.

"Even after my dying breath, I will protect him forever," the General got to his knees before us. His heart held such beauty and loyalty.

"You have been a wonderful friend." I knew the tears were falling, but I did not care, as they left clean streaks on my cheeks, clearing them of the black soot that covered my face.

"I'll see you when the Final War begins." He grabbed my arms, and as he reached for the locket, the fire in Danny's palm disappeared. My brother had willingly given him the locket, and I knew that my time had ended. Even Danny's unconscious body knew my time was over because the fire around us changed. It turned from the destructive red and yellow flames to the burning white and gold of celestial fire. The celestial flames began to restore the destroyed trees around us and pulled away from the willow tree. We watched as the fire healed the scars of the forest, and even pulled the smoke out of the air. My brother raised his hand, and the white fire flowed into his outstretched palm and disappeared into his body, leaving everything the way it was before. The only things that were different were our dead parents and our demolished, melted car.

"Will it hurt?" I just stared in complete disbelief at my brother's ability to recreate the forest around us.

The General didn't respond. He grabbed Danny's cold, limp hand in his own. I knew, like I had the first time I saw him, that he would protect my brother and succeed where I had failed in saving him. I looked into his eyes, and once again, I saw the truth in them. I saw what Danny might never see. This man, this General of Free Will, was the only one who could guide Danny into what was to come.

"Oh man, he's going to be pissed at me when the Final War begins." I could feel the strength of every General of Light, of Free Will with me. I could feel the strength in our combined hearts, even though most of them were thousands of miles away from me. I could hear that still, small voice telling me that it could be this way forever if I stayed in the light.

I looked into the eyes of the man who would take my place in protecting Danny. I pulled him closer to me and whispered in his ear. "I hope one day you will forgive us for not telling you, but we had to follow our orders, we had to follow the plan. I know that you will become a man who will inspire the world. You will lead millions and will be the peace that Creation needs. I know that you will become a phenomenal man."

The General placed the locket in Danny's lifeless hand, closed his fingers around it, and raised it to his chest.

"I want you to know that you will never be alone, Danny, and that we are always with you. We believe in you, and you have given us hope." I placed both of my hands onto his hand that held the locket, and I looked at the General. "He cannot know until he is ready to find the King, understand? And if you fail to protect him, so help me, I'll come back and kick your butt," I said, but I smiled and closed my eyes for the last time.

"I will see you soon, Matthew." I was glad he was with us in my final moments. It was good to be surrounded by family.

"Celestial Imperial," I whispered. The locket opened, engulfing Danny and me in a virtuous white light. I felt the light invading my body, and I felt my consciousness slipping away. In the distance, I was faintly aware of sirens that echoed through the night.

"I love you, Danny. Stay strong and remember that Creation is waiting." I felt death's warmth comfort my body. I was not afraid, though, because I knew my parents were waiting, and I was heading home to the Celestial Kingdom in the Realm of Light.

Chapter XII

Michael Shepherd

~Danny Elikai~

"Danny?" My brother's voice dissolved the memory as the Realm of Light returned, and I jerked back. I hadn't been able to see the face of the general who saved my life, but in my heart I knew him.

"I...I...I am so sorry, Matthew." My words were barely audible. "I am sorry you had to give your life for me. You should have let me die!" My brother pulled me into another tight hug.

"No, Danny, do not ever be sorry. I would do it again in a heartbeat," he said, but I pushed him away.

"Why!?"

"Danny, you are the only one who can bring the King of Light back," he said again, and I really heard him this time. I felt the anger leave my body, replaced with empty confusion.

"No." The panic was rising in my chest, and I felt my body beginning to tremble. "No, no, no, no."

Matthew placed a hand on my chest, looked me deep in the eyes. "Breathe." It took me a couple of minutes to regain my composure.

"Matthew, why am I the one responsible for finding the King and bringing him back? I only just found out about this myself! I'm still learning."

"Exactly, Danny. You and the King will share the same experience. By learning everything slowly, and by choosing Free Will over Destiny, you will help bring the King back. We had to be careful and take it slowly. Just as you panicked from discovering you are meant to find him, imagine when he has to choose to accept his role as King! If he is told before he is ready to accept it, he might never take the crown." My brother spoke with real sadness in his eyes. "We have to introduce him to this slowly and give him time to accept the truth. We must allow him to step into the war willingly. The Generals, the believers, and the host of light all have to be careful in how they present this information to him. You will understand everything soon enough."

"When I find him, how will I even begin to explain all of this?" I felt the pressure weighing on me.

"That is simple, Danny. He must first be guided to the truth."

"When the King is found, what will happen next?"

"The Crusaders are about to be unleashed upon the world. It is the choice and responsibility of the Generals of Free Will to defend humanity and the King until Phantonix is unleashed." My brother touched my face. "Then, the King will gather all his followers and wage the Final War to claim Creation once and for all."

"Why can't we stop the Crusaders from rising, and stop Phantonix from being unleashed?"

"We cannot stop this, Danny. The hearts of Creation have led us down this path. It is because of their choices that the war must be waged. Humanity must decide how they want Creation to be governed: Free Will or Destiny." He lowered his hand, and we stared at the crystal-clear ocean.

"The King of Free Will or the Emperor of Destiny," I finished for my brother.

"Yes. And unfortunately, Phantonix is winning the war."

"How? It hasn't even started!"

"That is something you will discover yourself as you try to help the world." I breathed out a sigh of relief because my mind could not handle any more information. "Also, please do not be mad at our aunt and uncle. They were just following the path the King has laid out for them." He gave me a soft smile.

"Where are mom and dad?"

"They are safe, and that is all you need to know for now. They love you, more than you will ever know," Matthew said. "But Danny, I cannot stress this enough. You need to find the King before the other Crusaders rise." He gently grabbed my hand and looked into my eyes. I felt the desperation in his body and the air around us. I knew the importance of this task, but I felt the dread that I would fail. "You are the only one who can find him."

I nodded in acceptance. "When will I see you again?" My voice came out shaky.

"We have exhausted our powers just to get you here, and now you know what to do. I will see you again when the King returns." He stood up and began to walk away.

"Wait!" Matthew turned back to me. "Who is the Crusader?" I asked. "I know you know who he is."

"I thought so, too, but the body the Crusader was using turned out to be a decoy. It was my friend Nick, the first friend I made in Grenoff. I told our uncle this, and when he went to Nick's house, he found that he and his family had been dead for over a month. We do not know who the Crusader is any more than you do, Danny. The last real face we know, as you saw, was Austin. But that's all we know for now."

"You are in the Realm of Light! How do you not know?!"

"In contrast to popular belief, we don't know everything, Danny," he smirked. "Everything we know has led us to this point, and the rest is up to the King and the Generals. That is the beauty of Free Will, after all. Our choices, our actions, and our faith will help us win this war. We have foreseen several possible outcomes that indicate we will win the war, but in reality, it comes down to Creation," my brother said. "Don't be fooled by numerous self-proclaimed 'people of faith,'" my brother used air quotes, "who preach that no matter what we do, the Light will win. They are false witnesses because the Victor has not yet been chosen, yet. The hearts of Creation will decide the Victor." He smiled. "Although, I am pretty confident that we are going to win. That is because Free Will, the choice to choose our path, has already won. Look at history, and you will see that."

"Okay," I nodded. "Where do I begin looking for the King?" My brother laughed a hearty chuckle.

"Oh, don't worry, Danny. The King of Free Will, of Light, is a lot closer than you think," and he faded away, taking the Realm of Light with him. I stood alone on the edge of Star Cliff back in Grenoff. The Final War, Phantonix, the King, the Crusaders, Free Will, and Destiny all raced through my head.

"Excuse me?" His voice was so beautiful it took the air out of my lungs. It sent a wave of emotion through me, and I felt every cell in my body respond to the man behind me. It was more beautiful than the wind in the trees, the roar of the ocean, or even the first cry of a newborn baby. The fire inside me burned brightly with exhilaration as if welcoming a long-lost friend.

I turned around and came face to face with a tall guy about my age. He stood there wearing the same white suit as my uncle as he made everything else around him fade away. Even the glorious Realm of Light could not hold a candle to his beauty, and I knew then who he was.

"Michael Shepherd."

"You dropped this." I wasn't sure if he had seen the Realm of Light, or if he just saw me standing at the edge of Star Cliff. His voice filled the cold night air around me, and he held the silver locket in his hands. The locket was open in his hand, giving off a small white light, that same lullaby playing around him.

I looked at the locket in his calloused hands. Even through this suit, I could see how impressive he was, the muscles rippling up his arms. His flawless white smile reached his eyes, which seemed to be fluid in color. In the few seconds I stared into them, they changed from green to blue to brown to golden.

He stood a few inches taller than me, and he was built like an ox. His midnight black hair was cut short, but the tips of his hair seemed to curl slightly. He had a young, gentle face with a strong jawline, and his warm ivory features seemed to have been sculpted by Michelangelo himself. I could see why everyone talked about him because he looked like he was from the Realm of Light.

"Thank you." My voice sounded like nails on a chalkboard compared to his, which made me winch. I moved closer to him, holding my hand out to accept the locket, and we watched as the locket slowly closed itself. As I reached to grab the locket from his hands, my skin came into contact with his for a brief moment. In that slight contact, I felt his loyalty to Free Will, the purity of his heart, and the unfailing love he bore for humanity. I looked into his eyes, and he stared back into mine.

"You must be Danny." His smile was immense and full of joy as I placed the locket into my suit pocket.

"Yes, Danny Elikai," I reached out my hand toward him. I felt a warm and steady feeling flow through me when he shook my hand.

"It's wonderful to meet you finally. My name is Michael Shepherd," he spoke, which set his multicolored eyes on fire.

"What are you doing up here?" I had to break the connection with him and took a couple of steps back. Michael seemed to mirror my movements, but then he passed me to stand at the edge of the cliff. Even with his hands in his pockets, it looked like he was about to reveal a set of beautiful wings and fly away.

"I had to get away from the celebration." He had genuine sorrow in his voice.

"Claire was your girlfriend, right?" I remembered the answer immediately after I asked the question. I felt pain and guilt in my chest as I looked at him. I could still feel the phantom pain from her death, and I remembered looking at her mutilated body after the Crusader was finished with her. I looked into his eyes, and I knew that I could never tell him what had happened the night she died.

"Yes, I guess you can say that. We were very close," he said, looking down at the concert in her honor.

I stood next to him, standing in the same place where the first Crusader had been created, and where Matthew had told me the truth about my task. Although the evil from this spot had faded, I still relived the atrocities as I watched the destruction of a beautiful soul.

"I am sorry for your loss," I put a hand upon his broad shoulder as he leaned into my touch, and it felt like my heart skipped like a smooth rock against a body of water.

"Thank you, Danny. I was truly sorry about Matthew's passing. He was one of my best friends. I hope he is at peace in the Realm of Light." Michael's eyes were trained on the bell tower.

"Trust me, Michael, he certainly is." My words filled the night air as we stood in silence for a few moments.

"Can I ask you for a favor?" His words were barely audible over the concert at the bottom of the cliff.

"Of course." Michael looked at me with his mesmerizing eyes and smiled.

"Will you help me lay her to rest?" A single tear fell from his long eyelashes.

"Yes, Michael. It would be my honor."

"Thank you." I did not hesitate to pull him into a hug, and I felt grief rip through him. I could feel his anguish, his need to be comforted. I could feel everything Michael felt as I felt his arms wrapped around me as my head barely touched his chin. He hugged me as if it were the only thing he had ever wanted, and at that moment, I wanted to be in his embrace, to hold him while he was sad, and I was not uncomfortable. I already knew that he would stand by my side for all eternity and that made me shudder. Michael pulled out of the hug and wiped away the tears.

"I'm sorry." He smiled sheepishly.

"Do-don't be. There's nothing wrong with needing to be comforted. You're going through something extremely difficult, and you need people to lean on. I'm glad you feel comfortable enough to lean on me."

"I am comfortable around you, Danny." His voice was soft, but there was something layered in his tone as if he genuinely had faith in me.

"Well, that's certainly kind of you to say to someone you just met."

"I don't feel like you are a stranger, Danny. I feel like I have known you my whole life." He said this without a hint of sarcasm. I stood at the edge of the cliff as I let his words sink in, and he was right.

"I know what you mean." The words fell out of my mouth before I had a chance to stop them. I knew they were true because standing here with Michael made me feel as if I was seeing a loved one who had been away for a long time.

"Why are you up here?"

"Honestly, I was up here to say goodbye to Matthew and Claire." My eyes were trained on the bell tower.

"Here lies," Michael's voice boomed through the night as he spoke to the stars, "the ones we have loved and lost! Here lies a part of our hearts that has been taken and delivered to the light! Rest in peace, Matthew Elikai and Claire Childs!" His words seemed to echo off the trees and rose to the stars on the wings of the wind. I felt peace wash over me, and I said a silent goodbye to them both.

"Are you ready, Michael?" He did not take his eyes off the stars.

"Yes, let's go." We turned and walked away from the cliff and descended the trail back to reality, and to honor the life of Claire.

Several hours later, just as the dawn began to lighten the dark sky, Michael and I walked in the funeral procession as we carried Claire to her final resting place. Two others were helping us carry the white coffin to the graveyard. Claire's mom walked in step with Michael, and my uncle was beside me. He was now dressed in an elegant uniform as the Sheriff. Everyone else walked behind us, and the celebration was over. I could feel their dedication to this beautiful soul.

No one spoke as soft drumming filled the morning air. I felt the fire coursing in my veins as we moved closer to the end. I had a bad feeling that the Crusader would strike, and I wanted nothing more than to face him.

We walked the rest of the distance in silence and arrived at the site where we would say our final goodbye. We placed the coffin on the lowering device over the hole in the ground that would be her final resting place.

Michael held Claire's mom as she broke out into sobs. I took a couple of steps back from the coffin, and everyone formed a supportive circle around Claire's casket and her grieving mother. This was another tradition in Grenoff, encircling those who had been lost, and those that were left to grieve. We were their shield, their protector, and their family in that moment.

The service passed by quickly with many tears, and we stood waiting. The first ray of sunlight broke the horizon over the lake, and the light slowly moved. No one said a word as we watched the light crawl toward us.

When the light finally touched the coffin, we all said in unison, "Goodbye, Claire. We will see you again in the Realm of Light." A gun salute echoed in the silent air, and we all held onto one another. Everyone watched as my uncle lowered Claire into the dirt. Many flowers were thrown into the grave, and many more tears were shed.

I looked up to see the graves of my family, and I saw her standing under the tree that shaded their headstones. Claire looked just as beautiful as always, but she was older and seemed to be at peace. She wore a simple white dress that danced in the morning breeze. She smiled at me, and I smiled back. Everyone said a final goodbye as I stared at the girl I had failed to save.

You made it to the Realm of Light?

Yes, I am safe. Her words filled my body, and I felt tears sliding down my face.

I am so sorry, Claire.

Don't be, Danny. I know you did everything you could. Just promise me you'll find the King, and end this. Her words hit me hard, and it sent a wave of determination through me.

I nodded, *I will. I promise.*

Make sure my mom knows not to be sad for me. I am home with Dad. She smiled that beautiful smile.

I will, Claire. I am glad you are no longer in pain.

She nodded, stepped into the sunlight, and just like Matthew, she disappeared. My eyes found Michael, who looked at me with a curious expression.

I let go of Izabelle's hand and walked up to Claire's mother. I wrapped her in a tight hug and told her Claire was safe and that she was home with her dad. She didn't question me, and she didn't call me a liar. She sobbed in relief and thanked me. I knew by the look in her eyes that she believed me.

"Thank you, Danny," Michael spoke through his sobs, and I let go of Claire's mother. I looked up into his mystical eyes and nodded. I walked away from the crowd as the sea of white and yellow began to disperse. We all needed to get some sleep. I felt him approach me from behind before he spoke.

"May I join you?" His words brought warmth to the cold morning air.

"I would like that."

"Thank you, Danny. I really don't want to go home to an empty apartment."

"You live on your own?"

"Yes. I was emancipated a couple of years ago," he said, and I nodded in response. I didn't want to pry. Michael would tell me his story on his own terms.

"You are always more than welcome to come back and live with us again." My aunt's words filled the silence. We stopped to look at her and my uncle, who had been walking behind us. They were wrapped tightly around each other, the love burning in their eyes.

"Thank you, but I have already benefited from your kindness, and I don't want to be a burden to you all." His eyes fell upon mine and then back at them. "I appreciate it, though."

"How many times do we have to offer, Michael?" My uncle's deep voice was clear in the morning crowd.

"Yeah, you could take the guest bedroom." He shuddered at my words as if it was too much for him.

"I'll think about it since you all insist," he said softly.

"Please do. We have two unused rooms," my aunt gave Michael a tight hug.

"Come on; we should go home." We all followed my uncle and walked back to the house.

Chapter XIII

The Warning

~Danny Elikai~

I woke up several hours later from a sleepless rest, emotionally drained. I rolled over to see Michael still fast asleep on the plush armchair in my room by the window. The sunlight shined on his black hair, and it looked like he had purple highlights. He was wearing a simple red T-shirt and black gym shorts that I had lent him. I was surprised that my clothes even fit him, considering I was lean while he was solid muscle, and he was a few inches taller than me. His suit was safe in Matthew's old closet. My aunt was trying to send a clear message to Michael, saying that he was more than welcome.

However, he was uncomfortable in Matthew's room, which was why he was asleep on the chair in my room.

I looked at him again, and I noticed he looked out of place. Or rather, he was the only thing that truly fit, and everything around him was out of place. I felt another weird wave of emotion, but I shook it off and got to my feet. I walked out of the room quietly and made my way down the stairs to find my aunt in the kitchen, looking more tired than normal.

"Coffee, honey?"

"Sure," I yawned. I took a sip of the tart black liquid, and the fire inside of me roared in disapproval. I added some creamer, and that seemed to be better. I had never been a coffee fan, but it was everything at that moment. I felt the energy radiate through my veins, tingling every nerve in my body.

"How are you feeling?"

"I am, honestly, not sure," I told my aunt everything Matthew had shown me and how I saw Claire at her funeral. My aunt began to tear up when I began talking and became an emotional wreck by the time I had finished.

"Oh, Danny." She grabbed my hand, and I felt the love in her heart. I could see how much light burned in her heart, almost as beautiful as Austin's had been.

"How can I see the Realm of Light? How can I see those that have departed?" I put my face in my hands, and I felt the exhaustion and confusion rip through me.

"With your heart," my aunt said softly.

"What?"

"Danny, everything will be explained when the King returns," she touched my face and it put me at ease. "I cannot wait for him to come back."

"Where do I begin to look for him?"

"I believe the King of Light is closer than you know." She poured more coffee into her mug.

"Would you mind if I had some?" His voice took our breaths away. I turned around, and Michael seemed to fill the doorway of the kitchen with a soft smile on his flawless face.

"Absolutely," My aunt went to grab a mug from the cupboard. Michael sat down at the table next to me, and the scent of honey filled my senses. I turned to face him.

"Good afternoon," he greeted. His eyes fell on mine, and for a second, his eyes flashed a deep emerald before they changed to honey-brown, and then to sapphire blue. I turned away because I was becoming lightheaded.

"Hey," I had to focus on drinking the coffee. The doorbell rang, and I looked at the door.

"Who now?" My aunt left the kitchen to open the door.

"Michael!" Izabelle yelled as she ran into the kitchen and threw herself into his arms, sobbing. Michael carried her to the couch, and I was left with my aunt.

"We tried to tell you," My aunt said softly, smirking at me while sipping her coffee. When I looked at her, I saw how she looked at where Michael had just sat.

"Yeah, I know what you mean. Does that happen with everyone?" I already knew the answer even before she nodded. "I think it's his eyes."

"Or his voice."

"Or he's from the Realm of Light." I turned away from her. I got to my feet and walked out of the kitchen. My emotions and my entire body were fried, as Matthew's mission burned in my mind.

Find the King, his words repeated in my mind.

I left the kitchen to go to my room, but I found Alvaro standing alone at the bottom of the staircase, looking up at the top. He had a small hand on the railing, and he stood still.

"Alvaro?" He turned to look at me and held out his other hand. I held his hand in mine, and everything else faded away.

I looked around, and I saw that I was standing in the same place in the house, but everything was different. Alvaro was no longer holding my hand, and the inside of the house was a blazing inferno. The thick smoke around me made it difficult to breathe, but as the fire licked my body, I was unaffected.

"Danny!" The agonizing scream from Alvaro made my heart plummet as the child ran past me up the stairs.

"Alvaro!" I choked as I ran up the stairs after him.

"He's coming!" My cousin screamed from upstairs as I stumbled to follow him.

"Who?!" An immense force picked me up and threw me into the wall at the top of the stairs in response. I was thrown through the wall and was sprawled on the floor of my bedroom.

My lungs burned white-hot, and I watched in horror as a figure crawled through the hole in the wall. My blood went cold when I looked at its face. It was a creature that only existed in nightmares. It was a human-shaped reptile that stood about seven feet tall and was covered in dark green scales. Its eyes were bright yellow, and its pupils were black slits. It had a long tail with spikes at the tip that snaked back and forth.

"W-Who are you?!" I trembled at the sight of the creature before me.

"Daimonas." His voice came out like sweet silk, and his tongue slithered like a snake between his razor-sharp teeth. I slowly got to my feet, fighting through the pain in my chest. I clenched my fists to take control of the surrounding fire. The fire danced around my enclosed fist. It felt alien in my hands as I forced it to form two blazing swords.

"You're a Crusader."

"Yes," the monster hissed, "I am a Crusader." The words spilled out of his lips as adrenaline rocked my body. I slowly moved into a defensive stance, ready for his first strike, but he seemed to be relaxed.

"How many Crusaders are there?" He raised his scaly hands with sharp black claws, indicating seven fingers.

"I am the fifth of the seven Crusaders," Daimonas said through his razor-sharp teeth.

"What do you want?" I had a feeling that he would not attack, and I slowly relaxed.

"A plea, Danny," he moved closer to me.

"What?" My body tightened with his response, and I snapped back to my defensive stance.

"Do not let my brother Ieiunium take me," he said softly. "Please, Danny. I need you to protect my heart." I could hear genuine fear in his voice.

"I don't understand." I looked into his reptilian eyes.

"I will be the last one he takes. Please, protect us. Protect the rest of us." He slowly retreated through the hole in the wall.

"What are you talking about?"

"Please," he whispered as he slowly backed through the hole, "protect the other three hearts, the three remaining Crusaders."

The monster disappeared into the flames as the burning swords twisted in my hands. I watched as the fire snaked around me and slowly began to consume me.

I felt the heat and the pain in the flames as they turned violet, and I heard Phantonix's high-pitched, ice-cold laughter. I watched helplessly as the dark fire bore into my eyes, and the smoke choked me.

I felt the pain all over my body before the small tug on my hand made it all disappear. The flames were gone, and the house was back to normal. My eyes flew up to see Alvaro standing a few steps above me. I was splayed on the floor at the bottom of the staircase. I could taste the smoke that was choking me only a second ago, and I desperately tried to catch my breath with fresh air.

"Alvaro, what was that?" I forced myself to say through the coughing fit. My cousin's eyes were burning with fear, and tears began to fall down his face.

"The future?" He threw himself in my arms, and I felt dread in his heart, for even he did not know.

"It's okay, Alvaro." I held him close. He cried in my arms, and I held him tightly.

"Danny?" My aunt poked her head around the corner. She saw me with her crying son. "What happened?"

"Alvaro showed me the fifth Crusader, Daimonas." I barely choked the words out.

"What?"

"He's coming."

"Daimonas?" My aunt said in fear, but I shook my head.

"Ieiunium."

"Why?" She got to her knees next to us.

"I'm not sure. Daimonas came to me and begged me to 'protect the other three hearts.' I don't know what that means."

"'The three other hearts?'" Her words didn't make any more sense than mine. There was absolute fear in her eyes.

"I don't understand, either. Daimonas said he didn't want to be taken by Ieiunium. He was afraid." Alvaro broke apart from my embrace, and Aunt Shannon wrapped him into her arms.

"How did he show you that?" My aunt looked at her son, but she was talking to me.

"I think," I said, trying to fit the pieces together, "Alvaro may be a General of Light." But my words sounded wrong, and my aunt gave me a questioning look.

"No, I don't think so. All of the Generals were born around the same time, and Alvaro is way too young." She shook her head. "No, Alvaro is not a General of Free Will."

"Then, how does he have these powers?"

"I don't know. He may have some natural ability like Matthew."

"Is that possible?" I looked at him. The white light burned bright in his heart.

"Yes, people can be born with spiritual abilities. But it's unbelievably rare."

"I think you might be right," I said. "I can see the light in his heart." My aunt rocked Alvaro, trying to comfort him.

"I'm going to take him to bed." She walked up the stairs. I got to my feet and turned to walk out the front door. The chilly evening air greeted me, and I sat down on the porch swing. I closed my eyes and let the cold air relax me. Everything was happening too fast, and I could not process it.

"Danny?" I opened my eyes and saw the navy-blue eyes of Jesse. He was standing right in front of me, smiling awkwardly.

"Hey, Jesse." I easily returned his smile.

"How was the funeral?"

"It was exhausting," I said. "I wish you could have been there with us."

"No, I didn't feel right going." Before I could ask, someone opened the door.

"Jesse?" Izabelle poked her head out of the door, and she smiled when she saw him.

"Hello, Jesse," Michael said warmly as he followed her out onto the porch. She wrapped her arms around Jesse, but he stood as still as a statue. I moved over on the porch swing to let Michael sit next to me.

"Hey," Jesse nodded at Izabelle and barely addressed Michael. His arms rested at his side, and he did not even attempt to hug her back. Michael sat down next to me, and we stared at them curiously.

"You okay, Jess?" Michael's words filled the awkward space between all of us, and Izabelle chuckled but pulled away.

"Sorry, I'm a bit out of it," Jesse said. "It's been a complicated couple of days."

"I don't blame you, babe," Izabelle came to sit on the other side of me. The three of us were squeezed tightly on the wooden porch swing. None of us said anything as we gently swung back and forth.

"It won't be the same without her," Michael said, and everyone nodded.

"What do we do now?" They all looked at me with a mixture of looks; Izabelle had a sad expression, Michael was peaceful, and Jesse looked tired and annoyed.

"We stick together," Izabelle said.

"We're in this together," Michael said confidently. I looked at them, but I felt disheartened. The Crusader had taken my parents, my brother, and now Claire. I looked at my friends, and I could not help but wonder which one of them I would lose to the Crusader next. Not to mention, I had to find and protect the King.

I forced a smile as the truth burned in me. I was a General of Free Will, and I had to find the King and protect my friends. I also knew that I would do whatever it took to stop and destroy Ieiunium, the first Crusader of Destiny.

Chapter XIV

The Song

~Danny Elikai~

"Danny!" Michael said with enthusiasm as he jumped on my bed, and my body groaned in the early hour. I pitifully opened my eyes, which immediately fell upon the green light of my alarm clock to show me it was 4:45 A.M. on a Saturday.

I rolled over and covered my head with the plush comforter in my feeble attempt to shut Michael out, but I knew it was pointless. As if to emphasize my point, he grabbed the covers and pulled them off the bed, letting the cold air swirl around me. The fire inside me groaned in annoyance. I curled up on my bed, wearing nothing more than gray sweatpants, as the cold October air drifted in through the open window that I had not left open.

I was doing my best to ignore him and to fall back asleep, but the raw excitement radiating off him seemed to be seeping into my bones.

"What?" I finally turned around to face him after a few more moments of pretending he did not exist. To no great surprise, he stood at the foot of my bed wearing tight running shorts and nothing else. He had a wicked smile on his face, and I swallowed hard as I watched the small bead of water travel down his sculpted abs to the tiny patch of black hair around his navel.

"Come on!" He had a level of energy that should have been illegal at that hour. I had an urge to throw my pillow at his puppy dog grin. He grabbed my leg and began shaking it until I finally sat up and glared at him. He just stood there with a big smile on his face. It was the same fake smile he had been wearing for a week now, a smile that hadn't let up since Claire's funeral.

Since the farewell ceremony, Michael had not left my side for a moment, not even to sleep. I usually found him sleeping in the chair by the window, but sometimes, I would wake up with him next to me. I could not mistake his sadness and his sorrow when I looked into his ever-changing eyes, but when he was next to me, he seemed to be at ease. I let him sleep next to me because he needed to be close to someone. I didn't mind it because when he was beside me, the darkness could not torment me. He was my friend, and it was comforting to have someone next to me in the dark. Except for last night, when he briefly returned to his rundown apartment to do chores and laundry. My Aunt Shannon had offered to take care of it for him, but he refused, saying she had already done enough for him.

"Come running with me!" He cheered, and he sat down on my bed next to me as I scowled at him in disgust.

"It's Saturday." The absolute revulsion was clear in my voice. I despised running, and it always made me feel like I was going to throw up. I had always loved cycling, though. I loved the feeling of speeding down the street on a bike like I could almost fly.

He sat cross-legged on my bed, his beauty and near nakedness, making my stomach flip flop. I looked at him and, not for the first time, I concluded that Michael's beauty was unworldly. He looked into my eyes and smiled.

"Yes, it is Saturday! And it's a beautiful day to go running!" I knew he was holding back what he was truly feeling. He was wounded by Claire's death, even though he would not admit it.

I grumbled again, and I looked out the window. The rain fell in dense sheets as lightning cracked the morning sky in a blinding light. The fire protested violently, and I had a feeling I would face the cold alone.

Michael sat on my bed, and I could feel his emotions next to me. I knew that I would run with him because it was what he needed. I turned to look at him and smiled halfheartedly.

"I love the rain," he said, not really to me, as he stared out the window. I sighed and put on a T-shirt and socks, noticing that Michael's eyes never left the rain. I could see his heart change as he watched the rain intently as if it could wash away his pain, the memories of the girl he loved, the memories that now brought white-hot pain instead of warmth and happiness. I watched him closely, but his heart did not open to me as it did with other people. I could only feel what was on the surface as if he were blocking me out. I shook my head and turned to the window.

"Did you crawl through the window?" I shut the window and sat in the chair to put on my shoes. Michael gave me a knowing smile with a wink, and he began to stretch as drops of water danced on his warm tanned skin. "Why? You have a key."

I thought back to last night when my aunt asked him if he still had the key to the house, and he responded by showing her the spare house key. I did not understand why Michael had a key to the house, but it was none of my business, and no one offered an explanation, so I did not bother to bring it up.

"I just wanted to be around you without waking everyone up." It was not the first time he had said something along these lines, but it always threw me off. I stood by the window with one shoe in my hand and shook off the feeling.

Michael had a beautiful heart. He was so giving and trusting, and when I was with him, I could not help but feel special and loved. His heart gave off a beautiful light, a light that I knew burned with a fierce loyalty that meant that once he was on my side, he would never leave.

"Me too," I said, and I meant it. I was glad Michael and I were becoming close friends. If I was being honest with myself, Michael was the truest friend I had ever had. It was weird to think about it because I had only known him for about a week, but it never felt that way. It felt like I had known him my whole life, and we were finally seeing each other after a long separation, almost like coming home. I knew he felt the same because he had said as much on the cliff during the celebration.

"Let's go!" He said as he opened the door and walked down the stairs. I watched him leave as a smile pulled at my lips. I walked out to join him in the cold downpour. I made sure to lock the door behind us, and I put the key to the house safely in my shoe. The rain sent goosebumps down my back, and the cold air hurt my lungs.

I tried to bring the fire out to bring me warmth, but it stayed buried in disapproval. It was probably for the best because I was not sure how Michael would respond to it. Even though it felt like I had known him forever, it was still not something I could just bring up casually.

Oh, my fire abilities? Don't worry about it. I'm just a General of Light to the King of Free Will, who is trying to stop an ancient entity from destroying everything we know and hold dear. The thought played in my head, and I laughed out loud at the stupidity of it.

Michael looked at me with a knowing smile, and I felt like he could read my mind.

We first ran to the school near the lake and doubled back to the center of town. We ran around the bell tower, turned northwest, and kept running until we ended up in front of the remains of Bear's Piano Diner. True to her word, Claire's mom had already sold the restaurant, and a new business was in the process of changing the inside and remodeling the outside.

Michael didn't say anything. He didn't even seem to be breathing as we stared through the rain at the place where Claire had been brutally murdered. I didn't say anything as we stood there, shoulder to shoulder, and we let the moments pass by. There was nothing to say, no words that could heal the events that unfolded here. I knew the Crusader would pay for this horrendous act.

I thought of Austin, and my eyes went up to Star Cliff, the place where the first Crusader had risen, and where Matthew finally told me the truth. I was not even aware that my fists were clenched until the sharp pain in my palm made me flinch. I had squeezed so hard my nails broke my skin, and blood began to bead in my palm. I angled my body so Michael would not see my hand, and I watched the fire reluctantly repaired the damage done by my nails. The rain washed away any evidence of blood.

"I miss you," Michael's soft words made me turn to look at him. He looked back to me with a sad smile. He didn't say another word as he turned and ran back the way we came. He ran a little faster than we had been running before, as if he was trying to run from her death or the memories. His long, powerful legs made it hard to keep up, but I would not leave him alone.

We ran in silence as my mind replayed her death, and I felt her pain tingling in my body. No matter how far or fast we ran, I would never outrun that horror. I knew I could never tell him the truth about her death, how horrific it was, or that I didn't save her.

We ran around Grenoff for what seemed like hours, and when we finally ran up the front steps to the porch of my aunt and uncle's house, I fell to the ground. The pain in my sides and legs felt like they would need a thousand stitches to repair the damage. I sprawled on the wet porch, breathing hard while Michael sat next to me, not even looking slightly out of breath. He had his legs crossed and leaned back to lay right next to me, not even an inch away from me. I had tears of exhaustion, sweat everywhere, and a burning in my lungs from the cold air, but Michael looked like a statue frozen in beauty. He listened to the rain, and even though he was already soaking wet, he reached out a hand to feel it. While he was enjoying himself, I was attempting to prevent myself from coughing up my lungs.

"I love a good storm." His voice was like a gentle breeze on a summer day. I rested on the porch in silence for several minutes until my breathing finally returned to normal, and I sat up.

"How long have you lived in Grenoff?" The cold air seemed to be numbing my entire body, and I felt my teeth beginning to chatter. Since Michael's eyes were focused on the rain, I released the heat from my fire, which had finally forgiven me. The heat flooded through me, and stability returned to my body.

"I moved here when I was younger." The tone and his body language told me he did not want to talk about his past. We didn't say much as we watched the storm hammer down on the streets of Grenoff.

"Michael." I reached up and touched his shoulder. He didn't cringe or shake me off. In fact, he moved into my touch. I felt his conflicting emotions, his longing for stability, comfort, and something I could not quite place.

I felt that protection around his heart slowly begin to fade as we sat there. He looked at me for just a moment before he smiled and turned away, and I felt him change. The walls around his heart had returned, and I watched as he sealed his emotions back inside him. He continued hiding behind a smile that I had worn countless times, a smile that convinced everyone that I was fine.

"Come on!" He exclaimed, getting to his feet. I looked at my legs, and I seriously doubted they were capable of lifting me off the ground. Michael held out his hand, and I took it without question. We walked into the house, and the smell of waffles drifted through the foyer.

"Danny?" my uncle called from the kitchen.

"Yeah!" I responded, and we took off our shoes. We were both dripping wet as my uncle came around the corner. He wore a checkered apron and had a goofy smile on his face. He was drying his hands on a kitchen towel with chickens on it when he said, "Oh, hello, Michael!"

"Good morning, Alex." Michael moved, and I hadn't even realized we were still holding hands when he let go so he could get towels from the small guest bathroom to dry off.

"Breakfast will be ready in a few minutes. Dry off before you get us all sick." He turned back and disappeared into the kitchen. In a few minutes, we were dry, changed, and standing in the kitchen with coffee.

"Any big plans for today?" my uncle asked as he shoveled eggs and bacon onto two different plates. On the counter beside him sat a breakfast tray for my aunt with a single rose in a small vase. I couldn't help but think it was such a simple, beautiful gesture for the woman he loved.

"Not much, probably homework," I mumbled.

Uncle Alex handed us our plates, and Michael and I sat in silence as we ate. My eyes found him, and I saw a strange expression in them, but he turned away, feeling annoyed. My uncle disappeared upstairs with the tray to eat breakfast in bed with his wife. When I looked up again, Michael was still giving me the same strange look.

"What?" I asked after I caught him staring at me the whole time.

"Nothing." He looked down at his almost empty plate.

"It's not nothing, Michael. You can tell me." He looked at me, and he smiled a goofy smile. Even with his ridiculous expression, his smile was more breathtaking than any other smile I had ever seen. I felt annoyed that no matter what he did, he looked beautiful. I knew it impacted everyone the same way, but it was not fading with time. It was almost as if I had forgotten the feeling until I saw him again.

"I was just thinking." He finished his breakfast, he got to his feet, and washed his plate before placing it in the dishwasher.

"What about?"

"What comes next, Danny." He turned to me and had real pain in his ever-changing eyes. He held onto the sink as he looked at me. A rush of emotion flooded me as I stared into his eyes. At that moment, I felt unbelievable pain and loneliness in him, but his hope burned hotter than the fire in my veins.

"What do you mean?"

"I'm not sure," he said softly. "I'm just not sure where to go from here." He stared down at the floor as he spoke.

"I'm sorry, Michael, but I don't understand. Do you mean what to do now that Claire is gone?" He shook his head.

"No. She is at peace in the Realm of Light," he said quickly, and he looked up at me. "I'm unsure about us." I felt something jump into my throat.

"Uhm." I had the deer-in-the-headlight expression on my face.

"Well, we are friends, right?" And I released the breath I did not know I was holding as I felt how clammy my hands were all of a sudden.

"Oo-of course, we are friends, Michael. I don't get out of bed at 4:45 A.M. on a Saturday for just anyone." I got to my shaking feet with my empty plate and walked toward him.

"That's a fair point. I'm just not good at making friends." He laughed so loudly that I almost tripped on the level floor as he moved to let me near the sink. "The majority of people can barely talk to me, let alone hang out with me as much as you have." He was not looking at me, and I didn't laugh. I didn't even speak as Michael opened up to me. I knew that Michael was incredibly comfortable with me, and he needed to talk.

"Because of how you look?" He nodded.

"Yeah. Most people either ignore me, stare at me, try to sleep with me, or become so distracted that they can't even function."

"Hey, don't worry about it. I have a hard time making friends, too. In fact, you, Izabelle, and Jesse are the first real friends I've had in a while." I placed a comforting hand on his shoulder. He chuckled, and I felt the vibration echo through his rippling shoulder.

"Well, I am glad we're friends," he turned back to me.

"Me too!" We hugged each other, and how his body seemed to wrap around mine felt more like home than the house around us. We broke apart to clean up the dishes.

"What are we going to do today?"

"We could just hang around the house and watch movies." He hand-dried the waffle iron.

"What's your favorite movie?" I asked as we moved into the living room, where my uncle's vast movie collection took up a large portion of the wall.

"The Green Mile," he said without hesitation.

"Never seen it." I felt his emotions run rampant like a child in a candy store.

"It's only the best movie ever!" I found the movie, and we sat on the couch, waiting for it to start.

"What is it about?" He turned to me and smiled as he hit play.

"Redemption, grace, and finding light in the darkest of places," and I laughed at that irony.

After three hours, the credits rolled, and tears fell both our faces, and Michael laughed as I wiped away the tears. "I told you."

"You were not kidding, that movie was incredible." He smiled even brighter.

"The book is even better if you could believe it," he stated, but I couldn't see how. I made a mental note that the next time I was at the bookstore, I had to buy a copy.

"What's your favorite movie?" Michael asked me, and I just shook my head.

"As of right now, *The Green Mile*." Michael threw up his hands in a touchdown victory.

"What was it three hours ago?"

"Life is Beautiful."

"What is it about?" I walked over, pulled the movie from the shelf, and put it into the DVD player. For the rest of the day, we watched movies, popped popcorn, and drank soda.

About half away through the day, Izabelle came over and brought candy, per Michael's request. We all sat on the couch and watched our favorite movies. We hardly spoke or did anything but let the day be filled with watching other people's problems. I looked at my friends, and I felt at peace.

"I'm hungry," Michael said as the credits of the last movie began on the screen. Michael jumped to his feet and disappeared into the kitchen.

"How can he be hungry?" I looked at the various plates, empty candy boxes, and discarded popcorn bags.

"He is a man of many talents, Danny," Izabelle said admirably. She sat next to me on the couch, and I could smell her enticing lavender-scented shampoo, and it sent a thrill down my spine.

"He certainly is unique," I nodded. "I'm really glad that Michael and I have grown so close over the last week."

"Told ya," she winked. "I'm just glad to be here with both of you." She lowered herself deeper into the plush leather couch and pulled a blanket around her.

"Me too."

Over the last few hours, we had all chosen deep and emotional movies, and a lot of the time, we all cried. I knew for myself that it was not just because of the movies, but also what we had gone through lately. We all had to say goodbye to a beautiful soul, and now we were leaning on each other for support, and I was grateful for it.

"How's Jesse?"

"I think Claire's death has affected him so deeply. He's so distant and easy to anger lately. I'm not sure what to do," she said as she looked at me.

"Just give him time and let him come back on his own terms."

"I know, and you're right. People deal with grief in their own way." She got up and put in another movie, and we waited for Michael to return. A few minutes later, he returned with a pile of egg salad sandwiches that my uncle had made for lunch.

I turned to Michael, who ate a sandwich and did a cheerful little dance, and I felt the laughter in my chest. I watched him as the movie started, and I felt the unease trickle through my veins. I felt he wasn't upset about Claire, not like I had convinced myself over the last week; now, looking at him, something felt different. I could feel his sorrow, yes, but he knew she was in a better place. He knew she was safe and protected and that he shouldn't be to upset about it. I knew she was, too, because I had seen her.

I kept my eyes on Michael a moment longer than I should have, but a thought, a single thought, came to life in my heart.

Is Michael the King?

My mind was racing in a million different directions, and my heart seemed to accept him as the King. It just made sense, since he was everything, a King should be. He was beautiful, gentle, loyal, and unbelievably kind. The longer I looked at him, the more I was sure he was the one I was looking for, the one who did not know who he was.

He chuckled at the TV, and I turned to the opening scene of the movie. A group of inmates in a French prison that were pulling a ship into port did not seem to be a laughable moment, and when I turned back to him, I met his eyes. They were royal blue, and within seconds they changed to an electric green. He smiled again at me and turned back to the movie. I looked at my hands, and I felt the fire burning hot in my veins as the idea took hold in my heart.

If anyone is the King of Light, it has to be Michael.

"Oooohhh, I love this part," Izabelle squealed, and we watched as the main character tore up his papers and threw them into the wind. I turned my thoughts away from the King of Light and tried to enjoy the day. The calm, peaceful, and beautiful moments with two of the best friends I had ever had, and it was just what I needed. We watched two more movies before Izabelle stood up.

"Alright, I need to go home. I've spent too much time here, and I think my dad is starting to get jealous." She gave us both hugs and left.

Michael and I sat on the couch, debating if we should put in another movie. I felt exhaustion down to my bones, even though I had not done anything strenuous since the run in the morning.

"Should we watch one of these?" Michael pulled out another stack of movies. I groaned and yawned at the same time. The clock read 10:30 P.M. Michael moved to the oak floor and crossed his legs as he pulled movies out randomly, reading the backs and then placing them back in the stack.

"Watch whatever. I'm probably going fall asleep any moment here." I grabbed the blanket that Izabelle had been using and curled under it.

My head rested against the side of the couch. I could still smell the intoxicating smell of lavender, and I took a deep breath. The room fell silent as my eyes became heavy, and I drifted to sleep.

****

I was not sure what had woken me up. Just a moment ago, I was dreaming of a beautiful meadow filled with white flowers, but now my eyes were staring at the ceiling. Everything seemed quiet and peaceful, but the stillness felt restless.

I looked around the room, but Michael was nowhere to be seen. The movies had been placed back in order against the wall, the TV was off, and the room was dark.

I sat up, and I found I had been resting on a pillow that had not been there when I had fallen asleep. I turned to the clock and saw it was 4:30 A.M. I got to my feet and walked to the front door and found it was unlocked. Michael's shoes were missing, but something told me that he hadn't gone home.

I stood in the entryway as a wave of conflicting feelings washed over me. I touched my cheek, and my hand came back wet. I wiped away the tears that did not belong to me. I felt his pain. His emotions were bouncing off the walls, and they were the reason the tears fell down my face.

"Michael," I said aloud as the front door opened on its own. I walked out onto the front porch, my fists clenched and ready for defense, but only the starry night sky greeted me. I quickly ran back into the house to put on my running shoes and grabbed a coat off the rack. I closed the door, locked it with a wave of my finger, and I ran down the street.

His emotions guided me through Grenoff with the accuracy of a compass as I ran down the deserted streets. The night fog drifted around me as I went to the place where he was breaking and found I was heading toward the graveyard.

I found myself standing outside of the old iron gate. I felt an aching pain in my side from running, but I didn't care. The iron gate was already partially open, so I pushed through, and it creaked in protest. I moved through the silent fog that covered the ground toward the place where I knew I would find him.

Michael sat down in front of Claire's grave, a small light coming from his hand as the locket's lullaby filled the foggy air around him. I didn't move, as my feet seemed to have planted roots to prevent me from approaching him.

His sobs echoed through the night. His sorrow, grief, and happiness washed over me in gentle waves. They filled my entire body, they echoed in my veins like a small drum, and I sat on the ground as I let his emotions flood me.

As he sat there mourning, the memories of the last couple of days came back to me, and I couldn't help but smile. While Michael was unworldly beautiful, he was also kind, humble, weird, and had the energy of a caffeinated Chihuahua. He was my best friend, almost like family, and I had never felt happier in my life. The darkness, my depression, and even Phantonix could not touch me. When I looked up, I saw that he had stopped crying and he wiped away his tears. I was about to pull together from where I was rooted when he began singing.

Everything else around me became silent. The wind stopped blowing, and the insects and small animals became still as his words carried into the night sky. His voice was deep, clear, and held such emotion and depth that I knew Creation itself was crying because of its majesty. I knew the song, a beautiful melody of love, and it would never sound the same again. Michael made it his own and changed it to be something new.

Tears fell down my face, and nothing else mattered in Creation except him and his song. I listened and watched as he stared at Claire's headstone. While his song filled my every thought, that still small voice echoed in the song's shadow, in the depths of my mind.

This song is not for Claire, that voice said.

Who is it for?

Michael finished, and I felt the thunderous applause from Creation echoing around me. I felt their standing ovation, and I knew I had to join them, to express their emotions for them, because Michael could not hear it. I started clapping in absolute astonishment, and he jerked up in surprise as he jumped to his feet. He spun around to face me.

"Danny, what are you doing here?" His eyes burned red with emotion.

"That was incredible, Michael." I walked up to him.

"Thank you," he did move away. He didn't even turn away from my gaze. "How long have you been there?"

"Not long," I said, "just enough for the song."

We stood there for several moments in silence, until he finally said, "I miss her," and turned to face the headstone.

"You really loved her." Michael laughed and my stomach did jumping jacks.

"Yes, Danny. I did love her. But not in the way everyone believed." I noticed he had set the locket on top of her headstone, and it was closed. "She was a beautiful, incredible woman, and Creation is worse off without her. But she could never hold my heart. She was one of my best friends, and that was all it would ever have been." He picked up the locket.

"Oh?"

"I wish she hadn't died without knowing the truth about me," he looked at me again, and I knew what he meant, and it didn't surprise me as my fire purred in joy. I felt my hands grow moist as he continued. "I was going to break up with her when I returned from my mom's funeral, but I was too late."

"I am so sorry, Michael. I'm sorry about you losing your mom and Claire. You've been through a lot, but at least you know the truth in your heart. "Not many can say that," I said sympathetically.

"Thank you, Danny. I miss my mom, I miss Claire, and I miss him." I followed his gaze and saw my family's headstones, and at that moment, I realized I was no longer sad or in pain. They were safe in the Realm of Light. Standing by their headstones with Michael, I no longer felt the overbearing sorrow that I had had for the last several months.

"It's okay to miss them, Michael."

"I've been conflicted, Danny. I have recently lost two people in my life, and of course, I'm sad, but strangely, I'm also happy. I am happier than I have ever been. I feel guilty, sometimes even disgusting in my happiness, in the wake of their deaths."

"Wh-why?"

"It's complicated, Danny." He smiled and I felt a warm tingle twirl up my spine. "But I'm sure I will tell you soon."

"Tell me whenever you are ready, no rush, okay? But please, Michael, don't feel guilty about being happy, even with them gone. They would have wanted you to be happy."

"Not my mother." He spoke without venom or anger but as a cold fact.

"Well then, Claire and Matthew would have wanted you to be happy, Michael." He turned back to the headstone and touched it.

"I know," he said softly.

"What can I do to help you, Michael?" He didn't say anything, but he turned around and hugged me. His arms trembled as his sobs touched the stars. Standing here with Michael, I knew what he wanted. It was the same thing everyone person wanted; every soul needed. He needed someone to be there for him, to stand with him through the darkest moments of his life, to fight with him, and to love him. I held Michael, and I knew that I would always be there for him. He was my best friend, and he was the King I had to find. When he stopped crying, he broke the hug, took a step back, and said, "Thank you, Danny."

"Always, Michael."

I turned to the night sky to give him a moment to pull himself together, and I saw the first rays of sunlight beginning to shine in the east.

"Looks like a new day has started."

"I have a feeling," Michael's voice returned to normal, "that nothing is ever going to be the same." His words rang with truth, and as we stood in the graveyard, we could both feel it. I knew it was because the Final War was coming. The Crusader's warning burned bright in my mind, and my time was running out.

But how would I tell Michael that he was the King of Free Will?

"Come on, let's go home." We walked back without another word. We both felt exhausted as we walked the streets of Grenoff. It was our home, the place where we found happiness in the depths of sorrow and darkness. It wasn't until we reached the front doors that I stopped him.

"Michael, you should move in," I said firmly.

"Danny, I can't."

"Why not? I've been inside your apartment, and it's disgusting. Plus, my uncle told me that your lease is almost up. You're not happy there, and I know you want to be here," I argued, looking up at the house. Michael looked at me.

"I'll think about it."

"Fair enough. But I won't drop it."

"I hope you don't," he said, and we continued to walk up to the house. When we walked in the foyer, I came face to face with my aunt. She wore a simple robe, and her hair was pulled into a bun. She gave us a quick hug.

"What are you guys doing up so early?"

"We decided to go for a morning stroll," Michael chuckled.

"Yeah, it was really enlightening."

"You guys are strange," she yawned and walked toward the kitchen.

"She's right," Michael followed her for coffee.

I shook my head, and the exhaustion set in again. I walked up the stairs to my room, stripped off my clothes, and slid between the sheets of my bed. I had never believed that I could be this happy, and it was all because of Michael.

Chapter XV

The Soldier of Darkness

~Danny Elikai~

Protect the other three hearts. Daimonas' warning scorched through me, making me tumble out of bed and smack my face against the floor. I was drenched in a cold sweat, and the constricting sweat-stained sheets were wrapped around me, making it hard to breathe in the humid room. My vision spun, and I needed some fresh air. I felt the fire explode out from every pore of my body. I watched as the fire burned away, not only the sheets but the gym shorts and the T-shirt I was wearing. I half crawled, half stumbled to the window, and my breath was dangerously short and harsh. The window almost broke its hinges as I forced it open. The cold October air filled my lungs and washed over my scorching hot skin.

Do not let my brother take me. Protect my heart. Daimonas' fear ran through my aching body. The acidic bite of bile numbed my mind as I threw up down the side of the house as I leaned out the window.

Lightning streaked across the deep purple storm clouds, and I knew I was running out of time. I was failing in my mission to bring back the King of Light, and to protect the remaining three hearts.

Watching the first Crusader rise has been a recurring nightmare whenever Michael was not lying beside me. I watched the lightning rip across the sky again as I slung over the window. I was filled with dread, and I felt alone and isolated in my mission. I knew I was not alone, because of the other Generals that walked with me up the hill during Claire's celebration of life. I could still feel them with me, their strength, and unfailing belief in the King of Light.

I had believed for so long that I was damned to the darkness and that the light had never cared for me. But I knew otherwise; I knew it had always been with me, but not in the way I wanted or expected. I believed in the King, the Final War, and Phantonix, whose existence filled me with a burning rage. I had let him convince me that I was evil and was destined for an eternity of sorrow. I had let him drag me down into the isolated frozen darkness, let him break me, and strip me down to nothing. I had believed him when he said I could only cause more pain and bring death to those around me. I had believed the Philosopher of Destiny, but I had been shown that I could choose to be in the light. This had also given me the drive to fight against the darkness and to fight for the Philosopher of Free Will.

"In order to fight for someone, they have to know who they are," I told myself as I was hanging out the window. My mind immediately went to Michael like it always did when I thought of the King.

I slowly pulled myself back into the house as I closed the window and turned back to the pile of ash that covered the oak floor. My aunt would kill me if she found out I had reduced more sheets and clothes to ash. I opened my fists and called out the fire from my veins, the fire to create. I knelt over the pile of ash, and let the fire descend upon it. I watched as it recreated the sheets and the clothes I had been wearing.

I looked down at my naked body, and then again at the open window, and a feeling of being exposed and on display ran through my body. I hastily walked over to the closet to pull out sweatpants and a sweater. I felt the fire finish remaking the sheets, and I walked over to the bed and threw them back on. The clothes I had been wearing were already folded, so I placed them back in my dresser. I knew my uncle would be home shortly, so I slowly made my way out of my room and down the stairs.

The house was silent in the early morning, and I walked past the room that Matthew had used almost every summer. The door was closed, and I knew Michael was fast asleep behind it. I was surprised Michael was sleeping in there because he normally crashed next to me. It took my aunt, uncle, and myself about three weeks total to convince him to move in and give up his repulsive apartment. Without any warning or explanation, he showed up last Tuesday with nothing more than a ripped duffle bag and a small suitcase under his arm. When he saw Michael, my uncle just smiled, hugged him, and we left him to get himself settled in the spare bedroom. We had moved Matthew's old things out to the storage locker with the rest of my parents' possessions.

I looked at my hands while I stood outside his door, and I felt a sting of shame. I wished I could just tell him the truth about my powers. I looked up at the door, and for the millionth time, I wanted to tell him everything. I hated hiding things from him, but how could I explain it without telling him he's the king?

I shook my head and walked away from the door, heading down the stairs to the kitchen. I started a pot of coffee because I knew everyone would be up soon. I poured myself a cup, added some creamer, and sat on the couch. I turned on the TV, and I began watching the news. A soft knock on the window made me jump, but when I looked over, I saw Izabelle waving at me.

"Morning." I opened the back door for her.

"Thank you!" She shivered as she walked past me.

"What are you doing here so early?"

"I couldn't sleep. I went for a walk and saw you were up," she helped herself to a cup of coffee.

I looked at her closely, and I saw the redness shined brightly on her flushed face. I felt that she had been outside longer than she wanted to admit. I could see the sorrow surrounding her and the pain in her eyes.

"Izabelle," I said quietly, "what's wrong?"

She looked into my eyes and began to sob. I moved quickly and wrapped her into a tight hug as she sobbed on my shoulder. She started to lose strength in her legs, so I picked her up and set her on the couch, wrapping her in a blanket. I grabbed a box of tissues and sat down next to her as she gripped my hand tightly. I waited for her to calm down. She cried for a long time before she could finally speak.

"He…he…" she said softly, "he broke up with me." She continued to sob with more force this time. I felt the pain in her heart, but I saw there was also shame.

"Jesse broke up with you?" She nodded tearfully. The fire in my veins fluttered.

"He's been acting differently since Claire died. He didn't even go to the funeral. He's been distant and angry, so I finally called him out on it last night, and he blew up on me. He said that he couldn't do it anymore. He couldn't pretend anymore and said that he had been unhappy for months. He told me that Claire's death made him realize that life is too short, and he needed time to figure out the future and that we both deserve to be happy."

"I am so sorry, Izabelle," I pull her into my arms.

"I just feel so stupid."

"Why?"

"I never thought I would be the girl to break down because of a guy, but here I am. I feel like a moron." Her words came out like acid as she pulled away. I saw the shame and anger in her heart that she felt toward herself.

"Izabelle," I looked into her tired eyes, "you can't blame yourself for who you fall in love with. You found something beautiful with Jesse, and that is all that matters. You have loved, and from what I saw, you loved him wonderfully. Jesse's actions are his own, and he did what he believed would let you both be happy in the long run."

"I just wish he would have talked to me. We could have helped each other through this. I mean, I miss Claire, too! I could have helped him!"

"Izabelle, everyone grieves differently after losing someone they know," I said. "I know that, even though he ended things with you, you will not stop being there for him. Your heart is kind and compassionate. That's one of the great things about you. But he's hurting, and he needs the people who love him." She gave me a tired look, but she kept eye contact.

"You're right, Danny." She sighed and tried to give me the trademark Izabelle smile, the one that reached her eyes and made them sparkle. "It just hurts."

"It's supposed to Izzy, and that's a good thing. You can't understand love without heartbreak. I know you're hurting now, but you will heal over time, and it will make you stronger." We hugged again.

"I'm so glad I know you," she said in my ear. "I'm grateful you're my friend."

"I'll always be here for you." She pulled out of my arms, and tears slid down her beautiful face. We looked into each other's eyes, and I felt a surge of warmth as the fire danced in my chest. Her hands were soft and warm in mine, and I had the urge to kiss her. However, when I looked into her heart, I saw she was not ready and needed time to heal. I broke our eye contact as I turned away and got to my feet.

"Would you like some breakfast?" I asked warmly. "Food always puts me in a better mood."

We spent the next half an hour making pancakes, eggs, sausage, and toast for everyone. My uncle came home while we were making breakfast, and he sat down and told us about how boring the night patrol had been.

My aunt joined us as I was dishing scrambled eggs into a large bowl, and the kitchen was filled with laughter. I looked around, and I saw Michael wasn't awake yet. I made him a plate, walked out of the kitchen and up the stairs to his bedroom, and gently knocked on the door.

"Michael, I have your breakfast."

Since Michael had been finally sleeping like a normal human being, he only responded to either food or coffee. I heard him roll onto the floor and let out a hushed exclamation of pain, and I could hear something dragging as he crawled to open the door. He opened it slowly, and he stood there in my black and red gym shorts. His beauty hit me like a freight train, and I felt the smile drop from my face as my stomach did the tango. He smiled at me and brushed his hair, which was longer than normal, out of his ever-changing eyes. I held the plate up to his face, and his smile touched his eyes.

He picked a piece of bacon off the plate and put it in his mouth. Even from the doorway, I could not help but notice his impressive physique, from his broad shoulders to his narrow, toned waist. I looked down at my own lean body and could not help but feel a little envious of his layers of muscle. However, I just didn't want to spend hours in the school gym as he did. He slid on a light-colored shirt over his body and turned back to glower at me. "I really hate mornings."

"Well, good morning to you too, sunshine," I said brightly, trying to annoy him. "Next Saturday, I will make you go running in revenge."

"I like to see you try, Danny, and good morning." He laughed before he took the plate of food from me. He moved as the smell of campfire hit my nostrils, and I felt my body burn before I followed him to the kitchen.

****

~The First Crusader~

The narrow streets were silent as the dense darkness slowly consumed the small Parisian neighborhood. The unnatural darkness even blocked the light from the golden tower in the distance, and the famine thundered in my veins. I felt my mouth water in anticipation of my prize, and I could not wait to sink my teeth into their delicious hearts.

I reached out to touch the barrier that had been created by the final Disciple of Light, and I felt a searing pain. I looked at my burned finger, but my laughter filled the night.

The barrier had been created to protect the child from the darkness, from Destiny, from me, but it was futile.

I had chosen my vessel well. I had been able to quickly move past the barrier and into the house where she dwelled. I had been working on these plans for a long time, and Creation would bend to our will tonight. This was the night I planned to take the fourth child.

I drummed my fingers as the darkness consumed a small alleyway, the stacked houses, and the streets of Paris. I reached out my hand and called the child's name.

"Allete." The French accent flawlessly rolled off my tongue, and I felt the beckoning. I called the child's name three times before she appeared in the small window. She smiled down at me as I removed my hood, and I smiled back at her. Her blonde hair was still in the braid I put it in yesterday, the last braid she would ever have. I had told her the truth, and she was ready. Her destiny would begin very soon.

I held out my hand, and she nodded. She moved quickly and silently down the stairs and unlatched the door. I watched as the door slowly opened, and I raised my hand to the barrier. I focused the darkness around me into an immense blast, but I knew it had to be her choice to remove the barrier. She stepped out of the door, and the barrier began to crumble. We watched in triumph as the barrier completely disintegrated around us, and I took a careful step toward the girl.

I rejoiced as my laughter filled the darkness around us, and I showed her my true form. She ran and jumped into my outstretched arms.

"Hello," I whispered into her ear.

"Hello, Ieiunium," she said sweetly. I pulled her out of the hug and looked into her baby-blue eyes. "I missed you."

"Are you ready?"

She looked up at me and nodded. "Yes."

"Good." I placed a finger to her forehead, and the darkness began to spread, rippling away from my finger. The shadows consumed her face and rapidly engulfed her into the Realm of Darkness, where she would wait until the ritual began. Famine coursed through my veins like lightning, and I knew my sacrifices would make my victory all the sweeter.

I turned back to gaze upon my prizes. I had been patiently waiting for this. I crossed the threshold, and I decided I would start with her father. The blood of her family needed to be shed, and I felt his deliciously pure heart call out to me, waiting to be savagely devoured.

****

~Danny Elikai~

"Jesse! Jesse!" My voice echoed as I walked out of my biology class. Jesse had just walked out of his chemistry class several rooms down the hallway. I ran past several posters advertising the Halloween school dance tonight, and he turned around as I approached. He looked up at me, and I saw that his eyes had a defeated, exhausted look to them. He waited for me as I jogged to catch up to him.

"Hey, Danny." His tone was rough and impatient. "I take it you talked to Izabelle."

"Yeah, she came over earlier this morning," I wanted to make sure my tone was soft. "I just wanted to check in on how you were doing."

"I'm tired, Danny." He turned on his heels to walk away.

"Jesse, wait," I grabbed his shoulder, and I felt the rage almost explode inside him. He turned his head to glare at me, and I could see a cold fury in his navy-blue eyes. I let go of his shoulder and took a step back.

"I wanted you to know that I'm here for you. You are my friend as well." He turned to me and stared for a few moments before sighing and gave me a small, forced smile.

"Thanks," he deflated quickly. "Sorry, I was so rude. When people break up, their friends usually take sides, and I was sure you would take Izzy's." The cold rage had disappeared in his eyes, but his exhaustion lingered.

"Jesse, you're my friend," I put my hand on his muscular bicep, and I shallowed hard. "Both of you are my friends, and I am not taking sides. I just want you to know that I'll always be here for you if you ever need to talk."

"Thank you, Danny." His smile quickly disappeared, and he looked over both of his shoulders. "I would actually love to talk to you now. Let's take a walk, and I will tell you what's going on."

He grabbed my wrist with his rough hand and led me away, and my body did not protest. We walked down the stairs, avoiding the offices and fellow students to the campus grounds. We slowly made our way toward the dense trees that lined the shore of the lake, and we were surrounded by complete silence. Jesse kept looking over his shoulder, as if he were afraid of someone following us.

After walking for several minutes, we came to a stop, completely hidden from view, before he let go of my wrist. We were standing near the ledge of a small cliff. After several moments, he finally spoke.

"I feel like a fraud," He was staring at the dark storm clouds in the distance. He stood at the edge of the small cliff. "I hate that I have to hide my true self." I could hear the pain in his voice. "Danny." He turned to stare me dead in the eyes as he trembled, "I'm... I'm gay."

"Jesse, thank you for telling me." I pulled him into a tight hug as a tingle swept through my body. "I know how hard this must be for you. I know there's nothing wrong with who you are, and you shouldn't have to hide your true self. I am here for you." My words came out strong but kind. He pulled out of the hug to look at me, and I could see pain buried in his eyes.

"You knew, didn't you?"

"No, I mean not really." I grabbed his shaking hands, and the conversation with Michael in the graveyard came back to me. "But I understand, and it's okay."

"It doesn't matter." He shook his head and turned away. "I look at myself in the mirror, and I can't help but feel like an imitation of my real self. I couldn't live a lie anymore just to make other people happy, and I didn't want to drag Izabelle down anymore. I know what I will face in the future just because of who I am and what I believe. I'm different than everyone around me, and I feel I can't be who I am without being judged."

"You should not care what other people think, Jesse. You need to be honest, and the right people, like Izabelle and myself, will stand by you and will accept you for who you are. She's your friend, and you need your friends when going through something like this." He nodded as a tear fell from his twinkling eyes.

"You know, I never told you, but you remind me so much of—" He never finished his sentence because his eyes went wide with fear. "MOVE!"

He pushed me to the ground as a black sword descended upon where I had stood just a second before. The blade slashed the front of Jesse's school uniform, blood pouring down from the wound, and he stumbled to the ground.

I hit the ground hard, but I spun around and sent a blast of fire in the direction where the sword had come from. My instincts and adrenaline flared to life as the Crusader used his blade to block the fire blast, and gently forced the tip of the blade into Jesse's chest, drawing another stream of blood.

"Jesse, no!"

"What are you doing?" Jesse yelled at the Crusader. The Crusader took off his hood, and Henry's dark eyes bore into Jesse.

"I'm doing what needs to be done, what everyone else is too weak to do." The blade tip sunk deeper into his chest.

I felt the fire rip out of my left hand and formed a flaming sword. Without wasting a single breath, I thrust the blazing sword into the chest of the Crusader, who had his eyes locked with Jesse. Henry's face twisted, and his dead eyes found mine. We stood there in limbo for a few seconds before he started to laugh.

"You weren't trying to kill me, were you?" We could feel my sword did not have any heat to it. "You will have to try harder for your fire to kill, and I don't believe you have that in you."

He drove his gloved fist into my face. I staggered back and fell to the ground again, but before I could get back to my feet, Henry had disappeared. He was right; I hadn't wanted to kill him. I just didn't want him to hurt my friend.

"Jesse!" I crawled over to where Jesse was sprawled in a pool of his blood. He stared at me with gasping breaths. Shock was clear on his pale face, and his eyes were locked with mine. I could see the fear in them as blood began to trickle out of his mouth.

Heal him, that still small voice echoed in my mind. I turned back to Jesse, whose eyes were losing the sparkle of life. I felt the fire in my veins roar to life, and I placed my hands on his wounds. I could not let him die; I could not lose another friend.

The heat penetrating the deep puncture wounds as the fire glowed inside of him. I watched as the fire repaired the damage to his body. I saw the slash disappear from his chest, and the stab wound began to close. I focused all of my energy into healing my friend as tears burned my eyes.

"No!" I turned in time to see the midnight blade descending upon me again, and without thinking, I raised my free hand to try to stop the blade from doing too much damage. I felt the tip of the blade crash into my burning palm and knew pain was not far behind. However, when the black blade made contact, it fractured and turned back into smoke. Henry staggered back; the surprise highlighted his face.

"No." The word was laced with anger and confusion. My hand was covered in a beautiful white fire with golden tips. I looked at it, and I could feel the light surging through me.

"Never again," I stood up. "You will not hurt anyone else." I knew the fire had repaired Jesse, and he was out of mortal danger, but he would still need a doctor. The damage to his chest was too extensive.

"Why weren't you there for me?" I could see the pain in Henry's eyes as he spoke.

"What?" I felt my heart tighten at the sorrow and fury in his eyes.

"You left me alone!" Tears fell down his face. "You let me be consumed by the darkness!"

"What are you talking about?" The adrenaline and my instincts were screaming not to let my guard down.

"Have you not figured it out yet?!" The darkness formed in his hands. "Just die already!"

He unleashed the darkness as a black wave flew toward me. I had to defend myself and Jesse. I dropped to my knees and formed a burning shield around us. The darkness slammed into it, and I felt the burning shield crack. I could feel the raw power behind the immense blast. I reached out so I could feel Henry's sorrow and anguish. I heard his soft sobs, and the feeling of despair was all around me.

The surrounding forest began to melt away, and I stood in a rundown house. Soft sunlight was coming through the holes in the motheaten curtains. An old-fashioned TV stood on milk crates as static rippled across the screen. I stood behind a pea-green couch that had several holes, with stuffing pouring out. The floor was covered in garbage and fast-food wrappers, and the stale air was filled with body odor and spoiled meat. The loud snores brought my attention to a naked man lying face down on the couch, covered in his vomit. I watched in disgust as the empty bottle of vodka in the man's hand dripped on the floor. The hot pink tattoo of a lipstick kiss on the man's right buttocks was like a beacon, the focal point of this nightmare. The environment around me was a train wreck, and it was impossible to look away. It was a nightmare that felt all too real as if this were someone's life.

The gentle cry of a child down the rotted hallway made me turn away from the grotesque man. I moved along the hallway and entered the kitchen. He sat on the floor, covering a bloody, blackened eye with a small dirty hand. He was wearing battered clothing that looked two sizes too big and had not appeared to have been washed in a month. His matted brown hair touched his shoulders, and the dirt on his feet was pitch black. His brown eye, the one I could see, did not have that raw hate and anger I had always seen.

"Henry?" I moved closer to the cowering child. He looked up at me, and I felt rage explode from behind me.

I spun around and saw the older Henry glaring at me. We stared at each other, frozen for a fraction of a second before he charged with the black sword in his hand. I formed another burning blade as the scene around us disappeared, and our blades collided. The trees and the lake of Grenoff snapped back into focus as I stared into Henry's enraged eyes.

"How dare you!" His animosity was dripping from his tongue.

"Henry," I tried to hold him back. Somehow, I had entered his mind and had taken him with me. Now we stood on the edge of the cliff, our powers on full display.

I looked into his furious eyes, which were ablaze with a murderous rage, and I couldn't help but think of something relatively insignificant at that moment. I wanted Michael to be here, to bear witness to this fight. I wanted him to be here, so I could easily explain to him about the Crusaders and Phantonix and hopefully guide him to his true identity as the King of Light. When I looked into Henry's eyes, I decided to tell Michael everything if I survived.

Henry's scream surrounded us, and with immense effort, he broke the connection of our swords, jumping back into the air. I watched as he placed the tip of the blade to his other palm and compressed the black blade into a small ball of shadows. He landed gracefully on his feet and quickly unleashed a blast of darkness. I didn't have time to react as it slammed me into the trunk of a tree that was on the edge of the small cliff. The wind was knocked out of me as I sat motionless on the ground, struggling to breathe.

I watched as he moved toward me, murder still clear in his eyes, as he formed the black blade again. Henry stood over me, the sword pointing at my heart. He didn't say anything as his chest rose and fell rapidly. I saw the glee in his eyes as he raised the blade high above me, ready to drive it deep into my chest.

Raise your hand, I heard a voice say in my mind. I felt the locket appear in my enclosed fist, burning hot in my hand, and I quickly raised it above me toward the descending blade. The locket opened to reveal a virtuous white light that eclipsed Henry and me.

Chapter XVI

The King of Free Will

~Danny Elikai~

"Danny?" It was that same voice that had told me to raise the locket to defend myself. That same voice that had been my guide through these last few weeks. I found myself falling through an endless darkness, and I felt frozen inside.

"Yes?" My weak voice was barely able to penetrate the solidifying darkness.

"Do you remember yet?"

"Remember what?" I choked. The air was thick, and I felt my head spin as I fell.

"The identity of the King."

"I believe I know," I said truthfully. "Do you know who he is?"

I opened my eyes, burning from the rushing air, and I saw a small ball of glowing white light falling with me.

"Yes, Danny, I know who he is," that still, small voice said, and the light made the darkness tremble as we fell for an eternity.

"Who is he?" I felt my heart aching for the truth.

"You already know, Danny. You just have to accept the truth." I looked into the ball of light falling with me. I reached out to touch it, to feel the warmth of the light.

"I do accept Michael as the King. I do not understand!"

"Yes, you do, but you are scared."

"Why would I be scared? Who are you?"

"My name is Eloheen." The light shined brighter as if it were the last rays of light Creation would ever see. I felt the darkness shatter and roar in protest as light flooded around me. The darkness was slowly melting away, and I could see a vast kingdom. As I fell, I saw that I was approaching a courtyard within a grand palace.

"I know you." I gently landed on my feet. I could feel his presence inside and all around me.

I spun around to try and look at the vast white kingdom, but it seemed to blur and stayed out of focus. The small ball of light in front of me was the only thing solid and clear. The kingdom around me looked as if it were not truly physical but was just a glimpse of something yet to come.

"Yes, you do know me," the small ball of light began to float away. My feet automatically began to follow as it led me along a blurred corridor. The small ball of light began to move faster as it approached what looked like stairs. It finally came to a halt, and I asked, the words burning on my lips.

"But you are not the King?" I looked upon the massive white doors in front of me. Except for the small ball of light, the doors were the only thing in focus. The doors were massive, grand, and beautiful.

They were made of an otherworldly white material that shined gold when small rays of light touched it. A seal was engraved on both doors, but I could not quite make it out, as if my brain refused to bring it into focus. My fire roared in excitement.

"You are correct, Danny." The massive doors swung inward with elegant ease. "I am not the King of Free Will. I am the one who created everything the King will rule." The small ball of light floated into the high-ceilinged room, which was lit by a soft light.

"You are the Creator." I was captivated as I looked around the unfocused but beautiful room. I could barely make out a few features, such as bookshelves, a painting around the domed ceiling, a large window, and a massive chair in the center of the room. I turned back to the floating ball of light. "Why are you here with me now?"

"Danny," Eloheen said in a soft, loving tone that filled me with a warm feeling, "I have never left you. I have always been with you." The small ball of light burned brighter than any other light around me. It floated toward me, and it settled into my open hand. The light faded away to reveal the plain silver locket.

"Why?"

You already know why, Eloheen whispered in my heart. *The King of Free Will, will return tonight.*

****

With a blink, I found myself lying on the ground a few feet away from Jesse's bloody body. The dark clouds around us boomed with the warning of a storm. I reached out to Jesse, and his body was ice cold to the touch.

"No! Jesse!" I looked into his fading eyes, and I knew time was running short. I placed my hands on his wounds, and I focused all of my energy into healing Jesse. My eyes scanned the vicinity, but the Crusader had vanished. The white golden flames danced around his chest in its frantic attempt to heal him.

"Danny!" The fear in his angelic voice made me look up. I looked into Michael's eyes and felt a wave of relief wash over me as tears fell down my face.

"Henry tried to kill him. Henry is the first Crusader," and he nodded as a broad smile touched his eyes.

"I guess we can finally drop the façade, then?"

"What façade?" He didn't say a word but pointed at the fire around my hands and in Jesse's chest. "You knew already, didn't you?"

"Yes, Danny, I knew. I was wondering how long it would take before we could be honest with each other."

He walked up to me slowly as a shimmering light appeared around his tall body and solidified into a white robe. It was the same white robe of the man who protected Matthew and me from the Crusader the night my family died and when I met Sun.

"It was you," I murmured, stunned as the memories flashed before my eyes. Michael knelt before me, and I saw the relief on his face. He raised his hand, and with a spark, an electric butterfly floated above his gloved fingertips. The lightning above us ripped across the sky in response.

"Yes, Danny. I was there the night your family died. I was the one who held you up when you tried to save Claire. I also walked up with you when you met

Matthew during Claire's funeral. I have always been with you, Danny." Michael lowered his hand, and he had a strange look in his eyes. It was a look that I couldn't figure out, but I knew then that he was not the one I was looking for.

"I thought," my heart fell in defeat. "I thought you were the King."

"No, Danny," he replied, "I am not the King of Free Will."

"Eloheen told me that the King is going to return tonight, but I don't know who he is!"

"Yes, I believe that the King will return tonight too, but you will find him soon," Michael's eyes flickered to Jesse and then back to myself.

"We need to get Jesse to the hospital, and you need to save your energy. We are going to need it." He removed my hand from the wounds. Michael gently picked Jesse up in his arms as if he were nothing more than a small sack of flour. The white robe disappeared, and his Grenoff High uniform returned. Michael began to move quickly, and I sprinted just to keep up with him.

"How long have you known?" I asked Michael as we sped toward the hospital.

"I have known since I was a child. I knew who you were from the start once the King told me the truth." He turned to face me. I could see the praise in his eyes, and an ache burned in my heart. I slowed as we cleared the trees back to Grenoff, the bell tower looming above us.

"Danny!" The voice had stopped me from asking the question burning on my lips. My uncle stood by the Jeep with my aunt, who had Alvaro in her arms. Alvaro looked panicked, and he reached out to Jesse as we ran up to them.

"Henry attacked them," Michael said to my uncle as he threw open the doors and helped us put Jesse in the Jeep. "He's the Crusader."

"What?!" I felt her pain and anger. She placed herself and Alvaro into the front passenger seat. Michael and I arranged ourselves around Jesse in the backseat to make sure he lay flat. Michael sat behind the driver's seat with Jesse's head in his lap, and I knelt on the floor behind the passenger's seat, holding Jesse's hand that was caked with blood.

"Danny." My eyes snapped to Jesse's fading blue eyes, which stared at me with a mixture of fear, shock, love, and pain.

"Are you okay?"

"Yes," he coughed up a small spatter of blood, "you are here." I saw relief ignite across his face, and a tear began to fall.

"Of course, I'm here," I tried to reflect comfort into my grip. His expression, apart from the mixture of emotions, looked as if that was the first time, he had ever seen me. He lifted his hand, which was still grasped in mine, and pressed our entangled hands to my cheek.

"Danny…please. Save me from the dark." Before I could even say a word, he closed his eyes, and his head fell back into Michael's lap.

"Alex," my aunt said gently. "We need to hurry." They held eye contact as he flipped on the sirens.

As my aunt pulled out her cell phone to call the hospital and warn them of our arrival, Jesse jerked his chest upward, and his wounds reopened as blood gushed out.

"No!" I dropped his hand and placed my hands over the wounds. I felt the fire trying to seal them, but my exhaustion kept me from completely healing him. The smell of blood filled the car, and it made me feel sick.

"Jesse." Alvaro's quiet voice filled the car. I craned my head to look at him, but no one else seemed to have heard him.

"He will be okay." However, he shook his head.

"No. His heart will soon rest with the Fallen," Alvaro whispered. He turned away without even the slightest look of remorse. I turned back to Jesse's pale body without learning who or what the Fallen were. His blood seemed to be all over my hands, our clothes, and the inside of the car. I shook away the exhaustion and put the rest of my energy into healing my friend. I felt myself slipping into oblivion as I forced my eyes to stay open, but my uncle slammed on the brakes.

"We're here. Danny, save your energy." Michael gently touched my hands. The back doors of the Jeep opened, and Jesse was pulled gently from the backseat onto the stretcher. He was now in the experienced hands of the doctors and nurses waiting for us. Without a word to us, they rushed Jesse into the hospital as my uncle called his deputies over the radio. He put out an alert for Henry for the attempted murder of Jesse.

Michael forced a nurse to check on me because I was losing consciousness from exhaustion. A nurse helped me wash the blood off my whole body, and after two hours of tests, I was cleared to be released and was sent to wait in the waiting room for news of Jesse.

I found myself alone in the empty room, surrounded by an assortment of handmade Halloween decorations. I had completely forgotten that today was Halloween.

I sat on a small couch near the door and closed my eyes. My body was exhausted, and my powers were drained, but I felt relief in my body. Eloheen's words burned in my chest, *The King of Free Will, will return tonight.*

"Danny." I cracked open my eyes to see Michael and Izabelle standing in front of me, his beautiful words made me twitch. They looked joyful, their eyes burning with praise, and I could feel the triumph coursing through their veins. I stared at them as something inside of me flickered to life, like a flower in bloom. A small voice began to whisper in my heart about the truth about the King, but I shook my head, dismissing the idea quickly.

"I'm glad you were with him when the Crusader attacked," Izabelle broke up the argument that was about to begin in my head. She grabbed my hand as she sat next to me.

"You know, too." A sigh of exhaustion escaped my lips.

"Matthew told me a while ago. I had pieced enough of the puzzle together, and I finally asked him. He then told me everything and introduced me to Michael. He told me all about you and asked me to keep an eye out for you, so I did. I'm glad I kept my word because you are an amazing friend." She pulled me into a hug. I held her tightly back and felt the warmth radiate off her body.

"I can't believe it was Henry," she said softly into my ear.

"I knew he struggled with the darkness, but I would never have guessed it was him," Michael said, but he didn't sit down. He stood in front of me, staring at me with the same weird look in his eyes as before.

"Me neither." I knew, just like Michael, about the darkness, but I would never have pieced together that Austin had disguised himself as Henry. I shook my head because none of this made any sense.

"I'm sorry we didn't tell you that we knew," Izabelle said sympathetically.

"When the Crusader murdered your family, we all promised each other not to tell you," Michael was embarrassed, and I felt the shame in his voice.

"I understand," I looked into Michael's eyes and thought of Matthew, and my heart felt a slight sting of pain mixed with warmth.

"How long have you known?"

"It was my seventh birthday when the King of Light appeared before me and told me the truth. Ever since then, I have been following his orders faithfully."

"Who is the King of Light?" He turned away and sat down in a chair.

"I can't tell you. You are the only one who can bring him back." Michael didn't look at me when he said this. I could feel his emotions, and they were screaming at him to tell me.

"Do you all know who the King of Light is?" I turned to Izabelle, and even she didn't meet my eyes as she nodded.

"It's another one of those things where I will find out in my own time?" I asked, and Michael looked up at me.

"You will know when you are ready." I could not help but sit there and feel annoyed because no one would give me a straight answer.

"Are you a General of Light, too?" I asked Izabelle.

"No, I am not a General. I don't have any celestial abilities like you and Michael. However, I fight for the Light, like Alex and Shannon. We are Soldiers of Light."

"It's funny," I began, the irritation burning hot inside me, "I didn't even know about any of this until a few months ago. Then, come to find out, I'm the only one who never knew anything. Everyone in my family was a believer, and they never told me about it." I buried my face in my hands, and hot tears of frustration leaked through my fingers.

"I know what you mean," Izabelle said softly. "My father believes too, and that's the true reason they moved here. They wanted to be here when the King of Free Will returned. I only found out the truth when I met Matthew. When I confronted my father about it, he said they never told me because I had to find out on my own. It had to be my own choice not only to believe but to learn about both sides." She took my hand into hers and gave it a squeeze. "It has to be our choice. We have to choose to want to know more and to believe in the King and the Final War. That's the whole point of Free Will."

I pulled away from her touch and ran my hands through my hair.

"Eloheen told me that the King would return tonight."

I glanced around the waiting room and looked at all the Halloween decorations. I could feel the irony rise in me as laughter quickly overcame me. Izabelle and Michael looked at me and then at the decorations, and they, too, began to laugh. A few moments later, we were found like this by my aunt and uncle. The stitch in my side was throbbing with pain.

"You guys are messed up," my uncle said as the laughter spread across his face.

When we finally all stopped laughing, we sat there in silence. No one wanted to break the soft calm that had washed over us.

"How is he?" Izabelle finally asked, and I felt that calm shatter like glass.

"The surgery went well, but they are worried about an infection that is spreading through his body," my aunt said softly. "He has been transferred to the ICU. They say he will have a good chance of surviving if he makes it through the night."

"Any news on Henry?" I asked, looking at my uncle.

"No word," he replied in a clipped tone, and I could see the fury behind his emerald eyes. "I am sure he is safe in the Realm of Darkness, waiting to make his next move."

"Coward," Michael spat with anger in his voice.

"I think I know what his next move will be," I said softly. I had been thinking it over ever since I sat down.

I had been reliving everything over the last few weeks, and it was the only thing that made sense. They all stared at me expectantly.

"What do you mean?" My aunt asked.

"There are seven crusades, right?" I watched them as they all exchanged looks.

"Yes, that is what the prophecy states," Michael said.

"Okay," I said slowly, "so, where are they?"

Now, their glances were directed at me, completely confused. "Why have we only seen the first Crusader? If there are seven, why haven't they attacked as well?"

"We don't know," my uncle replied.

"I think it has to do with the warning Daimonas gave me. 'Protect the three remaining hearts.'"

"The missing children," Izabelle said. "The seal of the Crusaders had appeared at the homes of those missing children all around the world." Her eyes weren't focused on us but behind us. I turned around to see what she was looking at, and my heart skipped a beat.

"No," I watched the breaking news story on the TV in the upper corner of the waiting room. The sound was muted, but the captions on the screen gave us all the information we needed to know.

"Another child has been taken." We all watched the news story. A family of nine had been brutally murdered in a small home in Paris. A young girl by the name of Allete was missing, and the symbol of the Crusaders was drawn in blood at the crime scene.

"Only two hearts remain," and the realization hit me as I counted the missing children.

"What do you mean, Danny?" Izabelle asked.

"The missing children are the Crusaders."

"The seven purest hearts will fall and be delivered unto Creation as the Generals of Destiny." Michael's words filled the surrounding space. Before I could even say a word, the doors to the emergency room burst open, and a bloodcurdling scream tore through the silence. A young woman was clinging onto the door, her right leg broken and bloody.

She wore a sexy nurse costume, on the account that it was Halloween, and her eyes were filled with terror. I looked into her eyes, and I knew who she was.

"Alyssa." She was a girl from my history class who had always sat next to the window and who I met at the bonfire before class started. She limped closer to me, making eye contact the whole time.

"I have…a message…to deliver." The horror was in her eyes as the tears fell down her cheeks, but she spoke with a forced dedication as she made her way to me.

"A message?" I moved closer toward her.

"Tonight…the innocent will die…and their blood will be spilled…in defiance to the King of Free Will." She hobbled over to me. "Phantonix…is waiting for you, Danny."

I felt fear course through me like lightning, and I found myself running out the door toward the school. I knew that was where he was waiting for me. There was a Halloween school dance that was tonight, and I had forgotten all about it. I could hear my uncle yelling, but I couldn't stop. I had to protect them. The exhaustion was now gone from my body, and the drive to end the Crusader was pounding in my heart.

I ran past the bell tower, and with a quick look at the clocks, I stopped dead in my tracks. Every face of the four clocks on the bell tower was the same shade of violet as Phantonix's eyes. The black marble walls of the bell tower began to crack around the clock faces, and spiderwebbed their way down to the base. Purple light began to stream through the cracks, illuminating the courtyard with a haunting glow.

"Beautiful, isn't it, Danny?" Standing on the steps at the base of the bell tower was Henry, dressed in a formfitting dark robe. He looked at me with triumph in his eyes and his heart.

"Are they still alive?" Henry looked at me and smiled wickedly.

"Alyssa gave a wonderful performance then, Danny." The black robe exploded into a cloud of black smoke, and I watched as it reformed and solidified into black armor. There was a purple symbol that looked like a seven-pointed star burning brightly on the chest plate over his darkened heart.

"I knew you would come running the minute we threatened innocent lives. You blindly left to meet the Emperor, without giving a second thought to those you left behind." His twisted smile grew, and my heart sank. "I'm sure at least one of your friends is still alive in the hospital. Alyssa is quite bloodthirsty, and she could not wait to pledge her allegiance to Phantonix."

"Michael will protect them." I saw the annoyance in his eyes.

"If she hasn't killed him, then I will take great joy in doing it myself. After I have killed you," he said with malice in his voice. He raised his gloved right hand, and it glowed dramatically as more black smoke formed a sword in his hand.

"I would love to see you try." The fire exploded out of both of my hands and formed two blazing swords.

"You will die on your knees, bowing to the true ruler of Creation, Emperor Phantonix!"

"Phantonix is not the true ruler!" I screamed at him. "The King of Light is the true ruler of Creation!"

Henry chuckled darkly and pointed the tip of the blade toward me.

"Here's the thing, Danny. I don't believe the King will ever return. You have failed to see the truth and ignored the facts staring at you in the face." He had been slowly walking toward me as he spoke. I could see the blade shaking in his hand, and I felt its anticipation.

"You don't know what you're talking about." He didn't answer, and he began to walk to my side. I mirrored his movement, and we circled each other while I raised my swords. We moved slowly until my back faced the stairs at the base of the tower.

"DIE!" He slashed the sword in the air as a black wave hurled toward me. I tried to defend myself, but the black wave hit me square in the chest, and I landed hard on the stone steps. I couldn't move, and my body throbbed with pain.

"Tonight," he said as he approached me, "I will kill the King and rid his petulant influence from Creation forever!"

I looked into Henry's eyes, and I saw someone who had been beaten and tortured his whole life. I even felt the harsh touch of loneliness. It was at that moment I saw the truth. I couldn't hurt him, and I wouldn't. The flaming swords disappeared, and I kept looking into his eyes as he stood over me, his blade ready to strike.

"You blame the King of Light for everything that happened in your life." Henry stopped and looked away. "You believe he left you alone in the darkness because you feel you weren't meant to be loved, that you are a wicked abomination."

"Shut up!" He slashed the blade again, and I felt blood leak from my chest as he ripped through my school uniform. I didn't even bother to defend myself.

"I know how that feels," I said without letting the anger pour out of me. "I believed the light didn't want me either, that I was destined for the darkness. I was tormented for years by Phantonix, and I felt like I was alone. I believed him, and I ignored everything good because I was convinced that I was worth nothing." I kept looking into his eyes, which were filled with pain and sorrow. He backed away from me, and I felt the fire inside me, repairing the cut on my chest. "Except, I am not destined for anything, Henry, and neither are you. The light saved me from what I did to myself and what I was made to believe." I got to my feet and fought through the pain. "I know the truth, Henry. I can see it in your heart." He backed away from me, tears falling down his cheeks.

"Shut up!" He roared again, but I knew I couldn't stop.

"You let the darkness take over you, and you ignored the light because you believed you weren't meant for it.

What your father did to you would have broken the strongest of men. You were shown nothing but cruelty and animosity, and you never learned anything else. But Henry, you are loved, you are wanted, and you can be a believer in the light if you just let go of the darkness. I know you still can because you are not the real Crusader. You are just a pawn he has been using to hide his true identity."

With these words, the tension in the night air softened, and the illusion disappeared. The cracks in the bell tower slowly receded, and the three other colors of the clock faces returned.

"I saw you in the corner of that disgusting house as a small, defenseless child. You cried to the light, and you wanted it to save you. Except the light didn't save you as you wanted. At that moment, you decided that the light didn't want you, and you turned to the darkness. What did Phantonix promise you if you followed him?"

Henry's eyes were focused on me with an intense shock as the tears continued to fall down his face. I could see the decision warring in his mind and his heart. I could see the light trying to sway his allegiance.

"He promised me a world without pain. A place where no more children would cry or feel alone. Destiny would remove that sorrow that runs rampant in Free Will."

After a moment, I began to approach him, but he screamed, raised the sword, and lunged toward me. A bolt of lightning collided with him and hurled him into a tree across the courtyard.

"Danny!" I turned to see Michael standing across the courtyard, lightning dancing around his hand. His eyes burned with an intense ferocity, and they blazed with every color of Creation, burning brighter than neon.

It was at that moment that I understood why his eyes were always changing colors. He wore the white robe of a General of Light. Small sparks of lightning rippled across his hand, and the thunder in the sky cracked in response. He moved gracefully as he quickly ran across the courtyard and up the stairs, stopping in front of me.

"Please remember the truth." His beauty radiated like an inferno, and I could almost remember where I had first met him, but it was not at the cliff during Claire's funeral. I could only see the outline of a beautiful kingdom, more beautiful than the one in the Realm of Light. There was emerald, green grass, and he stood at the edge of a cliff overlooking a golden sea.

"What truth?!"

"The truth that you won't accept. The truth that terrifies you, and the truth that will set Creation free." He opened his lightning-covered fist, and inside was the locket. "The truth that has set me free saved me and has led me here right now, praising you."

I looked into his eyes as he fell to his knees, the locket in his outstretched hand. The lullaby filled the night silence.

I brushed away the thought again, the one that had sparked to life in the waiting room. I stared into his eyes, and panic rose in my chest. *It couldn't be me, could it?*

Before I could say anything, another blast of darkness sailed toward Michael, who was looking at me.

I couldn't take my eyes off the blast that was going to take his life. I felt a timeless fear, the fear of losing someone I loved. I will not attend another funeral.

"NO!" I knocked him out of the way, and the blast ripped through me. I watched the horror form in Michael's eyes as he spun around and sent a jolt of lightning at Henry.

I closed my eyes as I hit the bell tower. The air had been knocked out of me, and I felt blood soaking my shirt. I could not move, and I knew my body was finished. I did not need to open my eyes to know Michael was fighting Henry.

"Danny." The soft voice made me open my eyes, and the scent of honey filled the air. I found myself looking into the celestial night sky as he looked down at me.

"Matthew." He smiled at me and held out his hand. "Am I dead?"

"You need to get up."

I reluctantly took his hand, and he pulled me to my feet. I looked at him, and behind him, I saw countless souls standing at the edge of a cliff.

"What's happening?" He took a step back, and he didn't answer me right away. "Matthew? I don't know what's happening." He just smiled and stepped out of the line of sight. My mother stepped out of the crowd and walked toward me. She appeared younger than I ever remembered seeing her, and her beautiful white dress danced in the light breeze.

"Yes, you do, Danny. We are all here to witness the return of the King of Free Will, The King of Light." She gave me a tight hug. I could feel the warmth in her embrace, and I felt the tears fall from her face.

"I don't understand, I haven't found him yet," but the fire inside me roared in disagreement.

"Yes, you did, Danny," Matthew said. "Have you never asked yourself why you can see into the hearts of others? Why you can see the Realm of Light when only a few living souls has ever been able to?"

"Why do you think Phantonix has tried to kill you or taunt you to harm yourself?" My mother asked.

"Why do you think they are here?" Matthew pointed behind me. Uncle Alex, Aunt Shannon, Izabelle, and countless others stood behind me.

"Why did Michael fall to his knees before you?" My mother asked.

"The King," they all said in unison, staring at me.

"The King," I repeated, and I closed my eyes tightly. When I opened my eyes, I found myself back in Grenoff, bleeding on the stone steps. Michael knelt before me with tears in his eyes.

"Please," he sobbed, "please come back to me."

He had his hands outstretched, and the locket was cradled in them. At that moment, I realized it was Michael's voice that had spoken to me from the locket, but it wasn't filtered and muffled like it had been when it came to me in my time of need. It was his voice that had guided me through the darkest moments of my life, but I never knew it had been him until that moment.

I looked to my left and saw my mother, Matthew, and countless other people garbed in white clothing. I turned my eyes to the right, and I saw Izabelle, my aunt, and my uncle just a few feet away, holding each other.

The King has returned, Eloheen's voice echoed in my body, and I felt the truth open in my heart. I reached out slowly, wincing from the pain, and took the locket from Michael, who had done everything to bring the King back. I looked at the locket, and those who had protected me, loved me, and kept the secret. Those who had guided me to the truth and allowed the King to choose to return when it was time.

I looked at the earthly realm and turned to the celestial realm, and I saw I was the force between them. I looked into the hearts of every person standing around me, and I was finally ready to find the King.

"I am the King," I said to the locket, and it opened. The light that escaped was more beautiful than Michael. I felt the light enter my body, lift me to my feet, and heal me. As I looked around, everything came into focus.

A proclamation burned hot within my mind, and I saw what they had seen.

> *Heed these words, those who have witnessed the return of the King of Light. In your hands is the locket of Creation and the proclamation of the two rulers. To those who know and believe, rejoice, for this is the beginning of the Final War. To the one who has opened this locket and used the light inside in a great moment of peril, rejoice, for your heart is pure and one*

of the few. To the hearts that have opened this locket and used the power within, you are called to arms to defend the innocent and your King. To those who have witnessed a child in his seventh year who has opened this locket, called upon by Eloheen, and have unleashed the power to his Generals, fall to your knees, for the one who stands before you is the King of Free Will. You will know him, for he bears the four lights of Creation within his eyes.

I looked down at the locket and saw the seal of the King—two beautiful white wings with a small ball of light centered between them. Scattered around the locket's face were eight jeweled stars that embodied different colors of light. I saw a yellow star and looked up at Michael, who had my glowing yellow seal on his forehead. I looked back at the stars, and I knew these stars represented the Generals of Light.

I felt the power of the light burn through me, and I let the light consume my body. I looked at the people in the courtyard, those who had come to bear witness to the King. I could see myself through their eyes, and I saw how beautiful and terrifying the scene was. I stood in an elegant white robe with swirling embroidered patterns of yellow and red around the collar and the sleeves. The seal of the King burned brightly on my forehead.

"Your majesty," I heard Michael say, and I looked at him. He was on his knees with tears in his eyes. I could see the praise, the love, and the loyalty burning bright in his heart.

"Please, don't kneel to me." However, he did not rise. He lowered himself in a bow, resting his face on the ground, and I felt immensely uneasy.

"Michael," I reached down and touched his shoulder. He looked up at me, and I could see everything inside him, and my heart ached. "Please, stand."

I let go of his shoulder and held out my hand. He looked at me, smiling, and took my hand as I pulled him to his feet.

I had the power of Light, and I felt Creation burning brightly in my veins. Even though I could see more than I ever thought was possible, I did not feel any different. I was still me, but the new power I felt terrified me.

I turned to see Izabelle and my aunt and uncle, who were on their knees as well. I then turned to my left and saw the other Generals of Light. They were all standing, looking at me. I could see into the hearts of every soul, and I knew all of their names.

They were next to Michael, with tears in their eyes, and they all fell to their knees.

"My King." I turned again and saw Matthew on his knees as well. His emerald eyes were alight with love and happiness. My mother knelt behind him, and her eyes filled with tears of joy. My father was not anywhere to be seen, but I could feel him with me. I looked all around me and saw countless faces that I recognized. I knew all their names at that moment, and I felt all of their struggles.

"Please, everyone, stand," I pleaded, looking at the countless souls around me. It felt vastly awkward to have everyone kneeling before me. However, everyone stayed on their knees, all except one.

"Henry." I walked toward him, holding out my hand. He stared at me in disbelief, his eyes locked on me, and his black swords faded in the presence of the light. I watched as a mixture of emotions flickered across his face, ranging from anger, fear, depression, sorrow, and finally defeat.

"Get away from me," he fell to his knees, but not like the others. I could still feel the rage he felt toward me, the one he felt had abandoned him.

"I am so sorry," I apologized. "I am sorry I wasn't there for you when you needed me." I got to my knees before him and touched his face. His whole life unfolded like the pages of a book before me. I could see everything he had ever seen, everything he had ever felt, and every time his father had broken him. I watched as he cried himself to sleep every night, and I was there every time he wanted to kill himself. I was there when the Crusader approached him and told him about Phantonix.

When Phantonix rises and wins the war of Creation, he will remove all pain and sorrow from this abysmal world, the Crusader's voice echoed in Henry's mind. *Everyone's destiny will be planned, and the hatred that is spread when Free Will runs rampant will be destroyed. There will be a designed order, and nothing will alter its course.* I could understand why he had chosen Phantonix, and I locked eyes with him.

"You are loved," I said gently, "and I want you to come home. Forgive yourself for the things you have done. You are not a Crusader, and you can return to the light." Tears slid down my face, and I could see the darkness beginning to fade in Henry's heart.

"But I killed Claire," he admitted under his breath.

My mind went back to that night. I could see myself standing outside of the diner as the shadow sat at the piano. I could hear my screams as I turned to look at myself. I saw the fear spread across my face as the truth hit me. I looked back at Henry and watched as the darkness created the illusion of the inky monster coming to life.

"I know, Henry." I held his hands, and we looked down at his palms to see the bloodstains upon them. I could feel Phantonix's anger burning in him, but I would not let the darkness touch Henry. I let the light burn brightly around us, shielding him.

"I am here for you, Henry." He looked into my eyes. "I am sorry for the sorrow that you have had to endure, and you need to know that you are forgiven."

As I spoke, Claire walked away from the host of light that surrounded us and came to kneel before Henry. There were tears in her eyes, and she touched both of our hands and nodded at Henry. Henry glanced up, and he stared into her brown eyes. He wore an expression of shock and confusion.

"Come home." She moved to touch his face.

"I can't," he said. In his heart, I saw two paths. One where he returned to Phantonix and rested in the darkness forever, and one where he forgave himself and would be sent into the Realm of Light.

"It's your choice, Henry," I said softly. "That is the beauty of Free Will. I cannot make you decide to come home or return to Phantonix." He looked at me. "However, I want you to know that whatever you decide, I will respect your decision."

He looked around and saw everyone staring at us. He looked at Claire, and he turned back to look me in the eyes.

"Then," he whispered, "I choose Phantonix."

With his choice, the darkness had conquered his heart, and the growing light faded. His decision magnified his voice as he got to his feet. "Free Will is the stain upon Creation, and it will crumble! I know Destiny is the true way." His words were not said in anger or spite but as his simple truth.

He turned away from me. I could see Phantonix standing against a tree in the courtyard, his shredded cloak floating in the darkness. I watched as his violet eyes blazed in victory. He opened his arms and accepted Henry again, moving him to his side. Henry stood next to him, and Phantonix roared.

"Tonight marks the fall of the King of Free Will! Tonight will mark the end of choice, of those arrogant fools who believe they are capable of choosing their own paths! The Final War is coming!" Henry turned back to look at me and yelled, "All hail Emperor Phantonix!"

They disappeared in a cloud of swirling darkness, and I felt the fight go out of me. The shining light that surrounded me disappeared. I knelt on the ground, wearing my shredded and bloody school uniform. I could no longer see the countless souls in the Realm of Light; all I could feel was defeat. I had failed to bring Henry back into the light. I failed him, again.

I felt Michael kneeling next to me. I knew it was Henry's choice, but his sorrow and memories were still fresh in my heart, and that had forced me to my feet.

"My King." I looked into his eyes, and he pulled me into a hug. "It's okay," he said softly. "He followed his own beliefs, and we must respect his choices."

"I failed him."

"No, Danny," Michael said softly into my ear. "You forgave him for everything he had done and gave him a chance to come home. It was his choice not to accept that gift, the freedom of redemption. He chose not to take it." I felt his words comfort my heart, and I pulled out of the hug and looked into his eyes.

"I want you to know, Michael, that I love you. You are my family and thank you for everything." I gave him a big smile.

"I love you too, my King." He had an honored look in his face, and he bowed slightly.

Before I could say anything, I felt a life-shattering pain rip through me. I felt a bloodcurdling scream rip out of me, and I grabbed my chest. My heart reverberated rapidly, and with every beat, a fresh wave of pain scorched through me.

"Danny?!" Michael's words sounded a million miles away. Grenoff, the bell tower, and my loved ones disappeared as I was surrounded by misery and pain.

****

~Danny Elikai~

I could feel every single tear that had ever been shed. I lived the darkest moments of every soul that had ever existed. I saw every face that had ever walked the Earth, and even those that had yet been born. I felt their pain as if I were experiencing it myself as I had with Claire. They rapidly flashed before me, one after another.

I was a young woman sobbing in her husband's arms after losing our newborn baby. I was a teenage boy who put a gun in my mouth, and the pain, sorrow, and anger flashed before me as I pulled the trigger. I found myself holding my young daughter's lifeless body after discovering her face down in the tub. I was an old man in a retirement home, staring at pictures of my family who hadn't visited me in many years. I was a little girl who was crying silently in a closet as my father beat my mother. I was a teenage girl standing in front of a mirror and was disgusted at my own fat body, even though I could see my ribs. I was a slave who was being lynched just because I tried to run away. I was a small boy that walked into a chamber full of showers and panicked as gas came out of the spigots.

I watched as countless people called out to the light and felt unanswered. This happened time and time again, and I experienced the pain and anguish of every soul that ever was or will be. I felt their pain for what felt like a million years until I finally heard his voice calling.

"Danny?" Michael's fearful voice broke through the endless sorrow. I looked up at him with unfocused eyes. My family surrounded me in the courtyard, and my uncle held my hand.

"I can feel them," I said weakly to Michael. "I can feel the sorrow of countless souls. Their pain, and even their deaths. I see them, and every bad thing they experienced." As I kept talking, the memories continued to flash before me. "I was an elderly woman weeping at the graves of her husband and child who died twenty years ago. I was a young woman who just killed herself because her family disowned her for simply being who she was."

I felt the hot tears sting, and the sobs came out harder as the pain intensified. I found myself as a young child in a war-torn country, and I looked upon the dead bodies of my loved ones. My papa was dead next to my mama, and my big brother didn't have a goofy smile across his face. I felt tears fall onto my teddy bear, the only one left in my life. I raised his dirty, burned paw to wipe away my tears. I turned away into the night, alone.

"No!" I screamed into the Grenoff night sky. "Please stop!" The pain was heartbreaking, and I could not continue. I wanted to save them, protect them, and ensure they knew I was there with them. But the visions changed so rapidly that I couldn't be there for them all.

"Danny!" Michael wrapped me into a tight hug that brought me back, but I immediately fell back into the visions. I was a young child in an orphanage staring at the night sky, alone, abandoned, and unloved. I was running up the stairs to escape the man trying to kill me, pleading to the light to save me as the knife pierced my heart. I was in a bathtub as I cut myself because I hated everything about my life. I was a teenager telling my family that I was a boy, not their little girl anymore; my father approached me with his belt in his hand, rage burning in his hateful eyes. On and on it went, vision after vision of the suffering of Creation.

I had felt everything everyone had ever experienced, but the worthlessness they felt cut the deepest. I felt unworthy of being their King as their sorrow coursed through my veins. I had left these poor people to suffer, bleed, and die.

"Danny," I found myself in my aunt's arms looking into Michael's eyes. "This is not your fault. You are not to blame."

I saw their lives flash before my eyes, again and again. Michael had the locket in his hands, and it was open, playing that familiar soft melody, the melody that had brought me so much comfort.

"Put the light back," he told me. It was then that I noticed that the power of light was still in my veins, burning brightly in every inch of my skin. I pushed away from my aunt's arms and knelt before the locket, but my emotions were conflicted. I wanted to end this, but I also wanted to be there for them, to help them.

"You cannot help them if you are broken. You need to put the light back." With incredible effort, I lifted one finger and placed it on the seal, my seal, and returned the power to the locket. I felt the power leave my body, and with a soft chime, the locket closed and went silent.

I looked into Michael's eyes and I felt hollow inside, exhausted, and broken. I closed my eyes and collapsed forward into his arms.

"You are safe, my King," he said quietly, and I felt the exhaustion trying to drag me into sleep. Before I closed my eyes, I looked up at the bell tower as it struck midnight, and one final vision ran across my mind before I passed out.

I stood in the light of a dozen torches as I praised the King of Free Will and cursed the Emperor of Destiny, the one I had believed in for so long. I looked over at my younger brother, lying on the cold ground, and knew I had done what I needed to protect him. I turned to stare my father in the eyes as I drove the knife into my heart.

Chapter XVII

The Corridors of Creation

~Danny Elikai~

I woke up without opening my eyes, and my body felt like lead. I did not want to face them—those who had protected me, who had fought for their King. I knew that when I opened my eyes, I would find myself in my bed, surrounded by my loved ones, but I felt like a fraud. I was not the King; there must have been a mistake.

I replayed the memory of last night over and over. I opened the locket, the power flowed through me, and I failed to save Henry. I had become the King, witnessed by the host and the Generals of Light. I could not recall their names, no matter how hard I tried, but I knew them and their stories when I saw their faces.

The memory of the small boy with the teddy bear looking down at his dead family burned the brightest. I could smell the burned stuffing of the teddy bear, and I felt his grief as if it were my own. I felt a sob escape me, and I shuddered.

I curled onto my side, and when my nose touched his shoulder, I felt his radiating heat. He was here next to me as if he wanted me to lean on him and use his strength.

"Breathe, Danny." Michael's words were soft as he whispered in my ear. "Take your time. We are here for you when you are ready." His words calmed my racing pulse as the exhaustion once again began to drag me back into the arms of oblivion.

****

When I woke up again, I felt alone. My body didn't hurt, and the sorrows of humanity no longer lingered in my bones. I cracked my eyes slightly open and found myself comforted by warmth.

I was lying on the floor that was made from the same white otherworldly material as the kingdom where I had spoken to Eloheen. As I looked around, I was in what seemed to be an endless hallway. There were millions of doors along endless corridors. Many were white doors with red script engraved on the door, while others were varnished wood, and a few within my sight were black with purple script engravings.

"Where am I?" My voice echoed along the corridors as I got to my feet.

"The Corridors of Creation," that still small voice spoke. I spun around and saw him. He wore dark blue jeans with a flannel shirt, the same clothes he wore the night he died. His electric green eyes looked at me with immense love and pride.

"Dad?" I asked, dumbfounded. His smile did not falter, but he shook his head.

"I am not your father, Danny." I stared at him, but my mind couldn't process his words.

"Are you Eloheen?" My voice echoed again along the corridors as his smile grew, and he nodded.

"Yes, Danny," he nodded. "I took this form because I knew it would bring you comfort. I thought you and I should talk, now that you know the truth." He sat on a small couch that had not been there a few moments before. "Please, Danny, sit." He motioned, and when I looked back, there was another small couch. I moved a few steps toward him and sat down, and the space between us shrank, so we were almost knee to knee.

"Why did you choose me?" I asked before I could stop myself. "I don't understand, Eloheen."

"I know, Danny. That is why we are here now. I am going to tell you as much as I can. However, because of the governing force you put into place, I am limited. Please be patient with me and understand that I am following your plan," he explained, and I nodded.

"I chose you to govern Creation because your heart was the purest out of every soul that had ever been created. You respect others, you guide them, and you help your fellow man. No one could hold a candle to you, and I knew when I formed life, you were the only true ruler." His words were calm and sweet, and everything fell quiet when he spoke. "I remember I was there when you were brought into existence, and I saw what the citizens of Creation would see. From that moment, I never believed anyone else could do it."

"Why did you have to choose anyone? Why didn't you take the throne?" He wiped away a tear from my father's face.

"You see, Danny, I never wanted the throne. I never wanted to rule; I just wanted peace. I believe that is why you are here, why you have suffered more than you remember, and why you will have to defeat him and fix my mistake."

"What was your mistake?"

"Phantonix," he had venom in his voice. However, his eyes were sad and held remorse, which was odd to see in my father's eyes. "When I told Phantonix you would rule Creation, he was not pleased. He believed that I betrayed him and took away his right to rule. You and Phantonix are as different as night and day. For the longest time, I led him to believe he would rule, and that was my intention. That is until I met you, and I knew the truth." He lowered his gaze to his intertwined fingers, and I saw the tears hit the ground.

"You promised Phantonix that he would rule Creation?"

"Yes, but again, I cannot explain more at this time. I am sure that one day, he will tell you his side of the story. But until then, that is all I can say on the subject. You will learn more and experience it again as the Crusaders rise and manipulate the world. Then you will become the man who will rule Creation," Eloheen said softly.

"You must have made a mistake, Eloheen. I can barely handle myself! I certainly can't govern the whole host of Creation. I don't know what I'm doing!" My voice rose in panic, and I felt the pressure pressing in on my chest.

"Breathe, Danny," he reached out and touched my shoulder. I stared into my father's eyes and felt a calm wash over me. I knew this was not my father, but those eyes, my family's eyes, had a way of calming me. I understood why Eloheen took this form, and I was grateful.

"At this moment, you are not ready to take the throne and govern Creation. You are just beginning your journey. You will have time to learn and experience what it means to be the King and how to handle the host of Creation." He smiled at me, but my mind could not comprehend what he was trying to explain to me. I looked at him, and I could see my own desperate, panicked expression in his eyes, and again he just smiled.

"Let me explain it to you another way. Right now, you found out that you are the King of Light, which is Point A. You are trying to jump to when the Final War is over, and you are ruling Creation, if you win, which is point Z. If the Final War were waged tomorrow, you would lose, because you are not ready to rule, and the people of Creation are not yet ready to accept what is coming. You see, people, the souls of Creation, are the true key to the end of the Final War, and your victory."

"If I'm not yet ready to take the crown, why did I find out I am the King of Light now? Why not just let me go along with being a General of Light until the time was right?"

"Danny," he said, giving me an expression that clearly stated he was going to have difficulty explaining this to me. "When Creation was on the verge of becoming a physical entity, just before the first light touched your kingdom, you approached me. We were spirits in the Realm of Light when you told me that you wanted to experience life the same as those you would rule. You told me that you had to be the embodiment of your philosophy, that you had to be an example. You wanted to show people not to follow you by what you said, but to follow your actions. You told me that you could not be allowed to remember who you truly were, and neither would the vast majority of Creation. You told me that this was the only true way to rule, to believe that you were one of the people so that you knew their needs. I did not understand at first, and I was afraid that you would crumble, and Creation would be lost.

"However, after several heated arguments, we came to an agreement. No matter what life you were in, no matter what happened, you would always be protected. You chose a select few to help guide you to the truth when it was necessary for the survival of humanity.

"For example, your family knew the truth about your identity, as well as your handpicked General, Michael. These protectors would help you discover the truth when the Soldiers of Destiny attempted to harm you or the other protectors. This inevitably came to pass when your parents and Matthew died when the Crusader interfered. Then, the responsibility fell to your aunt, uncle, and Michael to guide you to the truth about who you are. Matthew refused to stand by as you suffered and was granted the ability to interact with the physical realm to help you."

When he finished, we sat there in silence as he let me absorb the information he had presented.

"Does Phantonix know this?"

"Yes, he knows. And that is why he ordered Ieiunium to strike before you reached Grenoff. Your family was going to guide you to the truth this summer."

"If Phantonix knew that I would discover the truth if anyone from his side attacked me, why did he order the strike? Why not leave me in the dark to suffer like I was before?"

"This is only guesswork, but I assume since you would discover the truth eventually, he wanted to play it to his advantage. I am sure Phantonix wanted you to experience the unbelievable pain caused by the death of your family and hoped you would succumb to the darkness and end your life. He wanted to use your death as a weapon against Free Will. He believed that if you killed yourself because you could not handle life as you set it up, then it would prove to the souls of Creation that Destiny is the only true philosophy."

"He almost succeeded."

"No, he didn't, Danny." His smile felt like a lie.

"I wanted to kill myself! I didn't want to be alive anymore. I let the darkness in and let it overtake me!" The anger exploded out of me.

"I know everything you have experienced, as I have always been with you. I felt your pain as if it were my own, just like you did when you felt the sorrow and pain from the countless souls in the locket. However, I also know you. I know the depths of your heart, Danny. I knew, just like you did that, you would choose to be here, and from your actions and your strength, you are here now. You believe in the right to choose your own path, and you believe that you have to experience everything to know the truth. The pain you felt and the struggle you experienced will help you when you are trying to guide souls back to the light. You will be an effective leader because you experienced the pain with them. You will be their example."

I felt the anger slowly burn out of me. He continued, "You told me that even you had to experience the trials and tribulations of this world that were caused by the choices of Free Will. That way, you were no different from your people. You told me you needed to understand pain and love, sorrow and hope, and even death. You told me the only true way to bring people home to the Realm of Light was to fight, love, breathe, bleed, and die with them." Eloheen's message was sinking in, and I understood what he was trying so desperately to help me understand.

"'Do as I do, not as I say,'" I quoted, as my father's lesson burned hot in my mind. "My father always led as an example and told me that our words are only backed by our actions. Never believe people by their words; believe them when they deliver." My words were not meant for Eloheen, but rather for myself.

"That is correct. You said you had to choose to become the King, to fight, guide, and protect your people. You had to embody your philosophy for others to believe," Eloheen said, smiling again.

"It was my choice?"

"Yes, Danny. You can turn your back on this, refuse to be the King, and that would be your choice. However, I don't believe you will. You will take the throne to bring peace to a warring and devastated people. You will see the darkness and suffering of your followers and use the light to bring peace."

"How?" I was trying to absorb everything he told me, but my mind was hurting with all of this knowledge.

"That will come with time, Danny. You will learn this lesson again and again. You even told me you would fail, falter, and stumble, but that it was necessary. Right now, all you need to do is let your family, friends, and Generals guide you through the darkest times Creation will ever face."

"The uprising of the Crusaders?"

"Yes," Eloheen had a hint of anger in his voice.

"Do you know who Ieiunium is?"

"Austin is the Crusader, do not let that be mistaken. However, I am uncertain which face he is currently hiding behind. He can use the face of anyone whose heart resides in darkness," he said with a small smile and a wink.

"Thanks, that's really helpful," I sighed. "So, all I have to do is focus on the Crusaders, and the rest will come on its own?" Eloheen didn't answer, except to give me a warm smile and a nod. We sat in silence as I processed the information he had just laid out before me. I felt a calm feeling course through me as the truth settled in my heart.

"No one is expecting me to be King yet," I said softly to myself. I looked at the endless doors, and as I got to my feet, a name caught my eye.

"Do you know what these doors mean?" Eloheen asked. I didn't answer, because my eyes found a white door with a red engraving that read *Stephanie Elikai*.

"Mom?" I touched the door, and it slowly opened.

"Heads up!" I found myself standing on a beautiful beach.

The trees were bright with red, yellow, and orange leaves that fell to the ground. I stood next to Star Lake in Grenoff as a young woman with brown hair looked up in time to see a volleyball sailing toward her. She raised her book to block the ball from hitting her face. I noticed that the book was her favorite classic, and I couldn't help but smile.

I found I was staring at a younger version of my mom. She wore a simple one-piece bathing suit that belonged in a vintage store. Her brown hair was pulled up in a ponytail, and she rested on the beach as she deflected the ball that barely missed her. I noticed that she had not been aware of my presence.

"You, okay?" A young man ran up to us, and I stopped short. My dad stood before me. He looked so young, his strawberry blonde hair was longer than I had ever seen it, and his green eyes were ablaze with life. My dad had always had a chiseled physique, and his younger self was no exception. He had a huge smile on his face as he picked up his volleyball that landed a few inches from her. My mom stared at him without blinking. I was sure she had forgotten how to speak.

"You okay?" He sat down on the sand next to her.

"Watch where you're aiming next time," she huffed at him and turned back to her book.

"I'm Joshua," he held out his hand, "Joshua Elikai." She looked at it and then at his smile. My dad always said his smile was the only way for him to get out of trouble. I watched as the anger disappeared from my mom's face.

"Stephanie." She took his hand as love exploded between them.

"Do you want to play?" He held up the ball.

"I don't know how," she replied, but he grabbed her hand and pulled her up.

"Come on; I'll show you."

"Smooth." The scene dissolved, and I found myself in front of the white door with the crimson script. The door was completely sealed as I turned back to look at Eloheen, who had not moved from where he sat. I looked at the doors, and the understanding became clear.

"The white doors represent those who are dead and in the Realm of Light, correct?" Eloheen nodded.

I moved a few yards down the corridor until I reached his door. I reached out and touched a varnished wooden door with a red script engraved on it that read *Alexander Elikai*. It unlocked and slowly opened.

I walked into the light and found myself in my bedroom in Grenoff. My uncle was sitting in the armchair, his head resting on the wall, as a small amount of drool dripped from his mouth. I looked around the room and saw my aunt sitting in a chair next to my bed, her head on the mattress as she held my hand. Izabelle sat on the floor, and Michael was lying next to me, asleep. He was on top of the covers while I was under them, looking worse than death.

"Ah!" My uncle woke up with a start, but everyone else was still asleep. He looked through me as his eyes trailed along with everyone else. He got to his feet and walked through me to the edge of the bed. He gently touched his wife with two fingers on her cheek, but she did not stir. He sat on the edge of the bed and looked at my unconscious body.

"Please, Danny, wake up." Tears fell down his face. "Please, my King." He took my hand from my aunt.

I was uncomfortable with my uncle calling me King. I felt his sorrow, his worry that I would not forgive them for keeping this secret, but his biggest fear was that I wouldn't wake up.

I looked at them one last time before the scene dissolved around me. I stepped back through the open door, leaving my uncle's thoughts to himself.

"Well?" Eloheen's asked curiously from behind me. As I spun to face him, the corridors came back into focus.

"The wooden doors represent those who are still alive, but who have already chosen?" I said, noticing the red script that spelled out my uncle's name.

"Yes. The wooden doors represent the living, but the colors of the names are based on their beliefs. Alex, Shannon, and Izabelle's doors are engraved in red, whereas..." Eloheen waved his hand, and countless doors sped by. It was about twenty seconds before they came to a stop. To my left stood a wooden door with purple writing that read *Henry Lee*.

"Henry is alive but has chosen Phantonix." I looked at the other doors with purple writing. There were some names I recognized. A few of them were even famous. I felt sick, but before I could do anything, Eloheen waved his hand again. The speeding doors only lasted a few seconds, before a row of wooden doors stood before me. Their names were written in gray.

"These doors represent those who are undecided." There were countless doors, all engraved with the same gray color. "These souls will decide the true Victor of Creation. These are the souls who will decide if it will be you or Phantonix." Eloheen had a casual tone, but I felt the uncertainty in it. I stared at one of the gray names, and I felt the fire roar inside me with an ugly fury. I stared at the name, but I did not know its owner. I touched the gray engraved name of *Peter Stansbury*.

"Who is Peter Stansbury?" I asked Eloheen.

"I believe," Eloheen had a clinical tone, "he's a bartender in New York." I tried to open the door, but it wouldn't budge.

"That is something you do not need to see just yet." Before I could say another word, the doors began to speed by again. After a few moments, I found myself standing in front of a black door with a name engraved in purple.

"These are for those who are dead, but have chosen Phantonix?" I touched the scripted name of *Joseph Charles*.

"Yes. They are the soldiers in Phantonix's army. However, they may or may not be physically gone. They can still be alive, but dead inside." I nodded and began looking at the countless doors around me. I noticed there were many more doors with gray script than purple or red combined.

"Why are you showing me this?" Eloheen stood up. He waved both hands, and all the doors disappeared, except for two. The door on the left was beautiful, a sunshine yellow with red writing on it. The other door was a warm red, the writing engraved in yellow. I automatically moved toward the red door, and I noticed it had my name.

I looked back at the beautiful yellow door, and I chuckled when I saw the name *Michael Shepherd*. I walked up to his door and reached out. It opened eagerly at my touch. A soft yellow light shined in the corridor, its warmth similar to Michael's, and I stepped in.

The light was consumed by darkness, and I stood alone. I could not see anything, but I felt pain, sorrow, and loneliness. I blinked several times in order for my eyes to adjust to the dim light.

I was standing in a dirty room. After a moment, I saw a young child crying on a rotted bed.

"Michael?" To my astonishment, the child looked up at me, and my knees slammed to the garbage-ridden floor. I was speechless as I stared at my best friend. He couldn't have been more than nine years old, and his left eye was black and swollen. He wore ratty clothes and had angry rashes on his exposed skin.

"Wha?" His fear burned bright in me. "What's going on?"

"I'm sorry, I didn't mean to," he was cowering in the corner.

"Michael." His eyes were not focused on me but over my head. I turned around and saw an older woman standing in the doorway. She was livid and held an old leather belt in her hand. She looked nasty, unwashed, and very overweight. Her black hair was pulled into a tight bun, and a cigarette was hanging from her mouth. As I stared into her eyes, I could not help but feel as if I knew her, but I could not place from where.

"Liar!"

"I didn't mean to!" Michael tried to cower further, but he was already backed into the corner.

"Don't lie to me! Everything is your fault!" She charged at him and began beating him viciously with the belt.

"Stop!" I tried to stop her, but nothing happened. I could not save him from this, because I was not really there.

I watched as this woman savagely beat my Michael for over ten minutes. She whipped him, slapped him, and even punched him, before delivering a final kick to the gut. She turned around and left him in the room, slamming the door shut and locking it from the outside.

Michael cried on his bed for what seemed like forever. I walked over to him and sat down. I tried to touch him, but I was nothing more than a ghost in this memory.

"You are loved, Michael. I'm right here with you," I cried softly and repeatedly. I couldn't touch him, and I knew he couldn't hear me, but I did not know what else to do.

Michael stopped crying and looked at the door. Wiping away his tears, he took a deep breath. He got to his knees, folded his arms, and closed his eyes.

"My King?" I froze, and my heart ached. "I love you. Although I am sad and hurting now, I know you are with me. You are always with me, and you protect my heart from these nightmares. I know you are with me, even now, because I can feel you. You have never broken your promise; you have never left me. I know you are here holding my hand through the pain.

"I want to ask you for something. I want you to forgive her. She is not a bad mama, but she is sad, and she needs you. I know she is mad at me and believes I am the one who hurt them, but I didn't. I know you know that, and I am grateful for you choosing me to fight for you. I love you, and please forgive her." He spoke softly and wore a big smile on his bloody and bruised face as he pulled a book from under his mattress and began to read in the dim light.

The dark room and the pain melted away as I found myself staring at the yellow door. I felt the burning tears fall down my face, and I wanted nothing more than to go back to that child, to protect and love him. It was Eloheen's words, however, that made me turn away from the yellow door.

"He said that prayer every night for four years. His faith never cracked, no matter how bad the beatings were. He never lost his faith, and he always believed in you. He felt you there with him. You were the strength that kept him alive and gave him the chance to escape to Grenoff. He has been on his own ever since, even though his mother died only a while ago. Michael's absolute devotion to you is unfailing, like the sun rising in the east and setting in the west. No matter what happens, no matter what life throws at you both, he will never leave you." Eloheen waved his hand as another door appeared.

"Whose door is this?" I saw the scripted name of *Holland Shepherd* engraved on the door.

"Michael's mother," he said. I stared at the color of the door.

"Does he know?"

Eloheen shook his head and sighed, "He does not know for certain, but he has assumed correctly. He buried her with a simple headstone and hasn't looked back."

"Whose deaths did she blame Michael for?"

"His father and his twin brother," Eloheen said. "But I'm afraid that if you want to know more, you will have to ask him."

"Why did you show me this?"

"You need to know the severity of the task at hand. You need to understand what your followers have experienced and will experience before this war is over. However…" Eloheen's voice was fading, and he stopped talking. I stepped back in surprise. I could see through him as if his body were fading away.

"What's happening?!"

"It's alright, Danny," he gave me a weak smile. "I am nothing more than a final echo of my former self. My time has finally come, and now I can finally let go." He smiled. "Do not worry, Danny. I promise that before the Final War has been waged, you will see me again. Remember one thing: no matter what happens, what you see, feel, or experience, never forget that Michael will always be with you. His love and loyalty for you have no end. He will help guide you into eternity." Eloheen looked over my should before giving me a final wink, and then he was gone.

I stood in the corridors alone. I ran my hands through my hair and closed my eyes. I tried to bring everything that had just happened into focus. My brain hurt as I tried to recall everything, I had just learned and tried to put everything together. I stared at the place where Eloheen vanished, and I recited everything aloud to myself.

"I just found out I am the King, but no one expects me to be the King yet. I have seen the doorways to every soul in Creation. I had experienced a few of them, and just witnessed Eloheen's death?" I looked at the couch where he had just flickered from existence. "I am the final echo of my former self," I repeated. "Then there is Michael, who, even in the darkest moments of his life, found love and forgiveness. He unconditionally believes in me, the King of Light and Free Will." I got to my feet; my heart was ablaze with determination to face what was waiting for me. I pushed the red door open, my words echoing through the corridors of Creation.

"I'm coming for you, Ieiunium."

Chapter XVIII

The Children of the Solstice

~Danny Elikai~

The stillness around me was the first thing that I became aware of as my eyes slowly opened. I felt calm around the room, and I knew that my loved ones no longer surrounded me. I sat up, and my body protested due to the inactivity from my extended period of rest. I could still feel the remnants of the raw power of the light in my body.

My eyes fell upon a figure standing in my room, staring out the window. He wore the black robes of the Crusaders, the Generals of Destiny. I stared at him, but I felt the calming of the light radiating around him, and I knew he was not a threat.

"Hello." The figure turned to me, and all I could see was the darkness in the hood where his face should have been.

"I assumed correctly, then," his soft chuckle felt so familiar, but I could not place it. He walked away from the frost-covered window and stood next to the bed before falling to his knees. "My King."

"Please stand," I said quickly, as I was filled with unease. He jerked to his feet as if my words were lightning. "Who are you?"

"That is a long story." He sat on the edge of the bed. "For now, you can call me a friend, a Soldier of Light, even if I wear the armor of Destiny." I felt the shame in his heart and the disgust in his words.

"Soldier of Light?" I nodded. "Like Izabelle and my aunt and uncle?"

"Yes, I am a Solider of Light. We are the believers in Free Will who have turned to you. I will fight for you in the Final War alongside your friends and family. My heart is not strong enough to be a General of Light, and it never will be."

"If you are a Soldier of Light, then why are you wearing that?" I pointed to the black robe.

"My King, are you familiar with the Organization of Savina?"

"No. I have not yet explained Savina to Danny." His voice made my breath hitch in my throat, and we both turned to see Michael standing in the doorway, whose ever changing eyes held joy and were as bright as the sun. The man in black chuckled and turned to him.

"Hello, Michael."

"Hello, Targo," he said with a soft smile as they embraced. I looked back and forth between Michael and Targo.

"You know each other?"

"We met several years ago," Michael said, but his eyes never left me. "I assume you succeeded in your attempt?" He turned to Targo.

"Yes." The man in black turned his attention from Michael back to me. "My King, I will explain. The Organization of Savina are the foot soldiers in

Phantonix's Army. They have been manipulating humanity since the first light touched this world. Before I absconded to the side of Free Will, I was one of the most devoted of Phantonix's followers. I performed horrendous atrocities in the name of what I thought was, at the time, the true philosophy.

"When I turned from Destiny to Free Will, I went to the last of your disciples to confess and apologize for my crimes. I passed along vital information, secrets, and countless offerings to the light. In exchange, the information was sent out that I had been tortured and destroyed by that Disciple, and I was granted permission to live among humanity. I was given protection, a new identity, and was allowed to live as I saw fit. To be honest, I had some rough years. But I was given a wonderful family, and one day, I fell in love with a beautiful woman. I was truly happy for the first time since I was created.

"However, it wasn't until recently that I knew I had to return to the Realm of Darkness to retrieve vital information. It's been strenuous to stay under their radar, but I have succeeded." He reached into his pocket and pulled out several battered pieces of yellowing paper folded like a letter. "This is the reason, the spark, that turned my heart to Free Will."

He handed me the letter, and I gently opened it. The paper was delicate in my hand. I stared at a single name at the top, but the rest of the script was written in a strange language.

"What language is this?" I asked Targo.

"It's Icelandic."

"Danny," Michael said, and I looked up at him, "try to read it again."

I turned back to the letter, and my vision blurred. I struggled to read the parchment, and I had to rub my eyes. When I looked back at the letter, it had changed. It no longer contained the Icelandic characters but was written in plain English.

"The letter changed, didn't it?" I looked up and found Michael sitting on the bed next to me.

"How did you know?"

"Danny, you are the King. You can understand all languages and dialects." He pointed to the letter in my hands. "This letter was written in traditional Icelandic. The power inside your veins will translate it into your native tongue. This will work for every language under the sun. Even if you were talking to someone who spoke a different language, they would hear you in their native tongue," he explained simply.

"So, if I meet someone who only spoke Russian," I said softly, "then I would hear it as English, but when I spoke, they will hear in Russian?"

"Yeah, that's the general idea," Michael nodded.

"The letter in your hand," Targo said, interrupting an explanation that he probably felt was unnecessary, "is from the young woman who changed my life. She is the reason I decided to turn to the light." I turned back to the letter and began to read.

My beloved brother Otto,

It is with a heavy heart that I write to you, but you need to know the truth. I have hidden this letter from you until you are old enough to understand my actions, and hopefully, you will forgive me. It is the eve of your seventh birthday, and tomorrow at dawn, Creation will be forever changed.

We kept a secret from you and the other six children that were brought to Grenoff. We did not come here for the mining or the lumber, as I once told you, but rather to unleash unimaginable darkness upon the world.

I know these words will seem impossible, and maybe even terrifying, but I promise you they are true. Once the truth is told, I will not blame you for hating me. But I need you to promise me that you will do everything in your power to stop the darkness and to understand what I was willing to sacrifice to achieve this.

Otto, there is a war coming. This war will not only destroy Creation as we know it, but it will also bring everlasting peace. Right now, as we live and breathe, a powerful philosophy governs Creation, a philosophy that allows people to choose how they want to live their lives and what to believe.

This governing force is called Free Will. The right to choose was given to us by the King of Light. He is the one who will return to this world, after your children's children have long past, and unite the world in a time of great turmoil against the philosophy of Destiny.

Destiny is the reason I am writing you this letter because until recently, I was an agent of Destiny. I believed that I wanted nothing more than to overthrow Free Will, to unseat the King of Light from his throne, and to serve Emperor Phantonix. Papa had raised me to believe that Free Will was a stain upon the world, that it was against the true nature of humanity, and that we must serve Phantonix in all that we do.

I watched as war, disease, and famine ran rampant in this world. With Destiny, choice would be removed, and everything would be planned out. If Destiny were the governing force, our mother would have survived. I never dreamed that my heart would be swayed. I was even willing to sacrifice you to show my devotion.

You see, a member of Phantonix's inner circle approached our father and told him that your destiny had been foretold, that you were special. You and six other children were to be sacrificed on the Winter Solstice, and your blood would be marked. When the King of Light returns, our descendants will be called forth to become the Generals of Destiny, or as they would be known, the Crusaders of Destiny. When our father told me this, I was honored, and I knew this was the only true way to serve Phantonix. After your sacrifice, I was destined to go forth and bear children, and Savina would protect my descendants until the King returned, and the Final War began.

I am writing to you now because I cannot do it. I cannot let them sacrifice you. I made this decision a fortnight ago. I went into your room while you slept, to dream of the day when Phantonix ruled Creation. But when I looked at your innocent face, my heart broke. I felt the change rip through me like a wildfire. I tried to ignore the feeling because I knew Destiny was the correct philosophy. I woke up the next day, still determined to carry out the plan. I went about my normal routine and stayed on my destined path.

I did this for the next twelve days. On the night before your sacrifice, you came up to me. You said that you couldn't wait to grow up and have a family of your own and to raise them the way I helped to raise you. You smiled and walked away, and I knew that I had been defeated. I wanted you to have that family; I wanted you to grow up and be happy. I knew that your simple words had told me the truth. I wanted you to have the life you wanted, not what they had planned. I wanted you to have a choice. I finally understood what Free Will truly meant and understood that it was beautiful.

I know now that I am going to do everything I can to stop this, to make sure that you live a happy life. I plan to take your place in the sacrifice as soon as the ritual starts. I know that if we try to run, they will find us. This is the only way to make sure you survive because they will still need you to carry on our bloodline. I cannot stop this from happening, but I hope to change the plan to make it harder for the Crusaders to be unleashed.

I know I have no right to ask this from you, but I am begging you not to carry on our bloodline. I implore you to withhold from having the family that you desperately want. I am only asking, and not commanding, because it is your choice. I know this is unfair, because of what we had planned for you, but please. Fight Destiny, fight the darkness, and fight for Free Will.

I hope that, if I see you again, it will be in the Realm of Light. I hope that my sins can be forgiven and that the King of Light will grant me entry, but I will understand if he cannot forgive me for my crimes. I hope that you will forgive me, and I hope you know that I am sorry for everything. I wanted you to know the truth, and that my love for you and your happiness is why I have to fight. I am going to die to make sure Free Will wins the Final War so that I can see you again.

I am glad I am your sister, and I am grateful I have the choice to fight for you and countless others.

Praise the King of Free Will.

Your beloved sister,

Johanna

I finished the letter, and I could feel the sorrow, the shame, and the undying love from those words. I reread the letter several times to make sure that I fully understood it before looking up at the man in black.

"Were you the man who approached this family?"

"Yes." His voice was soft and filled with regret. "I was the one who picked them. I chose her father because of his devotion. The other six were not as easy to convince, but they all eventually crumbled." Michael touched my shoulder, and when I looked into his eyes, I felt his calmness snuff out the anger kindling in my chest.

"We will all make mistakes, Danny," Michael said. "However, he changed and became an ally to us. Without him, we could not have fought Destiny as effectively as we have." I listened to his words and nodded.

"Did she succeed?" I turned to Targo.

"Yes, and for that, I am grateful. The ritual was designed to mark the bloodlines of these families to allow us to find the Crusaders. It was at the peak of the Winter Solstice, and we were all prepared for the ritual. The seven who were to be sacrificed were asleep since we gave them a sleeping draught and were positioned around the stone basin in a circle. Their siblings were asleep at their feet while the families around them were chanting and ready to serve Destiny. I, the only one who knew the proper ritual, added all the necessary ingredients and was waiting for the proper moment to hit us. The ritual had to be performed meticulously, and if anything, even slightly changed, the outcome would be devastating. That was when it happened.

"The plan was to exsanguinate the seven children, allowing for their blood to fuse with their siblings. However, Johanna opened her eyes, got to her feet, and turned to look at me. No one interfered because she was the most loyal to our cause, but we would soon regret it. She pulled a knife out of her dress, and she shouted, 'Praise the King of Light! Praise Free Will!' She then stared her father in the eyes, smiled, and stabbed herself in the heart just as the solstice began. It sent a chain reaction through the other children.

"They all glowed white, and I knew I had to act fast to mitigate the damage. I slit their throats and continued the ritual. However, her actions changed everything. With her sacrifice, she protected the children and their descendants. Rather than being chosen by Destiny, the descendants had to choose to become Crusaders."

As Targo told me this story, a memory came rushing back to me. I remembered standing on the hillside with Austin after he had just killed his girlfriend, while Phantonix was trying to convince him to join Destiny, to allow the pain to end.

"It was their choice," I said simply. "Austin chose Destiny, and Johanna chose Free Will. She turned from the darkness to light, and he turned from light to darkness. It was a balance."

"Yes. Austin had to decide if he wanted to become a Crusader," Targo said. "They all must decide because of her sacrifice. Every child whose blood is marked must make a choice."

"There are only two children left who have not chosen yet," Michael said softly. "Five out of the seven have already chosen."

"We have to protect them!" I jumped to my feet.

"We're too late," said another voice in the doorway. We all turned to see my uncle standing there with a horrified expression. "Another child named Azareel in Jerusalem has been taken, and the mark of the Crusaders has been left. There is only one child left."

"Who is it?!" I turned to Targo as he shook his head.

"I do not know. When I confessed to the Disciple, he found them and procured another protective charm around them. It was his final act. He hid them, even from Savina, and they had been protected until this summer. I am not sure how the first Crusader found them, but I speculate that he has a unique connection to them all." He sounded defeated, and I felt frustrated.

"There is more you need to know." He looked up at me, and I could feel the shame burning through him. "If the final child is taken, the Crusaders will be unleashed during the upcoming Winter Solstice at sunset." I felt my blood run cold.

"All seven Crusaders will be unleashed upon the world." I slowly sat back down on the bed. We all sat in silence as we let the truth unfold around us.

"We have to find this child," I looked around the room. I turned back to Targo and stared into the blackness shrouding his face. "Thank you for telling me everything. I am grateful for the information. This will help."

"I am here to serve you, my King."

I felt like dismissing him, almost wanting to punish him for his crimes. I felt the rage in my fingertips as the fire screamed for justice. I closed my eyes and took a deep breath. I exhaled and opened my eyes.

"I forgive you." I knew it was the right thing to do, and because I knew he yearned to hear the words. "Michael is right; we all have made bad decisions, used poor judgment, and will do things we will regret by the time this is over. However, you have changed and have devoted the rest of your life to the light. It is because of your information that the descendants of those sacrificed children were found and protected from the darkness, and the Organization of Savina." I could feel the relief flood through him.

"Thank you, my King." He fell to his knees.

"Did Otto ever read this letter?" I asked Targo in an attempt to change the atmosphere.

"No. I needed to know what had changed Johanna's mind, and I found the letter after the ritual. I found it in a hollow tree by following the clues she left for her brother. Otto never learned the truth. He did, however, get married and start a family. He was happy and well-loved his whole life, and he lived to an old age. I kept an eye on him, and while he never knew the truth, he became a believer in Free Will. It wasn't for several decades after his death that I finally devoted myself to Free Will," he said.

"You loved her," I felt the truth burn hot in my heart.

"Yes, I loved Johanna, although I did not know it at the time. I did not realize it until I read her words." He talked to his hands, and then I felt his eyes found mine when he looked up. "I would like to know, my King, if she made it to the Realm of Light?"

"I am sorry, Targo, but I don't know." I looked at the locket that sat on the bed and went to pick it up. Michael grabbed my hand and looked me in the eye.

"No." I could see and feel the fear in Michael. "The raw power of light cannot be controlled yet." He turned to Targo. "I'm sorry, but I cannot allow him to find out that way."

"I understand." I looked at Michael's hand on mine, and he slowly released his grip, and I wanted to protest, and that confused me.

"We have to stop Ieiunium," I said, turning away from the confusion. "We must not allow the Crusaders to be unleashed."

"Danny," my uncle began before I interrupted him.

"No!" I knew what he was going at him to say. "I don't accept that we don't have a choice. We have a chance to stop this. The future is not set in stone," I glared at him, and he nodded.

"When is the Solstice?" I asked.

"December twenty-first at 4:23 P.M.," Targo said.

"We have until then to stop the rising of the Crusaders," I stood up and pocketed the locket.

"It is possible," Targo said slowly. We all looked at him as he was still on his knees before me. "Another ritual still needs to be completed. While the children have chosen Destiny, their hearts and bodies still need to be fully restored to their previous state. If you, like Johanna, alter the ritual, then you could stop the rising."

"We can't take that chance. We need to protect the final child," Michael said.

"I agree. The last child is our priority," I said. "Targo, I want you to return to the Realm of Darkness and gather as much information that relates to the Crusaders of Destiny, the Winter Solstice, or anything else that we need to know. I want to know what the Armies of Darkness are planning. I want you to return to Savina, reclaim your position, and reveal that you are still alive and that you had been spying on me." I spoke with as much authority as I could muster, and to my surprise, Targo laughed.

"I had a feeling this would be your command. I am willing to serve you forever, even if I die in the process."

"Targo, please be careful. I don't wish you any harm, and if you feel you are in mortal danger, return at once."

"I understand, my King. However, I must warn you, I will have to do things that are not becoming of a Soldier of Light." He lowered his head in shame.

"Do what you have to do to gain their trust, but don't let it darken your heart in the process."

"Yes, my King." He got to his feet. "I will have to be gone for an extended time, so I do not raise suspicion. I will have to gain their trust again,"

"I understand. Return when you are ready and when you know their plans," I said with a soft smile.

"Michael," Targo said, turning toward him. "I'll need your help." I looked at Michael and then at Targo.

Michael nodded and shot a bolt of lightning at him. Targo stood paralyzed as it tore through him, and he crumbled to his knees. Michael moved as he kicked him in the face. The force was deafening as it echoed in the room. I heard the sharp cry of pain from Targo, but he did not falter as Michael hit him again and again. We all knew that this had to happen; otherwise, it would be too suspicious if he returned unharmed.

I watched as Michael did what he could to protect the man before me, and with another spark of lightning, another scream of pain, we knew it was enough. Michael pulled back and looked sick but nodded when Targo thanked him.

He turned toward me, and I felt his devotion in his heart. "Thank you, my King. Until I see you again."

Without another word, he raised his hand as darkness formed behind him, almost like a door. It appeared to be breathing as it swirled around, and he limped right into it, disappearing from sight. I turned back to Michael, and my hands began to shake.

"Look, I know everyone believes that I am the King of Light, and maybe you're right. But for now, I am just Danny Elikai. I am just a fifteen-year-old kid, not a king, and I do not want to be treated any differently than you have been these last few months. If I wear a crown one day and sit on a throne, then we can discuss this again. But until then, I am no different from any other General of Free Will. Understood?" Michael and my uncle nodded in agreement.

"Good. Now, we have a Crusader to find." I turned toward the window. I could see that the first signs of winter had begun.

I felt Alex leave the room, and I was grateful. I didn't want to face him or for them to see my shaking hands. I didn't want them to see how much of a fraud I was, how unsure I was of sending Targo back to the Realm of Darkness. I might have just sent a Soldier of Light to his death, and I tried to fight off the wave of nausea.

"Danny." I couldn't move, as I struggled to breathe. Tears were stinging my eyes, and I felt as if I were ready to crumble like a house of cards. He placed his hand on my shoulder, and I felt the steadiness of his touch. "You did the right thing." His words were soft and gentle. "Targo knows what is at stake."

I didn't say a word as Michael stood behind me until I calmed down. I took a deep breath and sighed shakily. I turned back to my Michael, my rock, and my home. I looked into his ever-changing eyes and nodded.

"I have no idea what I am doing."

"You are the King of it all, Danny. Trust your heart, trust us, and we will get through this together." He pulled me into a tight embrace. I felt his warmth as my hands rested on his back.

"Thank you, Michael." I didn't pull out of the hug.

"I am sorry for not telling you sooner. I wanted to tell you from the moment we first talked on Star Cliff. And on one of the countless nights when you and I stayed up late watching movies. I almost told you everything that night in the graveyard. I wanted to tell you every moment we had together, but I promised I wouldn't. I could not lose you again." His tears fell and ran down my neck.

"I understand, Michael, I had to find out on my own. Honestly, I wouldn't have believed any of you if you told me, anyway." He pulled out of the hug and looked down at me.

"Do you remember that night in the graveyard when you heard me sing?"

"I don't think for as long as I live, I will ever forget that night."

"You are the reason that I am the happiest I have ever been." He took a step away to collect himself. "I am happy because I am with you, my King. I have known you are the King of Free Will since I was a young child—when I was neglected and starved in my mom's care.

"One night, when I was young, I cried out, and you came to me, comforted me, and showed me the truth. I felt your warmth, your love, and I knew that I belonged to Free Will. I knew that I was worthy to you and that I was loved." I felt my throat go dry as that scene of Michael's childhood returned in full force. "Everything I am, everything I have done, was to get here, to serve and protect you. I will continue to do everything for you. I will die for you if I must. You are my King, but you are also everything to me. I never thought I would be worthy enough to stand in your presence, let alone be considered your friend." He fell to his knees as tears streamed down his face.

I finally understood Michael's emotions and actions toward me over the last few weeks. I could feel his unconditional love toward me, his devotion to Free Will, and the burning white light in his heart. The swirling emotions in him were astonishing.

"Michael," I knelt before him while looking into his glorious eyes, "I was there the night you asked for forgiveness for your mom. I watched as she beat you, and I cried with you. I'm sorry you had to face that, but you were never alone. I will always be here with you, as you are my family."

"Thank you, Danny," his eyes were shimmering with tears. "I know you're confused and scared, but one day you will understand. You will sit on the Eternal Throne, and you will have brought peace to Creation. I will kneel in front of you, along with countless others. I know I promised you that I would not treat you differently, and I stand by my promise, but I need you to know I am yours now and forever." He wore a proud smile, and I nodded. I felt uncomfortable, not because of his heart or love for me, but his devotion to me as a King. He wiped away his tears and turned away.

"Michael," I pulled him into another tight hug. "Thank you," I whispered into his ear as his arms wrapped around me, and my skin burned against him.

He will guide you into Eternity, Danny. Eloheen's words replayed in my mind. I knew that Michael was mine, and with him by my side, I would never be alone. Whatever happened next, he and I would be in it together.

Chapter XIX

The Final Child

~Danny Elikai~

I stood shaking from pure exhaustion. The snow tried to cover the ground around me, but the fire burning in my hands melted it before it hit the ground. My clothes were nothing more than rags on my body, and the bruises from the relentless fighting were beginning to show.

I stood in a clearing on top of Grenoff Mountain as I waited. I knew they would strike again soon, and I couldn't help but smile. I felt happy, I felt powerful, and I felt loved, but mostly, I had never felt more alive. Even though my body felt broken, and I was bloody and exhausted, my heart and spirit were thriving.

I felt the static around me, and my arm hairs stood up a second before I saw the jet of lightning. Without thinking, I flipped backward out of the way and sent a blast of fire in response. He moved quicker than I could have thought possible, dodging the fire and sending a kick aimed at my head, which I barely deflected.

"Faster!" Michael charged me. I felt his punch collide with my ribs for the fifth time, but I sent a kick to his head before he could get out of the way. I watched him stagger and then stopped. He stood in the snow, the sweat glittering like diamonds off his broad-defined pecs with a gentle kiss of black hair that helped sculpt it. Michael was only wearing compression shorts that hung low enough where I could see how prominent that v-cut was. I had to force myself to focus on his goofy smile, not the black trail of hair descending south from his navel.

My mind didn't want to focus on anything other than that small patch of hair which meant I didn't feel the air change around me as she brought the crystal blade down across my back. I saw my blood splash on the snow as the pain ripped through me. Before she could attack again, I rolled out of the way. Izabelle mirrored my movements, and I barely avoided her second attack. I jumped out of the way, but I set myself up for Michael's kick. I faceplanted into the snow, my back and my nose bleeding. I stayed still in the snow, completely exhausted, and my fire began to repair the damage to my body.

Behind me, I heard a jet of lightning as Michael turned his attack toward Izabelle, who had become an expert with my family's sword. I heard Michael grunt as the crystal blade contacted his skin.

I turned around to look up through the snow and saw Michael and Izabelle trying to rip each other apart. I stood up, clamped my fists together, and slammed them into the ground. Fire exploded like wildfire as it sped toward them. Michael danced out of the way, but the blast slammed Izabelle into a tree. A jagged branch pierced her shoulder, and she began cursing as blood began to flow down her arm.

"Izabelle!" I stood up straight. However, she looked at me with a smirk and pulled herself off of the branch. Blood continued to drip from the hole in her shoulder and various scrapes and cuts on her body.

She twirled the sword and charged. She brought the sword down toward Michael, who caught the blade in his hands. I saw the pain ripple across his face, and his bloodstained the snow, but his smile stayed firm.

"You're going to have to do better than that," Michael laughed as he put both hands on the blade, his blood dripping toward the hilt. I watched the muscles in Michael's legs contract as he jumped from the ground, still holding the blade. He spun and twirled in the air, breaking Izabelle's grip. He hurled the blade with blinding speed, as it skewered a nearby tree with an ominous crack. He landed gracefully behind her as he formed lightning in his hand. Izabelle did not have time to react as he manipulated his lightning like a whip and brought it down across her back. The scream filled the night air as she crumbled into the snow in blinding pain.

"You need to move faster and be prepared for anything. The enemy will have powers that will rival your imagination. They will use them against you and will be itching to kill you. They will use their power to try to kill our King. You need to do better, Izabelle."

Michael stood over her as he talked, but right before he continued ranting, Izabelle flipped on the ground and brought her foot into his stomach with a staggering force. I sprang forward as he staggered back, and hurled my fiery fist into his stomach, right where Izabelle had just kicked him. Michael fell to one knee and took a deep breath. He raised a hand, and both Izabelle and I stopped.

"That's enough for today. Well done." That puppy dog smile did not leave his face. I felt the exhaustion finally bring me to my knees, and I watched Izabelle crumble again into a pile of snow with her eyes closed.

I crawled over to Izabelle, who had taken the most intense beating on this training session. I knelt over her, summoning the exhausted fire from my tired body, and touched her bleeding flesh. I surged the fire into her body and repaired the damage that had been caused. It only took a few moments until the wounds had been healed. I turned to Michael, stood up, and walked over to him.

"Save your strength, Danny," but I chose to ignore him. I placed a hand on his muscled chest, which was bleeding and burned from when I had sliced him earlier with my fiery blade.

"You did well." He held my gaze, and his eyes burned like a neon rainbow. I didn't understand why it was hard to swallow now, so I smiled back at him as I felt the fire finish healing his chest.

"Give me your hands," I said, the exhaustion wanting to drag me into a deep sleep. He held out his hands, and I saw the deep slashes across his palms from when he grabbed the blade.

I took a deep breath and touched the wounds, and he winced when I touched them. The fire left my veins and danced across his palms, and we watched as the white fire healed and restored his hands.

"Thank you, Danny." I turned away from his almost naked body as my pulse was ringing in my ears.

"Can you please put on some clothes now?" I felt the heat in my face. He laughed as he got to his feet and retrieved the small bag that was hanging on a low branch at the edge of the clearing. Izabelle was now on her feet as well, wearing tight shorts and a sports top, and began putting her regular clothes back on.

Both she and Michael decided that being practically naked was the best way to train as the clothes restricted their movements. I remained in my clothes, which were now completely ruined. I knew Aunt Shannon would not be pleased to see my clothes like this, but I didn't have any more energy to repair them.

"I can still feel the pain." Izabelle gently touched her shoulder, where she had taken the most damage.

"It's mental, it'll pass," Michael said in a flat tone, just like he did every time she complained about the pain after I had healed her.

I looked at both of them and felt a happiness course through my veins. It had been six weeks since I woke up and we discovered the truth about the Children and the Crusaders. The Winter Solstice was almost upon us, and things had been an incredible mixture of stress, school exams, and quality time with my friends, but we had no leads on the final Crusader.

"Danny." He walked up to me while holding the coat my aunt had personally customized for me. It was pearly white, fitted perfectly, and was a very similar design to Michael's celestial white robe. I had tried to create the same robe made from light but to no avail. I took the coat from him and felt the warmth in it.

He stood before me, and true to their word, everyone close to me had not treated me any differently than another General of Light. Michael told me that if I wished, he would train me like a warrior.

For the last six weeks, we spent every chance we had on this mountain clearing, practicing vigorously. Izabelle had joined us about a week into it, with many protests from myself and many others. She disregarded everyone and told us it was her job to protect her King. She wanted to train and be able to fight and protect me. Her father eventually came to the idea, and she had his permission to get beaten, torn, and abused every chance we could get.

He knew that it was her choice to be a Solider of Light, and he wanted to make sure she would survive. Izabelle never complained and never wanted us to show her mercy. She wanted us to come at her with full force, and Michael did. He wanted her to be able to protect herself, but mostly, to be able to defend me when the time came.

He turned back around and went to finish dressing, and I felt another surge of happiness pass through me again. Even though the Crusaders were about to be unleashed upon the world, the last few weeks had been the best of my life. My family, Izabelle and Michael, had never been closer, and we had created beautiful memories. There was nothing hidden between us, and all sorts of secrets had come out.

My uncle had given me journals, books, and countless other writings, all from the previous Disciples of Light and Free Will. The works that captured my attention the most were from the last Disciple, Elijah, who had sacrificed his life to protect the descendants Targo had mentioned. These books held countless spells, events, wars, prayers, thoughts, and much more. My uncle had them all hidden away until I was ready to take them.

"We should get going," Izabelle said, bringing my thoughts back to the clearing. She pulled the crystal sword, which had reformed back to the silver dagger, from the tree. She gently sheathed it and placed it into her backpack. "I promised Shannon that I would relieve her from her shift in watching Jesse." She smiled as she tied her black hair into her signature ponytail, and I felt the guilt burn through me.

"Izabelle," She looked at Michael with her beautiful hazel eyes. "You were amazing today," he gave her a warm smile.

"Thank you, Michael," she smiled back, "that means a lot."

We made our way down the mountain, which took us almost half an hour until we reached the Jeep. My uncle stood against the door, wearing all white like the rest of us, but he was drinking something hot out of a mug. He looked at us and smiled.

"Did you even practice on each other, or did you just team up against the King?" He asked with warmth in his voice. I looked at Izabelle and Michael, who didn't look any different than usual except for the exhaustion in their eyes while I looked like I went through a blender.

"No, he got in a couple of hits," Michael looked at me with a sense of pride.

"Well, that's an improvement from always ending up in the dirt," Uncle Alex said as we all entered the Jeep. Izabelle and I took the back seat so we could give Michael the front with the extra legroom.

"Oh yeah, now he just ends up in the snow," Izabelle smirked at me.

"Oh, bite me." Everyone laughed as my uncle turned the Jeep back down the dirt road, and we hit the base of the mountain within twenty minutes.

"I kept an eye out for you guys, but I didn't see anything that could cause the citizens of Grenoff to be alarmed," my uncle said.

"You didn't see the blasts of fire or the lightning?" Izabelle asked.

"Nope. I didn't see anything out of the ordinary, expect maybe a couple of frightened birds."

"I guess the mayor gave us the right spot then," Michael said, and we nodded in agreement.

The mayor was a fantastic woman who was a believer in Free Will. When I met her a few weeks ago, she was very kind and understanding of our wishes. She had a section of the wilderness on Grenoff Mountain closed off so we could train.

After I told Targo to return to the Realm of Darkness, I met many believers of Free Will, and all of them were incredibly kind people. They were there the night when I found out that I was the King. Most of the town was still blind to the truth, which was fine because even I was struggling with the truth.

We pulled into the hospital, and I turned to Izabelle, who had fallen asleep.

"Uncle Alex," I turned back to my uncle, "would you take Izabelle home? She took a beating today, and I think she needs to rest. I can stand guard tonight." I looked at my own torn and beaten clothes under my coat. I could repair them, but I wouldn't have any energy for several hours.

"Of course, Danny. I brought you a quick change of clothes, just in case this happened." He pointed backward as I reached over the backseat to retrieve the backpack and changed in the back of the car. He had even packed me the diary of Elijah.

"Thank you."

"I'll join you, Danny," Michael began to get out of the car, and I placed a hand on his shoulder.

"No, Michael. Go home and sleep. You can join me in a couple of hours." Michael looked at me, and I could see the exhaustion in his eyes. He nodded, and I got out of the Jeep, relieved as my pulse had returned to normal. "I'll send Aunt Shannon down in a few minutes," I said, walking toward the hospital.

The Grenoff Hospital was a trauma center that could handle almost anything. Even for a small town, there were a lot of bizarre accidents, and many people came from across the country for our renowned surgeons.

I moved through the hospital quickly and found his room in the pediatric ward. I stood outside the room, labeled 001. I took a deep breath and walked into the room. Whenever I saw him, I felt the guilt burning hot in my gut.

Jesse lay on the hospital bed, completely still. He had been in a vegetative state since his attack, and the doctors were unsure as to why he would not wake up. Even my healing fire could not heal what was wrong with his mind. His mother planned to transfer him to a long-term care facility in Texas in the morning.

We had been guarding Jesse as much as possible in case the Crusader attempted to attack him. We still did not know the true host of the Crusader, and Henry had not made an appearance since Halloween.

I stared into the seemingly empty room, where Jesse was alone, but I knew better. I closed the door behind me and stepped toward the bed. I raised my hand, making a sweeping motion, and they came into focus.

"Hello," my aunt said with a warm smile. I looked at her, sitting in the chair that had been empty a moment ago. She was knitting a wool hat, and Alvaro sat on the bed, holding Jesse's hand.

"It's good to know that the eclipse charm is still holding." From the diaries of the Disciples, there had been a few unique charms, and this one I had cast over the room. If someone entered the room, they would see nothing but Jesse alone. They would not see anyone else unless we spoke or made contact, and then the charm would break. It was a compelling charm.

"Yeah, it seems to work really well. We had a couple of nurses come in and check on Jesse, and his mom sat with him for a while. Luckily, Alvaro is a quiet child."

She motioned to him on the bed. Alvaro was just sitting there, holding Jesse's hand and staring at him silently.

"Alex is waiting for you outside," I said softly. "I will be taking over your shift." She looked up at me and smiled.

"Izabelle fell asleep again?"

"Yeah, she took a major beating today."

"Okay, honey." My aunt packed up her stuff and grabbed Alvaro off the bed. "I will make sure Michael brings you something to eat." She gave me a one-armed hug and left without another word.

I was left alone with another person I had failed to save. I looked at Jesse, and his words echoed in my head, *Save me from the darkness.*

I sat on the bed next to him and grabbed his hand. I looked at his closed eyes and took a deep breath. I tried to reach out into his emotions, but there was nothing there. I released his hand and went to sit where my aunt had been. I pulled out the diary and, with another glance at Jesse, picked up where I had left off reading this morning.

"Danny?" His words were barely audible, but I jerked into attention after an hour or two of reading. I looked at Jesse. He had not moved an inch, but something felt different. I got to my feet and walked up to him. I took his hand as the feeling of dread washed over me.

Danny?

"Jesse?" He gripped my hand tightly.

The darkness appeared from nowhere and rapidly began to swallow the entire room. I could not move, not only because of the iron grip from Jesse's hand but also the panic in his body. I found myself in thick, swirling darkness. I stood alone as I spun around in a circle. I was again lost in a dark void.

"Where are you?" I called into the abyss.

"Help me!" Jesse's voice echoed as if it came from a great distance and seemed to be fading. I began to run in the direction of his voice.

"Jesse!" The blackness shattered.

I found myself standing in an ancient dying forest. I could barely see the bright stars above me and felt the silence encasing me. I knew I wasn't alone as I could feel countless people, thousands of broken and hurting souls around me. I looked around me, but I saw no one.

"Jesse!" This time, he didn't answer me.

I felt someone behind me, and I quickly turned around, but no one was there. I felt an icy touch on my shoulder, but when I spun around again, I was alone.

"Where am I?" I looked at the ancient forest.

"It's your fault!" The furious screams filled the night air, but I could not see those who were screaming.

"What's happening?" Goosebumps rippled across my arm, and my fire growled in dread.

"You killed us!" The voices screamed louder in the dead forest. The atmosphere in the ancient forest was alive with animosity, rage, and sorrow.

"Danny." I felt the warmth and strength in his touch, and his voice quieted the forest. I turned and looked into Michael's ever-changing eyes.

"Michael, where am I?"

"You're in the hospital room." I could see the fear in his eyes. I blinked slowly, and the forest melted away. I was still sitting on the bed, holding Jesse's hand, and Michael was gripping my shoulder. I let go of Jesse's hand, and Michael wiped away a tear on my face.

"What happened?" Without hesitation I told him about the forest and the endless around me.

"I don't know what that means, Danny, but I believe it will be important." He touched my forehead; I felt a burning pressure.

I turned to look in the window to see my reflection, and I saw the seal of the King on my forehead.

When I looked beyond my reflection and out the window, I saw the sky had turned to night, and the stars were shining brightly. I had been trapped in that forest for several hours, but it felt like minutes.

"You're right, Michael, that forest is very important."

Henry sat in a chair by the door with a slight smile. Michael put himself between us as lightning began to spark around his enclosed fist.

"Relax, Michael. I'm not here to attack your King." He raised both hands in surrender.

"Why are you here?"

"I'm here to help." I saw the conflict in Henry's eyes. We stood there in an uncomfortable silence for a few moments. The only sound in the room was from Jesse's beeping heart monitor.

"I don't believe you, Henry," Michael took another step towards him.

"You don't, but your King does." I looked into his eyes, and I saw the truth in them, even though he was uncertain if this was the right move.

"Why do you want to help us?"

"I guess, consider it a thank you for forgiving me of my crimes." Another high beep came from Jesse's monitor. "To show my thanks, I am willing to give you information that will either give you a chance to save the final child or be prepared for the second Crusader's plan. It's your choice." Jesse's heart monitor beeped quicker in the silence.

"Do you mean that forest has something to do with the second Crusader?"

"Yes," I could see the fear in his eyes as his fingers twitched. "Honestly, it's an atrocious plan." The disgust was evident in his tone. He looked me in the eye, and the truth echoed in them. "I can tell you about it, or I can give you the name of the final child and attempt to prevent the rising. It's your choice, Danny." He gave me a cocky smile, but fear illuminated his brown eyes.

"I'm sure this won't end well for you, Henry."

"No. I know Phantonix and Ieiunium will not be pleased with me," he shrugged. "However, I want you to know that I am grateful that you gave me the choice, even though I still believe in Destiny. Your kindness did not go unappreciated, and I know it would not be the same if the tables were reversed." Michael gave me a look, and I knew what he wanted to ask, but we needed to focus on the present.

"Who is the final child, Henry?"

He sighed as he put his head in his hands and began to breathe deeply. Fear came off of him in waves, and he looked back up at me. His eyes shined with horror, but he quickly composed himself.

"I was hoping you would choose Metentis' plan," he shuddered. "It's the foundation of where nightmares come from."

He raised his hand, and darkness swirled next to him. A small oval doorway to the Realm of Darkness opened between us, and it moved as if it breathed. He moved toward the portal as if he were getting ready to leave. Black, purple, and green smoke swirled around the outer edges toward the middle.

I stared at the doorway to darkness, and an icy cold touched my skin. I felt my fire respond to its chilly attack as a warning bell went off in my mind.

I looked into the swirling depths, and an image appeared in the void.

"What?" I could see a decimated city, and I felt people around me. I wanted to look for them, but my eyes found Michael, who knelt before me. He wore white armor, and the seal of the King shone on his forehead, as two rainbows seemed to be emanating from his back, and in his outstretched hands, he held a broken object. Tears were sliding down his face as if his last hope had failed.

"Michael," I moved toward him. His eyes met mine, but his gaze quickly shifted behind me. When I turned around, I gasped. I found myself standing a few feet away from the doorway to darkness on the other side of the portal, the hospital room waiting for me.

"Michael?" I called him, and I realized how different his face was. He looked to be in his late twenties or early thirties. His black hair was short, and his thick black beard highlighted his honey-golden eyes. I was taken aback because Michael's eyes never stayed one color. My mind went into gridlock as I stared at him, and he smiled back at me as a silver object in his hand began to burn like a star.

"Danny!" It wasn't the man kneeling in front of me that spoke in a panicked voice. His inviting arms grabbed me from behind. I struggled in fear until I realized the younger Michael was trying to pull me back into the hospital room. All I could see was the older Michael, still kneeling before me, looking broken as he tried to tell me something.

"What?!" But it was too late as the scene from the portal disappeared, and I was back in the hospital room.

"Are you okay?" The younger Michael touched my face.

"D-did you see that?"

"See what?" he asked, "All I saw was you standing in darkness." His multicolored eyes showed fear, and I felt something dreadful was on the horizon.

"What was that?!" I turned to Henry, who looked at me with a shocked expression.

"No one has ever seen anything in the doorway to darkness. Whatever you saw, it can't be good for you." His eyes were wide, and something inside me told me I was the only one who saw it.

I stepped away from the darkness as apprehension burned in my veins because I had seen something I was not meant to see, something I really hoped would not come to pass.

Henry looked at us, and after the brief moment of confusion, he seemed to have put his mind back on track. He turned away from us as he pulled up his black hood. He spoke quietly, but his words were heavy.

"Danny, the final child is Alvaro Elikai." With those words, he disappeared into the darkness, and my blood ran cold.

Chapter XX

Alex's Secret

~Danny Elikai~

The Jeep sped down the road as I tried desperately to call my aunt and uncle, but I kept getting an error message. Michael and I had run out of the hospital, making sure the charm was still in place to protect Jesse. My uncle had lent Michael his Jeep so we would not have to walk home in the middle of the night.

We had to get to Alvaro and protect him before the Crusader could get to him. Fear burned hot in my body as we arrived at the house, drenched in panicked sweat, but everything looked normal. I threw myself out of the Jeep, ran up the stairs, and almost broke the front door as I tried to open it. The house smelled like my aunt's cooking, and I ran into the foyer.

"Aunt Shannon! Uncle Alex! Izabelle!" My voice boomed through the quiet house, and to my relief, all three appeared from different parts of the house. They all looked worried. Michael had walked through the door and stood behind me.

"What's wrong?" my uncle said from upstairs. Izabelle had come out of the study, and my aunt had run out of the living room.

"Where is Alvaro?"

"I just put him down for the night." He started coming down the stairs.

"You need to go get him. Now." The authority was clear in my voice.

"Danny, what's going on?" My aunt's voice was filled with fear.

"Alvaro is the final child. He is a Crusader! He is Daimonas." The truth had hit me in the car, and the ground beneath us shook violently. I turned back to look out of the open door, and what I saw took my breath away. A beautiful white shield surrounded the house, and the shield was cracking.

"That must be the protection that Elijah had placed to protect the descendants," my uncle said as the shield shook again, and the cracks began to spread violently. "I think the first Crusader has finally arrived." He stood next to me, his gaze transfixed on the shattering shield.

"Yes," a high-pitched, monstrous voice said from behind us, and we all spun around and saw him standing on the top of the stairs wearing his favorite pajamas, the ones with the yellow fire trucks. The trucks matched his glowing canary yellow eyes.

"Alvaro."

"I tried to warn you, Danny. Now it is too late. The first Crusader is here." His voice chilled the atmosphere, and I felt the shield crack again. For a split second, I looked out the front door to witness it. The shield had crumbled and disappeared, leaving us exposed to the powers of Destiny. Standing in the street was a hooded figure with darkness surrounding him.

Izabelle and Michael charged the Crusader without hesitation at the same time. Izabelle pulled the silver dagger from its sheath, and the shimmering crystal blade formed. Michael's white robe appeared in a flash as he hurled lightning at the Crusader. I turned to face Alvaro while Uncle Alex grabbed his wife, who was sobbing and pulled her from sight.

"You have a choice, Alvaro," I had to convenience my cousin. "I know the truth. You can still stand in the Light. You don't have to join Destiny." I was trying to remain calm, but Alvaro did not look at me. His yellow eyes were focused on the fight outside.

"You continue to fail in your understanding, Danny," Alvaro began to slowly walk down the steps as if he had all the time in the world. "I remember now. I remember everything, and I know who I am. My true memories have returned to me, and I can see the truth."

I was horrified as I watched Alvaro's skin become transparent and begin to reshape itself. The formless mass grew until it was seven feet tall, as the transparent liquid began to solidify into dark green scales.

His massive hands were topped with razor-sharp black claws, and a long narrow tail curled around his chest. His mustard-yellow eyes held malice and cruelty. The laughter felt abnormal as a long tongue licked his razor-sharp teeth. The Crusader Daimonas loomed before me, and the shredded remains of Alvaro's pajamas were at his scaled feet.

I pulled my fire into my left fist. The burning sword that formed was feeble due to my exhaustion but my apprehension of harming a family member.

"Even your celestial fire knows it's too late, Danny."

"I don't want to fight you, Alvaro," I stepped into a defensive position. "You're my family!"

"That is truer than you know, Danny," he hissed.

"Alvaro!" My uncle broke the tense atmosphere as he walked through the hallway. I glanced at him, and I saw he looked not only terrified, but ashamed, and I saw the guilt eating away at his heart. There was something there, something like a broken promise.

"Hello, Father," Daimonas said without taking his eyes off me.

"I am so sorry, I failed you, son." He ran down the stairs with alarming speed and grabbed Uncle Alex by his throat. His black claws broke the skin, and tiny drops of blood escaped down his back.

"Your feeble attempts to protect me have failed. The Elikai bloodline is tainted. You saw to that, and it is because of you that we will rise!" He threw my uncle through the wall leading to the living room, his blood staining the floor.

"What do you mean it's his fault?"

I had been trying to walk around him slowly, but his tail collided with my jaw, and I was hurled across the floor, landing on my leg. The shattering of my jaw and my right leg left me paralyzed with immense pain on the floor as Daimonas laughed harder.

"When you became the King of Light on Halloween night, did you not see the stains upon his heart?" I could feel him standing over me, his raw power and hot breath washing over me, but my vision kept blurring out. "Or were you too distracted trying to save that misguided and easily corruptible plaything that Ieiunium has?"

"You mean Henry?" He grabbed me by the throat and raised me to eye level, my legs dangling freely. My vision came back at the wrong time, and I stared into his yellow snakelike eyes.

"You can still come back. We're family!" I forced the words out with great difficulty through my broken jaw and the strangling force crushing my windpipe.

"Family is the reason that I will not kill you or your soldiers tonight."

A flash of lightning appeared from the doorway and hit Alvaro, but it didn't cause any damage. The lightning danced around his scaly body and then ricocheted back at Michael. His own lightning blasted him into a wall, and Daimonas chuckled in amusement.

"There is only one General of Free Will that can harm me. Unfortunately, for you, Michael, that is not you." Daimonas looked at me. "Gather your wounded and prepare, Danny. The end of Free Will is finally at hand."

He dropped me to the ground on my broken leg, and pain shot through me, leaving me gasping for air. I gritted my teeth because I knew I still had to fight; I had to stop him. I had to save him or die trying.

I crawled across the floor. I watched as his illusion disappeared, and his body became translucent again. Daimonas returned to the diminutive form of Alvaro, who walked out the door. I crawled to the front door, and I saw the Crusader hold Izabelle by the throat, ready to strike.

"Enough, Ieiunium." I watched as the first Crusader looked at the small child and obeyed without question. He released Izabelle, who crumbled on the brick walkway.

"Did you spill the blood of your father?" I heard Ieiunium's voice, and its deep familiarity rang in the night air.

"It has been done," Alvaro held out his bloody hand.

"What about their hearts?" Ieiunium turned to look at Izabelle on the ground, and I could feel the desire on his lips.

"They are not to be harmed. Phantonix has told you this," Alvaro commanded, and Ieiunium almost seemed to cower under his command. Without another word, he took Alvaro's hand, and they disappeared into the surrounding darkness.

"Izabelle!" I desperately tried to crawl out of the front door. I knew Michael was unconscious in the house after he had taken a direct blast from his lightning, but he was not too badly harmed from being thrown into a wall. I could hear Aunt Shannon taking care of Alex, who was sobbing in the living room. I knew I had to heal Izabelle. Slowly crawling down the front porch and across the lawn, I finally reached her. I painfully forced my legs into a seated position, and I put her head on my uninjured leg.

"I am not important, Danny. Use the remainder of your strength to heal yourself. I will be okay." Her voice was almost a whisper, but I knew it was not true. "I held him off. I protected you."

"You were amazing," I nodded as my fire entered her body. There was not much damage except for a couple of broken bones and some internal bleeding. I felt the relief flood through me as the fire finished healing her.

"Can I sleep now?"

"We have to get you back in the house." My beaten body could not carry her. Michael was lying motionless on the floor inside the house, and my powers were almost drained again. I could not fix my body now. I knew that we could not stay exposed like this, no matter what Daimonas said. I had a feeling that Ieiunium would come back as soon as possible.

Please, help me, I closed my eyes and called out to them with my heart. *I need your help.*

"Hello, Danny." I looked up in response to the deep Scottish voice, as he wore the white robe of a General of Free Will.

"Hello, Conall." The guy pulled down his hood, and I stared into his light hazel eyes. I had never met him, but I knew him the second I saw him. He had been there the night I discovered I was the King of Free Will. He could not have been older than me, but he already looked like a fully grown man, with his solid ox build and a thick red beard that matched his short red hair.

"My King." He knelt on one knee, and a tear fell down his face, and his smile was luminous. I had the feeling he was the type who did not cry often.

"Please, I need you to bring her into the house."

He looked at my broken leg, and without another word, he gently picked up Izabelle and me into his steely arms. He moved us gracefully and delicately as if our weight didn't even register to him. He moved around the house, almost like he had already been there, and went into Alex's office. He sat me down on an office chair by the window and placed Izabelle on a futon that Alex slept on when he was in the doghouse.

"Thank you, Conall."

"My King," he bowed deeply without his knees touching the floor. "It is my absolute pleasure to be here with you and to serve you in any way I can."

"Please, Conall, do not bow to me."

"I will kneel before my King."

"Alright," I did not want to argue with him after he saved us. "I could use your help with the rising of the Crusaders." He smiled and raised himself up so he could touch my face. The look in his eyes told me he could not believe he was here with me.

"You have everyone you need. It is not my time to join you, Danny. I will soon trust me. One day, I will be by your side forever." He smiled.

"I don't understand."

"The other Generals have work to do before we join you, my King. Many of us are not yet worthy to stand with you." The shame consumed his eyes. "While we are your Generals, some of our faiths have crumbled. We must rebuild our foundation again before we are worthy to stand by your side."

He turned toward the front door and pointed toward the living room, where Michael remained unconscious. I could feel the regret that surrounded his heart. "His faith never waned. His heart is the example we strive for. He is worthy to stand with you. He is all you need for the moment. But I promise you, I soon will be worthy."

"You are worthy," I reached forward in the chair and hugged him. I felt joy burning bright in his beautiful heart, and when I pulled away, he had disappeared.

"I will see you soon, Conall," I said to the space where he had just been.

I looked at Izabelle, who rested peacefully on the futon. The exhaustion I felt threatened to drag me unconscious, but I needed to protect my family from the darkness that threatened to return. I also needed the truth about what my uncle had done to cause this.

I wheeled myself in the office chair out of the room and closed the front door. I closed my eyes and focused. I had to seal the house. I had to use the rest of my energy to protect them, to keep them alive. I trusted Alvaro, since he spared us this time, due to our being family, but I did not trust Ieiunium.

I tried to create the shield, but I could barely hold myself up. My powers had been completely drained, and I could not seal the house.

"Please," I said again, and no one answered except for that small, beautiful lullaby. I turned around and watched a soft light escape from Michael's pocket.

I wheeled to where Michael was lying unconscious. I reached into his pocket, and I felt the warmth of the locket. I held it in both hands as it slowly opened. This time, the raw power of light didn't overtake me. The beautiful white light touched my entire body, and I felt its warmth emanating within me. It restored my energy and healed my broken leg and jaw. I felt the fire roar back to life in my veins with full force. The locket's lullaby seemed to reach Michael, and he opened his eyes.

"My King." He was in awe and joy.

"Stay there," I got to my feet as I raised the locket. The light spread until it touched everything in the house. It illuminated the shattered wall and everyone in the house. I let the light restore everything and everyone. I held the locket even higher as my fire encased it, and the combined power created a shield around the house. I sealed the protection with the promise that nothing under Destiny's banner would enter this house again unless invited. The light faded back into the locket, and it closed itself. I put it in my pocket.

"Thank you, Danny," Michael groggily got to his feet, and I looked into his eyes. Even though the light had healed him, I could see how physically and emotionally exhausted he was.

"You should go to bed, Michael."

"I'm okay."

"Michael, please go to bed. I need to talk to my uncle alone." He looked into my eyes and then nodded, then walked up the stairs and sat on the top step. Even in his exhausted state, he would still protect me.

I took a deep breath and turned to the living room. When I walked in, I saw my uncle lying on the couch. I knew the power in the locket had healed him, but he looked broken. My aunt sat next to him, crying into her hands. His electric green eyes found mine, his blonde hair and beard were stained with blood, and I could see the shame burning bright in them.

"Alex, what did he mean when he said, 'the Elikai bloodline is tainted?'"

"I... I knew... I knew Alvaro was a Crusader," he put his face into his hands. I felt my fire roar in anger, and my breath caught in my chest.

"What?!" Aunt Shannon looked stunned.

"It happened a long time ago," he began, and I could feel the regret radiating from him. "It was when we found out that Shannon couldn't bear children. I felt defeated and that I wasn't meant to be a father. I went to the local bar and started drinking." Tears began to fall down his face. "There was a beautiful woman there. I had never seen her before, and she made me feel special.

"The next thing I knew, we were back in her hotel room. That night, I broke my commitment to my wife and to the light," he said, looking at me. "I slept with her, and afterward, I fell asleep. When I woke up the next morning, she was nowhere to be found, and I knew what I had to do. I went home and confessed what I had done to Shannon. She, by the grace of light, forgave me and gave me a second chance." He looked at his wife, and she touched his face. I saw the unconditional love in her eyes and her heart.

"It was about nine months later when we received a phone call," she began, but Uncle Alex grabbed her hand.

"I need to finish," he told her, and he turned back to me. "We received the call that my son had been born and that his mother had died in childbirth. She had put me down as the emergency contact and noted me as the child's father. We drove to New York, and when they showed me the body of the woman, I knew it was her. I knew at that moment that the child had to be mine.

"We met the child, and when he looked at me, his eyes flashed yellow. They performed a paternity test and confirmed what I had felt in my heart: Alvaro was my son. We took him home, and Shannon adopted him, and he became part of our family. I was so overjoyed that we were blessed with a child that nothing could break that happiness.

"However, Alvaro began to change when your parents and Matthew died. When Shannon told me what he had shown you, it only confirmed my dread. When we found out about the descendants, I began to dig into his mother's past. I found the last descendant on record and checked it with the books you have, and I found it. She was a direct descendant of a man named Otto. I knew then that he was one of them." Shannon wore a shocked expression as he spoke, with my fury burning in her eyes.

"Why didn't you tell us?"

"I was afraid!" He began sobbing into his hands. "I didn't want anything to harm our son."

"We could have protected him better! Our son is gone, and you knew the truth!" She slapped him across the face, and my anger disappeared.

"Aunt Shan-Shannon!"

"What did you think was going to happen!?" Her anger burned so hotly it looked like she was going to burn him to ash. "That the King was going to destroy him? Or that we would disown him? Danny and Michael could have protected him! Danny is the King of Free

Will! You should have trusted him, and you should have trusted me! He could have saved our son!" She slapped him again, even harder than the first time. My uncle just sat there because he knew he had failed.

"Aunt Shannon," I was trying to show a level head, "that's enough." She looked at me angrily and nodded.

"Yes, my King." She quickly walked out of the room. I knew how much inner strength it took to turn and walk away. Uncle Alex continued to sit there, holding himself as tears streamed down his face.

"I understand what you were trying to do." I tried not to let my anger get the best of me right now. "However, you should have told me. Aunt Shannon was right; we could have protected Alvaro. We could have done more before it was too late." He looked up at me, and I could see the shame in his eyes.

"I am sorry, my King." My uncle fell to his knees and continued to sob. I got to my knees with him and pulled him into a hug, and I let him sob into my chest until he calmed down.

"Please, save my son," he pulled out of the hug, and I looked into his green eyes. I could see the desperation, regret, and pain. "Save him from Phantonix."

I knelt in front of my uncle, the man who withheld critical information from me, who had known for weeks that his son was a Crusader. He wanted to do what he could to protect him.

I could see his belief in me, but the fear for his son's safety overshadowed his faith in Free Will.

"I will try to save Alvaro."

"Thank you." I placed a hand on his shoulder.

I got to my feet and walked out of the room into the kitchen to allow him privacy and to let him pull himself back together.

I knew where I would find my aunt, but as I walked through the kitchen, the phone rang. I looked at it, I looked at the time, and I knew it was not going to be good news. I reached out and picked up the phone.

"Hello?"

"Hello. My name is Ruth, and I am a nurse at the Grenoff Memorial Hospital. I was hoping to speak to Sheriff Elikai?" The voice was kind, but it sounded urgent.

"My uncle is currently indisposed. Can I take a message?" I turned away from the living room, so he could not hear me.

"Son, I am sorry, but this is urgent. I *really* need to speak to Sheriff Elikai." She sounded on the verge of panic as she emphasized the word 'really.'

"Hold on, I'll see if he's available." I walked back into the living room. My uncle was getting to his feet, wiping away the tears.

"A nurse from the hospital is on the line for you, Sheriff," I held out the phone to him. He grabbed it and answered professionally. I waited a few seconds and watched the fear spread in his bright green eyes.

"I will be right there." He hung up the phone and looked at me.

"What's going on?" The dread was tight in my gut.

"Jesse is missing."

Chapter XXI

The First Crusader

~Danny Elikai~

The Crusaders of Destiny will rise at the Winter Solstice. Come, King of Free Will, to where you allowed true love to perish and bear witness to the fall of your regime.

I stared at the message written in blood that had been waiting for me in Jesse's hospital room. I could not take my eyes off it. The hospital staff tried frantically to explain how a comatose young man could be kidnapped under their watch. My uncle had spent several hours trying to figure out what had happened, even though we both knew the truth. The evidence had been written in blood.

I had not moved since we arrived. I saw blood on the sheets and the wall. I stood there while a nurse consoled a distraught Mrs. Daniels as the mayor and my uncle talked. I was there all night, unable to take my eyes off the warning.

I looked at the rising sun and knew I would have to face them tonight. Uncle Alex was right; I could not stop the rise of the Crusaders, because I could not force them to change their hearts. They had to choose to come back to the light. Alvaro proved to me that they all had decided.

The door to the hospital room opened, but my eyes could not be taken away from the warning.

"We know what we have to do now." I turned and looked at Michael as his beautiful voice filled the room. He stood in the doorway and looked at me, his black hair reflecting purple highlights in the sunlight.

"What is it we have to do, Michael?"

"It's simple, Danny." He came to stand by me and took my hand into his, and it steadied my heart. "We are going to stop the rise of the Crusaders." I couldn't help but laugh because he made it sound as if it was no more challenging than riding a bike.

"How do you suggest we do that? Just go in, guns blazing?" I turned towards him, and my stomach hitched into my chest.

"Yes, we could go in gun blazing, or we could stall the ritual. We could figure out how to disrupt it or even try to save just one child." His eyes never left mine, not even to look at the blood on the wall.

"You make it sound so easy."

"I know it will not be easy, Danny, but we must try at least, right?"

"Do you truly believe we can stop this?" He smiled.

"I believe in you. You are the light of my world, and together we can do this. You never know, maybe all it takes is a simple act."

"Or we can just kill the Crusader," Izabelle stated as she walked into the room. Her hair was tied up, and she wore clothes that made her look like she was ready for a fight. She twirled the silver dagger in her free hand.

"Let's use that as the worst-case scenario." I hoped it would never come to that.

Izabelle read the message on the wall, '*The fall of your regime.*'

"'Come, King of Free Will, to the place where you allowed true love to perish,'" Michael added.

"Where did you let true love die, Danny?" Izabelle winked at me.

"Star Cliff," I responded slowly as the memory of Austin and Lily returned to me. "The Crusaders will be unleashed on Star Cliff."

"Then what are we standing around for? Let's go!" Izabelle looked ready for war.

"No, Michael is right. If we can stop this, we don't want to give them time to undo it. We have to do it during the ritual. We have to be there at just the right time," I said. I sat down on the plush armchair near the bloody bed.

"So, we just sit here and wait?" Izabelle threw her hands up as Michael moved a wooden chair and sat down.

"Yes, we will have to wait." She nodded as she sat down to my left.

We sat in the bloodstained room, and no one seemed to be bothered by us, even though many people came in and out of the room. I was unsure how long we sat there, but I knew I had fallen asleep for a few hours. My mind needed to rest, and I needed the comfort of oblivion.

When I woke up, I saw that Izabelle and Michael were asleep too. We all knew what we would have to do, and we needed to rest. I looked at the clock in the room and knew it was finally time.

"We need to get going," I got to my feet, and Izabelle and Michael woke up. I looked out the window up at the sky and knew this was the last sunset when the world would still be at peace.

"Tonight will decide the future and when the end begins," I turned to look at my friends. "Are you ready?" They nodded, and we set off toward Star Cliff.

****

Snow covered the ground, but the sky was clear as we walked toward the cliff where the Generals of Destiny waited. We walked past the courtyard with the black bell tower, and I could not help but think about the last few months in my head. Everything I had learned and what was still to come made me want to run home and hide under my bed. I kept walking, though, because the three of us were the only people who had a chance to stop the rise of Destiny. I was glad the other Generals were not here with us. In case we did not make it out alive, there would still be others who could take on the Crusaders.

I thought about the other Generals as we approached the entrance to the path that led up the steep hill. I knew they were with us in spirit, and I could feel them with me at that moment. I felt Matthew, my aunt and uncle, my mother, and even the host of light watching us.

The Crusaders would be unleashed within the hour as the sun dropped and we approached the path.

"You know, six months ago, if you had told me that we would meet the Generals of Destiny and that I was the King of Free Will, I would have thought you were insane."

"We all had to find out when we were ready," Michael said. "We can do this, Danny."

I looked at him and nodded. "I am glad to be here with you both. You are truly the best, and I don't think I would want anyone else with me as we go toward the beginning of the end."

"I'm glad we're in this together," Izabelle said as she hugged me. Michael wrapped his arms around both of us, and we stood there holding each other for another moment before the task ahead of us drove us apart.

"Let's go," Michael said, and without another word, we walked a few steps up the path to meet the Crusaders of Destiny.

The minute we set foot onto the path, the darkness consumed the entrance, and there was nowhere to go but up.

"Well, that's a good sign." I laughed at her sarcasm.

I turned away and began to walk up the path, my heart thundering in my chest. We walked in step up the hill, and the memory of when I had made this trek swam before my vision. It was the night of Claire's funeral when I had first met Michael and the other Generals of Light. Now we were to bear witness to the rise of the Generals of Darkness.

The silence overtook us as an eerie feeling washed over me, and I could feel thousands of eyes watching us. I watched as the darkness around us began to manipulate and disfigure the beautiful surroundings into a vision from a nightmare. The trees began to rot, and a dense fog spilled down over the ground. The clear sky overhead was blotted out with dark purple storm clouds.

"They know we're coming," I said as we approached the top.

"Do you think it's a trap?" Michael asked, and not even a moment later, we knew the answer.

Henry stood at the entrance, now framed with two massive and rotting trees blocking the cliff from view.

"Where is Alvaro?!" He just leaned against one of the trees and gave a small smile.

"They're all here." He motioned behind him to the cliff that overlooked Grenoff. "I was convinced you wouldn't show up, but Phantonix disagreed," Henry said softly.

He held out his hand, and a small black ball of darkness formed. He raised it toward us, and without warning, the darkness blasted out in a wave of black and purple. Michael moved quickly, forming a white shield that reflected the blast. The darkness was thrown into a tree, and the earsplitting noise reverberated around us.

When Michael dropped the shield, Henry had already started to charge, and his black sword slashed the front of Michael's chest.

Blood began pouring from the wound that reached from his left hip to his right shoulder. Michael staggered back, and Henry moved to strike again.

In desperation, I turned and sent a blast of fire at him, but he dodged it with a quick backflip. He landed on his feet near the tree where he stood when we arrived. For the first time since knowing Henry, I finally saw a playful, genuine smile on his face.

"You may enter now." Henry turned and walked past the clearing.

I was stunned until I heard Michael's sharp gasp. I turned back and saw him lying on the ground. His wound glistened with swirling darkness, and the pool of blood was growing around him.

"I-I...can't...move," he said through clenched teeth.

Izabelle and I ran toward him. I let the fire rip out to heal him, but when I placed my fiery hand on the wound, the darkness began to crawl up my arm and quenched my fire. I pulled away quickly and looked at Michael.

I tried again, but even though the darkness consumed my hand, I kept my hand on his chest. I knew I could heal him, but pain ripped through me. I pulled my hand back again and looked into Michael's eyes.

"Don't worry," Henry's voice echoed down from the hilltop, "it won't kill him. It's just a paralyzing agent. The darkness is there to stop you from healing him until after the Solstice." The darkness seemed to amplify his voice. "Trust me; a few Crusaders want to get their turn at Michael." I could hear his playful tone as if he knew the truth I did not quite understand.

"Go," Michael said painfully, "stop them." I turned to Izabelle, who stood next to us with the crystal sword out and ready.

"I need you, Michael." I grabbed his hand.

"No, Danny, you'll be fine. Izabelle can protect you until I figure out a way to move." Michael tried to smile, but I could see the rage and conflict in his eyes. He did not want to let me go without him by my side, but I could not heal him.

"Don't worry, Michael, I'll protect him," Izabelle said confidently, and I got to my feet.

"I will be fine," he winced. "Go."

I turned back to the entrance and began walking. I didn't want to leave Michael behind, but time was running out. The silence around us was deafening as we approached the two ancient dead trees that stood like a gate protecting the cliff. We were just about to step through when Henry's bloodcurdling scream filled the silence. Izabelle and I ran past the trees and around the corner, only to stop dead in our tracks—the sight before us made our blood go cold.

The seal of the Crusaders burned on the ground. It was a seven-pointed star in front of an unbroken circle. The bases of the seven points were interwoven, making it look like a blooming flower. Six unconscious children were floating around the basin, the Crusader's symbol shining brightly on their heads in different colors. Alvaro's was yellow, while the others were maroon, magenta, emerald, rust orange, and royal blue.

However, the children or the symbols didn't make us stop cold—it was him. He stood in black robes, his arm almost elbow-deep into Henry's chest. He looked up and smiled at me.

"Howdy, Danny!" he called with his thick Southern accent as he pulled Henry's heart out of his body. Henry crumbled to the ground, and Jesse leaned against a black stone basin, holding Henry's heart. He was soaked to the elbow in blood.

"What took y'all so long?" To my disgust, he took a bite out of the heart like it was an apple.

"No," I heard Izabelle say in horror, as I felt a scream rising in my throat.

"Hey, Izzy! I didn't expect to see you here." His mouth was full of heart, and his teeth glistened with blood when he smiled.

I felt Izabelle shudder and recoil under his navy-blue gaze, and my stomach dropped to my toes. We stared as Jesse continued eating Henry's heart. I felt my mouth drop open in disbelief as blood ran from his lips to his chin.

"You look a little stunned. Don't worry; it'll pass." He took another bloody bite. He reveled in the taste of another's heart. He looked at it and dropped the half-eaten heart into the basin.

"I'm sorry," he wiped away the blood from his lips with a white handkerchief, "I've been waitin' a long time to taste his heart." He smiled another bloody smile.

"I don't understand." My mind was slowly returning to me, but it barely made sense. "What's going on?"

"Danny, please don't be dense. It's elementary. I'm not Jesse; I'm Ieiunium, the first Crusader!" I noticed he no longer had a Southern drawl to his voice. "Well, technically, this meat suit isn't." He indicated his body, but my brain went into gridlock again. "You still seem confused." He leaned against the basin, smiled, and his eyes flashed a haunting pale gaze.

"No! I refuse to believe you! Jesse is a believer in the light!" Izabelle's disbelief brought me back to reality.

"Yes, I know all about Jesse's beliefs, emotions, and thoughts. I've had to endure them for months." He rolled his eyes as if the memories annoyed him. "You see, I needed a body that could easily penetrate the defenses set forth by Elijah. I tried many hosts over the last several decades, but none seemed to work. I had almost given up hope, but then I found Jesse." He touched his chest where his heart was. "His heart was so pure that I could easily hide my true essence behind it," Ieiunium said gleefully.

"If Jesse's heart was pure, why did he let you in?"

"Danny, you already know Jesse's little secret." He waved a finger at me. "I'm surprised you didn't tell anyone, not even our dear Izabelle."

My mind went back to the day at the lake, the day he broke up with Izabelle. He had told me he was living a lie and could not handle it anymore—he was gay. However, a different thought about that day crossed my mind.

"On the cliff, were you telling me something about Jesse or yourself?" I asked accusingly. "When were you talking about making other people happy and being different than everyone around you, about living a lie and being judged by others?" The venom was now evident in my voice. "Was that about Jesse being gay, or are you manipulating him to Destiny?!"

"Both, Danny. I told you Jesse's little secret while still expressing my discomfort in the light, my hatred of you and your followers. When I met Jesse, I told him if he allowed me in, I could cure him. I could make him 'normal.'" He emphasized his point with air quotes and another roll of his eyes.

"Danny," Izabelle touched my arm, and I turned to look at her. "What is he talking about?"

"I'm sorry, Izabelle," I turned back to Ieiunium. "He believed you?!"

"Yes, he believed me," he rose his arms in triumph. "He let me into his heart when he was weak, and I took over. I manipulated him, and I broke him. When he had lost all hope, I told him there was nothing sinful or abnormal about him. I told him that the King of Light wouldn't care who another loves and that he was created this way. His heart crumbled, and his body became mine completely."

"What are you talking about?!" Izabelle screamed, but he merely shrugged and looked at me expectantly.

"You were playing him this whole time." My words were flat and lacked emotion. "You preyed upon his worst fears, deepest insecurities, and desire to be normal? You promised him you would cure him of his homosexuality when you only wanted to control his body?!" The rage exploded out of me with every word and the disgust at the monster before me.

"There was nothing wrong with who he was, and you broke him! You made him feel disgusting like he was an abomination when there was nothing wrong with him!"

I broke away from Izabelle as the fire exploded out of my hand, forming a recurve bow. I pulled back on the fire string as a flaming arrow appeared in the notch. I released the burning arrow, trained at his heart. Ieiunium did not flinch as the flaming arrow sped toward him, and I knew it would hit its mark. The fire exploded before it hit him, revealing an invisible shield before fizzling away.

"Did you really think we would not protect them from your interference?" After I looked a little closer, I could see the slight discoloration around the barrier.

"How long have you been inside, Jesse?" Izabelle asked painfully.

"About a month before I started dating you, Izzy," he winked with a cruel smile. I looked up at Izabelle, who had hot tears streaming down her angry face. "You see, King of Free Will, I needed Jesse to enter the descendants' houses, be around the children, and show them the truth slowly. I needed to be someone people trusted and allowed into their homes. I needed someone even you could trust. Danny." Everything came into focus, and I knew he had played us all. He had been there this whole time, babysitting Alvaro and being in class with me. He had even been one of my closest friends. I saw the truth pour in over the last few months.

"You know, Jesse almost gave me away. I had lost control after Henry attacked me, and Jesse slipped out. He told you to protect him from the darkness." The fire in my veins and my hands died away.

I had failed to realize the truth right in front of me, and I had failed Jesse. I fell to the ground in shock and complete disarray.

"I knew then I could not allow him to continue to share his body in case Jesse told you the full truth. Once I was secure in the hospital and regained control, I gave Jesse's soul to Henry and ordered him to throw it into the Forest of the Fallen, where he would rot for eternity in misery!" His cold laughter echoed through the night, and I stared in revulsion.

"My plan has worked perfectly." Ieiunium turned around and looked at the other six Crusaders of Destiny. "I have been using different hearts, different faces to keep you and your believers off my trail. Your brother played into my trap the night he died when I used the face of his friend Nick. Incidentally, Nick led me to Jesse."

"Why did Henry try to kill you if your plan worked perfectly?" I looked at the dead body at his feet as the rage sparked the fire in my heart.

"I hate to have to admit this, Danny, but I was not as strong as I initially thought. The plan was for me to stand by your side until the ritual began, but I grew tired. I could no longer stand your company; I could not tolerate being your friend. I could no longer pretend to have respect for the King of Free Will. The days passed, and I watched as you pulled yourself out of your depression and self-hate and turned into the young man who would soon discover the truth. My hatred toward you grew, and I knew I could no longer keep up the act.

"Once you found out you were the King, there was a chance you would be able to look past Jesse's heart and see me hiding behind his light. I asked Phantonix for guidance, and he agreed to have Henry attack me, and my timing was impeccable. I was safe in the hospital when you discovered the truth that night, and Jesse's body was devastated by the attack. I had regained full control and could remain in hiding as a comatose patient. I was still able to communicate orders to those around me, and when you cast your eclipse charm, I altered it so it would appear that Jesse was still there.

"However, I knew time was growing short, and I had to tell Alvaro the truth and help him remember. I did not want to heal Jesse or to be in your company, and I began to panic. My chance came when I saw Shannon bringing him to the hospital. Alvaro held Jesse's hand, and I told him everything."

"You bastard!" Izabelle charged.

"Izabelle! No!" I screamed, but I was too late. She let her anger get the best of her and slammed into the barrier. Ieiunium laughed as he walked up to where Izabelle lay bleeding on the ground, dazed from striking the barrier.

"Poor Izzy," he looked down at her. "I forgot to tell you how much I enjoyed playing you along. I enjoyed watching you fall for a man who could truly never love you. If it weren't for me, this miserable little faggot would never have even given you the time of day. I knew how you felt about him and how important you would be to Danny. It was too perfect, Izabelle.

"I relished that it was a General of Destiny that kissed you, held you, who you confided in, who you loved. The betrayal you feel made the whole thing worth it. You will make my victory so sweet, and I cannot wait to taste it, so I have to thank you." He winked at her, and she glared at him. I could feel the anger and betrayal from several yards away.

"I wish you could have seen the turmoil and conflict that Jesse felt every time he looked at Michael." He pointed beyond the trees where Michael was bleeding out. "If only you knew how Jesse's heart fluttered when Michael spoke or when he thought of him. It ate away at him every day, and he felt so ashamed. I cannot recall a time I had more fun!" He turned away from us.

"We will stop you!"

"No, you won't, Danny. I have already added the final ingredient." His eyes fell on Henry's body and then back to me. "My brothers and sisters are about to be unleashed, and then Creation will be laid to waste."

"Henry was the last ingredient?" The anger was burning so hot it threatened to burn me alive.

"Henry was a critical piece that I needed. When Johanna sacrificed herself, her heart turned from darkness to light. However, I'm sure you know all about that, Danny." He looked at me with a knowing smile, and I felt my stomach fall again.

Does he know about Targo? My mind panicked as his smile sent a rippling fear through me. Regardless, he continued as my fear intensified.

"To complete the ritual and allow the rest of the Crusaders to rise, I needed to undo her sacrifice. I had been grooming him for a long time. I prepared him and allowed him to believe he was important. I gave him a fraction of my power, lent him my cloak to disguise him, and ordered him to do what I could not. Then, he was surrounded by your light when you found out you were the King, and he still chose Destiny. His heart was the heart of someone who had looked upon the King of Free Will and still chose Destiny, which is rare. Henry was a piece of the final ritual. He didn't know, of course. He thought he would stand with us until the end.

"All I wanted was his weak, pathetic heart. He was nothing more than a puppet. But don't worry too much about him; he's enjoying his reward in the Dark Realm." He waved nonchalantly at Henry's mutilated body.

"See how easy it is to corrupt the hearts of humanity, Danny? I had beautifully and carefully crafted Henry's entire nightmare of a life."

He looked down at Izabelle. "This is why we will win Creation, why Phantonix will rule forever. Destiny is the true philosophy!"

"I am going to stop you." I stared into the eyes of Jesse, the poor young man who had been manipulated, tortured, and betrayed. I could see past the disguise and saw Ieiunium, and I saw the boy who once loved a girl on this cliff.

Ieiunium's laugh was cruel. "It doesn't matter now, Danny." He looked at the bell tower that indicated the coming of the solstice. "The time has come! Rise my brothers and sisters in arms! Be reborn in Destiny and rise to serve Emperor Phantonix!"

He turned toward the floating children. However, nothing happened. The children floated in the air, and the sky was thick with ominous purple storm clouds as the ground quaked. We stood there as the bell tower chimed and the solstice passed.

"N-No! I did everything perfectly! Why have they not risen?!" His question was answered with a burst of cold laughter. We all looked down at Henry's body, and I was frozen in horror. Henry rose to a seated position despite the gaping hole in his chest. His eyes were open and alert, but not the hate-filled brown I remembered. They had changed to the violet, victorious eyes of Phantonix.

Chapter XXII

The Two Philosophers

~Danny Elikai~

"Emperor." The first Crusader fell to the ground in praise as Henry's body got to his feet and brushed off the dirt. Izabelle had stopped crying as she stared horrified at the mutilated corpse of Henry. I looked into Phantonix's eyes, the eyes of the other Philosopher.

He looked at me and smiled.

"I will be with you shortly, Danny." He then turned to his Crusader, whose nose was touching the ground.

"Rise, Ieiunium." The Crusader stood up and stared into his master's eyes. I could see the devotion, the love, and the power in Ieiunium's eyes as Phantonix touched his face. "You were wonderful, my child."

"Emperor, I do not know what happened, but the ritual failed. The Crusaders have not yet risen."

"I know, Ieiunium, but soon they will rise. And it is all thanks to you." He had a soothing tone as he patted the Crusader's shoulder.

"You took great liberties in presenting Creation to the other Crusaders." He turned to the barrier Ieiunium had placed, and with a flick of his finger, it disappeared, and Phantonix slowly walked over to the cliff's edge to stare down at Grenoff as he took in the surroundings. "But I prefer Creation's natural beauty, Ieiunium."

He raised his hand, and with a snap of his fingers, all the transformations disappeared. The dead trees returned to normal, the thick fog vanished, the dark clouds faded, and the silence disappeared. He didn't say a word as he closed his eyes and took a deep breath of fresh air. No one moved as Phantonix stood at the cliff's edge, admiring the town below.

"Emperor?"

"You will have to excuse me, Ieiunium. I have not been in a physical body in what feels like an eternity. I've walked this world as a phantom, which meant I could never truly experience it. I am just enjoying the time you have given me. This is truly a wonderful gift," he gestured to everything around him. When he turned back to us, we could not mistake the wonder and love in his piercing violet eyes. My skin began to crawl when his gaze fell upon me.

"I had forgotten how beautiful Creation truly is, how beautiful Eloheen made it." Phantonix walked around the edge of the cliff, taking in everything he could see. When I looked closer, I noticed Henry's skin was turning gray, almost ashy in color.

"Tell me, Danny, how does it feel now that you know the truth? Now that you know that you are the King of Free Will?" He looked at me, but I couldn't answer. My voice was caught in my throat. "I assume you still find it hard to accept. I would also wager that you still have not truly accepted your role and continue to pretend you are nothing more then a General of Free Will." He then turned to Izabelle. "Has he asked you to treat him in such a disrespectful manner?" He laughed as if he already knew the answer, and Izabelle remained frozen with fear.

He turned and smiled nostalgically at me. "You did the same thing the first time you learned that you were to rule Creation. I always did admire that about you, how humble you are. You let your humility guide you but see yourself as no better than these disgusting peasants." He waved a gray hand toward the town below the cliff.

"They're beautiful, kind, and wonderful people." I stood my ground, and I stared at the Emperor of Destiny. "And I will not allow you to degrade them that way.

"Yes, I knew you would see it that way. You always have, Danny. You see beauty in the unworthy. They are filthy animals who have betrayed, murdered, and cheated just to get what they want or to save their own skins," he said with pure loathing in his voice. "Don't you see that they cannot be left to make their own decisions? What about the genocide and terrorism you hear about every day? Have they not proven to you, time and time again, that they are unworthy of deciding what is best for themselves?!" His voice had risen in anger.

"Never! You may see us as murderous, cheating, lying pieces of filth, but we aren't." He stopped and stared at me with disbelief.

"*Us?* Why would you degrade your status by categorizing yourself with these contemptible, disgusting swine?" Phantonix bellowed as if he were insulted. "You were chosen by Eloheen, so act like it while you can!"

"Yes, I do associate myself with them. We may let the darkness get the best of us sometimes, but we are good. We are willing to put others before ourselves. We are willing to do what it takes for the benefit of all of humanity. I have seen kindness, the generosity, the selflessness in the hearts of those around me. I know what they have done for me, and I believe in them."

"You do not know their hearts as I do!" Phantonix roared.

"I do know them." I could see the hatred burning in his eyes. "And I believe they will end the war in favor of Free Will."

"Well, Danny, I guess I will have to continue to prove my point. Then, when you are forced to recognize the truth, you will hand me the right to govern them, to plan their entire lives." He turned away from me and moved toward his Crusader.

"I apologize for not informing you of this earlier, but I feared you would not perform the ritual if you knew the truth." He turned back to the starry sky.

"Em-Emperor?" Ieiunium spoke again, and his voice betrayed his unease and confusion. "How have you escaped your cage? How are you here tonight?"

"That is a complicated question, Ieiunium. The ritual to raise the Crusaders can only be completed by the Emperor of Destiny. The spell you cast was a two-part spell. The first part would allow me to briefly break free of my cage that the King of Free Will sealed me in." He looked at me with disgust before continuing. "I would walk free in a vessel for a short time to complete the second part of the spell. I just wanted to enjoy my time in the physical realm before I was sent back."

He took a deep breath, but when he smiled, a piece of gray flesh fell off Henry's face. I could see the exposed jawbone, and the rest of his face looked like it could crumble at any moment.

I acted without thinking. I sent a blast of fire to try to destroy Henry's body before Phantonix could finish the ritual, but he swatted it away without even looking at me. A small piece of his flesh flew off his hand with the quick motion.

"Come now, Danny, you know you cannot stop this." He reached his decaying hand toward me, and I felt something tighten in my chest. I couldn't breathe, and I fell to my knees. "You cannot stop what has been foretold. I will rule Creation because it is my Destiny," Phantonix grinned while walked closer to me.

He knelt in front of me as he held his grip in my chest, and I struggled to breathe. "You wanted it this way, to let this world be governed by Free Will, by choice. You allowed people to choose their paths, to ignore and refuse what they were preordained. While Free Will is a plague that will tarnish Creation, certain events are set in stone. They will come to pass because of the hearts that are involved. The choices of the heart will end you. You will be impaled upon your sword."

Phantonix looked into my eyes. As he reached out to touch my face, the crystal sword sliced off his hand. Phantonix didn't even flinch or scream in pain.

The rotting hand smashed into the ground, but no blood escaped from his veins. Henry's body was dead, and the blood had stopped circulating. Phantonix looked at his forearm and then at the hand on the ground with mild interest. He looked up at Izabelle, who was afraid, and revulsion engraved on her face.

"Izabelle, this flesh is dead," Phantonix chuckled. "What did you think that would actually do?" He got to his feet and turned to face Izabelle. She raised the sword, ready to fight.

"Keep your hands off him," she snarled. I could see the rage in her heart, and another piece of flesh fell off Henry's face. The pressure in my chest did not dissipate as he turned to approach Izabelle.

"My dear, Izzy, I have missed you. It has been far too long." Izabelle lunged at him, but he acted quickly. He ducked as she swung the blade at him. Before she could strike again, he placed two of his fingers to her forehead, and she immediately crumbled to the ground. The crystal blade dropped next to her, reforming the dagger.

"Try to keep this one alive, Danny. She may come in handy in the future." He turned away from me, picked up the dagger, and faced his Crusader, who was standing next to the stone basin. I felt the pressure disappear from my chest, and I moved to Izabelle while attempting to refill my lungs with air.

Please don't be dead, please don't be dead, I touched her neck and felt her strong heartbeat. Relief washed over me as I turned around to look at the basin.

I watched in disbelief as Phantonix grabbed his Crusader by the hair and slashed Jesse's throat with the dagger. He turned to me, winked, and tossed the blade back at my feet.

"Master…" Ieiunium choked. Phantonix put his hand around the wound and pulled out what looked like pale smoke that seemed to tremble in his hand. I stared at it and realized that it was the Crusader's soul.

"Thank you," he spoke lovingly to the essence in his hands. He turned away from me, and his voice boomed, "Tonight, my chosen six will be unleashed upon the world and will help me bring Free Will to its knees. Together, we will establish the rightful philosophy upon Creation." A fire came to life underneath the stone basin. "I have sacrificed the first to give birth to the rest. I will use his soul to awaken yours and to awaken the Destiny in your hearts. You six will be the first to be sealed by Destiny. You will obey the true philosophy and the true ruler of Creation! Free Will—the choice to falter and stumble has been stripped away from your hearts. You will be the messengers of Destiny, my living examples, as you bring the world to order." He gently lowered Ieiunium's pale soul into the basin, and the potion began to bubble violently.

The seals on the children's foreheads began to glow brighter. Phantonix turned to where I rested, and he smiled as he raised his remaining hand. The severed hand twitched, rolled over, and then levitated off the ground and floated into the basin. "I willingly give the flesh of the miserable, the pawn, as an offering to you, my children, to restore your true bodies, to break the chains of the flesh that bind you. The blood of each of your families has been paid to restore your powers."

The children's bodies became transparent, and they all began to shimmer and transform.

I had to do something; I had to find a way to stop the darkness from taking over these children. My answer came in the form of a bolt of lightning that came from behind me. It pierced another hole in Henry's chest, which seemed to speed up the disintegration process. Phantonix spun around, and I saw his fear as he looked at Michael. Michael was clutching the violent wound on his chest with one hand, but he was up and moving. The paralysis spell that Ieiunium had cast seemed to have been lifted with his death.

"No!" Phantonix raised his hand and unleashed a wave of darkness exploded toward Michael. He dodged it and launched another bolt of lightning at Phantonix.

Their fight waged before me, and I knew time was running out. I looked at the children, and I knew the Crusaders of Destiny were almost reborn. I watched as these children would be bound to Phantonix's will.

Maybe all it takes is a simple act. Michael's words played in my mind, and I knew it was their only chance. Phantonix had said that he stripped away their Free Will. *But what if I gave it back?*

I looked at the stone basin, and I knew it was the only way. I picked up the dagger Phantonix had thrown at my feet after he killed Ieiunium, and I acted quickly.

Phantonix was standing next to the stone basin and was distracted by fending off Michael's lightning, and without hesitation, I threw the dagger at him. The blade flew quickly, but he spun in time and caught the handle of the dagger, which he held directly above the basin.

"You will have to do better than that, my King." He wore a sarcastic smile.

"I wasn't aiming for you." I raised my sliced palm as a few drops of my blood dripped from the tip of the silver blade into the basin.

He looked back at me, but before he could stop me, I addressed the rising Crusaders. "With my blood, the blood of the King of Light, I give you back the gift of Free Will. I give you back the choice that Phantonix has stripped away from you. Destiny does not bind you. You have the freedom to decide!" I felt the rage explode from Phantonix as each of the children shuddered, as they became solid once again. I got to my feet, squared my shoulders, and looked into the eyes of the other philosopher.

"That changes nothing, Danny! They will still lay waste to Creation and will begin the Final War! You could not stop the rising, and you will not stop the Final War! I am destined to rule Creation!"

"You're right, Phantonix. I couldn't stop the rising, and I won't be able to stop the coming Final War. However, my blood has changed your Crusaders. They now have the chance to return to the light if they want. The restoration of their Free Will, will be your downfall, Phantonix," I looked into his violet eyes.

"NO!" He roared. He raised his hand to strike me down, and a mass of darkness formed in his gray hand, but a flash of lightning hit him in the chest. Henry's body disintegrated and became nothing more than a pile of ash. The Emperor of Destiny had been sent back to his cage.

I turned around as Michael staggered toward me and fell on the ground beside me. I touched his chest, which was no longer coated with darkness, and I was able to repair the damage with my fire. Izabelle was still on the ground, unresponsive.

We looked at the six floating before us. They were all older, and some of them were not human.

"We have risen!" The Crusaders of Destiny spoke in unison, and their voices echoed throughout Creation.

I looked into the reptilian eyes of Daimonas, my cousin, and my family. I looked at him, and I could see at that moment Destiny still governed his heart. However, amid the swirling darkness was a light, a flicker of Free Will. I looked over to the other five Crusaders and saw it in their hearts as well. While the Crusaders had risen and the battle had truly begun, I knew there was a chance, a single choice that could turn their darkness into light.

"We will follow Phantonix's orders," again they said in unison. "We are the messengers of Destiny, and we will lay waste to this world. We will destroy the Soldiers and Children of Free Will." They lowered to the ground and stared at us.

Michael put himself in front of me, ready for the assault, when one of the Crusaders stepped forward. This Crusader was a woman with high cheekbones and long brown hair, and she raised her hand. In a flash of crimson light, the basin vanished, as well as the burning seal of the Crusaders.

"What now?" I asked them after an extended period of silence.

"Now, King of Free Will, we will begin our assaults against you and those like you." The response had come from the Crusader that seemed to be made of wisping darkness, its piercing blue eyes sweeping us over.

"However," Daimonas spoke, "we must follow in the order that we were sealed."

"What order?" Michael asked.

The other female Crusader, the one with black hair and magenta eyes, laughed in response. "When the King of Light sealed us away, he did so to ensure we could not all lay waste to the world at once. We must return in the order he sealed us. Ieiunium was the first to be sealed, and I was the third."

"You can only assault the world in a particular order?"

"Yes," the elderly man with green eyes answered. "It is the only way to release our Emperor from his cage. Our hearts and destinies are sealed upon the door to his cage. You made it so, King of Light. While Free Will governs Creation, we must obey its laws, even if we are the Crusaders of Destiny. All living things must obey its laws, even Phantonix. However," he said with a wicked chuckle, "that doesn't mean we cannot manipulate the rules."

"The rising of the Crusaders was the first seal on his cage, which is now broken," the third Crusader said with love and devotion that reminded me of Michael. "Each of us will fall and in doing so will unleash unhinged carnage upon Creation, allowing Phantonix to rise and unite the children of Destiny under the banner of peace and harmony."

"The Fallen will soon rise, Your Majesty," the middle-aged man said. He had rusty orange eyes with black hair that looked like it needed to be washed.

"We will grant you a small window of rest before the second Crusader's plan is set into motion, King of Free Will." Daimonas had a nasty grin, exposing his razor-sharp teeth.

They all raised their hands, and in a flash of darkness, they disappeared. We were left alone at the edge of Star Cliff, at the edge of Armageddon.

"We failed," I took a deep shuddering breath. "The Crusaders have risen. Creation is about to be torn apart because we failed to stop the rising."

"No, Danny," Michael put an arm around me, and I felt the panic exploding in my chest. "The rising was always going to happen. But you changed the tides, and you did the only thing that could be done. You gave Phantonix's Generals, the embodiments of Destiny, the opportunity to have the choice to abscond to Free Will. You never know what that gift will turn into or how that flickering light will grow in their hearts. You gave them a gift, a gift that will hopefully be the end of Phantonix."

I turned back to where Alvaro had stood, a Crusader of Destiny. "I hope Alvaro comes back. I hope my small action was enough to bring him home."

"I believe he will." He smiled at me, and I could feel his devotion as his words filled me with hope. "But only Alvaro can make that decision. However, hope is a powerful weapon."

I nodded in response. I could sense his unease but knew we would not be attacked. "Come on, let's get off this cliff."

I turned to look at Jesse's body. We walked up to his broken and mutilated corpse, and I got to my knees and touched his face. It felt cold, and I lifted him into my arms. I knew there was no more life in him. His heart and his soul were gone. I would not leave him. He was my friend, and he deserved better. I felt tears threatening to fall from my face, but I put my grief behind a wall. Michael picked up Izabelle, and we began our descent back to Grenoff.

Chapter XXIII

The Third Funeral

~Danny Elikai~

We walked in silence down the path as we carried the dead weight of our friends. I held back the tears and my emotions as we headed down to the town that had protected me, the town I had failed to protect. I knew there hadn't been a real chance of stopping the rise of the Crusaders, but I had convinced myself that we could do it. I could not help but believe that the good guys would save the day in the nick of time, due to the countless happy endings that every story taught us to believe.

I carried Jesse down the hill, and a dark feeling began to consume me. It was the feeling that my story would not end happily. I tried to push that feeling away, but it lingered as we reached the end of the trail.

I was not sure what I expected when we reached the entrance to the path, but it certainly was not this. My uncle and aunt stood in front, holding each other tightly as their eyes widened in shock as they saw us. Mrs. Daniels stood alone, clutching Jesse's cowboy hat, and she crumbled to the ground in sobs at the sight of her son. Mr. Pescador also started crying as Michael carried his daughter. Several others were waiting, including the mayor, a couple of deputies, and some EMTs in an ambulance.

"Danny," my uncle said as he pulled away from my aunt and rushed to help us.

I looked him in the eyes and said, "They have risen." My words were gentle, but they rang clearly. The mayor looked sick, and my aunt cried.

The EMTs came up to me with a stretcher to take Jesse. I backed away, grunting in protest as flares of fire escaped from my nostrils in a warning. They stopped dead in their tracks.

"Danny," Michael said gently, "let them take him. There is nothing more you can do for him." I turned to Michael and saw he had sympathy in his ever-changing eyes.

"I cannot let anything else happen to him."

"He'll be okay, my King," one of the EMTs said. "I will make sure nothing else happens to him." His words were soft as he approached me. The EMT was an inch or two shorter than me, but he had kind brown eyes that matched his amber complexion. I felt my body relaxed, and I nodded as they approached with a stretcher.

"Thank you, Alec." I didn't know his name, but it somehow escaped my lips. He smiled at me as he gave me a slight bow and loaded Jesse onto the stretcher.

The other EMTs placed Izabelle onto a stretcher. Her father gave me a grateful look as he disappeared into the ambulance. Mrs. Daniels hugged me and thanked me for bringing her boy back home. She then entered the other ambulance and disappeared. I looked at the small group of people around me.

"They said they would give us a small window of time to prepare for the next attack." I looked at the mayor, who nodded and left without another word. She looked like she was on the verge of a mental breakdown.

I turned to my uncle as he dismissed his deputies because there was nothing for them to do here, and they bowed to me before leaving. I felt uncomfortable with everyone bowing, but I didn't say anything. I was physically and mentally exhausted to do much more than recount the events of the last couple of hours. The wall behind which I had buried my feelings would crumble shortly, but they needed to know everything.

"Tell me everything." My uncle's expression made it seem like he had read my mind.

"Not here," I looked up at the cliff face. "I can't be here right now." I walked away toward the Jeep. They followed me without question, and I slowly got in the back as Michael sat next to me. I knew he would not leave my side no matter what.

I thought of everything that had happened over the last few months as my uncle drove us home. The past was replaying on repeat as I tried to understand and rebuild the story, so I could accurately tell them everything. We needed to prepare for the coming struggle between Free Will and Destiny. I felt the tears threatening to dissolve the wall, and my heart began to protest against my ribs. I remembered how Ieiunium killed Henry with Jesse's hand, Phantonix's rising, and Ieiunium's death.

The walls began to close in as the realization hit me that I had failed to save Jesse not only from the darkness, but from lies he had believed. I reached out and grabbed Michael's hand as the scream built in my throat.

"It's okay," his grip was tight. "You just have to hold on a little longer." His touch calmed me just enough to breathe and to put my thoughts back into focus.

We pulled into the driveway of our house, and I tried to reassemble everything. I got out of the car and walked into the house. I didn't stop until we reached the living room. I sat in the plush recliner while my uncle, aunt, and Michael sat on the couch.

"Start whenever you are ready," my uncle said.

I took another deep long breath before beginning to explain everything from the moment we received the phone call. I told them how we hiked to the top of the cliff and how Michael was unable to continue. I told them about the scene with the basin and the children. I hesitated and then explained how Ieiunium had overtaken Jesse for about a year, and how he ripped out Henry's heart. I explained how the Crusader used Jesse's heart to enter the protected houses and to interact with the children that would become the Crusaders.

They were an incredible audience. As I told them the story, they gasped, became angry, cried, and sat deathly quiet when I explained how Phantonix had taken over Henry's dead body. I told them how he finished the ritual, how I had used my blood to restore Free Will in their hearts, and about the seals on Phantonix's cage. When I finished, my throat hurt from speaking so much.

"Seals on Phantonix's Cage?" My uncle asked.

I shook my head and explained, "From what the Crusaders said, they are the keys to unleashing Phantonix."

"That's worrisome," my uncle shook his head.

"My question," Michael began, "is how the first Crusader knew we knew about Johanna?"

I felt that tightening grip on my stomach as fear coursed through me.

"I don't know, but I hope I did not send Targo to his death."

"I would not worry about Targo, as he can take care of himself," my uncle said thoughtfully. "We have to assume the Crusader knew you knew about Johanna because you are the King of Light. Maybe you saw the past or saw that it was written in Elijah's diary since he was the one who sealed them away. There are countless ways you could have figured it out. Regardless, if we try to make contact now, we will be putting his life in jeopardy." I nodded in agreement, but something about his smile told me he knew something else about Targo that he wasn't sharing. I pushed it from my mind because we had more pressing issues to deal with.

"We need to focus on the second Crusader," Aunt Shannon tears brimmed her eyes. "Do you know who the second Crusader is? Or what their plan is?"

"It has to do with something called the Forest of the Fallen," I said hesitantly, but none of it made sense.

My aunt sat on the couch and cried over her lost son. She curled up in her husband's arms, and I could see she had forgiven him. Her forgiveness held no end, and it brought happiness to my saddened heart.

"How much time do you think they will give us?" Michael asked.

"I think they will give us enough time to bury Jesse."

"Well," my uncle said gently, "you two should get some rest. There is nothing more we can do tonight. You both did everything you could. We have no idea what will come from you giving them back their ability to choose."

"I just hope it was enough," I placed my face into my hands.

"It was, Danny. You just need to trust your decision," my aunt said. I nodded, too exhausted to continue.

Michael and I got to our feet and walked out of the room. I walked up the stairs, and Michael followed me. I was correct in saying he would not leave my side, now that there were six Crusaders unleashed upon the world. The memory of Alvaro's warning flashed before my eyes as I reached the landing. Alvaro had shown me the truth, and I knew I had failed to save him. It seemed I could not save anyone.

I opened the door to my room, my only haven, stepped in, and stopped in my tracks.

"Matthew!" I saw him sitting on the window seat. Michael and I entered the room and closed the door. I stared at him in disbelief.

"What are you doing here?" Michael asked as my excitement echoed in his words. I stood there as I stared into my brother's bright green eyes, and his strawberry blonde hair looked shorter than the last time I had seen him.

"Hello, Danny," he was only looking at me.

"Matthew," I walked slowly toward him, "what are you doing here?"

"I came here for you," and I nodded because he wanted to make sure I was okay. "I wanted you to know that you did everything you could." I sat on my bed, running my hands through my hair.

"The Crusaders have risen, Matthew."

"We know, and that is okay, Danny, because they were supposed to, Danny. Phantonix was right; the war is coming no matter what. Even though Free Will is the governing philosophy, there are some things we cannot change," he said softly.

"Why could we not stop this?"

"The only way the Final War will end is when the hearts of Creation decide the Victor. It will be either you or Phantonix. The only way to avoid the war is if every soul unanimously decided right now the Victor."

"Which will never happen because the hearts of Creation are not ready." Michael's truth rang clear.

"Michael is right. The Final War must be waged so Creation can finally be at peace."

"I understand." I moved to lie down on the bed, and I closed my eyes. I felt the exhaustion in my bones, and I wanted nothing more than to sleep.

"I cannot come to you anymore, Danny." His words made me jerk back up. I looked up at him in stunned silence.

"I am surprised the host of light allowed you this much," Michael said solemnly as he sat on the bed next to me.

"My job was to help guide him, but the rest now falls on you, Michael. I am no longer needed."

"I'll always need you, Matthew." He looked back at me and smiled.

"I love you, Danny."

"I love you, too, Matthew." He smiled as he moved to touch the blonde streaks of hair above my ears.

"I believe in you, my King." Tears filled his bright green eyes, and then he disappeared. I closed my eyes again because my heart could not process anything more, and to my great relief, sleep finally overtook me as Michael lay next to me.

****

The soft knock on the door made me look up as Izabelle entered the room. She wore the same white dress with yellow embroidered flowers from Claire's funeral. Her black hair was pulled back into an elegant braid with daisies woven in. She looked breathtaking, and I could not help but tell her so.

"You look handsome, my King." Her words made me blush. I wore the same white suit, but with that red shirt and violet pocket square for a third funeral of someone I failed to save. I understood that I technically never knew the real Jesse, but I felt like I had. My mind kept returning to the one interaction I had with him when he pleaded for me to save him.

When Izabelle returned from the hospital two days ago, she had told me everything about the real Jesse before the Crusader possessed him. She said that the whole time the Crusader was in control, he kept Jesse's actions, beliefs, and personality the same. I knew that he would have been a true friend.

I had the heart-wrenching experience of telling Mrs. Daniels everything before the funeral. She had a right to know what had happened to her son, and I held nothing back. She deserved the truth, and I could not disrespect his memory by lying. I told her everything about him, allowing the Crusader into his heart, his coming out, and how the Crusader had manipulated and tormented him. I explained what Ieiunium had done and what little I knew about the Forest of the Fallen. She sobbed harder than ever as I explained everything, but I also made her a promise that I would do whatever it took to save Jesse. I would bring his soul into the Realm of Light, even if it killed me.

"It's time, Danny," Izabelle said, pulling my thoughts back to the present. She placed her soft, warm hand on my face. I looked into her tear-stained hazel eyes, and once again, I wanted to kiss her. I knew that it was not the time for that, and maybe it would never be. "It's time for us to say goodbye."

I looked at my reflection in the mirror, one that I had hated, which now represented Free Will, the Light.

I pulled the violet handkerchief out of my pocket, folded it into a square, and placed it in my jacket pocket.

"Let's do this." I held out my hand, and she took it without question. Michael stood in the entryway, wearing his white suit with a yellow shirt, and my breath caught in his grandeur and beauty.

"Are you ready?" he asked, and I nodded.

He pulled me into a warm hug, and we held each other for a long time. Michael and I had been distant for the last week since I needed time and space to put my head back together. After I woke up from Matthew's farewell, I told him I needed to be alone. To my great astonishment, he agreed, and I had not seen him since. However, as we stood there hugging, I realized how much I needed him by my side. I pulled out of his embrace and took the hands of my two best friends.

"Let's go." We walked out of the house and found my aunt and uncle standing on the sidewalk, waiting for us. They wore the same colors as us, the colors of Free Will, and were ready to say goodbye to the young man they had known for so long. We walked up to them, and without saying a word, we all walked to the concert to celebrate Jesse's life.

Jesse's ceremony was everything it should have been. We cried, we danced, and we celebrated the life of a young man who had fallen at the hands of darkness. I felt immense sorrow in my heart, and I did not know where to go from here or what tomorrow would hold. Just for a moment, before the next horrendous event, we would heal and mourn.

I was grateful that the majority of Grenoff did not know the truth about what had happened to Jesse. The official story was that Henry kidnapped, killed, and left him on the cliff as he escaped into the night.

No one would know that Henry was dead and was nothing more than ash in the wind. There would be no celebration of life for Henry, and I could not help but wonder where he was now. Ieiunium has said he was getting his reward in the Realm of Darkness. Was that a good thing, or was he curled up in a fetal position in the icy darkness? I did not know, and I tried not to think about it.

We joined the crowd that had come to say goodbye to Jesse. I stood in the audience as the mayor, Izabelle, and his mother gave speeches. We listened, held each other, and were given the time to mourn and say goodbye to our friend. I listened to the speeches, but my mind kept creeping back to the next battle with the Crusaders and Phantonix. I wondered where the second Crusader, Metentis, was hiding, which out of the six he was, and what he was planning. I could not stop obsessing over the Forest of the Fallen, or how it played into his plan, and what we could do to prepare for it.

I thought of Jesse, and I looked toward the graveyard at the base of the mountain. My eyes raked over the graves until I found the fresh one that sat two rows away from Claire's. I looked at the place where they would bury him, and I saw a man standing next to the plot, his gaze fixed on a headstone. He looked familiar, so I let go of Michael's and Izabelle's hands and moved toward him.

Even in the great distance, I could see he wore a black suit with red trim. Michael did not follow me, but his eyes watched my every move. I knew he would be there in a flash if something happened to me. I could feel the static in the air building in me, and I knew the lightning was ready to strike at any moment.

I reached the graveyard within minutes. I opened the rusty iron gate and walked toward where my friend would rest.

"Hello, Danny." The man greeted me as I approached from behind. He turned around, and I gasped at the sharp outline of his skull. Silverish-looking skin looked as if it were loosely draped over a frail skeleton. He looked as old as time, but his stone-gray eyes were filled with life. He wore a ring on every finger, and his suit looked new and expensive.

"Do I know you?"

"I am not surprised you do not remember me, my King." He held onto his elegant walking stick. I looked closer at it and saw that it was shaped like an old-fashioned scythe.

"Who are you?" I felt uneasy in the company of this man, and I saw the terror on his face.

"My name is Ankou, but you will know me better under my official title, Death."

"Wh-What?"

"My King," he collapsed to his knees as he grabbed my hands, and I flinched under his icy touch. The tears were falling down his ancient face, and his eyes were wide in desperation. "I need your help."

To be continued in

The Memoirs of Elikai:
The Ritual of the Fallen

Book Two in
The Memoirs of Elikai Series

Now Available

The Memoirs of Elikai: The Children of the Solstice

Please write a review on *Amazon* and *Good Reads*! Your reviews mean the world to Indie authors, and we would love to hear your thoughts.

The Memoirs of Elikai: The Ritual of the Fallen.

Available Now

****

~About the Author~

D. Alexander received his bachelor's in humanities from Washington State University in Pullman, Washington, and his master's in library science from the University of Wisconsin.
He enjoys diverse sections of Literature and the imagination that goes into these vast stories.

Made in the USA
Middletown, DE
19 April 2024